The Last Yard

A Sports Grumpy Sunshine
Second Chance Football
Romance

CK Franco

Blurbs

"One last play. One broken team. One chance to rewrite everything."

Once, Jaxon Reyes was football's golden boy.
Now, he's a headline everyone remembers for the wrong reasons.

Redemption Valley is supposed to be the end of the line—a forgotten town, a fractured football program, and a locker room full of men who don't trust second chances. But when Jaxon is offered one final shot to step back onto the field, walking away is no longer an option.

The problem?
The team doesn't want him.
The town doesn't forgive him.
And the woman who believes in him most shines far too bright for a man drowning in regret.

As grit replaces glory and brotherhood is forged through pain, Jaxon must decide what matters more—winning the game, or becoming the man worthy of a future beyond the final whistle.

The Last Yard is a heartfelt, slow-burn football romance about second chances, found family, and discovering that redemption isn't earned in stadium lights—but in the quiet moments when no one is watching.

"For anyone who was told their best days were behind them—
and chose to keep going anyway."

"The scoreboard remembers wins.

But character is built when no one is counting."

Prologue

The stadium lights were still on when Jaxon Reyes realized
the game was already over.

Not the one on the field—the one inside him.

The cheers had faded, replaced by silence so loud it rang in his ears.
Headlines would come next. Opinions. Judgment. Everyone would
have something to say about how he fell.

But none of them would ask what it felt like to lose the only thing
that ever made sense.

As the field emptied and the night swallowed the noise, Jaxon understood one brutal truth:

Football had taught him how to win.
But it had never taught him how to survive the loss.

Contents

The Day the Game Ended

The bar sits heavy with the smell of stale beer and worn leather. Its low-hung ceiling bears the stains of decades—smoke, neglect, and time itself settling into the cracks. Against the far wall, televisions flicker above dusty bottles, casting a jaundiced glow over tired faces.

At the counter's end, Jaxon Reyes is slumped over scratched wood, an empty glass crushed in his grip. His knuckles have turned white. Stubble shadows his jaw—the mark of a man who has stopped bothering with the small rituals of care. His hair is tousled. His eyes, when they open fully, burn with something sharp and broken.

The televisions erupt. The championship crowd roars like a ghost chasing him backward in time.

Bright stadium lights flicker across the screen. Sweaty, triumphant bodies. Players he once called brothers. The commentators' voices cut through the bar's hum like dull knives.

"There's no denying the impact Jaxon Reyes had whenever he was on the field," one says, reluctant nostalgia threading through the words. "But the scandal that tore through his career? That's a different story—a reminder that no star shines forever."

The scandal had splashed across every headline, turning cheers into whispers overnight and stealing him from the field—and the spotlight—for good.

Another commentator name-drops the fall that followed, framing Jaxon as a cautionary tale. The screen cuts between slow-motion replays of aerial passes and touchdown dives, then—sharp and cruel—his replacement hoists the trophy. The crowd erupts in a unified cheer that fills the bar like poison gas.

Jaxon's eyes burn into the screen, not really seeing, forcing the image in—a ritual as punishing as the grip now crushing the empty glass.

The subtle scrape of glass against worn wood is the only sound he makes as his fingers flex involuntarily.

Memories flit through him: grass beneath cleats, the thud of a perfect pass, a roar that shook the stadium, then the crash, the fall, the headlines screaming his name, the whispers that followed, the betrayal, and the silence after the storm.

His breath flattens; his muscles seize.

Around him, a handful of other patrons keep their distance. A man with a cracked cigarette hunches in a corner, while a woman two stools away taps her fingers absently on a grimy ashtray. Nobody turns to look; nobody sees the fallen star crumpling in the dim light.

This bar is both his hiding place and his cage—a place where no one expects the hero who once ruled the stadium's roar.

His shoulders fold inward further. The ache in his chest pulses like a second heartbeat. He can taste bitter regret on his tongue—acrid, like cheap whiskey swallowed too fast.

The humming chatter from the TV drones on, glory and ruin weaving through the stale air. The moment stretches, taut and unforgiving.

The door rattles. A gust of cold night air slips inside, brushing against Jaxon like a reminder. Outside these walls, life keeps moving. But here, in the shadows of peeling paint and faded "No Loitering" signs, time folds back on itself. Here, he is frozen.

He tightens his grip again; his nails leave crescent marks in the glass—a silent invocation of pain. The tension hikes through his fingers and settles rigid and clenched in his jaw. The empty glass trembles slightly—a fragile echo of his resolve breaking.

Somewhere in the smoky haze, a jukebox clicks and sputters before falling silent, swallowed by the edge of night.

The commentators' voices flicker with something sharp—memory bait, teasing the wound. "Jaxon Reyes. Remember the name. Remember what might have been."

He snarls the words under his breath, defiance and regret blending together, bitter as ashes.

In the darkness, keys clatter, and boots thud against scuffed floors. The bar's rough clientele breathe and move around him, indifferent and oblivious. Their lives hum far from the haunting glare of televised stadium lights or the crushing weight of a faded reputation.

A shard of neon light slices across the counter, illuminating a bead of sweat traced along Jaxon's temple. His gaze flickers—not away from the screen—no matter how much it hurts—but inward, to the scars beneath the surface, worn and raw both.

The bar's dim glow digs into his skin: cold and biting. The stale air tastes faintly metallic, mixing with the sour note of broken dreams that linger like smoke.

The faded "Happy Hour" sign, the scuffed floor, and the buzz of flickering bulbs overhead—none of it moves him. The room contracts around him until it's just Jaxon, his empty glass, and the ghostly echoes of past cheers reverberating from a world he once commanded, now just out of reach.

His jaw tightens one last time. The glass slips, sliding with a dull scrape back into its resting place, emptier than before.

And there he stays: hunched, silent, and alone, while the television blares on, recounting the rise and ruin of the quarterback whose name the night still carries, even if the bar's few witnesses do not.

The door creaks open, letting in a colder draft that scatters empty napkins across the sticky bar top. The grizzled man who slides in carries the scent of grease and cigarette smoke—work boots scraping against the linoleum, the sound grating against Jaxon's nerves. He slaps his cap down beside him, settling onto the stool as if he owns the place.

Jaxon's fingers pressed against the grimy bar, the sticky residue clinging to his skin like the night's regrets. A faint hum of stale beer and cigarette smoke hovered in the air, settling in his lungs like unwelcome memories.

"Are you the new local ghost story, or just another washed-up athlete chasing the bottom of a bottle?"

The man's tone was casual yet loaded, the kind of contempt reserved for men who once had it all—and lost it.

Jaxon didn't look up. His jaw tightened, and a muscle twitched beneath his skin.

"Athlete?" His voice came out low and brittle, like rusted wire snapping. "Not exactly the comeback story anyone's waiting for."

The man snorted, then laughed—a sharp, brittle sound that rang off the cracked bottles and cheap tile. His eyes were fixed on the TV, where the broadcast looped shots of the championship, roaring crowds, and flashes of Jaxon's replacement—the one who took everything.

"Wait a minute... Reyes? You? Shit." His expression twisted, and then his voice dropped into that ragged sneer reserved for legends turned cautionary tales. "Look at you, man. I thought you were the big star. Once the golden boy, now just a cautionary headline. Public disgrace, drug bust, all that garbage. And here you sit, rotting away in some dive that forgot better days."

His breath smelled of stale beer and self-satisfaction.

Jaxon's muscles coiled beneath his threadbare shirt. His gaze narrowed into a hard, razor-slice glare. His knuckles whitened around the glass, fingernails digging in like a silent scream. Years of bottled-up frustration threaded through that grip—emotions he refused to let spill into the open.

He fought the urge to shove the man backward into his chair. Violence burned like static beneath his skin.

"Funny how lives like mine are entertainment for their whole damn town," Jaxon spat through clenched teeth. "You ever wonder what it's like to have a target tattooed on your back? To be the guy everyone's waiting to watch crash and burn?"

The stranger leaned in, his voice dropping to a conspiratorial growl. "Well, maybe if you hadn't pissed away your chances, you wouldn't be the joke everyone's still laughing about. You had the world at your feet,

Reyes. Instead, you took the easy way out. Shows what you're made of."

Around them, the few late-night patrons glanced over—not dismissive, not sympathetic either. Their faces were etched with hard nights and harder lives, none willing to pick a fight that wouldn't add anything to the tab.

A muscle twitched in Jaxon's jaw—flame-flickering anger, barely contained. The bar seemed to stifle the swell of something fierce, raw, and rusty.

He breathed in slowly, forcing the tempest back into its cage.

The game's roar on the screens faded into background noise. His world shrank to this corner, this man, this moment. The stranger's success on that television screen amplified every wound—a stark, undeniable contrast to Jaxon's fall from grace. It was a public reminder that someone else had claimed what should have been his.

He hauled his gaze from the man's mocking grin and lowered it back to the jagged seam of his empty glass.

A brief hush fell across the bar. No one moved. The weight of a thousand unspoken judgments pressed down, heavier than the smoke in the room.

"You don't know me," Jaxon finally snarled. His voice cut cold and sharp. "So don't pretend like you do."

His words carried the wound that kept bleeding beneath every moment.

The older man's smirk faltered. Recognition lurched into something closer to respect—ugly and grudging. He leaned back, crowding just a bit less now, as if the bar itself wanted to close ranks around Jaxon.

"Guess I know enough," he muttered, his eyes flicking back to the screen. "But you? You're just a ghost now, one nobody wants to remember."

Whispers crawled through the room for a split second—faint like a stifled gasp—before settling back into the murmur of clinking glasses and the hum of flickering neon.

Jaxon's gaze remained fixed on the jagged edge of his glass, the only steady thing in a world turned hostile.

The glow from the television reflected the tired lines beneath his eyes—years of battles lost, fights not just on fields but within himself. He reclaimed his glass as if it were the only thing left that belonged to him.

The grizzled man slid his stubby fingers down the counter, nursing his own bitterness like a drink gone cold. Around them, life in the bar trundled on, oblivious and relentless.

Jaxon sat, a shadow folded beneath the flicker of the TV light, simmering in quiet fury and faded pride.

###

Jaxon's breath hitched—rough, a whisper beneath the television's low hum.

"Nobody wants you anymore," his own voice echoed, shaking in the stale air. The bar pressed around him—the clink and murmur, the thick weight of bodies and regret. Images flashed behind his eyes: headlines screaming betrayal, crowds turning sour, the searing sting of boos swallowed whole into his skin.

That one mistake played like a shattered record, that instant break where everything cracked wide open, where he let himself fall apart.

He squeezed the empty glass tighter, his knuckles blanching.

The worn bar top scratched beneath his calloused fingers. Sticky spots of spilled beer mingled with burnt tobacco and cheap whiskey.

Above, the screen flickered—the broadcast spitting victories and celebrations that no longer belonged to him. Former teammates flashed by, their faces shining in the glare, basking in the glory that once etched his name in headlines.

He recognized the truth clawing at his insides: lost. Forgotten. No longer part of the game he once ruled.

The bar's gritty undercurrent pressed down on him: faint sweat, stale smoke, and the ghost of cheap cologne mixed with spilled liquor. Suffocating. Yet beneath it all lay that ache—a fragile pulse of something he dared not name.

His eyes darted to the glow of his phone, the screen lit in the dim light. Messages piled up like burdens. From his agent came terse texts reeking of impatience and dwindling faith. Bank alerts blinked red—a cold numerical echo of all the times he had fallen short. Then there was the blocked number.

"Emma" flashed stubbornly on the neglected call log.

It had been three months since he blocked her, three months since she had tried to talk sense into him, since her voice had cracked when she said, "You're not the man I thought you were." The words had hit harder than any headline or any crowd's turning. He swiped past it without a glance, but the tightening in his chest refused to untangle. She had given him chances he had squandered, given him love he hadn't known how to hold.

His throat tightened. The taste of copper rose as he swallowed hard, the sting settling like grit behind his eyes.

"Why'd you even bother showing up, huh?" The stranger's voice sliced through the quiet—sharp, sneering.

Jaxon's jaw locked, and his gaze remained fixed on the empty glass. Heat rose from somewhere deep—old anger, stubborn and fierce. His voice came out low and clipped, breaking the silence.

"Because some things aren't that easy to walk away from."

"Easy? You had it all. You blew it." The sneer deepened. "Now you're just the punchline nobody laughs at."

He tasted the bitterness behind the words but kept the storm inside—barely. The threat of a fight hovered unspoken, a raw charge that tightened his shoulders. Then he uncoiled himself instead.

"Punchlines get rewritten," he muttered, his voice rough. But the words wavered like a half-forgotten promise. "If you're patient enough to listen."

The bar shifted. The dim light caught brief flickers of surprise and disdain among the few patrons scattered in the corners, but none stepped closer. None bothered.

His isolation tightened like a noose.

The stranger leaned away, satisfied for a moment, and the atmosphere slipped back into its usual lull. Jaxon's shoulders dropped. He pulled out his phone again, fingers trembling slightly as they scrolled through the day's reminders. Every ding and buzz felt like a tiny avalanche. Another text from the agent demanding updates. A flurry of bank notices flashed insistent warnings: overdue, pending, failed.

The numerical dance of decay.

On the screen, "Emma" still beckoned like an unreachable shore. His thumb hovered, refusing to tap. He was trapped in a limbo of memory and regret.

A fight raged beneath the surface—between escape and endurance, between the poison of drink and the fragile thread of something unnamed pulling at his shadows. It was a struggle between the man he had been and whoever he might become if he had the guts to try.

The television crackled louder as the championship game continued. Crowds roared, and helmets clashed in vivid cascades of sound that seemed distant and foreign. Jaxon's eyes never left the screen, but the images blurred, merging with the steady throb in his chest.

Another drink whispered seductively in the haze, a promise of numbness waiting just beyond his reach.

But he didn't reach for it.

Instead, the empty glass caught a jagged reflection of him: unshaven, worn—a man tangled in the fallout of yesterdays. His fingers released the glass with a soft scrape against the wood, the contact cold enough to rouse the frozen silence that blanketed him.

The words came raw and harsh, private and unyielding:

"Maybe it's time to look forward instead of backward."

Silence pressed heavier. The game's relentless chant filled the space between heartbreak and hope. Jaxon remained rooted at the far end of the bar, shadows folding around him like a faded promise, caught between the weight of old ghosts and the fragile ache of a new beginning waiting just out of sight.

The bar's low hum—muffled voices and clinking bottles—blurred into a dull drone behind the sudden pulse from Jaxon's pocket. His fingers, rough and twitching, fished out the phone with reluctant precision. The screen blinked to life, cutting through the smoky haze near the cracked window. A text glowed harshly against the chipped wood of the bar counter, where his elbow rested on sticky residue, faint traces of spilled whiskey clinging to the grain.

One shot left. Redemption Valley. You take it, or you're done.

Marcus Hale's name sat stark and unforgiving above the message, as if the words themselves could slice through Jaxon's defenses. The digits glowed colder than the stale air around him. No congratulations. No pleasantries. Just the blunt truth: pick up the pieces or settle for nothing.

His thumb hovered over the screen. Muscles knotted in quiet defiance. The promise of a last chance—a final throw—was an alien ache against the ringing silence in his mind. His thumb trembled, hovering over "delete" before retreating, fingers curling tight as a hard pulse quickened beneath his ribs.

Beneath the terse line, two attachments blinked. A travel voucher and a thin digital contract. The voucher looked slick and clinical—a one-way ticket out of the ruins, stamped with barcodes and dates. Last stop for fallen players. Make or break. Jaxon swallowed, dry as rust, his gaze locked on the glowing screen as shadows flickered over his grimy hands.

The contract's words hovered just a swipe away, waiting to bind him with their cold formality. His wariness stirred—past experiences had taught him that binding obligations came with traps. He had learned that lesson more than once.

"Don't even think about it," the older man beside him muttered, scorn thick in his whiskey-soaked voice. He leaned in like a vulture circling. "Is this what you're banking on? Another washed-up ballplayer's circus act?"

Jaxon's jaw tightened, muscles drawn taut beneath his skin. He didn't look up.

The mocking continued, dripping like poison. "Last shot, huh? Gonna drop it just like every damn time before? I'd bet a beer you'll screw it up."

The bar's stale smell wrapped around Jaxon—spilled beer and sticky floors—but beneath it, something harsher clawed at his gut. A sudden rising heat he fought to smother beneath practiced indifference. His fingers curled into fists, knuckles blanching.

"You've got me all figured out, huh?" His voice came out sharp and cold. "Maybe I'm just saving my best for last."

The man snorted, dismissing the threat like an old joke. Murmurs from other patrons shifted for a moment, curiosity flickering before retreating to their own shadows. No one stepped in. No one cared. The weight of their indifference hit harder than the insults.

Jaxon's lips pressed into a thin line. The sting of humiliation folded him inward. He didn't respond. Instead, he let the phone lie face-up on the scratched bar top, the glow of the offer bleeding into the rough grain like a secret left exposed.

"Just a joke," the stranger sneered under his breath, his eyes flickering with cruel anticipation. "Don't waste your pity party here."

Jaxon's breath hitched, his nostrils flaring against the burn of cheap smoke. He lowered his hand slowly, his muscles stiff as granite, and pressed a sharp finger against the screen, magnifying the tiny print on the contract. Lines of fine text spelled out rules and ultimatums—deadlines that snapped shut like trapdoors.

His gaze drifted to the travel voucher—a cold promise to a place where dreams went to die or find a new heartbeat. Somewhere beneath the weight of nearly lost years, a flicker of something like hope stirred: tentative, fragile.

The television overhead blared on, blending the roar of crowds and adrenaline-drenched voices into a relentless stream. The championship game marched through its final moments, with crowds cheering for players who wore the glory Jaxon once claimed. The announcers' voices were a distant echo now, names and highlights scratching at the back of his skull like ghosts refusing to rest.

The strain in his eyes deepened, revealing pools of exhaustion and stubborn fire. He forced himself to meet the flickering screen for a moment, willing the past to fold away. His fingers trembled, but he didn't swipe the offer away.

"Looks like you've got a choice," the stranger's voice cut through again, laced with bitter amusement. "Last chance. What, are you going to take it, or just fade into the shadows?"

Jaxon's lips curled into a humorless half-smile—tired but sharp.

"Doesn't make it easy, does it?"

The man grinned wide, the leer of a gambler flipping his last card.

"Nah. Not for a man who's been down this road before."

The air between them shivered with tension, the bar's dim glow casting long, uneven shadows across the scarred wood. Around them, the night pressed in with indifferent weight—a room full of ghosts and lost chances. Jaxon's fingers brushed the edge of the phone screen again. The details remained stark, still real.

He set the phone down carefully and deliberately, just so, with the screen facing up and light spilling over the dark wood. The truth lay bare between him and the buzzing neon.

His eyes narrowed, tracing the edges of the offer he couldn't yet accept or deny. The sting of pride clawed alongside the whisper of possibility—an ember in the cold, fragile night.

He didn't look away—not yet.

The television blares during the final moments—the whistle slicing through the roar of the crowd like a blade. On screen, a fresh-faced quarterback raises the championship trophy high above his head. The stadium trembles. Cheers erupt. The camera swings over waves of elated fans, their faces lit with unfiltered joy. Jaxon Reyes sits rigid, his eyes locked on the screen as the commentators' voices echo with heavy nostalgia, fingers of ice crawling the length of his spine.

"There he goes, the new hero of the Hawks," one voice intones, flooding the room with a hollow kind of celebration in which Jaxon once basked. "Remember when Reyes led this team here? Before the fall—it was electric."

The close-ups shift. Faces gleam—players who once shared his fights, now ghosts etched into highlight reels. Perfect passes flicker across the screen. Touchdown dances. Roaring crowds blur into one another like a fever dream he can no longer touch.

His knuckles whiten as he grips the empty glass, fighting the pull of the bottle on the shelf behind the bar. The rims bite into his skin. Stale whiskey clings to the air between breaths, acrid and accusing.

Behind him, the bartender reaches up and snaps the power off the television. The harsh click breaks the spell, plunging the bar into a dull fluorescent hum and peeling paint shadows.

"Closing time," the bartender muttered without looking. He nodded toward the door, his voice flat, somber as a judge delivering a sentence.

Jaxon's fingers lingered on the rim of the glass. The hollow clink against the worn wood beneath the counter was stark in the dim light. The bar felt colder now, the remaining patrons scattered like ghosts, their faces veiled in quiet detachment.

He dragged a slow breath, tasting the dry leather of his throat and the acrid tang of regret swirling beneath it. Another drink twisted inside him—dangerous, familiar—but something else threaded through the ache beneath his ribs: a brittle flicker of resolve, or maybe just desperation wearing resolve's face.

His gaze drifted across the cracked linoleum floor. He heard a scrape of chair legs nearby and the faint murmur of voices dissolving into nothing.

The sharp shortcut back to numbness beckoned, while the slow, uncertain step forward toward something he'd barely dared to name whispered just as loudly. The glass suddenly felt heavier, colder—the weight of empty promises pressed into its fragile frame.

He set it down with a soft thud. The act was small, deliberate.

"Last call, Reyes," the bartender said, the words carrying a sharper edge now, thin as a challenge. Jaxon nodded, pulling the hood of his beaten jacket tighter against the chill crawling in from the cracked door.

His fingers found the phone in his pocket, feeling the sharp edges of the message Marcus Hale had sent hours ago—an offer dangling on the thin line between salvation and surrender. He didn't trust Marcus—not entirely. But beneath the distrust lay something fragile and dangerous: a reluctant flicker of hope, the kind of hope that could unmake him if he let it.

He rose, his joints stiff from the weight of too many hours spent folded into a barstool.

Outside, the city breathed beneath the dim glow of street lamps. This corner of it, anyway—rundown and fading, with storefronts boarded or abandoned and cracked concrete mapped with years of neglect. The air swirled with the scent of wet asphalt, distant car engines, and the faint promise of rain. The atmosphere hung thick with the stale perfume of decline, gritty and unforgiving—the kind of place where men like him came to disappear.

Jaxon stepped into the night. Every noise was sharp against the darkness: the scrape of footsteps behind him fading, the muted hum of neon signs flickering above closed storefronts. His shoulders tightened against the cold, the weight of the day folding into the shadows beneath his hood.

The glow from the bar's window behind him was a river of harsh light spilling onto cracked concrete. He moved away from it and the bar's whispered judgments, carrying the offer like a fragile ember tucked deep inside a stained pocket. The raw residue of tonight's bitter humiliation clung to him like a second skin.

His breath formed ragged clouds as he blended into the night, the city swallowing him whole but not quite erasing the ghost of all that had come before.

The air outside the bar clings to Jaxon's skin like a damp shroud, sour with spilled beer and winter's bite lingering in the night. His boots scrape against gravel as he steps onto cracked pavement bathed in the sickly yellow fog of the streetlights. Long shadows flicker and twitch in the cold, as if the darkness itself is restless.

He tugs the hood of his worn jacket tighter around his face, trying to fold himself smaller and less visible.

A sharp click breaks the tentative silence—the quick, accusing snap of a camera.

Jaxon's pulse hammers against his ribs as his head snaps sideways. Victor Cross stands a few feet away, the lens aimed like a sniper's scope. His grin stretches thin, teeth sharp as broken glass.

"Figured you'd sneak off unnoticed, Reyes," Victor says, his voice low and oily, blending into the hum of traffic and distant sirens. "Ain't luck exactly waving your flag tonight, is it?"

Jaxon's shoulders stiffen. His eyes darken, a flicker of heat igniting behind the dull ache. His jaw tightens until it aches, but no words come.

Victor steps closer. The camera flashes relentlessly, capturing every grimace and every shadow. He is portraying Jaxon as a haunted ghost, chasing the mirage of a glory long gone.

"So tell me," Victor presses, his voice louder, sharp enough to cut through the murmur of the night. "Where did it all go wrong this time? The scandal? Or is it just your ego finally losing the game?"

Jaxon's gaze locks onto Victor's smirk, his eyes dark pools thick with years of bitterness. "Why don't you try that question on yourself?" he spits back. "You build careers out of ashes and scorched reputations."

Victor's chuckle slides into the night like a snake curling through dry leaves. "Smart mouth, Reyes. You know that's why people keep watching. The fall is always juicier than the rise."

He steps in closer, the camera raised like a weapon.

"Tell me—are you going to crawl out of that hole, or just keep digging?"

Jaxon's fists curl into tight balls at his sides. His voice drops to a controlled snarl laced with an icy edge. "I'm done playing your game. Move aside."

The street holds its breath. Passersby glance at the confrontation, their eyes flicking between the broken man and the relentless journalist. Few intervene. The world is too tired, too numb.

But Victor, relentless as a shark sensing blood, leans in undeterred.

"What about last week's headlines?" Another flash. "Do you think Redemption Valley's ready for your comeback? Or will you set fire to another chance?"

Jaxon spits out a curse. His muscles coil like those of a cornered animal. A heartbeat longer. Then he turns, his hood marking him as an invisible scar against the streetlight's glare. His steps are quick and sharp, desperate to widen the gap.

Victor's camera whirs behind him—a volley of clicks and flashes that rain down like missiles. Each one ignites a prick of anxiety deep in Jaxon's chest.

His breath comes unevenly. The cold air freezes every nerve ending as memories dart like restless cats behind his eyes—tabloid covers, stadium boos, the bitter sting of betrayal layered beneath each exhale. These moments always hit the same: the flashes, the footsteps, the sensation of being hunted. His chest tightens as adrenaline surges, threatening to pull him under.

He rounds a street corner, glancing over his shoulder. Victor stands firm, updating the world with every captured frame.

Jaxon's fingers itch for warmth, for anything but the cold. His mind throttles down the adrenaline surge as the bar's rough edges dissolve behind him, swallowed in murmured conversations and stale cigarette smoke drifting through the alleys.

Years of intense media pressure have taught him this: panic feeds the sharks. Keep moving. Don't let them see you crack.

His car looms ahead—a battered relic of better days, its worn leather seats waiting like a refuge. The keys press cold against his palm as his fingers tremble, his heart still rattling in his throat.

Before the hood drops, he throws one last harsh glance over his shoulder, catching Victor's silhouette outlined in the crumbling city glow. Persistent. Unforgiving.

The driver's door groans as he pulls it open. The faint scrape against the asphalt is sharp in the silence that stretches between flashes and footsteps.

He slides inside and closes the door behind him. The metal is cool against his spine. His breath comes shallow and tight, the weight of the encounter heavy in his chest.

Outside, the night presses in with cold indifference. The streetlights sputter like dying stars as the distant hum of the city carries on, indifferent to the war waging in a quiet corner—between a fallen man and the greed waiting to consume whatever flicker of hope remains.

Jaxon leans back in the cracked vinyl seat. The night's damp chill seeps through the thin fabric of his jacket. The engine's hum is muted now, with streetlights casting lazy orange pools through the windshield.

His phone screen glows in the darkness—a pulse against the quiet. He taps it awake, his fingers rough and unsteady. The message from Marcus Hale pops up again, stubborn and blunt like the man's voice.

One shot left. Redemption Valley. You take it, or you're done.

He stares and scrolls through the terse lines—no fluff, no promises. Just the barest outline of his last chance.

A travel voucher is attached, along with a contract thin enough to slice pride like a knife. His thumb lingers over the text, tracing where hope blends with humiliation. The weight of those harsh words settles like rubble pressing on his chest, constricting in sudden waves.

Smoke curls from the ember of his cigarette, a fragile dance in the car's stale air. He flicks ashes with a nervous twitch, scattering them across the cracked dashboard. Pain flickers through his fingers as he fumbles for another match, striking it quickly. The flame flares and dies, mirroring his own flickering resolve. His fingers fumble as he lights the next one, shadows leaping over his clenched jaw.

This is it, he thinks, bitterness licking the back of his throat like cheap whiskey gone sour.

His mind conjures the ruins: roaring stadiums now muffled by silence. Public disgrace carved deep in headlines and hushed whispers. The faces of the crowd blur into faceless mobs, their cheers replaced by jeers. Championship rings slip through his fingers, replaced by the cold weight of regret.

He imagined Redemption Valley—not the faded field or battered goalposts; he had seen those before, years ago, when he was still hungry and whole. Now? Now it was something else—a place where maybe he could claw back something: respect, a future, maybe even a shred of himself. Back then, Redemption Valley had been a stepping stone; now it felt like his last ledge before the fall.

The thought ignited a flicker—faint but alive—in the cave of shadows he had been digging into for months.

Dawn crept in slow and gray, spilling light over cracked sidewalks and shuttered windows. Silent city streets rolled past as he lit another cigarette, smoke curling around the rearview mirror. His reflection caught and held—eyes sharp and haunted, jaw clenched as if he were biting back the past.

The travel voucher's bright icon beckoned on the screen. His thumb hovered, pride wrestling with desperation. He fought the urge to backspace, to delete the message, to let this chance dissolve into the night like so many before.

But the ember in his chest pulsed stronger now—fragile but alive.

He tapped open the voucher. The digital ticket unspooled like a lifeline, the cursor blinking an invitation.

Finally, with a breath that shook the air, he pressed "Confirm." The screen blurred with confirmation—a one-way ticket to Redemption Valley, to a place wired with more ghosts than hope.

His phone vibrated softly, stirring the stillness. He glanced at the screen—an unopened message from Emma. The name flickered at the edge of his vision like a ghost he couldn't quite reach. Cold blue light bathed his face. He stared. For a long moment, the urge to open it thrummed deep inside him, a silent ache threading through his ribs.

But his fingers curled shut around the phone instead. He wouldn't crack. Not yet. Not when the last thread of control was slipping through his hands like smoke. He tapped the screen, closing the message without reading it. The phone dimmed like a fading heartbeat.

Outside, the city yawned awake. The faint scent of damp pavement rose with the wind, and early traffic swelled in the distance. Inside the cramped car, Jaxon sat rigid, his breath shallow but steady. His eyes were fixed not on the road but on his reflection in the glass.

Somewhere deep behind those eyes, something began to stir—a cautious ember. Neither fierce nor certain, but enough to tilt the night's balance.

His fingers curled into fists pressed against his thighs, nails digging faint crescent marks into his skin. The cigarette between his lips burned low, its last tendrils twisting upward, fragile and thin.

Then two rough voices broke the silence.

"Didn't think you had another in you, Reyes. Thought you were done for good."

Jaxon's eyes snapped to the passenger side. No one was there. The barbs were a memory—the echo of a man's sneer from a few hours ago when the stranger's words had cut too close. Too sharp.

"Yeah? Looks like you don't know when to quit. Think you have this one all figured out, huh?"

"No thanks to any of you," Jaxon muttered under his breath, his voice rough with fatigue. "This one's mine. Or it's nothing."

"Better not screw it up like everything else."

The words hung, bitter and heavy. But Jaxon's grip tightened—not on pride, but on the thin thread pulling him from the edge.

He exhaled slowly. The cigarette's glow winked out.

His eyes flicked back to the ticket blinking on his phone. The path ahead was neither mapped nor promised, but it was real.

One step. One choice.

Then the screen went dark.

Welcome to Redemption Valley

The bus grumbled to a stop. Tires crunched against cracked asphalt, stained with oil and scattered leaves. Jaxon Reyes swung his duffel off the worn seat, the fabric faded from years of hauling gear and sweat.

The humid morning pressed around him like a wet blanket, with gray light settling low and thick. He set one boot onto the uneven parking lot, where cracked concrete wove snake-like fissures beneath dull puddles.

Ahead, the football field stretched out—a patchwork of scorched grass and muddy dirt, with lines blurred from neglect. The goalpost leaned crooked, its peeling yellow paint no more than a brittle memory. A cluster of crows hovered near the base, their hushed caws blending with the distant hum of the awakening town. Once, this field had mattered. State champions for three years running. Now, it was just rust and regret.

Jaxon lifted his chin, his eyes narrowing at the decay. The air tasted faintly metallic, sliced by the sharp tang of freshly cut grass struggling to grow in stubborn patches. His fingers tightened around the strap, the worn leather rubbing raw. Nothing worth saving ever came easy.

The taxi waited at the edge of the lot, a battered sedan with faded navy paint chipped at the edges. Sliding into the passenger seat, Jaxon stared out as the car lurched forward, cutting through the twisted veins of Redemption Valley's main street.

Mismatched houses leaned into cracked sidewalks, their windows dark or shuttered, and the paint formed a patchwork of chipped pastels and harsh neutrals. Rust gathered on the edges of mailboxes. Overgrown lawns reached for attention in vain.

Locals cast sidelong glances as the taxi rolled by—weathered faces worn into thin smiles or scowls. A woman at a corner store gripped a faded headline from a crumpled newspaper, her eyes flicking up as the car slowed. A teenage boy leaned against a cracked storefront, his gaze sharp and unblinking, as though he knew the story by heart and wasn't done telling it.

Recognition ignited in a few eyes—bitter and reluctant. That old disappointment and scandal thrummed through the town like a restless ghost, refusing to be laid to rest.

Jaxon swallowed against the tightness creeping up his throat. The engine's low drone and the murmurs from the town settled into a dull ache behind his ribs. He retreated into himself, his shoulders hunching and drawing inward. Even the dust hanging in the air tasted of grudges and faded hopes.

The stadium emerged around a bend—a battered monument to faded glory. Weathered championship banners flapped listlessly from rusted poles, their once-vibrant colors dulled by restless seasons and relentless sun. The sign above the entrance bore cracked paint and a missing 'R' in "Redemption Valley," with the steady drip of rain having etched stories into the masonry. Graffiti sprawled across the cinderblock walls—tags and furious scrawls like a language of defiance scratched into stone.

A cold shiver slid down Jaxon's spine. Torn banners whipped limply in the breeze, their faded names barely readable beneath grime and peeling paint.

The taxi slowed as they neared the entrance. The driver, a middle-aged man with sun-splashed skin and a cigarette dangling from the corner of his mouth, glanced over with a warning glint in his eyes.

"You'll want to watch your back here," the driver muttered, flicking ash from his cigarette with a wary glance in the mirror. "Folks remember the news. And not all of them want you here."

Jaxon's jaw clenched. He knew what they remembered—the fumbled play, the missed block, the interception that should never have happened. The shame burned like a scar reopened. He met the driver's gaze, offering nothing—just a nod, just steel.

The car sputtered to a stop near the heavy gray security doors. Jaxon fished coins from a weathered pocket and paid the driver with a crisp bill. He stepped out, his duffel slung low, leather scuffing against the cracked asphalt.

The air clung thick with heat and unease as he locked eyes on the looming building. It towered—a hulking silhouette of peeling paint and barred windows, sharp edges softened by the misty dawn. The faded blue "Home of the Hawks" banner drooped above the entrance, sagging like a forgotten promise.

His boots echoed hollowly against the concrete steps. Fingers grazed cold metal on the security gate, worn and unyielding.

The facility waited—heavy, silent—a crucible of second chances and whispered threats. A place where redemption tasted bitter and the stakes were carved deep.

Jaxon breathed in slowly and steadily. Damp earth mingled with distant leather and sweat. He crossed the threshold—the first step into a story already fraying at the edges.

The heavy security doors groaned open with a reluctant hiss, swallowing Jaxon Reyes into stale, suffocating air. The smell stole the air from his lungs—a sharp mix of sour sweat and damp concrete that twisted his stomach and made his throat tighten. He tasted decay beneath his tongue.

Overhead, the fluorescents sputtered—buzzing like a swarm of restless flies—casting flickering green shadows that danced over cracked cinderblocks. Near the corner, a janitor leaned against peeling walls, mop handle hanging slack from one hand. His eyes remained glued to a cracked phone screen. When Jaxon passed, the man's gaze darted away, sharp and dismissive, as though this newcomer irritated the very walls around him.

Jaxon shouldered his worn duffel—leather scuffed, strap frayed from years of use—and stepped forward. His cleats clicked sharply against the concrete, each sound swallowed by the long, narrow corridor ahead. Dust motes scattered in the patchy light. He walked through them like ghosts.

Along the walls, yellowed motivational posters cling desperately to their places. "Discipline Over Everything." "Pain is Temporary, Pride is Forever." The slogans have faded to ghostly whispers, their edges curling like dead leaves. Some are slashed, others folded, and a few are smeared with dirt or streaked with water stains that run like tears down cracked paint. Graffiti layers beneath—a tapestry of past hopes and lost fights, each mark a small rebellion against this place.

The facility itself bears the weight of its own decline. Paint peels in long strips, and concrete blooms with water damage. This building has witnessed dreams die before. That history seeps from every corner, a silent testimony to athletes who came seeking redemption and left with less than when they arrived.

As Jaxon trudges deeper, voices drift through the thick air—sharp, coarse, and carnivorous laughter that ripples louder with each step. Bursts of profanity and rough shouts claw at his nerves. The sound isn't the electric roar of a team united; it's ragged, raw, and chaos masquerading as camaraderie.

Bitterness pools at the back of his throat. The ghost of cocky optimism from moments before crumbles, fragile as cracked glass.

His breath comes slow and steady—a practiced rhythm learned from years under center, a way to ground himself. The thin promise whispered before he arrived, the one about this being his "last chance," feels distant now, almost naive, as though some younger version of himself had believed in such things.

His hand rises, rough fingers grazing the chipped metal of the locker room door. The temperature shifts. The air presses heavier with years of sweat and whispered disappointment. He can feel ghosts sewn into the fabric of these walls—the fracture lines of dreams that never took flight.

A low hum of static buzzes through the flickering lights above. The promise still claws at him—hope tangled with grit, defiant even here. But for the first time since he touched down, it dims, obscured by the taste of dust and broken echoes surrounding him.

"Don't get soft, Reyes," a low voice hisses from the shadows. "This place will chew you up."

He swallows hard, his jaw clenching as if to lock away whatever hope he still carries. Hope may be scarce here, but it's all he has. Slowly, he grips the door, feeling the rough metal bite into his palm.

"You think this place can fix you?" Another voice cracks like static, mocking, from somewhere deeper in the echoes.

Jaxon doesn't reply—not yet. The distant noise carries on—a cacophony of broken promises and wild laughter—while the dim corridor holds its breath, waiting. He pushes the door open and steps inside.

Jaxon Reyes yanked the locker room door open. A jagged blast of bass rattled the cramped space. Towels swung through the air like feathery boomerangs, scenting the humid room with stale sweat and the sharp tang of liniment. The damp air clung heavily, sticky against his skin, and the uneven thud of cleats on scuffed concrete echoed off metal lockers dented from years of frustration.

The players' posturing, shouting, and laughing filled every inch of the room with unruly energy. Their voices bristled like static electricity in the thick heat.

His eyes caught sight of Brick. The team's human wrecking ball hurled a scuffed football into a dented steel locker. The thunk echoed, sharp and accusatory. Brick's scowl sliced through the air when he caught Jaxon's glance. His massive frame cast a shadow that cooled the humid air. Behind that glare lived a man shaped by past struggles, with a need to prove himself that festered beneath every frustrated gesture.

The room felt fractured before Jaxon even stepped inside—a once-proud program crumbling under the weight of its own failures. Redemption Valley. The name used to mean something. Now it meant this: chaos, indiscipline, and a team teetering on the brink of collapse.

His gaze drifted across the room to Caleb, who was seated alone on a splintered bench. The kid wore headphones large enough to swallow his ears. But the silence betrayed him. His eyes flicked up, harboring a tangled mix of awe, resentment, and something like guarded hope. Caleb's fingers jittered over his phone, and hesitation trembled in every tap. Watching Jaxon was a silent challenge—or maybe a plea he didn't dare voice aloud.

DeShawn's voice boomed from deeper within the chaos, slicing through the racket. "Look alive, boys! The washed-up legends have arrived!" The room erupted in hoarse laughter, ice shattering. Eyes darted nervously, and hands flexed. The tension lingered just beneath the noise.

Jaxon's breath caught.

Eli Brooks stood across the room, his eyes narrowed, cold and calculating. A smirk tugged at the corner of his mouth, as if he held a secret just out of reach. His lips parted slightly, whispering something to a teammate nearby. Suspicion clenched Jaxon's chest; Eli's skepticism was a storm waiting to break.

The whiteboard on the far wall hung crooked. Instead of diagrams or plays, obscene doodles splattered across the surface—crude sketches and graffiti mocking any hint of order. The marker's faded black trails sank into the peeling paint, confirming what Jaxon already sensed deep in his bones: this team was fractured, undisciplined, and on the edge of collapse.

He stepped fully inside, and the door thudded shut behind him, muffling the outside world. The room swelled with noise—raucous laughter, sharp voices, and the thud of cleats on scuffed floors. Most faces avoided his gaze; eyes flickered away, shoulders tightened, and conversations dipped into hushed tones. The distance between him and this fractured tribe felt like a chasm opening wide, swallowing any fragile hope he brought with him.

A young voice called out from near the back, "Hey Reyes, are you lost or just scared of the noise?"

"Nope. Just figuring out where the hell I'm supposed to fit in."

The chuckles that followed felt hollow, echoing off concrete walls and faded locker stains—weightless gestures that barely concealed the simmering challenge. Jaxon's jaw tightened, his lips pressed into a thin line as he scanned the faces again. Each one was a stone in this fortress of distrust. Some flinched under his stare, while others met it head-on with veiled hostility.

Brick stepped forward, his massive frame blocking half the room. "You sure you're ready for this? This ain't the big leagues, Reyes. Time to get real—or get gone."

Jaxon tipped his head slowly, his eyes locked onto Brick's. "I don't need a pep talk from the locker room security guard."

Brick's glare sharpened. "Security guard? Is that what you think of me? Maybe I'm the only one who remembers what it takes."

DeShawn snorted, nudging Caleb as he wiped sweat from his brow. "Yeah, man, he's like a brick wall—only messier. That's why they call him Brick."

Caleb shrugged, tension riding every muscle. "You hear that? Bringing more drama than a soap opera."

Jaxon's hands curled into fists at his sides. "Drama's just part of the game, kid. I'm here to play."

The room roared back with laughter edged in skepticism. But within the noise, something unspoken wove tightly—a challenge, a dare, a reluctant invitation wrapped in barbs and jabs.

The bass dropped again. Music pulsed like a heartbeat beneath the verbal sparring. Jaxon's gaze slid once more to the whiteboard. No plays. No plans. Just chaos scribbled in ink, a visual echo of this room's fractured soul. The scent of old sweat, cheap cologne, and damp fabric lingered, wrapping around him as he stood planted near the doorway.

In the clamor, some players nudged each other. Eyes bounced between Jaxon and Eli, caught in a silent war of strategies and alliances under the fluorescent lights buzzing overhead. The raucous energy swelled, swallowing him whole and tightening the cage of isolation threading through the locker room.

A quiet voice broke the din, barely audible. "Good luck, Reyes. You're going to need it."

Jaxon didn't flinch. He knew this was just the opening play—a gauntlet thrown, a battle line drawn. The locker room noise rose again, a roaring tide of challenge and reluctance, sealing him into this crucible of grit and ghosts.

He stood alone but unbroken, at the edge of a chaos that would either forge him anew or shatter what little hope remained.

The racket in the locker room shattered like glass caught in a fist when a sharp whistle cut through the chaos. Jaxon froze mid-step. The echo bounced off concrete walls, muscles tensing as all eyes snapped toward Coach Marcus Hale.

Hale fills the doorway like an immovable wall—shoulders squared, spine rigid, eyes hard as flint. His jaw sets like a trap closing.

"You're Reyes," Hale's voice cuts across the room, cold and raw. "I don't care what the papers say. Here, you earn everything."

The words drop, weightless yet heavy. An unspoken challenge drifts between the players, who simmer in the hush that follows, afraid to breathe loud enough to break the tension. Jaxon's jaw tightens, muscles beneath his skin twitching. He locks eyes with Hale's steady glare, measuring the steel behind it.

Somewhere inside, doubt claws at his ribs. Can he actually earn it here? After everything?

Hale steps deeper inside. The cement floor creaks—decades of sweat and will pressed into its surface. "This isn't about what you did or who you were," he says, stripping every pretense from his voice. "There's zero tolerance for drama. You want respect? You earn it with sweat and grind, not headlines and past glories."

Jaxon swallows. The acrid sting of stale sweat and liniment floods his nostrils, thick and choking. Each syllable slides down like a bitter pill. His fingers curl into fists, nails digging into calloused palms, trying to quiet the heat rising from his chest.

The room feels tighter. Fluorescent lights buzz overhead like an accusation.

"Players will test you," Hale's gaze drops briefly to the worn floor before rising back up, flint unyielding. "Coaches will test you too. That's how this works. If you can't stand the heat, don't bother stepping onto my field."

They don't sound like empty threats. The warning seeps into the locker room, threading through every dented locker and scarred bench. Then Hale's shoulders pivot—sharp and precise—as he strides away without another glance. His footsteps fade down the corridor.

Behind him, a static-charged silence settles. Thick. Waiting.

Jaxon watches him go. Footsteps echo and fade, but the weight in his chest remains. He's no prodigy handed a spotlight. No star whispered about in awe. He's rough stone—stubborn, unrefined. Waiting to be carved or shattered.

The crowd's gaze feels like a slow burn across his skin. Judgment settles in layers, thick and unforgiving.

The locker room noise, once wild and chaotic, dims to murmurs—a low tide pulling back but never quite silent. Jaxon steps forward. The weight of the room presses in, heavy on his back like a linebacker's tackle.

The scent of sweat, old leather, and faint rusted metal curls in the stale air. Flickering bulbs hum overhead like broken wings, adding texture to the moment. Players shift, eyes darting between Jaxon and the empty doorway, measuring this new piece in their battered puzzle.

"You ready to shut up and work, or are you planning on being another headline?" a voice mutters from the edge of the room, sharp as a thorn. Laughter ripples, but pockets of silence hold firm.

Jaxon doesn't answer right away. When his voice comes, it cuts through like gravel scraping against steel.

"Not here to be anyone's cautionary tale."

He lets the words hang, low and rough, daring them to challenge his silence.

A ripple of surprise. A few stunned glances. Hale's words spin in the air, mixing with Jaxon's quiet defiance.

The pause stretches thick, the weight of a thousand unwon battles.

Coach Hale's whistle blares again, sharp as a gunshot, slicing open the moment.

Between the siren call and the stuttering fluorescent buzz, Jaxon catches it—the raw edge of what this place demands: survival through endurance, forgiveness earned by sweat, respect carved from chaos.

He isn't a savior here.

He's a player now.

One more gauntlet to run.

One more fall to rise from.

The buzz in the locker room swells. Players size him up—some with grudging respect, others with roiling resentment. The scent of liniment and sweat sinks deeper into Jaxon's skin, clinging as stubbornly as the skepticism etched into every face.

He tightens his grip on his duffel. The coarse fabric bites into his calloused hands. The game has just begun.

Jaxon Reyes threads his way between battered rows of green metal lockers. The air hangs thick with stale sweat and lingering tension. Muted conversations ripple like an undercurrent—sharp, mutinous murmurs that make the space feel cramped and breathless.

Heads swivel. Eyes narrow with suspicion and simmering disdain. His footsteps clack across the splintered wood bench. The hostility brushes against him like something alive, a silent warning that settles in his chest. It triggers an old wound—the one that never quite scarred over. This is what betrayal tastes like: cold and familiar.

A rough shove digs into his shoulder. Deliberate. Not subtle.

"Watch it, Reyes," a gruff voice hisses just behind him.

The jostle isn't accidental. As he steadies himself, a second bump follows—rougher. A quiet threat wrapped in cheap theater. Caleb, sitting nearby, shifts urgently. His open palm reaches out in hesitant solidarity. A subtle offer. A break in the icy wall.

But Brick's broad frame cuts between them like a living blockade. The defensive lineman's glare burns sudden and fierce—sharp enough to freeze Caleb's hand halfway. "Don't," Brick snaps low, his eyes locked on Reyes with a warning promise etched into the hard line of his jaw. Caleb withdraws, frustration wetting his quick breaths. The room's low murmur swells once more.

Jaxon's ears catch fragments of wagers whispered in dark corners. Rough voices dare to guess how long the former pro's resolve will last. The clink of imagined coins rings metallic and cold. Each calculated bet is a hammer striking isolation deeper into his ribs.

The room breathes around him—resentful, restless, ready to turn.

He reaches the far end, where his locker leans lonely against the peeling cinderblock wall. The nameplate rattles loose, barely clinging to the dented metal door. Someone has spray-painted jagged letters over his last name like a cruel scar: *FALLEN* screams in splattered black. The graffiti echoes the public scandal, the moment everything fractured. Of course, they'd use this insult now. Of course.

The silence hangs heavier here, thick with rancid expectation.

Fingers tightening, Jaxon pulls the locker door open. The rotten stench of mold and decay assaults him—a tangled mess of foul, unfurling athletic tape, sticky and blackened with age. Nestled amid the ruin lies a dead rat, curled and stiffened as if frozen in a final, bitter sneer.

His locker, once a haven, is now a grotesque shrine to mockery.

Laughter shatters the air—sharp, with jagged edges that scrape his nerves. It ricochets off the concrete—a relentless volley of mockery that presses against his skin like cold steel. Voices twist into cruel jokes and taunts that rake through the piercing silence.

Jaxon lifts his gaze and locks eyes with Eli Brooks across the chaos. Eli is a shadow at the fringe of the crowd, his lips curled in a smirk. There is triumph lurking there—a silent admission. This vandalism is no accident; he orchestrated it. He probably did. The cold calculation in that glance digs deeper than any physical jab.

Movement from the corner catches Jaxon's attention. Coach Marcus Hale steps into the room. His sturdy frame halts as his eyes scan the vandalized locker and its gruesome contents. His jaw tightens, flint-hard.

He says nothing—no intervention, no protective shield.

The heavy silence between them spreads like wildfire, delivering a clear message: this fight, Reyes, is yours alone.

Jaxon closes the dented metal door slowly and deliberately. The clang echoes hollow and final. His shadowed face stares back from the worn surface—grim and unyielding beneath furrowed brows.

Around him, laughter buzzes like vicious insects—stinging, circling, relentless.

But amid the storm of jeers, Jaxon stands firm, ice and steel against the tide.

Jaxon's jaw tightens until the muscles knot painfully, his eyes locked on the dead rat splayed grotesquely atop his gear. The foul, damp stench of decay bites at his nostrils, mingling with the sour tang of rotten athletic tape clinging like a second skin to battered pads and cleats.

A sharp flicker shudders through his mind. Ease and respect once crowned this space—trophies gleaming, nameplate pristine. Now, that memory shatters against the cruel graffiti sprawling across his name, smeared in spiteful strokes like one last jab from ghosts he thought he had left behind.

His throat tightens, and his jaw muscles contract as he swallows the rising fury, locking it behind a quiet mask. No storming out. No shouting down the jeers crowding the room's cold air.

Instead, his hands move deliberately, almost ritualistically, peeling away the cloying tape in stiff strips. They scrape away decades of dust beneath and press rotten fragments into a battered corner. The rat's lifeless eyes stare accusatorily, but Jaxon hesitates only for a breath before bending to scoop it up with cautious fingers, wincing at the slick chill. He carries the grim cargo across the room to a dented trash can. The scrape of plastic rubbing against his palm is the last unwelcome sound before silence settles back in.

Over the low rumble of locker room banter and the occasional crackle of half-hearted chuckles, the room's poisoned atmosphere seeps through. Some players toss half-mocking glances; others pretend to show pity, their faces an unsettling blend of schadenfreude and sympathy. Jaxon's silence slices through their noise—cold, impenetrable—a barrier forged by years of bruised pride.

He folds his battered jersey with precision. Each motion is measured; each second is a promise to himself that he won't let this break him.

Pausing, he smooths the wrinkles from his weathered pants, his fingers lingering on the worn fabric as if it might anchor him to something solid.

A shadow detaches from the cluster. Footsteps, lighter but deliberate, echo softly against the concrete floor. The scrape of Eli's sneakers on the worn concrete sharpens like a knife against the din of muffled jeers.

Eli Brooks steps closer, his eyes sharp and unblinking, his mouth curling into a smirk that tastes of envy and disdain. His words hit like a cold fist.

"Welcome to Redemption, Reyes. Try not to choke on your comeback."

The locker room holds its breath for a heartbeat. Then laughter follows—a brittle veil over venom.

Jaxon's hand freezes mid-motion, his palm pressed flat against the rough metal face of his locker door. The pocked surface presses cool against his skin, catching his trembling reflection—shadowed eyes, jaw set hard, a man stripped down to bare resolve.

Humiliation claws at his insides, harder than the public scandals and televised rebukes ever did. But beneath that raw sting, something quieter and fiercer stirs, like ash puffed toward life.

For a moment, Jaxon wonders if this is just the beginning; if Eli's taunt is the worst this place has to offer, or if things could get even harder from here.

He pushes the thought aside.

His voice finally breaks the heavy silence: low, gravelly, but unequivocal.

"That's where you're wrong, Brooks."

Eli's smirk falters ever so slightly, his eyes narrowing as he steps back into the crowd's uncertain murmur. Jaxon straightens, muscles taut—not in triumph, but in defiance.

Around him, the half-lit lockers loom like silent sentinels, once a shrine and now a battlefield. He stands immovable against the noise, a dark silhouette etched into the dented steel—flawed but unyielding.

His breath comes steady, exhaling a quiet promise to himself: no matter how deep the wounds, no matter how loud the jeers, he'll carve his place here by grit and bone.

His gaze drifts briefly to the worn edges of the nameplate; the spray paint is still smeared but powerless against the man who refuses to fold.

He's not just here to survive.

He's here to last.

Shock Therapy

The building squats low against the murky blue of pre-dawn. Emma slips through the narrow door of the Redemption Valley medical facility, the damp chill wrapping around her like a thin cloak. With a soft click, she flips on the pale LED lights. They hum to life, casting a sharp-edged glow against the sea-glass green walls. Shadows retreat, making the small room feel sterile yet quietly alive.

She moves to the treatment table, her fingers reaching for the paper roll. The scent of aged liniment drifts in from the field beyond, layering over grass and earth—care and hard use braided together. Emma pulls the paper taut. It whispers against itself, crisp and alive. She smooths it flat beneath her hands. From the nearby counter, she plucks clear plastic bins labeled with neat print—tape, bandages, foam rollers, and icy-hot cream—and arranges them carefully. Each container lines up like sentinels, waiting.

A soft hiss escapes as she plugs in the diffuser on the windowsill. Sharp, clean peppermint unfurls into the sterile air. The contrast soothes and sharpens at once. The little succulents perched beside the diffuser glisten, their waxy leaves fragile and green. Emma's fingers pause mid-air, resting lightly on one leaf as a flicker of something—doubt, maybe—tugs at her. She shakes it off and nudges the row straight, as if imposing order on the morning's impending chaos.

She pulls open the worn binder. The leather spine is cracked and softened with use, and the pages are yellowed and dog-eared from seasons of aches and rebounds. Her eyes skim down the list, tracing names inked in black: Brick Turner, DeShawn Price, Caleb Monroe. They are familiar enough to carry weight. Next to each name are scribbled notes: "old sprain right ankle," "turf burn, watch swelling," "shoulder tightness, limit load." These players matter. She knows their bodies the way some people know maps. Her pen flicks quick tick marks, creating a quiet rhythm that steadies her focus.

"I need you to get it together today," she breathes to herself. Her lips barely move, and the words dissolve into the quiet room.

She straightens, and the binder closes with a soft, final snap. Her hand moves to the row of succulents, cold and glossy beneath her fingertips. The dawn light catches their leaves—pale, fragile, and holding steady. She steadies her breath. Her shoulders stiffen slightly, and her hands remain firm despite a flicker of doubt behind her eyes.

The peppermint scent tastes faintly sweet on her tongue. Low murmurs drift through the walls—voices stirring and metal clanging softly. Echoes of a restless morning begin to wake.

She pockets the pen, and her fingertips linger briefly on the binder's worn leather. Then she moves to the door handle. Cold metal meets her palm. She pauses for a heartbeat as the first ripple of life from the training facility spills in—shouts rising, laughter echoing, and the unmistakable cadence of early morning grit.

Outside, the day was already beginning.

The quiet smile she holds is tight and measured. Her jaw is set. She's ready.

A raucous chorus pushes against the heavy medical room door. A slam of lockers shards the air—metal banging against metal with a clatter sharp enough to make Emma's hand freeze mid-reach on the worn doorknob. Somewhere beyond, Coach Hale's gruff voice cuts through the jumbled noise, a sharp bark above the overlapping laughter and the clang of iron weights.

"Get your heads in the game! No horsing around!"

His tone is all iron and command, unmistakable and charged with urgency. Emma's pulse shifts into alertness. There's weight in that voice—the kind of pressure that settles into her shoulders before the real work begins. Coach expects readiness. He expects control. She exhales slowly. Today, they'll need both.

Emma leans forward, easing the door open just enough to peer into the hallway. The fluorescent lights bleach the narrow corridor in dull white, flickering faintly overhead like a pulse syncing with the chaos. Voices rise and fall in fragmented bursts, sharp as boxers' jabs and twice as quick.

"Move, Brick! You're blocking me!"

"I didn't touch you—quit whining!"

A string of salty epithets ricochets off the concrete walls, creating a rough-edged symphony of men who are tired and wired, aching and restless. The tension vibrates in the air, thick as dust motes swirling in the stale light. Emma's jaw clenches just enough to still the tremor beneath her skin. Something's on a hair trigger—frustrations fraying like worn rope, ready to snap.

She closes the door slowly and turns back to the whiteboard fixed on the far wall of her office—a practical battlefield map of healing.

She flips it open, unfolding the day's priorities: bleeding, concussion checks, and mobility assessments. Her pen races through the list in quick, precise strokes. The faint scratch of the marker against the whiteboard feels tense and focused.

Bleeding: control first. The open wounds that bleed faster than hope.

Concussion checks: watchfulness above all. Silent threats that aren't bloodied but break all the same.

Mobility: measure every grimace and twitch. A delicate balance of pain and will.

Emma breathes deeply. Her shoulders relax. The space within her settles. The faint scent of peppermint curls from the diffuser, warding off the clinical sterility with something softer—bracing and clear. The corners of her mouth flatten in resolve.

A storm is coming. Time to stand steady or get swept away.

The door swings wide as she steps into the hall. A cold draft stirs the papers clipped to bulletin boards, mixing with the smell of sweat, rubber cleats scuffing the linoleum, and a faint trace of turf glue lingering from the morning drills. The distant thud of feet pounding the stairwells layers beneath the sharp chorus of voices.

Emma moves with a calm born of long practice. Each step is deliberate as she heads toward the swirl of noise—a beacon of order amid the coming storm. Her hands flex at her sides, subtly ready to transform chaos into care.

The hallway stretches ahead, lined with scuffed lockers battered by the weight of seasons past. Redemption Valley's football program wore its history on these metal doors—the echoes of broken promises and worn dreams hung like jerseys on rusted hooks. Even the air seemed to carry the weight of what had come before.

She pauses momentarily before the training room entrance. The quiet before the surge holds, brittle with heat and tension.

It's time.

###

The door to the medical room slams open. Metal clangs. Heavy footsteps thud across the linoleum.

Brick Turner bursts through, a soaked towel clamped against his eyebrow. His gruff curses spill like wildfire, filling the cramped space with heat. Blood seeps through the fabric—dark and fast. Emma's stomach tightens, that familiar flutter of controlled urgency, but her hands move without hesitation. Sterile gauze. Antiseptic. She steps forward before the anger in Brick's eyes can fully ignite, her voice firm and steady.

Behind him, DeShawn Price limps exaggeratedly, his grin betraying the theatrical hamstring pull. His voice cuts sharp and loud. "Nah, man, you're trippin'. I had the line wide open—try again."

Caleb Monroe trails beside him, his jaw tight. "I was running my route. You didn't even see me coming."

Emma raises a steady hand. Her jaw tightens, and her breath comes measured and controlled. When her voice cuts through—hard as cracked leather—there's no room for argument. "Sit. Stay. No fights in here."

The doorway swells as more players shuffle in. Groans and complaints tangle like wires in the heavy air.

"Hamstring," someone hisses.

"Turf burns got me," whispers another.

Fingers flex awkwardly; a pinkie is sprained, tucked carefully away. The room clings to the bitter tang of sweat mingled with sharp liniment. Torn jerseys hang damp and heavy against slick skin. Emma's voice cuts through again—just loud enough, just firm enough. "One spot each. No crowding the door. Everyone, take a seat—isolated and quiet. Help me keep this room from turning into a brawl."

Reluctant bodies scatter to the benches. Shoulders bump and settle. The player storm begins to calm under her steady gaze.

Emma kneels before Brick first. Her fingers are deft as she peels back the towel. A jagged red cut splits the heavy ridge above his eye, angry and raw. She swabs it with antiseptic. The sting makes him grunt, but he doesn't complain. Her fingers stay steady as she threads butterfly stitches across the wound—each loop a quiet battle against his simmering irritation. The clipped humor she laces through her words is dry, deliberate, and designed to redirect his fire.

"Try not to bleed on my floor next time, tough guy. Cleaning that up is a royal pain."

Brick grunts something between a curse and a truce. His glare softens as the sharp edges of pain dull beneath her care. Tension ebbs from his frame, leaving space for something like relief.

Emma's hands shift to DeShawn next. She bends his foot gently, examining the swollen ankle beneath scuffed, turf-strewn socks. "You're milking that limp more than the injury," she says with a smirk. "Ice it. Don't audition for a drama club."

DeShawn's laughter bubbles out, filling the cramped room with warmth. He lowers himself onto the bench, the exaggerated limp melting into a genuine wince. Relief settles over him like a balm.

Beside them, Caleb edges toward DeShawn again. Voices rise, threading with frustration. Emma cuts between them, her eyebrows drawn tight.

"Enough." Iron edges her voice. "Caleb, lie down. You've got a shoulder I need to check. This bickering isn't helping anyone heal faster."

She points toward a worn treatment table, its vinyl cracked but serviceable. DeShawn's retort catches in a chuckle as he relents, sinking back with an exaggerated sigh.

"I promise—I'll take care of everyone in the order they arrived. No one's getting left behind."

She calls softly to one of her assistants, gesturing for ice packs to be handed out to restless hands and sore limbs. There is quiet precision in motion. The room exhales under her control.

Emma pulls out the worn binder. Her thumb flicks through notes as she scribbles beside each player's name—Brick's eyebrow cut, De-Shawn's ankle swelling, Caleb's tender shoulder. She pockets a strip of tape with the rhythm of hours spent in hurried care, her mind ticking through the next steps. She takes a breath, steadying herself. This work—endless, necessary, exhausting—never completely leaves her shoulders. But the players need her to remain steady. So she stays steady.

Footsteps shuffle. Voices soften. The shuffling of bodies becomes still.

"Brick, hold still. Almost done here." She snaps tape over the final stitch. The paper rustles softly—a small victory in the lingering tension.

DeShawn's foot nudges gently against the ice pack. "You think you're the only one who hurts, huh?" he grins, nudging Caleb playfully.

Caleb barely smiles but nods, his eyes flicking to the floor. Vulnerable. A quiet strength masks something deeper.

Emma watches them all. She notes their exhaustion and defiance tangled together. The task ahead isn't just healing bones and muscles; it's binding fractured minds and bruised egos.

As she tucks the tape away and closes the binder, her eyes scan the players, calm enough to listen. Her authority is established. Her space is held. Awareness is sharp, and her presence is steady. The room breathes with tentative order now, subdued conversations rising like ripples on still water.

She brushes the binder flat on the table with care. The faint rustle is a whispered promise: this is where they heal. This is where the fight for second chances begins.

Coach Marcus Hale lingers at the threshold of the medical room, arms folded tightly across his chest. His jaw is a hard line—the kind that rarely cracks, especially not here.

His steel-blue eyes lock onto Emma. The look is sharp—like morning light slicing through the narrow window. A silent challenge, or maybe a test.

Emma doesn't flinch. She keeps her gaze level, absorbed in the steady rhythm of care, her voice clipped into commands that slice through the chaos. She feels that old familiar grip tighten—a reminder that Hale's scrutiny isn't just about this room, but about every hint of weakness she refuses to show.

His stance doesn't waver. After a long beat, Marcus offers a brief nod—wordless, thick with meaning. A quiet acknowledgment—not just of the work, but of the fact that this room, this space, is hers when the storm hits.

Emma lets a tight smile flicker—quick and controlled. She responds with a sharp nod of her own.

Without missing a beat, her hands move back to Brick's bleeding eyebrow. She peels back the edges of his cut with practiced precision.

"Alright, I need five ice packs, and someone's going to help me keep track of vitals." Her voice is steady, with no room for hesitation. "Eli, Caleb—you two organize the ice. DeShawn, clean up the gauze. Let's keep it tight."

The players flinch slightly at every clipped command. Their eyes flicker to Emma. The slightest hesitation melts beneath her steady presence. They shuffle with reluctant efficiency—ice packs clinking, players murmuring under their breath. The weight of authority isn't shouted here; it's felt in every terse instruction and every measured glance that pins theirs, sharp and unblinking.

Bracing gauze around Caleb's swollen shoulder, Emma finally breaks the tension. Her voice is dry, cutting through the thick air.

"Someone tell these boys the turf isn't a wrestling mat. At this rate, we'll need a soap opera, not a football season."

A few terse chuckles ripple through the room. Caleb offers a wry grin, shaking his head as he shifts against the table.

"Man, I'm just rebranding the old turf special," DeShawn says, limping over with an ice pack. "Drama with every step."

Brick snorts. His eyes are still fierce but easing with humor. The room exhales. The edge blunts just enough to settle nerves. The bickering softens into muted conversations, and the players start to sink into acceptance—not of the injuries, but of the care Emma commands.

Emma's gaze flickers toward the doorway where Hale remains, watching with that unyielding stare. A subtle shift in his posture and a relaxed breath that he doesn't let escape fully speak volumes. This nod isn't just about the wounds—it's about trust built in moments under pressure.

She pulls a strip of tape from the dispenser, pressing it lightly against Caleb's skin as she finishes wrapping his shoulder.

"Next time, try not to treat the grass like an opponent you're trying to take down."

Caleb smirks, his voice low. "No promises. You therapists always have to act like superheroes."

"That's because we deal with the aftermath," Emma shoots back, glancing up at Hale. "Someone's got to pick up the pieces when your guys decide to reinvent football as a brutal art form."

A rough laugh escapes from Brick. The tension is now diffused to a simmer.

One by one, players gather their ice packs, casting sideways glances of grudging gratitude. The air hums with soft murmurs—pain laced with respect for the woman who commands this space. Emma watches them file out, shoulders squared, eyes steady and clear. The quiet after the battle. The fragile peace earned with care and sweat.

Alone now, she leans back against the edge of the treatment table. Her clipboard rests heavily in her lap. The faint scent of antiseptic and peppermint oil lingers, mixing with the copper tang in the air from scraped skin. These smells are constant companions—sharp reminders of battles fought on battered bodies and the fragile hope stitched into every injured player's recovery.

She allows herself to take a slow breath, the kind that sinks past muscle and bone, grounding her.

Marcus Hale's nod still weighs in the room, a silent seal on a hard-fought truce. Authority is established—not with words, but with presence.

"I'm not here to play nursemaid," she mutters quietly, her voice threading through the stillness.

"But damn, if I'm not going to make sure they don't destroy themselves while they're at it."

"Yeah, well, you better keep that pep talk ready," Brick calls from the doorway, his voice rough but appreciative. "Because these boys don't do easy."

Emma allows a tight smile, her eyes sharp.

"Easy's not on the menu. Never was."

She slides her clipboard closed, the faint scrape of paper edges the only sound in the room besides the distant echo of footsteps moving down the hallway.

Outside, the day waits—rugged and unyielding—but here, for a few waning moments, Emma holds the line.

The room hums with an uneasy quiet now—the chaotic shouts and groans from minutes ago fading into a distant murmur. Emma sits at the chipped desk, her fingers tapping across the injury log, her pen sliding between the neat columns as she traces the last of the players' names: Brick, DeShawn, Caleb. The stale scent of antiseptic lingers around her, sharp against the faint floral hint of peppermint still rising from the diffuser in the corner. The overhead LEDs buzz softly. Her eyes lift just as the slow scrape of the door's hinges breaks the silence.

Jaxon Reyes steps inside carefully, each movement cautious, as though he is testing old cracks in his body before committing. His dark, guarded eyes settle immediately on Emma's, holding hers in a steady, unblinking stare that feels like an unspoken dare. The air thickens. Their history presses between them, charged and suffocating.

Emma's shoulders draw taut, her fingers curling into loose fists at her sides. Her lips press into a thin line, and her eyes sharpen with practiced calm. She does not invite softness—just clipped questions that skim over their tangled past: "Any new pain? How is the rehab going?"

He shifts his weight, his jaw tight. "Same old aches. Rehab is a godsend and a curse."

The barest edge of impatience flickers behind Emma's steady gaze. "Have you been staying on schedule?"

Jaxon steps forward, his boots thudding softly on the linoleum. He lowers himself heavily onto the narrow treatment table with a grunt, that familiar, stubborn resistance evident in his posture. His hands tug at the hem of his jacket, peeling it back with deliberate slowness before ripping off his shirt.

He hesitates for a fraction of a second—that split-second refusal before surrender—bracing himself as if exposure itself might wound him. The sharp smell of sweat and leather fills the room. His skin is pale under the harsh white lights, scattered with scars. Silent battlefields.

Emma reaches for the examination gloves, her voice flat. "Show me your shoulder."

Her fingers trail over the taut skin there, pressing lightly to test for tenderness and muscle tone. She scrutinizes the jagged old scars—furrows deeper than surface wounds—that ripple beneath her touch. Her breath catches when her fingertips brush something raw beneath the layers of scar tissue. A flicker of empathy crosses her features, but she clips it back, burying the feeling beneath clinical focus.

Jaxon's attempt at levity falls flat. "Still got the band-aid charm, huh?"

Her lips quirk in a ghost of a smile, but she doesn't rise to the bait. "Pain level?"

"Doesn't hurt if I don't move." His voice came out low and dry. "The couch hears all my complaints."

She pressed a finger along a muscle knot. "And rehab? How honest are you being with me? With yourself?"

His gaze shuttered. "Let's just say... I'm flexible with the rules." He shrugged, a half-smile tugging at the corner of his mouth. "Creatively, maybe."

The tension in the room thickened. Emma's voice faltered, her strength on the edge. "If you want to stay in the game," she said, her voice low, "you have to start telling the truth about the pain. You can't fix what you pretend isn't broken."

Her hand jerked slightly as she fumbled with a bandage wrapper. The rustle felt deafening. Then, steadying herself, she wrapped the strip neatly around his shoulder, the soft swish of gauze punctuating her measured words. "Expectations aren't suggestions, Reyes. If you keep lying, you'll cost yourself more than just this team."

Jaxon's eyes darkened, shadows pooling beneath tired lids. He barely whispered, the words almost swallowed by the quiet. "Got it."

Emma pulled back, already gathering the scattered tools. She folded the crinkled white paper on the treatment table with careful precision. The soft clink of metal filled the space as she returned the instruments to their trays fragile and charged.

She watched him there on the table, shoulders curved inward like a wall against the world. Respect flickered through her for his stubborn refusal to quit, mixed with frustration that he wouldn't let her help him do it right. The conflict twisted in her chest—professional distance warring with something she had spent months trying to bury.

She moved to the door, her voice low but firm. "No more secrets. Not if you want to make it."

Without waiting for a response, Emma stepped out, pressing the door shut behind her. The heavy click reverberated in the empty hallway. Outside, her breath escaped in a shaky exhale, and her hand trembled as it fell from the doorframe.

Inside, Jaxon sat alone at the table, one hand cradling his swollen shoulder. His eyes were fixed on the closed door, a silent battle waging behind his stoic mask.

A Team of Broken Men

Jaxon Reyes stepped onto the practice field. The worn grass crunched faintly beneath his boots. He stopped at the fifty-yard line, hands stuffed deep in his pockets, his eyes sweeping across scattered figures shuffling on uneven turf.

The sky hung low—gray and unbroken. It dulled everything below; the faded white lines blurred beneath neglect, worn down by time and too many half-hearted seasons. The wind carried the scent of damp earth and old sweat, mingling with the distant hum of cars passing the chain-link fences.

He breathed it in. The smell reminded him of something he had tried to leave behind—how far this place was from anywhere that mattered.

Across the field, players slouched, their shoulders sagging like heavy weights. Their footsteps dragged, slow and uneven, as if the air itself pulled at their limbs before the whistle even blew. Some lumbered toward a huddle, while others clustered in small groups, pockets of half-formed laughter and sharper undertones threading through the air.

Jaxon didn't call anyone over; he stayed rooted. The chill pressed against his skin—more from the atmosphere than the weather.

Watching. Waiting.

Coach Marcus Hale's voice cut through like a whip crack. "Get it together, Hawks! Huddle up, now!"

The tone sliced sharply. Several players flinched, their bodies tightening as if the sting were almost physical. Jaxon recognized that flinch; Hale had drawn blood before—recent practices still stung, losses that hadn't stopped burning.

"Hands in," Marcus barked, pacing, his eyes cold and unforgiving. "We don't have the luxury to play soft today. Not with what's waiting for us at the season's end."

His jaw tightened. The words hung in the air. No mercy.

Players squinted, their shoulders tense beneath worn jerseys. Warmth drained from the air. The coach's frustration settled in—heavy. Thick.

A few yards away, knots of players exchanged banter that barely scraped the surface. Voices bobbed back and forth—some chuckles forced, others brittle with tension. One joke landed flat, swallowed by awkward silence. An eye roll sharp enough to sting.

"I swear, Brick's gonna lose it if Caleb fumbles again," DeShawn's voice carried across the grass, tinged with the resigned amusement only exhausted teammates could muster.

Caleb snorted, his cheeks coloring beneath his helmet. He said nothing.

Brick stood apart, scowling, arms crossed, his body coiled like a spring.

"Maybe if Eli actually threw the ball instead of staring holes in the dirt, we'd have a chance," another player muttered, low enough to skirt direct confrontation but loud enough to be heard.

Laughter flickered unevenly, undercut by murmurs and sharp groans. The collective mood hung on a knife-edge. Fractures appeared like spiderweb cracks across the team's façade.

Jaxon leaned back against the chipped blue paint of the bleachers. The metal was cold against his shoulder blades. With his hands still deep in his pockets, he remained quiet. His breath rose in slow clouds.

No sudden commands. No false encouragement.

He tasted the faint grit of dust drifting up from the turf and heard the scrape of cleats on cracked concrete by the sidelines. He caught the scent of liniment carried on sudden gusts from the training table nearby.

It all felt raw and unvarnished—the truth of where this team stood, and maybe, by extension, where he stood too.

An unraveling football thumped weakly against a leather-clad palm. Jaxon's eyes flickered toward the players. Caleb's shoulders slumped, and restless feet circled around Brick's tight frame. Eli made a hollow, quick step toward the bench, his jaw clenched.

The roles were set without being spoken.

He resisted the urge to step forward, to fill the silence with his voice and his presence. Not yet. The weight of his last choice still hung in the air like damp fabric against his skin, reminding him that authority doesn't come free, and maybe not without scars.

A sudden burst of laughter, brittle and too loud, drew his gaze to the younger players trading disjointed jokes. Their smiles were fleeting and forced. The empty space between intention and connection widened again.

"You think this hellhole is going to see a win this year?" a voice muttered near the bench. Sharp. Quiet. More a statement than a question.

"Only if the ghosts of past losses finally decide to leave us alone," another replied, their tone flat, glancing at the fading scoreboard behind the end zone—a permanent, silent witness stuck on a lost game.

Jaxon let the murmurs wash over him. He focused instead on the shape of the sky, the slow crawl of clouds hiding the sun but not the threat of rain. The sticky press of humidity clung to his skin beneath the rough wool of his jacket.

This place. This team. None of it was clean. None of it was easy.

Coach Hale's voice sliced through the air again. Sharper. Harder.

"Focus up! Left side! Right side! Use your heads, Hawks!"

His bark sent a shiver through the lineup. A few players blinked against the rawness. Some clamped their jaws. Others let their eyes drift away, unwilling or unable to hold the coach's brutal gaze.

Jaxon's jaw pressed tight. He leaned further into the shadow of the bleachers, his silhouette etched against the stubborn banner sagging above, its faded letters whispering promises long since frayed.

He didn't move. He didn't call out.

He folded his arms, feeling the rough fabric bite into his skin, and let the scene play out in its slow unraveling.

He watched and waited.

Coach Hale's whistle cuts sharply and clearly through the humid morning air. The routine drills begin—half-hearted and sluggish. Lines of wear crack the turf beneath tired cleats. Above, thunder rolls low across gathering clouds, a warning the field seems too weary to heed.

Jaxon Reyes lingers near the sideline, his hands buried deep in his pockets. His eyes scan the scattered shapes of his teammates like a detective assembling a fractured puzzle. He throws to a backup receiver—tight spirals, precise, with no wasted motion. But he doesn't call out; he doesn't snap anyone to attention.

The detachment costs something. Jaxon feels the weight of it and sees it reflected in the shuffling feet around him. A quarterback who won't lead leaves a vacuum. The team moves through it like ghosts, synthetic energy failing to ignite.

At the ten-yard line, Caleb Monroe stretches for a routine pass. The ball slips cleanly through his hands. It thuds against the faded turf paint, soft and final.

Nearby players exchange murmurs, and a sharp exhale punctuates the air.

Someone rolls their eyes audibly, that sound dragging through the tense quiet like a knife.

"Seriously? Again, Caleb?" muttered someone from the back, barely suppressing exasperation.

Caleb's fingers twitch against his helmet's chinstrap. He drags it lower, as if trying to disappear beneath the padded shell. Every muscle stiffens under the strain of tired eyes watching him.

Not far off, Logan "Brick" Turner hurls himself into a tackling dummy with the force of a sledgehammer. His bulk crashes through the worn vinyl. The impact shakes the gray steel frame and rattles it. Brick heaves breaths—his chest rising and falling like storm waves beneath a dark sky—but doesn't stop. His jaw clenches, and raw anger flickers across the sharp edges of his gaze. He gives a slow shake of his head, as if wrestling the fury back inside where it belongs.

On the sidelines, Eli Brooks shifts his weight restlessly. His dark eyes narrow beneath a heavy brow. His lips move quietly, low grumbles scraping against the constant hum of restless voices.

"Where's the damn leadership?" His voice barely rises above a hiss, but it threads through the gathering discontent like cool poison. Eyes shift toward Jaxon.

The corner of Jaxon's mouth twitches—frustration or indifference, it's hard to tell. His gaze drops again, returning to the crisp arc of his pass. He knows what they're thinking. The silence between his throws feels like an accusation.

DeShawn Price plucks at the dry grass near the sideline, stepping forward to inject something—anything—into the tangle of tension. "Hey, Caleb, you're just pacing yourself. Saving the big catches for the game, right? Gotta keep Coach Hale guessing."

His grin is wide, full of mischief, meant to spark a reaction. Instead, it lands flat.

Caleb's almost-smile barely registers before evaporating. He shoves his helmet further down, his eyes cast downward. The moment slips away like smoke, leaving DeShawn's words hanging unclaimed in the heavy air.

Coach Hale's sharp gaze cuts through the faltering energy like a shutter snapping shut.

"Focus! Again!" His voice is taut with thinly veiled impatience. The whistle shrieks—piercing, rattling the ragged edges of the bleachers. The team falters. Scattered attention drifts like loose leaves caught in a weak wind.

Players glance sideways at one another. Shoulders tense. Hard breaths puff in the damp air, mingling with the sour tang of sweat and freshly cut grass. Jaxon's arms rise just a fraction. He sends another ball launching toward his receiver, fingers curling tightly around the leather as if squeezing the last drops of control from the moment.

From the sidelines, Eli's dissatisfaction morphs into sharp, quiet murmurs traded among a muttering cluster: "No one's stepping up." "Just a bunch of ghosts out there." "The season's already lost."

"Come on, Caleb, maybe you should stick to defense," DeShawn jabs, but his grin doesn't quite reach his eyes anymore.

"That's rich, Price. You run like a busted lawnmower," Caleb fires back under his breath, his voice low enough that only a few catch the crack in his humor.

A flicker of anger pulses through the crowd. It's swallowed quickly beneath the weight of weariness and unspoken doubts.

Jaxon's gaze snaps briefly to the group. Something flashes across his features—disdain, exhaustion, maybe regret—before he turns back to the sideline. The drill collapses into fragmented moments. Players break ranks. Voices rise in small clusters of complaint and quiet resentment.

Coach Hale surveys the fractured gathering, his jaw tight. He had hoped Jaxon would step in by now, would do something—anything—to anchor the team. Instead, his quarterback stands apart, throwing passes into the void like a man trying to outrun his own shadow. The leadership gap yawns wider with each dropped ball and each muttered complaint.

The whistle blows once more. Sharp. Insistent.

The energy fails to rally. It remains fractured and aimless. A ragged pulse barely beats beneath the surface.

A heavy silence settles over the field. The humid air thickens with unspoken frustrations and the scent of sweat and rain-washed grass.

The team is far from whole. It shows in every dropped pass, every muttered complaint, and every moment Jaxon refuses to bridge the distance between them and whatever they are supposed to become.

The first real test of the morning has already failed. Nothing remains but the tight knot of defeat tightening in Coach Hale's jaw.

Caleb's feet pound the cracked turf, pumping hard as he cuts sharply toward the sideline. The sharp scent of damp earth and worn leather presses into his nostrils. The sky hangs low, a slate-gray ceiling casting the field in a muted glow. Distant bleachers rattle faintly in an indifferent breeze.

His eyes hunt for the route marker. The pattern drilled into muscle memory slips. He veers too wide. Too late. His break is clumsy and desperate.

Then—Brick.

A wall of muscle appears, solid and immovable. There is no time to adjust. Bodies collide. The violent clang of helmets reverberates through Caleb's skull, a metallic screech that vibrates down his spine. The impact rattles bones and steals breath. The world tilts.

Caleb stumbles backward. Shock flickers across his face. Dizziness stings the edges of his vision, sharp and nauseating. His shoulder explodes with pain.

Brick plants his feet firmly, steady despite the collision. His jaw clenches tight, muscles standing out along his neck in raw relief. His breath hitches—each exhale ragged and rough. His eyes bore into Caleb, cold and unforgiving.

"Are you kidding me?" Brick's voice booms like thunder rolling off distant hills. "Man, you don't even know the damn plays, and you're out here acting like you belong?"

Before Caleb can steady himself, Brick shoves him hard. The force carries the weight of a man's frustration, disappointment, and simmering rage. Caleb stumbles back several steps, his arms flailing briefly before he regains his balance. His shoulder throbs where Brick's palm made contact—a burning ache spreading across his collarbone.

Caleb's throat tightens. His fingers twitch as he rubs the fresh sting blossoming along his shoulder. But the words burn deeper than flesh. His breath catches—disbelief and hurt mingling beneath flared nostrils. His lips part. He hesitates. Silence pins his voice down like lead.

Coach Hale's boots skid sharply on the turf as he storms toward them. The man's presence slices through the rising tension like a whip crack. His gaze burns with ice, cutting through both players' focus with surgical precision. Coach Hale has built his reputation on discipline—twenty years of molding boys into soldiers, of crushing weakness before it can spread through a roster. He doesn't tolerate fractures on his field.

"Enough!" The coach's voice rips through the discord, sharp and unforgiving. "This isn't a playground. This is a damn team, and you two are acting like children. Discipline means something here. You *will* play as a unit or get the hell off that field. Caleb. Brick. Take your squabble to the side and figure it out like men. No more distractions!"

The words ripple outward, crashing over clusters of players. They scatter uneasily, forming pockets of murmurs and sidelong glances. The energy fractures—like shattered glass catching dull light at sharp, unpleasant angles.

Some mutter criticisms low enough to be swallowed by the wind. Others fold into silence, their shoulders tight with unspoken grievances. The team splinters further. The fragile thread of unity snaps under strain.

Brick's jaw clenches tightly. The muscles stand out along his neck in raw relief. He turns away in a slow, deliberate pivot. His broad shoulders heave once—a breath stolen and held, then released in a gust of pent-up fury. His heavy strides eat up the distance between him and the far sideline, his helmet tucked tightly under one arm. His shadow looms long and stony across the cracked grass.

Behind him, Caleb stands still. His fingers work the ache around his shoulder. His gaze lingers on the ground as if searching for words buried beneath dirt and sweat. The silence presses down between them, cold and hollow, charged with the weight of things left unsaid—feelings too tangled for easy fixing.

No apology comes. No bridge. Just separation, carved deeper by the harsh edges of frustration and pride.

The whistle had barely stopped echoing when Jaxon slid away from the turmoil, his cleats crunching softly over the patchwork grass dotted with brittle dandelions. He found the orange cone marking a far corner of the practice field—weathered and leaning slightly, like everything else here—and his shoulders tightened. The scattered murmurs and stifled frustration of the main group buzzed distantly behind him.

Caleb and Brick's collision had left a fracture in the team's fragile unity. Jaxon wasn't ready to weld it back together. Instead, he gripped the football tighter, ready to do what felt safest: throw.

The backup receiver—a wiry kid with quick feet and nervous eyes—slid into position thirty yards away. Jaxon's throws were sharp, snapping through the thick air. But there was none of the easy rhythm that once came without thought. Each flick of his wrist felt measured. Controlled. As if he were trying to harness a storm inside him—one he wasn't sure he wanted to unleash.

Around him, the field was scattered with bodies and distant voices. Jaxon kept his gaze locked on the receiver's outstretched hands. The worn laces bit into his palm with a dry sting. The faint scent of grass, damp with morning dew, drifted upward with each breath he took. He forced himself to keep tossing. Over and over. As if repetition could drown out the memories of eyes—Emma's eyes—the way they had pierced through his defenses just moments before.

"Don't care," he tried to tell himself. "Just throw." But the buzz of emotions wouldn't dull, prickling beneath his skin like nettles. The heat of those hazel eyes lingered, sharp and unrelenting, stabbing at the walls he'd built. His chest tightened, a bitter knot twisting beneath his sternum as he pushed the thought away. Focus. Control. Distance.

From the bench along the sideline—a battered metal frame sagging under reluctant bodies—Eli Brooks sat with his arms crossed and lips pressed tight. His stare slashed across the field, sharp and cold. The resentment in that glare gathered traction, infecting a few others until the usual slap and call of drills dissolved into a careless shuffle of feet and drifting attention.

No one was listening. No one was looking to Jaxon for guidance.

The vacuum of leadership rippled through the scattered players, an invisible rift widening with every missed catch and half-hearted route. Jaxon's jaw tightened. The ball felt heavier in his hands—almost reluctant.

His arm coiled and unwound. The leather snapped through the air toward the receiver, who caught it with clumsy hands. Their eyes met for a breath. There was an unspoken challenge in that lingering glance, a question hanging between them: Are you really here to lead?

Jaxon didn't answer. His gaze was locked on the receiver's hands, deaf to the ripple of wind chasing the chain-link fence nearby or the sharp clang of a helmet hitting the turf. Around him, the chaos of the field was a distant hum he refused to acknowledge. The sky hung low, thick with gray clouds that swallowed the sun's bite whole. Damp air clung to his skin, mingling sweat with the earthy scent of crushed grass and mud. Somewhere, a dull thud echoed—the heartbeat of a fractured practice.

Another throw. The ball spun tightly, catching a whisper of the chilly breeze. The receiver stumbled but managed to catch it. Jaxon didn't allow himself the relief of a nod or a grin. His shoulders remained rigid, and his breathing was shallow and steady. He inhaled the damp morning air with clinical detachment.

He settled into the rhythm of throw, retrieve, throw again. The repetitive motion was both a balm and a barrier.

In his mind, Emma's voice—calm, firm, tinged with frustration—floated unbidden. She had named the fractures: the worn spots in the team's armor, Brick's fury, Caleb's panic, DeShawn's jokes hiding fear, and Eli's simmering bitterness. She had looked past his walls and saw the weight he carried—maybe better than he did himself. The team's losing record had left them raw, bleeding into every drill. Their morale had fractured long before Caleb and Brick collided today. She had understood that. She had tried to make him understand.

"Don't let it in," he ordered silently. "Not now. Not here. This isn't your damn fight—not yet."

Yet with every toss and every calculated pass, the distance he cultivated felt thinner, not thicker.

"You're just here to play," he muttered under his breath. The words tasted sour on his tongue, barely acknowledging their lie.

From the corner of his eye, he caught movement on the sideline. Eli shifted, his eyes still fixed hard and unyielding. The undercurrent of discontent ebbed and grew, catching like wildfire as others shifted their stares away from the drills—rolling their eyes, shrinking back, and carelessly kicking dirt into the sparse grass.

The team had become a ragged constellation of fragmented stars, no longer blazing with shared purpose. Jaxon knew the space between them wasn't just physical; it yawned wide emotionally—a chasm he could neither bridge nor ignore.

The receiver jogged back, panting lightly and wiping a sheen of sweat from his brow.

Jaxon took one last breath. The leather ball felt rough and familiar in his palm. He threw everything he had—sharp, precise. Then he let the ball drop carelessly at his feet. The muted thud punctuated the rustling field.

He didn't move to retrieve it.

Instead, he stayed planted by the cone, shoulders squared but somehow slumping beneath the weight of invisible burdens. His eyes flickered to the distant huddle where voices rose and fell in uneven cadence. Still, he kept his distance—not just across the field, but deeper, where safety meant shutting down.

I'm not their damn leader—not yet. Screw that. That thought was a brittle shield, protecting him from every pull to step up. The ache of isolation settled like a stone in his gut as the practice field around him hummed with fractured energy and half-spoken resentments. The gap between him and the team felt endless.

He turned his gaze from the far side of the field, biting back the knot of questions and the echo of that daring look Emma had thrown his way just moments ago.

The sky pressed down, heavy and indifferent. Jaxon stood still, the ball forgotten at his feet, his body and mind alike retreating to a place beyond reach.

###

The damp grass squished under Emma's sneakers as she threaded through scattered clusters of players. Above, the afternoon sky hung slate-gray, blanketing the sun's heat.

With a clipboard pressed against her hip, she scanned each stance: tired shoulders hunched too far forward, eyes flickering with frustration or boredom. The faint snap of elastic bands stretched through the air, mingling with sharp liniment and sweat, while earthy dirt clung to everything.

"Keep your back straighter, Caleb," she said to the young receiver slouched near the sideline. Her voice was firm but careful. She touched his upper arm lightly, nudging it back. "We all have to be ready, or it falls apart."

Caleb nodded, his cheeks flushing as he adjusted his posture.

Emma's gaze swept across the field. The worn lines beneath their cleats had lost any fresh paint—cracked and layered like topographic maps of past losses and forgotten victories. Players chatted in half-hearted bursts, their energy leaking like the faded scoreboard's dead bulbs. She caught DeShawn Price's eye, noted the slight sag in his spine, and gave him a sharp look.

"DeShawn, eyes up. Fear has to come off the field before the next snap."

The corners of his mouth twitched—tempted to respond with humor—but her steady gaze shut that down.

The practice hummed low around her, filled with footsteps and muffled grumbles. Emma's feet carried her to the forty-yard line just as Coach Marcus Hale's bark cut through the restless noise. The older man's face was a worn map of hard lines and stern creases, his graying hair damp with sweat. He planted his hands firmly on his hips.

"Jaxon," he called out.

The field held its breath.

Jaxon Reyes lifted his chin, tight-lipped. He trudged through the scattered squad, shoulders hunched and hands shoved deep into his pockets. A ghost of a scowl shadowed his features. The faint leather scent of his gloves rose when he pulled one out to rub at his palm—but not at his eyes, not at his mouth. There was no concession to the frustration clawing at his back.

Coach Hale's gaze pinned him down, unblinking and relentless. "I'm not here to babysit. You get that? This—" He gestured broadly to the fractured group around them. "—this mess? It needs a leader. Not—"

"Yeah, yeah. I'm just here to play," Jaxon cut in. His voice was sharp and clipped—a wall as solid as the cracked bleachers behind him. He stepped back and turned on his heel before the man could finish, distancing himself from the weight of unspoken expectations.

Coach Hale exhaled, his lips thinning. He said no more.

Not yet.

From the periphery of this tight exchange, Emma's eyes caught Jaxon's. A flicker of recognition sparked in the space between them. His glance held hers longer than necessary—raw edges of something unsettled swirling behind the dark storm of his gaze.

Then she broke from the hesitant cluster and strode toward him.

Her steps were measured but filled with intent, carrying the quiet authority of one accustomed to holding her ground. The chatter and shuffling of cleats dulled as she approached. A subtle watchfulness rippled through the players—the unspoken signal that something had changed.

Emma stopped a few feet from Jaxon, her stance solid, arms relaxed but ready. Her steady hazel eyes never left his.

The humid air seemed heavier with possibility. Even the fading light felt less oppressive here.

Around them, the field hummed with tension—a suspended breath in the fractured rhythm of the day's practice.

"You say you're just here to play," Emma said, her voice low but clear. Shadows of past conversations threaded through her words. "But this team isn't just about plays or yards. It's about more than football."

Jaxon's jaw tensed. His eyes narrowed like a storm about to break. He shifted his weight, readying the usual deflection—but for once, the words didn't tumble out. His lips parted, a war raging inside him. No sound came.

Emma let the silence settle—unblinking, unrelenting—like the steady tick of a clock counting down beyond the scoreboard's frozen numbers.

Then, as if she were both shield and challenge, she waited. The unspoken dare hung in the still air between them.

Behind her, the players glanced over. Their own unease crackled like static as the gap between fractured loyalty and hesitant hope widened.

Jaxon's fingers twitched at his sides. His breath caught for the briefest second before he pulled tighter into himself, turning away just enough to veil the storm raging behind his eyes.

The field felt colder in that moment, not because the sky had darkened, but because authority and vulnerability were locked in a fragile, clenched dance, neither willing to let go first.

Emma approached through the haze of dust kicked up by cleats, each step measured and steady. Her clipboard was tucked under one arm, and the sun-beaten field stretched around them—thick with tension and heat despite the overcast sky. The faint scent of damp grass lingered in the humid air, clinging to her skin. She stopped a few paces from Jaxon, who stared at the worn midpoint of the field, hands jammed in his pockets, shoulders tight beneath his weathered practice hoodie. The scattered players dimmed around them—jerky movements, low conversations tinged with frustration—their noise fading beneath her voice when she finally spoke: low, unwavering, as crisp as a whistle cutting through chaos.

"They're damaged, Jax. But not hopeless—not if you let yourself see it. You're looking right at the cracks, but you haven't crawled beneath the surface. You need to tear down those walls you've built around yourself."

His jaw tightens. A muscle jumps beneath the stubble shadowing his cheek. He doesn't meet her eyes; instead, he tracks a worn spot on the field where the white lines have faded into chipped scars in the turf.

"I'm not here to babysit broken boys."

Emma's breath shifts, but she keeps her tone calm and clinical, leaving no room for softening. "It's not about babysitting. It's about reading the room—you, me, this team." She pauses, allowing weight to settle into the space between them. "Take Brick. Anger simmers like a storm cloud. He bangs against every tackling dummy he sees, carrying that fire as if it's the only thing keeping him standing."

Her gaze flicks to the cluster of players where Brick stands, fists clenched tightly at his sides, nostrils flaring with every ragged breath.

"Caleb panics over mistakes that wouldn't rattle most guys." Emma's voice folds into a steady rhythm. "He fumbles that ball, and his shoulders collapse as if the weight of every eye in the stadium is pressing down on him. You saw it today."

She turns back to Jaxon, and there's something in her expression—a flicker of history, of knowing something he doesn't want to examine.

"Then there's DeShawn, hiding behind his jokes, turning nervous energy into laughs but never fooling anyone who watches closely. And Eli—the quiet resentment behind that gaze—like he's holding his breath, waiting for everything to crumble."

Jaxon's eyes snap up, sharp as shattered glass. He steps forward slightly, his fists releasing their grip on the hoodie. Heat rises under his skin, irritation flooding his veins like a tide.

"You're painting them as victims," he spits quietly, his voice rough. "Like they want a damn parade for messing up."

Emma doesn't flinch. Her lips press into a thin line, and her eyes harden—the burden of knowing what has been left undone hanging between them like storm clouds pregnant with rain.

"They're pain-wrapped, sure." She holds his gaze steady. "But pain shifts. It's a lever if you know where to push. You can't pretend they're just problems to fix. They're people, and they're screaming for someone to *see* it—the anger, fear, resentment—because no one is calling them out, and no one is offering a hand."

A silence swells, thick enough to catch the distant rattling of the bleachers and the faint hum of the scoreboard's broken digits. Jaxon's chest tightens, the discomfort of raw truth settling heavily. His mouth opens, a sharp retort on his tongue, but the laughter of a nearby player and the clatter of equipment fade against the steady beat of Emma's words anchoring inside.

He swallows back the impulse; the words lodge in his throat like stubborn grit.

"You think I don't see it?" His voice dips, rougher now, bruised by the accumulation of things unsaid. "I'm not some damn coach-pass-through. I'm here to play—not to play shrink."

But beneath the defensiveness, there's something else—fear, perhaps. Or the weight of knowing she's right and hating that she can still read him like that, the way she always could.

Emma inclines her head slightly. She doesn't soften, though something passes through her expression—history weighted behind the measured challenge now hanging between them. All the times he'd pushed her away. All the times she'd tried anyway.

"If all you're willing to be is a player," she says slowly, "then you're wasting your shot—and theirs. This team needs more than arm strength and stubborn grit. They need you to care. Or step aside."

Her words land softly but razor-sharp, cutting through the discomfort and forcing a pause.

Jaxon blindsides the urge to push back. Irritation curls beneath his ribs, prickling and hot. But beneath that, the muscles around his heart clench—a fragile thing trying not to fracture. The heat of the humid air presses against his skin as the afternoon drapes over the field, heavy with expectation.

For a heartbeat, the space between them is thick with the unsaid: the fractured past, the shards of trust barely held together.

He breathes in sharply. His fists clench again, just below the surface.

The words hover between them, suspended and unanswered.

###

The snap came quickly and cleanly, the ball slipping from the center's hands into Jaxon's waiting grasp. Around him, the linemen shifted, the practiced dance rehearsed countless times. Yet something already felt off—a brittle edge in the rhythm that had gone unnoticed until now.

Jaxon scanned the field, his eyes catching Caleb Monroe pulling in for the handoff at the ten-yard line.

But Caleb's fingers fumbled, a slick slip beneath the turf's uneven blades. The football skittered free, rolling erratically across the patchy grass like a wild animal escaping its cage. Shouts erupted—sharp and panicked. Players lunged forward chaotically, scrambling to snatch the ball before it tumbled into enemy hands.

The offense was fracturing. Jaxon felt it in his bones—this team was barely holding together.

A burst of clattering cleats and frustrated curses spilled over the field. "Come on, Caleb!" Brick thundered, his voice raw, fury threading through each syllable.

Brick ripped his helmet free. Sweat and dirt streaked his scowling face, his breath ragged in the chill air. His hands trembled at his sides, barely holding back the storm churning inside his chest. Then, with a roar that shattered the tense quiet, he hurled the battered helmet—steel clanging off the cold goalpost. A sharp crack echoed across the field as his palm slammed against the yellow frame, vibrating through the chilled autumn air. Veins throbbed at his temples; his eyes burned with a dark fury barely contained.

Amid the tension, DeShawn Price didn't just stay quiet. He shifted the mood with a loud, mocking laugh that split the charged atmosphere like a knife.

"Look at this circus," he called out, his voice rich with sarcasm. He cocked his head as if daring someone to take him seriously. "Maybe we should just hand over the trophy now and save ourselves the trouble."

The jibes rolled across the turf, half in jest but stinging with truth. They pulled strained smiles from some while igniting fresh sparks of resentment in others. Caleb pulled his helmet lower, his cheeks burning—not merely from exertion but from the weight of every pair of eyes flickering with disappointment and impatience.

Coach Marcus Hale's whistle cut through the din, sharp and urgent. Even his strident commands skittered weakly in the chaos. "Settle down! Enough goddamn noise!" His voice cracked, strained from repeated barks that fell on deaf ears. The team was splintering before his eyes, and he knew it. Authority meant nothing when discipline had already broken.

The team fractured further. Shards of argument sliced through the air like fists—accusations met with dismissive grunts, and murmured slights flared into open confrontation.

Jaxon stepped forward. He hesitated at first, the practiced authority in his voice faltering under the weight of fractured attention. "Alright, regroup! Let's focus—everyone, listen up!"

His words hung in the air, met with a smattering of indifference and whispered barbs. Some players turned their backs, while others exchanged eye rolls thick with sarcasm.

DeShawn's gaze flicked over to Jaxon with keen amusement. He stepped into the center of the growing unrest, his grin sharp and cutting.

"Guess fallen stars can't fix us either, huh?" he said, loud enough for the entire field to hear, his voice dripping with mocking finality.

The laughter died instantly, and the field fell into a brittle silence. All eyes snapped toward Jaxon.

The ball at his feet seemed to pulse with tension. The uneven grass pressed cold against his worn cleats. The world tilted slightly on the edge of something fragile—hope, anger, a challenge unspoken but deafening.

Jaxon swallowed hard, his jaw clenched, muscles taut beneath his weathered jersey.

His fingertips curled around the fabric of his practice towel—a pale white against the stained earth beneath him. Slowly and deliberately, he let it slip from his grip.

The towel hit the ground with a muted thud, and dust motes swirled briefly in the stale air.

Jaxon turned sharply on his heel, his shoulders squared in a rigid line. He stalked off the field, each step a distant drumbeat away from the chaos he had never quite learned to tame. His booted feet thudded against the worn patches of grass and cracked dirt.

His back was a wall to the rest of the team. No glance back. No lingering hesitation. The locker room beckoned like a fragile refuge beyond the broken field.

Every step away felt heavier, as if the ground were pulling him under. He couldn't fix this—not now.

Voices buzzed low behind him, but they faded into the hum of distant traffic and the stubborn rustle of dry leaves clinging to the chain-link fence.

The tension hung thick, like a wounded beast pacing restlessly. The practice field, once a ground of promise, now held only echoes—fractured calls, bruised pride, and the sharp tang of failure mingling with dampened hopes.

The storm wasn't over; it had just begun to break.

Jaxon's cleats crunched through the uneven grass, patches worn thin enough to reveal stubborn dirt beneath. His broad shoulders carried the weight of the morning's mess—frayed nerves, snapped tempers, and a team splintering instead of uniting. He kept his hands stuffed deep in his jacket pockets, fingers clutching the fabric against the slight dampness in the air.

Emma stood rooted near the forty-yard line, arms folded loosely across her chest. The muscles in her jaw tightened, her gaze steady beneath the thick, low-hanging clouds. Her breath drifted out in quiet plumes, mingling with the scent of crushed grass and faint liniment clinging to the humid breeze. There was no softness in her eyes—only a silent challenge pressed into the curve of her lips. A lone sentinel mid-battlefield, waiting for the slightest sign that the man walking away might stop running.

Jaxon slows near the sideline. The clatter of cleats and shuffles dulls behind the charged silence between them. He stops, his body tense, and pivots his head slowly, locking eyes with Emma's unwavering stare. The world between them narrows. Teammates' murmurs dissolve into a mute hum, swallowed whole by the gravity of this shared moment.

Her eyes hold him, steady and unyielding. No words, just a silent dare buried beneath the weight of everything they have avoided.

The heat of her look blazes through the cool air, catching beneath his skin like an ember he has buried too deep. His breath hitches, and his chest tightens as memories flash—her calm firmness in the training room, her words sharp and impossible to ignore. He is not sure if it is defiance or exhaustion that colors his face, but the corners of his mouth pull taut, his jaw clenched so hard that his teeth ache. Beneath the surface, something stirs—an echo of the man he used to be, trapped behind years of scars and silence.

"I'm done." His voice is low, ragged, barely breaking the fragile stillness.

Emma doesn't blink. "Done running, then? Or just done pretending it matters?"

He stiffens, the question landing like a strike between his ribs. For a heartbeat, he considers turning on his heel, swallowing his pride to vanish into the narrowing corridor toward the locker room. But she is waiting—not pleading, not judging—waiting for something more. Something real.

Silence stretches heavily, punctuated only by the distant clink of a helmet dropped on the turf and a sporadic burst of laughter too brittle to carry warmth. The damp grass whispers beneath their feet. A chilly breeze twists through the bleachers, lifting loose paper and carrying a faint tang of sweat and liniment.

"You always do this," he finally snaps, his voice shading into bitter humor. "You show up just when I'm about to check out."

Emma swallows a smile barely held back. "And you always push when you're scared to pull close. When are you going to stop treating everyone like they're a damn draft pick you can cut?"

"Because it's easier than admitting I need help." His words come out sharp, sharper than he intends. "Because trusting someone—especially you—means risking everything."

Her posture softens fractionally, her shoulders relaxing just enough for vulnerability to flicker in her gaze. There's something unspoken in that shift, a hint of old hurt neither of them has quite buried. "Trust is earned, Jaxon. Not begged for in desperate moments."

His eyes flick toward hers, his jaw slackening under the weight of that truth. For a breath, the anger dulls, replaced by a raw, aching openness he's fought to bury. Exhaustion bleeds through the cracks, and beneath it lies something that looks like fear.

"I'm not asking for easy," he murmurs, his voice nearly lost in the thickening air. "Just a chance to prove it."

Emma steps forward, the space between them shrinking. Charged. Unbreakable. "Then start playing like it matters—for them. For you."

He nods slowly, not out of capitulation but from a hard-won resolve settling into his bones. The haze over the field lifts in the periphery. Players move with muted purpose, their figures distant but unmistakably tethered to this fragile moment.

Jaxon turns his face away. The first step toward the locker room is heavy but deliberate. Behind him, Emma watches—steady and unwavering—the unspoken question lingering like a pulse beneath the cracked sky.

Will he run, or will he finally step up?

Ghosts Don't Stay Buried

Emma's footsteps scratch softly against the linoleum, sharp and steady beneath the harsh fluorescent lights that hum above. Her phone buzzes again, restless and unimpressed—a thin pulse echoing in the hollow corridor. She snatches it up: another missed call from Jaxon's number. The screen blinks insistently, but no answer comes. She stares at it as the glow dims, watching the battery's slow surrender. Her thumb hovers but doesn't dare to press dial. The night around her stretches long and restless, shadows pooling at the edges of sterile walls.

She stops, sliding a palm flat against the cool paint, grounding herself. The touch is sharp, a cold anchor in the middle of everything unspooling inside her chest. That curtained room doesn't feel far away—her mother's pale face lies still beneath the thin hospital blanket, fragile as spun glass. The machines beside her bed pulse with a mechanical rhythm that Emma has learned to dread, each beep a reminder that her mother's breathing has become a negotiation rather than a certainty. Hope and dread tangle in her chest, neither one winning. Emma's fingers flex and clench like a silent prayer, kneading the hem of her sleeves over and over, the fabric soft beneath her trembling hands. The antiseptic scent lingers like a ghost, sharp and a little cloying, mixing with the faint, sour tang of old coffee left too long in forgotten mugs.

A nurse rounds the corner, her footsteps light but tired. Her gaze meets Emma's, laden with wordless sympathy that cuts sharper than any phrase. Emma swallows the knot pressing at her throat.

"Have you heard anything about Jaxon?" Emma's voice cracks slightly, swallowed by the sterile air.

The nurse shakes her head, tight-lipped and guarded. "Nothing yet." Her eyes flicker away, unwilling—or unable—to offer more. The hallway swallows her footsteps as she moves on, leaving a hollow quiet behind.

Emma exhales, a slow, shuddering breath, and turns her head toward the glass doors at the end of the corridor. Dawn bleeds in, thin and pale, with fingers of soft gray weaving through grimy panes. The world outside seems smaller here, compressed into a sliver of fading night and reluctant light.

She steps forward, drawn toward the fragile morning like a moth circling a dim flame. The chill bites through her thin sweater as she pushes open the doors, the cold air rushing in, sharp and immediate, carrying the scent of wet pavement and last night's rain. The breath she exhales clouds the space between her and the awakening day.

Her grip tightens around her phone, now dead and dark in her palm, a small weight that feels heavier than it should. The hospital behind her shudders in the silence, the buzzing machines and distant voices reduced to a muted murmur.

Jaxon is gone.

No message. No explanation. Just the echo of footsteps lost somewhere between those endless halls and the vast, uncertain sky that stretches above the town. She remembers the last time someone she loved disappeared without warning—her father, slipping out before dawn one Tuesday, leaving nothing but a coffee cup in the sink and a silence that had swallowed her childhood whole. The same hollow abandonment blooms now, ancient and fresh all at once, and she understands with sudden, crushing clarity why his vanishing has torn something vital loose inside her.

Her heart pitches erratically, a desperate beat against the void where hope used to stand. Numbness creeps in, slow and insidious, settling over her like a fog.

She whispers, barely audible against the morning's chill, "Why did you leave?"

Her voice scatters on the wind, unanswered and fragile.

The hospital steps feel colder beneath her feet—hard edges biting into the soles of her shoes—as she stands rooted, staring out at where the sun climbs awkwardly over the streets of Redemption Valley. The blue and gold banners twitch silently in the cool breeze, mocking the quiet void left by his absence.

Her throat tightens. The weight of the night presses down and refuses to let go.

Her phone—a lifeline now severed—rests heavily, powerless, and silent in her hand.

Jaxon has disappeared without a word. There was no goodbye to soften the hurt, no hint of where he might turn next.

A shiver ripples through her as the first slender shafts of light catch the moisture on her lashes. The sun rises, indifferent and impassive, while all she feels is the empty space he left behind.

Emma methodically lays out sterile wipes across the treatment table, their crisp edges cool beneath her fingertips. The walls around her shimmer softly in muted sea-glass green, the color offering a calming contrast to the tension coiled just beyond the door.

She flips open Jaxon's injury chart. Her precise fingers scan the notes without hesitation. Each entry is a stark reminder of the work ahead—three weeks of setbacks, incremental gains, and the stubborn resistance of a body that refused to heal on schedule. She had seen athletes like him before: driven, reckless with their recovery. But Jaxon was different, and that terrified her.

The door creaks open.

Jaxon steps inside, his tall frame rigid, shoulders squared with a tautness that speaks of tension not yet eased. His dark eyes flicker toward her, betrayed by a guarded sheen—watchful, cautious. The weight of their history hangs unspoken between them, a rope stretched taut, threatening to snap if either of them pulls too hard.

Emma's gaze lifts to meet his, then immediately returns to the chart, her fingers tightening around the paper as if it anchored her composure.

"Range of motion remains limited in the right shoulder," Emma begins, her voice clear and steady. "Pain is reported as moderate—six on the scale this morning. The recommended focus is on controlled mobility exercises, concentrated stretching, and light resistance training."

His lips twitch, almost breaking into a half-smile, a crack in his usual guarded demeanor. "Practice today was..." His voice lowers as he leans forward slightly, testing the waters. "That last drill—the lateral sprints? It nearly wiped me out." His eyes darken ever so slightly, not quite matching the levity in his tone.

Emma's gaze sharpens. She meets his attempt with gentle firmness, clearing her throat. "These sessions are for treatment, Jaxon," she says quietly but resolutely. "They are not for revisiting the past or team banter." Her hands move to the chart again, jotting down the next note with a brisk stroke. Signal received.

His body shifts, weight settling unevenly. Fingers curl against a faint, pale scar etched into his palm—an automatic gesture, his silent concession. He watches as Emma pulls a fresh roll of kinesio tape onto the table, the adhesive gleaming under the soft lighting.

"I'm here as your sports therapist," Emma states, her voice unwavering. "My responsibility is physical care, which means no personal history discussions during treatment."

She picks up the resistance bands. The elastic stretches with a sharp whisper as she loops a bright red band over her palm, preparing for the exercises ahead.

Jaxon's gaze flickers toward her hands, simple professionalism grounding him back in the present moment. He holds his silence, deferring the weight of unspoken words for now. His jaw tightens imperceptibly as he watches her work—fingers tightening, then relaxing in time with the steady rhythm of tape strips being pulled and smoothed across his shoulder.

The team's arrival murmurs through the thin walls. Lockers clang, and laughter rolls down the hall.

Emma finishes securing the tape. The fabric grips his skin in a neat, supportive line. She steps back, sliding the chart closed with a quiet snap.

"That'll have to do for today," she says softly, her voice clipped but professional. "You'll feel the difference during practice tomorrow."

Her eyes flick toward the doorway, where echoes from the corridor swell with urgency and restless energy. "Session's over."

Jaxon nods, the corners of his mouth barely lifting in acknowledgment. He turns, muscles tensing as he heads toward the door. The faint scrunch of tape under his shoulder moves with him—a tether to a healing he's reluctant to claim but cannot deny.

The room hums low and expectant once more. The scent of liniment and antiseptic hangs steadily as the sounds outside swell—a distant rally of voices, the scrape of cleats on linoleum, the heartbeat of a team still scrambling toward redemption.

Through the cracked-open door, cleats clattered. Voices murmured low, then sharpened into laughter—a sharp, booming guffaw laced with rough camaraderie. Emma's ears caught Brick's unmistakable voice: loud, unapologetic. It carried down the corridor like a gunshot.

"...and then I told him, that's not a slippery slope—that's an avalanche!" Brick's laughter shook the narrow hallway, bouncing off cinderblock walls.

The sound hung heavy in the air. Emma breathed in the sharp scent of sweat and turf, the faint metallic tang of lockers slamming shut with a rhythmic clang. It sounded like thunder—like heavy boots marching home after a battle lost.

The echoes stirred the corners of the sterile room, where antiseptic mingled with the lingering musk of muscle strain. She clenched her jaw and used the rising racket as cover.

The session had to end. Now.

With steady fingers, she pulled a final strip from the roll of tape, pressed it in place on Jaxon's shoulder, and let out a slow breath.

"Caleb!" Her voice cut through the din, sharp but practiced. "Don't forget the quad stretches before you hit the field again. Keep those muscles loose."

Caleb, the lean receiver with quiet intensity burning in his eyes, pivoted on worn sneakers and nodded. He turned back toward the squad without hesitation.

Emma's clipboard felt solid in her grip—a map of minor pains, progress notes, and treatment schedules she had memorized by now. More than that, it was a shield—a record of control in a space where control was all she had.

She glanced up. The hallway outside breathed with movement—shuffling feet, jingling lockers, and murmurs of encouragement tangled with mock complaints. The pulse of the team tapped against the gray walls, electric and unpredictable.

Jaxon didn't head for the exit.

His broad frame lingered in the threshold, shadowed. Dark eyes tracked her every move, hesitant but clear, as if weighing the distance between them.

"You... holding up, Emma?" His voice was low, words clipped as if he were keeping something locked inside.

She tilted her head slightly, not fully meeting his gaze. "The training schedule is brutal. You know the drill. We all grind through."

"Yeah." His voice dropped further, raw with unclaimed meaning. He shifted his weight, heel tapping a restless beat against the linoleum. His fingers twitched at his side. "Any downtime for you?"

Her hands moved automatically, peeling a disinfectant wipe from the packet—a ritual born of habit and necessity. The cool swipe against the pale laminate interrupted any conversation. She turned her back to him strategically, that edge between professionalism and old wounds forming a quiet barrier between them.

The scent of alcohol and mint lingered as she cleaned in measured strokes—the sterile swish of fabric against the surface, a sound that blotted out unspoken words.

Jaxon's toes scraped softly against the cracked linoleum. The tension coiled beneath his composed exterior, visible in the set of his shoulders and the way his eyes wouldn't leave her hands. He seemed poised on the edge of saying something heavier, something that might crack them both open. Then he swallowed it instead.

Footsteps passed by—a pair of players laughing and challenging each other's boasts. The hum of team life pressed close, relentless. Yet Jaxon and Emma remained anchored just outside its rhythm. Silence settled between them, taut as a wire about to snap.

She finished the last swipe, folded the wipe deliberately, and slid it into the small trash bin tucked beneath the counter. The crisp crinkle punctuated the quiet.

"I need to see the next player." Her tone was flat but not unkind. The clipboard lifted like an invisible line drawn between them.

Jaxon's shoulders stiffened. There was a brief hesitation. Then he stepped back, surrendering the doorway. The faint scent of liniment clung to his jacket sleeve as he moved away, swallowed by the corridor's relentless pace.

Emma watched him go. The door remained ajar. Laughter and challenge drifted inward once more. The space between them, thick as the air before a storm, held a promise of conversations yet to come—and those better left untouched.

She turned toward the next appointment, her breath catching under the weight of the unspoken.

Emma moved past him. Her sleeve brushed his arm—a whisper of contact that sent electricity through her chest, sharp and consuming. Jaxon felt it. His gaze tracked her like a moth drawn to sudden light, but neither broke the silence that enveloped the room. Outside, pale sunlight pooled through the window, scattering muted gold across walls the color of sea glass.

He leaned against the doorframe, shoulders weighted, muscles loosening just enough to crack the armor he had worn for so long. Emma's jaw clenched as she reached for the resistance bands, her fingers tightening into fists before she gripped the faded rubber instead, grounding herself. Her eyes found his—still guarded, but hesitant now. The weight between them hung thick as honey.

"About earlier," he said, his voice rough around the edges. "Sorry I bailed."

His eyes traced the hard lines of her face, searching for softness, for any fracture in the professional wall she had built.

Emma's jaw tightened as she dropped the bands onto the counter. The sharp thud echoed in the still room. Her voice turned colder. "Sorry doesn't fix it, Jaxon. You walked out mid-crisis. One word won't change that."

He flinched, his jaw tightening, a scowl flickering across his face like a shadow on rough stone. The memory surfaced without warning—the last time she had looked at him like this, disappointed and distant. He looked away, his gaze settling on a scuff mark on the floor as if it held answers he couldn't articulate.

"I'm sorry for everything," he said in fragments. The words felt hollow in his mouth. "You wouldn't understand. Not yet."

Emma's hand hovered before the sanitizer bottle, trembling just enough that the rim caught a glint of light. She reached for it, her fingers closing around it. The sharp antiseptic smell bit at her nostrils, mingling with the faint rubber tang of the bands and the distant hum of late-night machines. She inhaled it back, pressing her spine stiff against the cold counter, her voice clipped with refusal.

"This isn't the place. Not now. I won't discuss the past here, Jaxon."

She turned away. Her shoulders rose as if to swallow back a sigh, her eyes fixed beyond the windowpane. The rising sun threw shards of light across her face—light enough to hide what she wouldn't show.

Jaxon's boot thudded against the faded linoleum. His hand brushed the chipped doorframe—an anchor in the silence. The weight in his chest made each step feel heavier, as though gravity itself had shifted. His breath hitched just enough for Emma to catch it, a tremor beneath the gruff exterior. His lips moved without sound at first.

Then he said, "I'm sorry."

The words came fragile and raw. Sincerity pulled taut between them, but the why and how hung suspended—unspoken, just out of reach.

Emma glanced away, her throat tightening. A lone tear bloomed at the edge of her eye. She blinked it back, the taste of salt bitter on her tongue. Her fingers found the edge of the clipboard, curling around the papers as her body betrayed what her voice would not. She breathed out, steadying the swell beneath her ribs.

Job first. Boundaries intact.

She would not let the past—or Jaxon—fracture her focus today. Not after she had finally rebuilt what he had broken.

He lingered where the cool hallway light bled into the warm quiet of the room—shadowed, hesitant. Then his voice cut through the fragile stillness, soft and almost swallowed by the muted hum of the building.

"Emma."

Each syllable was a tentative bridge cast across years of unsaid things. It drifted closer, but he stepped back before the space could narrow. His figure blurred into the corridor's gloom.

No follow-up. No explanations handed over like gifts.

Only distance that stretched taut.

Emma's gaze followed his retreating shoulders—rigid, guarded. Then he vanished into the corridor.

The door swung softly shut behind him, the click sharp in the stillness.

Alone now, the sterile air pressed in—cool beneath the glow of the overhead LED lights. Her heart pounded unevenly, each beat a jagged pulse in the quiet calm. His footsteps echoed faintly from the hall-way—steady, purposeful, weighted with the gravity of what remained unspoken.

She lowered the clipboard onto the treatment table with a firm hand. Her fingers trembled but steadied with resolve. The scent of peppermint from the diffuser mingled with faint antiseptic, ground-ing her in the present moment. This clinical room—once a sanctuary and battlefield in equal measure—waited in brittle silence.

Emma's whispered words sliced through the stillness, brittle and resolute: "Ghosts don't stay buried."

Her eyes lifted, sharp and determined, tracing the pale sunlight threading through the slatted blinds. Golden bars spilled across the sea-glass walls. The weight of memory hummed in the quiet—unshed apologies, fractures of trust, and the raw edges of what could be or what once was.

Yet somewhere beneath it, a flicker pressed against the dark.

Small. Hesitant.

Not yet defeated. Not yet lost.

Jaxon's apology lingered like a fragile ember in the cooling air. Emma pressed the clipboard tightly against her side as the echo of his voice faded completely, swallowed by the distant bustle of the team outside.

The door remained closed now, a barrier between past wounds and present duty, firm as stone.

For all the cracks beneath, Emma's resolve hardened: no ghosts would dictate her tomorrow.

Not today.

Not ever.

The Locker Room Test

The coach's whistle blasts sharply through the thick, humid air, like an electric shock.

The drill dissolves. Players' legs falter, feet dragging through battered grass streaked with mud. Heavy shoulders slump beneath grime-streaked jerseys plastered with sweat. Each step carries the weight of another failed play. The field blurs—exhaled breaths, muted curses, a slow migration toward the shadows where the bleachers stand as silent witnesses.

Boots slap against cracked concrete as the team files into the locker room, a cavernous shell of peeling paint and flickering fluorescents. The overhead lights stutter, casting ghostly pulses over worn green lockers and splintered wooden benches stained by seasons of spilled water and bruised tempers.

The air hangs thick; liniment bites sharply. Damp jerseys cling sourly against skin.

Dirty cleats scuff the cold floor, a steady, dull rhythm punctuating the collective silence.

Jaxon lingers near the back, unzipping his duffel with stiff fingers. His palms tighten around the strap as if anchoring himself against something building inside the room. He watches players shuffle past, their shoulders hunched, their eyes anywhere but on each other.

Eyebrows knit tightly. Fists clench mid-pat on benches. The air tastes like tightened nerves and unshed words.

Jaxon knows the drill didn't fail on its own. He can feel blame gathering in the corners like a storm about to break.

"Long day." A low murmur, barely audible over the fluorescent hum.

A faint scrape echoes. The last helmet clatters to the floor—a metallic clang, sharp and sudden against the concrete. The locker room falls instantly into stillness. Every breath seems to hold a question.

The door thuds shut behind the last player. An uneasy silence seals them in.

Jaxon's throat tightens. He remembers the last real blowup—three weeks ago, when voices had shattered against these same metal lockers, and nobody had known how to piece things back together. This silence feels different. Fragile. Like standing on thin ice.

"You know what? That was a mess." Caleb's voice breaks the quiet, small and caught somewhere between apology and defiance. His fingers tremble slightly as he fumbles with tape near a bench, nerves bleeding through his stoic mask.

"Mess doesn't cover it." Brick's voice comes low and rough from the corner, his eyes on the ground but carrying the weight of frustration. "That was sloppy."

Jaxon shifts. The thick leather of his duffel creaks beneath his grip.

His voice cuts through the room—steady but hard. It carries the weight of a man no longer willing to fade into the background.

"This isn't where we're supposed to be," he says, his eyes scanning the circle of faces. "Not by a long shot."

Eli leans against a locker, his shoulders rigid. Something unreadable smolders beneath his wary eyes—anger, perhaps, or something closer to betrayal.

"We all know why this tanked." Eli's voice bleeds resentment, sharp as broken glass. "Slow calls. Missed adjustments. You weren't tossing out fixes when protection crumbled on the snap, were you?"

DeShawn shifts. His usual easy grin flickers uncertainly before tightening into a hard line. "Man, maybe nobody was really 'there' when the drill turned into whatever that disaster was."

Jaxon's jaw tightens. He holds his ground, his eyes steeling as he prepares for what comes next.

"Blaming each other won't fix a damn thing," he says. His voice rises just a shade—controlled but firm. The first real crack of leadership since he walked into this room. "We're dragging ourselves down with it. You're all better than this. I missed an adjustment. I dropped the ball on that play. But this? This finger-pointing? It ends now."

The flickering lights catch the glitter in Brick's narrowed eyes. The defensive lineman exhales slowly, tension coiling tight around his fists.

"You ready to prove it, Reyes?" Brick's voice rumbles, quiet but sharp.

A charged stillness settles over the room. Players shift uneasily. The room teeters between an uneasy truce and the next explosion.

Then something shifts. The chatter begins to ebb. Caleb exhales a shaky breath, looking anywhere but at Jaxon. DeShawn's mouth tightens—a silent acknowledgment that something has changed, that the battle lines have been redrawn.

"No fancy excuses," Jaxon continues. His voice carries more weight than words alone. "Respect each other. Take responsibility. We start now."

The locker room begins to empty. Feet scrape. Gear shuffles. The metallic clatter of helmets and locker doors punctuates the tentative retreat from the stifling heat of frustration.

Yet beneath the slow exodus, a new tension hums—a boundary freshly marked. A challenge is thrown down in the shadows and flickering light of this worn battlefield.

Brick's boots thud against the gray concrete. Each step pounds like a distant drum. His jaw is clenched tight, muscles taut beneath dark skin that gleams with sweat. His nostrils flare—sharp, ragged breaths snatching the stale air.

The worn wooden bench groans beneath empty helmets and water bottles. Brick doesn't pause. He rips his helmet free from the peeling leather strap and grips it like a cudgel, his eyes darkening as he heads toward the cracked cinderblock wall.

He stopped a breath away, coiled like a snap wire.

Without warning, his arm arced back in a raw, savage swing. The helmet tore through the air—a hollow thud against cold concrete. The noise ricocheted sharply, clanging off the walls. It sucked the breath from the room. Bits of cracked plastic rattled across the floor, shards scattered like the aftermath of his shattered temper.

It might as well have been a gunshot.

Voices near the benches faltered. Players froze mid-motion, their skin slick with grime and fatigue. Caleb, crouched low over fraying tape, flinched. His hands trembled. His eyes snapped up—wide, alert—locked onto Brick's rigid silhouette outlined by the flickering fluorescent lights.

Caleb's breath caught. He had seen this before. Last month in practice, Brick had thrown a dumbbell hard enough to dent the rack. The defensive lineman carried something volatile just beneath his skin, and today it had cracked through the surface.

Conversations hissed and sputtered, then collapsed into silence.

The locker room felt suddenly suffocating. Humid heat clung like a wet blanket across raw skin and worn jerseys. The faint musk of sweat mingled with the sharp tang of liniment and dust, settling thick between them.

DeShawn cleared his throat. He had developed a reputation as the unofficial morale officer—the one who broke tension with humor, though anxiety always threaded beneath his attempts at levity. He forced a grin that didn't reach his eyes.

"Yo, Brick—save some of that fire for the game, will you?" His voice quivered, a high-pitched stab in the heavy quiet. "Or do you think the wall's our secret weapon?"

The room held its breath instead of breaking into laughter. No one cracked a smile. The joke died, struck down by the weight of brick-hard resentment radiating from the defensive lineman's clenched frame.

Brick's chest heaved unevenly, his shoulders jerking with each ragged breath. His fists slackened just a fraction—the fine tremor in his knuckles betraying the storm beneath his skin. His glare never shifted, but the fire behind his eyes flickered uncertainly. A taut wire stretched between anger and exhaustion.

The echo of the impact still lingered in the charged silence—an unspoken challenge hanging thick between them, waiting to be answered.

Eli leans against the front row of lockers, his arms crossed so tightly that his sleeves wrinkle. His jaw sets hard—a blockade. His eyes are sharp, focused on Jaxon's retreating figure near the back. The air still thrums from Brick's outburst, that crashing helmet's echo lingering like a storm rumble.

Eli's voice cuts through the tension—sharp, biting.

"You think just showing up and barking orders makes you a leader?" His words slice like a whistle. "'Cause all I saw today were slow reads. Slow, man. Second drill, play twenty-three, shotgun spread—you froze. You didn't call the audible when Brick was open. You didn't adjust protection on the left flank. We got burned because your head was somewhere else."

Murmurs ripple through the crowded room. Players scrape their sneakers across the scuffed concrete, shoulders twitching like coiled springs. Near Eli, a cluster of boys nod, their whispered voices thick with discontent.

"Yeah, and the snap count?" Someone's voice cracks, rough and clipped, breath catching amid the heavy stench of sweat and liniment. "Totally off. We're stepping on each other out there. Brick almost got blindsided twice."

Another voice slips in—quiet and cutting. "We needed direction. Instead? Chaos."

Eli's glare dares to meet Jaxon's, waiting, daring him to respond.

Brick steps forward—tall and looming. His knuckles whiten as he slaps the dented locker beside him. Metal screams. The sound booms like a gunshot, demanding silence.

"Fancy pros who don't care," Brick growls, his voice thick and dark. "They think they can waltz in, toss plays around like confetti, and we'll just catch them. That doesn't fly here." His eyes burn, frustration flickering into something deeper—betrayal, maybe, or the weight of shattered hopes.

DeShawn shifts near the wall, pushing a loose sweatshirt strap past his wrist. He tries to cut the rising tension with humor—a thin veil stretched over nerves about to snap. "Well, hey, at least we're consistent at screwing up, right?" His grin shakes, and his voice pitches high when he laughs, forced but desperate to lighten the room.

The room doesn't loosen. The joke dies. Players talk louder over him, returning to heated grumbles, blame crackling like dry kindling catching fire.

"You kidding? This isn't a joke, DeShawn. It's survival," Eli snaps back. "We either fix this, or we're toast." Every syllable is a pointed jab. "And it starts with you, Jax. If you can't call plays right, can't lead, then what the hell are you even doing here?"

Heads swivel. Sneakers rattle on concrete. Eyes dart between Jaxon and the group—searching, accusing.

Caleb's fingers tremble over tape near the benches. His eyes flick up—wide, uncertain, searching for any sign of mercy beneath this storm. DeShawn's smile vanishes. His jaw clenches into a stiff line.

The air thickens—hot, sharp. It tastes of frustration, the salt of sweat, and the metallic edge of tension corralling men who want to believe in a comeback but don't know where to find one.

Jaxon's gaze holds steady for a breath—rare vulnerability buried under layers of hard edges. The room swells with shouts and accusations, overlapping and unyielding. A relentless tide dragging him under.

The line between leader and adversary draws itself clear—razor-thin, unforgiving.

The locker room feels smaller now, walls closing in with every word landing heavier than the last. Voices rise until the air hums with the buzz of a storm ready to break loose.

The divide yawns between the man who once led and the team wondering if he still can.

No one moves to break the swell. Instead, they brace themselves, each man caught in the pull of raw frustration and unspoken hopes tangled tight, waiting to see who blinks first.

Jaxon stepped away from the cold metal locker. His boots scraped against the cracked concrete floor. The harsh buzz of flickering fluorescents overhead caught the glint of sweat on his brow, mixing with the stale locker room air that tasted like old tape and regret.

He squared his broad shoulders, swallowing the knotted urge to disappear into the shadows. Instead, he strode to the center of the room, planting himself where every eye could latch onto him. The air hung thick with heat and tension.

His gaze sliced through the cluster of restless players—some sharp, others defeated. Their silence pressed heavily.

"This—" His voice cut clear, steady but hard. "This isn't some goddamn blame game."

Heads pivoted. Murmurs stilled. He let the silence stretch, then continued, his voice rising with measured fire.

"Every time we point fingers, every time someone looks to dump the mess on someone else," he stepped forward, his boots thudding softly. His eyes locked on Eli and Brick, their faces carved with skepticism and simmering frustration. "That drags us deeper into the hole. We can't win on that bullshit. We need accountability, not excuses."

The low scrape of a taped hand gripping a bench shifted the mood. Attentiveness flickered through the room.

Jaxon swallowed against the grit in his throat. The familiar knot twisted inside him—part fear, part stubborn defiance. He refused to back down this time.

"I'm not above it. I missed the adjustment on that last drill. Yeah, I screwed up." He exhaled, letting the weight settle. "That's on me. But that ends now. If we're going to pull this team out of the gutter, we all own our mistakes. Respect is earned here, both on the field and off it. No more passing the buck."

The silence crashed back, heavier than before, like a dropped weight in the already cramped space.

Brick's jaw clenched. Eli's eyes burned with a cold challenge. Neither moved, but the electric undercurrent of testing pulsed in their stances—old frustrations and unresolved power struggles tightening the air between them.

Among the cluster, Caleb's lower lip trembled. He hunched forward as if the weight of the room were pressing down on him. DeShawn's mouth clamped shut, a stiff line cutting through his usually easy grin—clearly bracing against the honesty hanging thick between them.

"You expect me to just swallow all that?" Eli's voice cracked the fragile stillness. Sharp. Cold. "Pretend this mess didn't burn us all? Lead us? When the quarterback can't even read a damn defense?"

He leaned forward, his breath hot with accusation.

"Slow reads. Missed calls. We lost ground because you weren't there."

Brick's steps rumbled heavily, filling the space between Jaxon and the lockers. His fist banged into a dented metal door—stark punctuation that echoed through the room. "Yeah. You're preaching respect now, but all I see are fancy pros who don't give a damn about this team." His voice cut like edged steel, raw and jagged. "About us."

The room pulsed. Shouts began brewing, voices threading through layers of frustration.

DeShawn stepped between the rising storm, his voice light but trembling. "Hey, come on, man. We're all on the same side here, right? No need for a war zone."

His joke landed flat, swallowed by the growing storm.

Players exchanged glances. Tension coiled tighter with every breath.

Jaxon didn't flinch. He planted both feet firmly, his fists unclenching at his sides. His voice came steady and uncompromising.

"Enough." It reverberated through the walls.

"You want to whine about missed reads and 'fancy pros'? Fine. But that isn't leadership—that's whining." His eyes swept over them, icy and unyielding. "This team's sinking because we let blame rule. No one's keeping score on who messed up worst. Except maybe you, Eli. Always ready to pounce."

Eli's lips pressed tightly together. He bit back a retort, his glare unwavering.

Jaxon exhaled—a breath that tasted like dusty turf and the metallic tang of sweat.

"I won't pretend I'm perfect. I never said that. But if you want to win, you need to start by owning your faults." He paused, letting his gaze find each face in turn. "And respecting the guy who is trying to pull you out of the fire."

A pause thick enough to choke on.

The players shuffled, some exchanging wary looks. Caleb's eyes flickered up—a mix of uncertainty and grudging respect rippling through his guarded expression. DeShawn's jaw twitched again, tight and thoughtful.

The room's tension didn't break into relief or ease; it shifted. The boiling undercurrent simmered down to a steady, uneasy pulse.

Instead of fracturing, the team began to break apart slowly. Feet scraped against the floor, and jerseys rustled as bodies moved toward the exit. The scent of sweat and worn leather filled the space, mingling with the buzz of cracked fluorescent bulbs overhead that cast a sputtering glow over faces etched with surprise and a new kind of wariness.

Jaxon watched them go—not with relief, but with the weight of boundaries newly forged—tense, fragile, but real.

No chaos unfurled—just a quiet, hard-earned pause.

Coach Marcus Hale's boots scraped against the cracked concrete as he crossed the locker room threshold. His face was flushed from the walk across the practice field. The tension knotted tighter the moment he stepped inside.

He hadn't needed to listen long; the voices had carried clear, sharp as the whistle's final blow.

Now his dark eyes surveyed the scattered players—sweaty shoulders hunched, mud streaking their jerseys like battle scars that wouldn't quite fade. Without a word, Marcus climbed onto a battered wooden bench near the center. The grating creak sliced through the low murmur and shuffling feet.

The room fell silent—brittle, broken only by shallow intakes of breath and the distant hum of flickering fluorescent lights overhead.

"Enough," he said, his voice rough and clipped. Each word was loaded with authority. "Discipline isn't a suggestion around here; it's the goddamn foundation. Do you think this program's a joke?"

The question hung in the stale air, heavy with the weight of lost seasons and shattered dreams etched into every flaking piece of paint.

"Division like the crap I just heard? It'll sink us—all of us. Your last chance isn't some abstract concept; it's what we're fighting to keep."

The players shifted uneasily at the edges of his stare. Brick's jaw clenched, his eyes burning with frustration. Across the room, Caleb's gaze dropped to his scuffed boots, his fingers tapping nervously against the bench.

Marcus's hands curled into fists at his sides—knuckles white beneath sweat and grime. His voice dropped but did not soften. "You want to point fingers? Fine. But don't expect to keep wearing that Hawks jersey if you can't own your part. Accountability isn't optional; it's damn mandatory."

"The board is watching us," he continued. "The whole town is breathing down our necks. Every misstep, every hissed insult, every helmet thrown in anger—that's money drying up. Fans are turning their backs. Your teammates are breaking down."

He paused, letting silence settle like weight on their shoulders.

"So get your asses moving. Clean up your gear. Meet the standard we set, or don't bother showing up next time."

The room exhaled collectively—tight, reluctant. Boots scraped as players began to rise, reaching for worn cleats and crumpled jerseys. The sharp scent of liniment and stale sweat filled the air, faint echoes of the day's hard work mingling with something rawer, something like fear.

The racket of zippers and rustling fabric filled the pause between order and actual movement. Voices emerged low now, stripped of the earlier explosion's heat, but an uneasy undercurrent lingered.

Jaxon's eyes met Brick's across the cluttered room. There was grudging respect mixed with simmering frustration—an understanding between them that ran deeper than words.

Caleb remained seated for a moment longer, his fingers working at nothing, as if wrapping tape around invisible seams of resolve and nerves. When he finally stood, his movements were measured and controlled.

DeShawn shouldered his bag, his jaw tight. He caught Jaxon's glance and gave the faintest nod. The message rang loud and clear.

One by one, the players filed toward the exit. Some exchanged sullen nods, while others lingered just long enough to absorb the weight of combined demands from their coach and their reluctant leader.

The locker room gradually emptied, with fluorescent lights casting longer shadows in the space they left behind.

When the last echoes of footsteps faded, the door thudded shut with a final, metallic clang that reverberated off the concrete walls. A charged stillness clung to the air—thick with sweat and unspoken promises, testing the fragile limits of tolerance and trust.

The new rules hung like a silent edict. The ghosts of the past retreated, but the cost to come cast a long shadow over battered benches and cracked lockers that witnessed it all.

No one moved.

Not yet.

The locker room door thuds shut, muffling the last echoes of footsteps. Coach Hale gestures sharply for Jaxon to stay behind. The thud isolates them, sealing in the harsh fluorescent buzz and the faint, ever-present scent of stale coffee and old sweat.

Paper, taped playbooks, and scattered empty Gatorade cups clutter the cramped office like the debris of a program slowly sinking. Budget cuts are made visible, sponsors are abandoning ship, and the supply closet reflects it.

Coach Hale swings his chair around, settling behind the desk with the precision of a man accustomed to commanding attention. His eyes lock onto Jaxon's with the cold fire of expectation—no softness, just raw, unfiltered demand.

"This is it, Reyes." Hale's voice cuts through the cramped space, clipped and unyielding. "One more blow-up—on the field or off—doesn't make a damn bit of difference. You crack again, you're done. No ifs, no buts."

Jaxon feels the words land like ice against his skin. A cold knot tightens in his chest. His mouth opens—ready to argue, to defend—but the words catch, stuck tight in his throat. He swallows grit and lets the silence hang thick between them.

Hale folds his hands atop the desk, his jaw tight. "You think this is just about wins and losses? Think harder." His gaze sharpens. "The program's bleeding money. Sponsors are jumping ship. The community is sliding closer to turning its back on us. We're riding the edge, and if you can't steady the damn ship, that's it."

The drone of the flickering fluorescent light weaves into the tension, a low hum underscoring everything. Jaxon can taste the faint bitterness of liniment from afternoon practice, mixing with the stale office air and coating his tongue with the flavor of failure.

"You don't get a clean slate here. Not really."

Hale's voice lowers, each word deliberate. Jaxon's fingers twitch at his sides, fists threatening to clench but held stubbornly loose. The pressure of knowing that every eye in this program—every player, every sponsor, every person in this godforsaken town—is fixed on him, waiting to see if he'll fold again.

"The town's watching. The sponsors are watching. Hell, even the players are watching." Hale leans forward, his eyes narrowing under heavy brows, his voice dropping to a razor's edge. "If you keep acting half the way you did today—breaking the team down instead of building it up—you'll find yourself out on your ass faster than you think."

Defense curls its claws in Jaxon's chest, but he holds it at bay. This isn't a council to be won with excuses or deflection.

"I'm giving you one shot at this. One." Hale's words hit like a steel rod—threat and opportunity wrapped tight. "The rest of the program? They're counting on you to be more than a player clawing for a last shot at glory. They need a leader. Prove you're that man—don't just play like one."

The office lights flicker again. Shadows tangle in the corners, stretching out as if to swallow the moment whole.

Jaxon's chest rises and falls in slow, deliberate control. He inhales the stale, bitter mix of coffee grounds and frustration that props up this grim little fortress. The quiet tick of a battered wall clock taps out seconds heavy with meaning.

Hale's steely gaze never wavers. "All eyes are on you, Reyes. Your move."

No further words come—just the hum of fluorescents, the muted sounds of the distant emptying locker room, and the weight of a future hinged on a single choice—one mistake away from the edge.

Jaxon pushes open the office door and steps back into the gray cavern of the locker room. The air feels thicker now, heavier with the ghosts of the storm just passed. His boots make soft, deliberate thuds against the cracked concrete floor, echoing under the low hum of flickering fluorescents.

Rows of green metal lockers stand like solemn sentinels, some doors scratched and dented, others ajar, revealing the day's sweat-soaked jerseys and scuffed cleats strewn on broken benches. Damp grass and worn leather linger in the air; faint traces of liniment mingle with the musky ache of exertion. The silence tightens like a noose around him.

He strolls past the scattered gear, his eyes tracing the trails of dried mud that cling stubbornly to cleats abandoned in haste. A half-empty water bottle rattles faintly when a draft moves it. Distant footsteps echo in the hall outside. The space feels hollow—prayers whispered in stillness, the battleground of their fractured team.

Jaxon pauses in front of his locker. The chipped paint on the metal door feels rough under his fingertips. He pulls his helmet free with a slow, almost reluctant grasp. It is heavy in his hands. Sweat clings to the inside of the padding, sharp with liniment and old fear. He lifts the helmet off, and wet heat spills from his hair into the stale air. His fingers clench damp strands against his skin, then drag down his face—calloused knuckles scraping over gritty stubble. His jaw tightens. Salt stings his lips, and he tastes it: the bitterness of sweat and the lingering edge of liniment.

His gaze falls to the cracked floor as his mind rewinds over the afternoon's fractious moments. Coach Hale's clipped voice still cuts through the noise at the back of his skull—a scalpel finding bone: *last chance, no exceptions*. The threat is real: funding is on the line, community trust is fraying, and the future hangs by a thread.

And the team. Their eyes flash with resentment and raw hope alike. Brick's jaw is clenched, and his fists tremble. Eli's sharp accusations are like barbed arrows. Caleb is caught between doubt and expectation. DeShawn's forced levity cracks under tension. Each face imprints itself in Jaxon's mind, etched with the electric charge of unsaid words and unclaimed blame.

The boundary he established moments ago—the demand for accountability, respect, and change—feels fragile, like a whisper poised on a knife's edge. Can he hold it? Can he actually lead them out of this mire, or will he fold back into the familiar shadows of cynicism?

A voice breaks the silence from the door. "You good in there?"

Jaxon startles, then exhales. "Yeah. Just—processing."

Emma's figure stands framed by the doorway, her hazel eyes steady and warm in that harsh fluorescent light. There is something resolute in her stance—a calm strength that both steadies and unsettles him. He has seen that look before, in moments when she stood between his worst impulses and whatever good might still be salvageable in him. It unsettles him now as much as it ever did.

"You shook them up," she says softly, stepping inside.

He shrugs, his helmet barely cradled in one hand. "Maybe they needed it. The truth is ugly."

She nods, walking further into the room. "And you? Do you believe it'll stick? That the team will actually step up?"

Jaxon meets her gaze. The space between them crackles, unspoken words hanging heavier than the stale air. "I don't know." His voice catches. "But I have to try."

Emma studies him for a long moment. "Trying is the first damn step. Just don't let the past pull you under again."

"I'm not sure I have the luxury of falling back," Jaxon admits, his voice tight. "Coach laid it out plainly: one more fuck-up, and it's over."

Her lips press into a thin line—equal parts warning and encouragement. "Then don't fuck it up."

A weight settles in his chest, heavy enough to bend him. Yet beneath that, a fragile ember stirs, fighting the smothering dark. He looks away, his eyes catching the flicker of a single overhead bulb struggling to keep its light steady, casting long shadows that dance like memories across the locker room walls.

The faces rise again: Brick's fiery glare, Eli's sharp edge, Caleb's uncertain hope, and DeShawn's nervous charm. Their trust is tentative, a fragile thread linking them all. The future is an unknown field, every step a gamble.

Jaxon lowers his gaze to his helmet lying in his lap. The scent of sweat and liniment rises—a sharp reminder of effort and pain. He breathes in deeply, feeling the sharp sting of adrenaline mixing with fatigue.

Suddenly, the silence fractures. A fragile resolve builds from within.

But the next move? That could tip everything.

"You do realize," Emma's voice cuts gently through the charged stillness, "we're counting on you."

"And if I don't come through?"

"There's no plan B."

His eyes snap up, meeting hers. No comfort. No evasion. Just cold truth.

"I'll figure it out," he says, though the tremor in his voice betrays the uncertainty lurking beneath.

Emma smiles faintly, a quiet flame in the oppressive dusk. "Good. Because this team—they need you."

Jaxon slides the helmet carefully onto the bench beside him, hands folded, shoulders squared. The locker room hums softly around him, the fluorescent light above flickering—on, off, back on—like a heartbeat caught in a stuttering rhythm.

He stands still beneath it, stretched between promise and peril. The weight of all those watching rests squarely on his shoulders.

His next move will write the first real line on the blank slate they all stare down—the last yard between failure and redemption.

For now, he just breathes in the sharp, aching stillness and waits.

First Snap, First Fall

The motel clock glows 4:37 a.m. in muted red, its dull buzz swallowed by the thick silence of the room. Jaxon lies on his back, the thin blanket tangled between his long fingers. The fabric is rough against his skin, with threads worn bare in spots, providing a poor shield against the chill seeping through cracked windows.

Outside, the world holds its breath—no birdsong yet, just the distant hum of a restless town.

His eyes burn from trying not to close them, stinging as if the plays themselves are scraping under his lids. In his mind, the field unfolds—splayed beneath a steel-gray sky that mirrors the gloom creeping under his ribs. He traces routes, his fingertip shivering across the blanket's crease, imagining receivers cutting sharp and smooth like shadows darting through fog.

Snap. Drop. Release.

The familiar rhythms feel brittle today, as if they'll shatter if he holds on too tight.

His throat itches dry. A whispered threat slips past trembling lips. "Discipline or destruction, Reyes. One more misstep, and the whole damn program goes under."

The words stick like shards between his teeth. His chest tightens, breath shallow—each syllable a stone sinking in his gut. Coach Hale's warning isn't just a caution; it's a verdict disguised as hope. Jaxon tastes fear, thick and acrid, mingling with something sharper: the weight of a team's last chance pressed tight against his ribs, demanding more than he knows he can give.

He rolls onto one side, fingers lingering on the stained blanket. Silence leans close. He pushes himself upright, muscles taut with the tension of a man threading slow needle holes through his own skin. No jerks. No wasted movement. His body is a machine in slow, careful startup.

His hands find the box of tape beside the faded duffel bag. Each strip peels off sticky and hot against his wrist, winding tight with practiced care. The ritual steadies a mind roaring with second guesses and ghosts.

Buckles click. Cleats tighten. The familiar scrape of laces against rough leather anchors him in the drifting fog inside. Every knot tied feels like an act of defiance against the doubt gnawing at the edges.

A thin whiff of stale motel carpet laces the air, mingling with the faint metallic tang of his own sweat. The room shrinks as he pulls on faded practice pants, the fabric whispering against hardened calves. His shirt, damp from last night's restless sleep, clings—smelling faintly of liniment and old grass. Ghosts of fields that once felt like home.

The laces cinch tight on boots that have carried him through better days, now worn, with edges fraying like the frayed edges of his resolve.

His shoulders jerk in a brief, stiff shrug, then settle into a tight, squared line beneath the threadbare fabric.

The mirror above the chipped dresser catches his tired glare. Dark eyes are locked hard. His jaw is set like cast iron.

Ready.

The chill outside nips at bare skin as the door creaks open. He shoulders the duffel, its worn strap biting into his flesh, and steps out into the fracturing dawn. The sky is a bruise of cold purples and pale blues, with faint light whispering against the horizon. The air smells of wet earth and restless wind, crisp enough to burn his lungs with each breath.

Streetlights flicker against the cracked pavement. Each footfall is steady, measured like the ticking seconds before battle. The motel stands forgotten behind him, dull and anonymous, swallowed by shadows.

Ahead, the stadium's silhouette waits—dark and unyielding beneath the early sky. It's more than just a field now; it's the vessel for a whole town's pride, for seasons lost and ghosts that haunt the bleachers, for every failure and false hope that has seeped into the concrete. It represents everything Jaxon carries on his shoulders, everything riding on hands that have stopped believing they can save anything.

His mind churns with silent commands and broken rhythms, plays folding and unfolding like origami beneath his skin. The quiet thrum in his chest is a slow drumming—the pulse of a soldier readying for war.

A breeze stirs the scattered leaves along the roadside, carrying distant echoes—murmurs of a past he's still trying to outrun and a future as uncertain as the rising sun. His gaze never falters, his eyes locked on the faint lights beyond, where everything waits to be claimed or lost.

"Cut the crap, Reyes."

The voice hovers low, almost lost in the wind—a ghost-seed planted in the soil of his thoughts. He doesn't answer. The words twine with the cold air, sharpening his focus.

There is no room for doubt. Not today.

His hands clench the strap harder, his knuckles pale beneath rough skin. The earth beneath his boots seems to pulse with the heartbeat of a thousand lost chances. Still, he walks—each step a promise breathed into the dawn.

The stadium looms larger now, each yard a battlefield stretching beneath the stirring light. The quiet buzz of early preparation hums from within, the scent of fresh-cut grass mingling with equipment musk and anticipation.

Somewhere deep, the fragile seed of resolve takes root—fragile but fierce.

Jaxon squares his shoulders, his jaw tightening. The plays still roll in his mind:

Snap. Drop. Release.

A silent war rages before the crowd ever gathers.

Cold air cracks in his lungs as he breathes in the coming day.

Time to move.

Jaxon stepped through the narrow locker room entrance. The scent of sweat, leather, and liniment coiled heavily in the thick air. Fluorescent lights flickered overhead, casting sharp, sickly halos over concrete walls scarred with decades of drill markings and graffiti. His boots thudded on the cracked tile as helmets and pads clattered—a cacophony born from nervous energy. He paused at his locker, its cold steel rough against his fingertips, and took a slow breath. The humid weight settled around him like a shroud.

Around the room, players moved through their rituals. Caleb sat alone on a splintered wooden bench, his fingers twisting absently over worn tape. His shoulders folded inward like a shell closing. The knot in his gut tightened with each passing second. Nearby, Brick paced by the lockers, his jaw clenched tight. Each step fell deliberate and heavy, his boots scraping the floor in an angry rhythm. DeShawn draped himself against a row of lockers, forcing easy grins that didn't reach his dark eyes, tossing out jokes that flitted and fell, unclaimed by the others.

Players shifted uneasily, their weight moving from foot to foot. Knuckles whitened as helmets clattered. The air grew thick, almost suffocating.

Coach Marcus Hale strode into the center like a storm breaking. His hard-soled boots scraped against the concrete. Every head lifted. Murmurs hushed as his voice cut through—brittle, clipped, with no softness in it.

"Discipline. That's your first and last play tonight." His eyes swept the room like flint seeking steel. "Accountability isn't optional for any of you. If you fumble, miss your mark, or don't cover your man—that's on you. It's on all of you. We win as a team, and we own every damn loss as one. No excuses."

The players stiffened. Shoulders straightened under an unspoken weight. Eyes flicked toward Jaxon, heavy with silent questions, a fragile hope balanced on the edge of a blade.

At the doorway, Emma appeared. Clipboard in hand, she moved with quiet purpose. She stooped briefly to inspect a scraped knee on one of the younger players, who was flushed with nerves. Her touch was gentle but efficient—peppermint and antiseptic mingled softly in the stale room. Her hazel eyes found Jaxon's for a moment, steady and sure. He looked away, his gaze sliding past her protectively, unwilling to meet the warmth that sought him out.

Whispered conversations died to a tense hush—the kind that pressed cold and sharp in Jaxon's chest like the first bite of winter. Only the faint hum of faulty fluorescents overhead remained, flickering like a broken heartbeat.

"In this room," Coach Hale's voice rasped, "we don't just play football. We fight for respect. For each other. For redemption. You're here because every second counts."

The pause stretched between his words, heavy with unspoken truths. Eyes locked across the team. Heat pulsed electrically across faces glistening with anticipation and fear. Jaxon felt the weight like a furnace—every pair of eyes burning into him, testing, demanding.

Caleb's hands tightened around the tape. His gaze drifted toward Jaxon, silently pleading for guidance amid the silent storm. Doubt spiraled through him—could he live up to what they all hoped he would become? Brick stopped pacing, folding his massive arms. His gaze held a fierce resolve that barely masked the worry beneath. DeShawn shifted his weight, forcing a crooked grin, but inside, the tight knot in his belly refused to loosen.

Jaxon exhaled slowly. His fingers flexed against the cold locker metal. The air tasted sharp—varnished wood and the metallic sting of sweat-soaked gear. Restless thoughts spiraled through his mind: the plays, the stakes, the betrayals of past mistakes.

He spoke. His voice broke the silence, rough and low, but steady.

"You think Coach Hale isn't watching *you*? Every slip, every hesitation?" Jaxon's words hung in the thick air. "This team's about trust—and right now, we don't have enough of it."

Caleb swallowed hard. His voice came out small and uncertain. "Coach says we have to own every loss... but how do you own it when you're already broken?"

Brick's booming reply cut through the doubt. "We're not broken, kid. We're raw. We're unfinished. And that means we're ready to fight."

DeShawn tried to lighten the mood, chuckling unevenly. "Yeah, raw and maybe a little bruised... but we've got heart. And at least I'm still the best at telling bad jokes under pressure."

Jaxon met DeShawn's forced grin with a sharp nod. The tension softened just enough to allow them to breathe.

Coach Hale's gaze swept across the group again. "Jaxon," he said, his voice tightening, "this locker room is watching. They need to hear your reckoning as much as mine."

The room seemed to lean in. Breaths grew shallow. A locker slammed, punctuating the silence like a pulse reverberating through the charged air.

From the corner, Emma's eyes flicked back to him. A quiet vow flickered there beneath layers of professionalism and buried feelings. She stepped away, the faint scuff of her shoes retreating as the room's focus snapped back to the grim line of men standing ready.

Jaxon felt the heat of every pair of eyes settle on him—heavy as judgment, sharp as a promise. The flickering lights hummed overhead, restless. The humid air wrapped around him, thick with possibility and the sting of what was to come.

The stadium lights fight through the stubborn grip of fog, their beams fracturing in the damp, cool air like shards of broken glass. Jaxon's breath curls in uneven puffs as he falls into an easy jog, the cracked turf thudding beneath his cleats. Around him, the team moves in a loose cluster—uneasy and restless. The crowd's hum is a thin thread, mostly local press and scattered fans huddled in threadbare jackets, their murmurs a low static weaving through the crisp dawn. It is a far cry from the roaring stadiums he once commanded. That absence speaks louder than any cheer.

Jaxon's eyes snap to the bleachers. There, Victor Cross sits alone, a slim notepad in hand, fingers dancing across the page. That sharp gaze is locked on him, calculating and waiting. It is the kind that collects dirt to fling at exposed skin. Jaxon has learned that lesson before—Victor's write-ups have a way of finding the soft spots, the moments that matter most. The weight folds tight across his ribs, cold iron pressing down.

He shakes it off and angles toward the line, his voice firm and low.

"Conservative—strong run, off right. Keep it tight. Let's test the communication."

The center nods, shoulders tensing as fingers flex on the laces. The familiar choreography unfolds—the subtle shifts of bodies, silent glances, a breath held just before the snap. But there, just before the ball flies...

The center blinks, eyes flickering off cue.

His snap cadence stutters, creating a crack in the rhythm.

The running back hesitates—brief but fatal, like a falcon missing its dive.

The handoff is sloppy; fingers fumble. Leather bites the air before thudding to the ground.

Chaos blooms. Bodies collide, hands clawing frantically over the loose ball. Breath catches—sharp, quick, desperate.

Jaxon's jaw tightens, and his fists clench at his sides. The sudden urge to shout is swallowed by the tightness in his throat, but he forces the words out anyway.

"Get it together! Eyes up, stay sharp!"

The line strains, shifts, and murmurs—but his shout shrinks in the damp air, swallowed by confusion like leaves smothered in mud. The play dissolves, sputtering and stalling, resulting in a net loss punched onto the scoreboard. Faces flush with frustration, and shoulders slump beneath invisible weights.

He steps back, scanning the field, looking for steadiness in the jittery jigsaw. Finding nothing but hesitation.

The crowd picks up a ripple of discontent, murmurs rising into an unsettled tide as Jaxon jogs toward the sideline, his shoulders tight and his jaw clenched like a vise.

Victor's pen doesn't stop moving—a relentless scratch, cataloging every falter, every hesitation, and every crack in the foundation Jaxon is trying to rebuild.

The knot in Jaxon's gut twists tighter. The season's long shadow stretches farther already, swallowing what little daylight the dawn offers.

The ball thudded softly into Jaxon's palm. The huddle dissolved into controlled chaos. He pivoted and handed off to DeShawn, whose legs pumped with a familiar rhythm—but something wasn't right.

DeShawn faltered in the exchange. The ball slipped, slapped against his forearm like a live spark before gravity claimed it. The sharp whistle sliced through the damp air, thick with sweat and turf dust. The crowd's murmur faltered, replaced by a collective intake of breath—an invisible crack running through the huddle.

A bright yellow flag arced onto the turf like a fallen leaf.

The referee stepped forward, his voice clipped and harsh: "False start on number fifteen. Five-yard penalty. Repeat third down."

Eli's gaze burned into Jaxon like a flare. Nostrils flaring beneath his helmet, Eli's lips pressed into a hard line, his jaw tightening with silent blame. A palpable chill snaked through the huddle—thicker than the dampness from fresh-cut grass. Teammates shifted uneasily, their shoulders tightening, some stealing quick glances at Eli's simmering anger. The atmosphere stiffened. A brittle silence stretched between them, fraying the edges of focus.

Jaxon met that glare briefly. Irritation flickered across his face before he turned away, focusing on the growing crowd noise—a muted swell of uncertain and expectant voices.

Brick burst through the opposing backfield with crushing intent. A fractured play scattered chaos down the line, but Brick was re-lentless—torquing his massive frame into the breach. He crashed into a ball carrier with the sound of breaking wood and grunted breath, finishing the tackle with a certainty that shook the turf. Dirt churned underfoot, speckling his jersey with bruises of mud.

Caleb stood nearby, vulnerable on the edge. Brick responded with a shove to an encroaching opponent's chest and a growled warning to back off. His gaze flickered toward Caleb, a mixture of feral anger and protective fire burning behind it. "Keep your head up, damn it." Brick's voice came low and ragged, his breath catching like gravel scraping against boots.

Emma appeared along the sideline like a steady balm, striding with quiet urgency. She knelt beside DeShawn, whose forearm bore a thin scrape crusted faintly with dirt. The sharp scent of antiseptic mingled with sweat and leather. Her gloved fingers moved deftly—a cotton pad soaked in cool disinfectant traced the raw skin, followed by a precise fold of white bandage wrapped reassuringly around the injury.

DeShawn forced a crooked smile at her, his breath ragged and his eyes catching the flicker of concern in hers.

"Gotta keep you in the game, huh?" she murmured, her voice a low thread of comfort against the clamor.

"You're making me sound fragile," he grinned, flexing cautiously.

Emma's smile tightened. Her eyes caught Jaxon as he stood nearby, tension drawn sharply across his jawline, distracting himself too well.

Back on the field, the offense reset. But the echoes of unease lingered like the chilly breath of early autumn fog. Eli's glare remained—a dark stain on the fabric of teamwork. The scoreboard flickered coldly. The visitors' numbers climbed slowly, unnerving in their quiet inevitability.

The players breathed heavier now. Chests rose and fell with effort and strain. Cleats scuffed at grass dampened by recent rains, the smell sharp and earthy. Around them, the stadium held a lingering mist in its breath, fragile as whispered promises.

Eli's resentment was a live wire coursing silently between teammates braced for the next snap. The team skirted close to fracture, held only by the thinnest thread of discipline and unspoken hope.

The game's pulse quickened. Uncertainty wove its cold fingers through every motion, every glance. The scoreboard's numbers shifted. The visitors inched ahead. Tension tightened, ready to snap or mend the fragile bonds woven under relentless pressure.

The huddle thinned, crunching underfoot with cracked cleats and nervous breaths. The sky swallowed the last blush of dawn, casting a cold silver wash over the field.

Jaxon's fingers tap a restless rhythm against his thigh, muscles corded beneath fading sweat. Scarred jerseys cling to bodies he is supposed to command. The weight of miscues hangs thick in the air, sharper than the biting wind threading through the stands.

Coach Hale's warning echoes like a hammer behind his eyes: *No more mistakes. Don't let this team crumble.*

It's not a threat; it's a pulse he cannot ignore, thrumming along his ribs and settling like stone in his gut. The crowd's murmur barely scratches the chill, and sparse applause is drowned by the pressing silence of expectation. Each breath feels borrowed. Each second ticks toward the edge of something irreversible—a final chance he can taste like copper on his tongue.

Third possession.

Jaxon's Adam's apple bobs against the swell of silence as he swallows hard. He slaps his palms together and shouts the call—a throwback to plays ripped from his pro days, reckless and daring. The kind of play that demands trust. The kind of play that could ignite the spark or scorch everything to ash.

Caleb shifts on the line, a flicker of flame breaking through the gray. Jaxon's eyes lock on him—lean, lithe, a shadow slipping wide open in the downfield zone. But there is danger there too: two defenders close in fast, chests heaving like pistons.

Jaxon's breath catches. Hesitation slices through the chain of decision-making.

A fraction of a second bends taut. Fingers twitch. Then, with a grunt ripping free from his throat, Jaxon snaps his arm forward, the oval spiraling into the chilled air like a missile aimed at hope.

Caleb's jaw clenches; his eyes flick back over his shoulder, breath quickening. He darts forward, legs pumping hard. Over the leather of his gloves, desperation stitches every feature as the ball arcs—a gleaming promise and a swift threat all at once.

His fingers brush the leather—a slick, fleeting touch.

The world tilts as the ball slips past him, spinning wide—curling into the waiting arms of an opponent whose smirk darkens the field like a shadow crossing sunlight.

The stadium exhales in stunned silence.

Time distorts—gasps and shuffling feet create a jagged soundtrack to the chaos unfolding. Cleats drum a relentless beat against the turf, that wet grass-and-leather smell mingling with the sharp tang of crushed earth. The opposing returner takes off, a thunderous rumble shaking the ground. Redemption Valley's players scramble, lungs heaving, hands grasping at air and turf as desperation claws at them from every angle.

Sweat beads cold at Jaxon's temple.

His legs churn beneath him as he jogs back to the sideline, the knot in his stomach tightening with every step. His chest hammers under the weight of unsaid words. Teammates' eyes bore into him—raw, unfiltered disappointment. The pressure coils inside like a serpent, squeezing harder, unforgiving.

His jaw clenches, lips pressed thin. The cold air tastes like regret, biting sharply at his teeth. Around him, fractured murmurs ripple—phrases half-heard, fragments of blame flung like knives in the half-light.

"Reckless," a voice mutters. "Too soon."

"Not the time, Jax."

Doubt gnaws at the edges. He shoves it down. Not now.

"Come on, man," DeShawn's voice cracks from nearby, laced with humor forcing its way through the tension. "We aren't out yet. You've got this."

Jaxon shakes his head behind tight lids, something raw and ragged unspooling in his chest.

"Did you see Caleb's footwork? He had no angle. You threw him under the bus." Eli's voice hisses with quiet accusation, sharp and cold as frost.

"That's on me." Jaxon's voice comes out low but firm. "My call. Not Caleb's. Not anyone else's."

"Yeah? Your call just cost us field position and the whole damn drive." Eli steps closer, his hands restless at his sides.

"Take it all." Jaxon's eyes burn into Eli's, fierce and unyielding. "Better than seeing you eat it."

No one moves. The tension clings like smoke, thick and choking.

Caleb stands further down, arms crossed, his eyes pulled tight shut for a moment—a rush of vulnerability slipping beneath the surface. Brick drops beside him, his shoulder heavy with shared weight.

"You good?" Brick grunts, his voice low.

Caleb only nods, his voice caught somewhere between grit and ghosts.

Jaxon breathes in the smell of cut grass, liniment, and the faint tang of blood mingled with cold sweat. His fingertips itch, restless for control that slips just beyond his grasp. The wind catches his hoodie, pulling it around his frame like a fragile shield.

The stadium lights flicker faintly through the haze settling low—ghosts of missed chances hovering where the ball had flown, away from hope and into shadow. The field feels colder now, underfoot and in his chest.

"Next play," Jaxon mutters, his voice rough but steady, his eyes narrowing as he stitches resolve from the frayed threads inside. The weight of the game presses in—a storm gathering—and beneath it all, a whisper of possibility, fragile but alive.

Coach Hale's voice cuts through the noise, sharp as a blade through fog.

"Timeout."

His jaw clenches so tightly that the skin pulls taut over his cheekbones. He holds his silence, letting the moment swell. The players freeze mid-motion—some tightening their gloves, others pressing their palms to their knees. The stadium's buzz hangs low and thick.

The press swarms forward, a tide of cameras and microphones. Lenses snap, and flashbulbs punctuate the gray afternoon like distant thunderclaps. Victor Cross swivels his notepad with predatory focus, his eyes narrowed on Jaxon. He's hunting, waiting for the crack in the armor, the perfect quote that will sell tomorrow's story. His fingers drum against his leg—impatient, calculating.

The air tastes of turf dust and sweat, with a sharp sting of antiseptic from the medical tents nearby.

Jaxon steps away from the huddle. His boots crunch against the gravel as he speaks.

Roughly, above the roar of engines and voices surrounding them.

"That interception—my call."

The words hit hard, each syllable a stone dropping in still water. "I wanted to push the momentum. That was on me, not Caleb."

Heads turn. Eyes flicker between Jaxon and Caleb. The quiet kid slumps midway down the bench, shoulders drawn inward, trying to disappear beneath peeling paint and scuffed hardware. His fingers twitch against his leg, avoiding. Every gaze feels like a weight he can't hold.

Brick slides beside him with a low grunt. His cleats scrape the dirt. Without looking up, he leans close, his voice rough, a murmur.

"Don't you listen to them. You did your part. Everyone knows it."

His hand comes down on Caleb's shoulder—solid, a wall of silent support, grounded and unwavering.

Caleb's jaw tightens—steel, barely holding the fear and shame at bay. But the firm press of Brick's palm beneath it settles something. His breath slows, and the quick thuds pounding in his ears ease.

A flicker of trust surfaces—small, fragile, but existing.

DeShawn leans against the lockers with a half-grin that doesn't quite reach his eyes. His arms are crossed, fingers twitching with restless energy.

"Well, looks like I'm still sitting on the bench for the highlight reel, huh?" His voice attempts levity, brittle as a dry leaf. It draws a couple of weak chuckles scattered from the sidelines like fragile sparks in a storm. But the smile doesn't touch his eyes; the weight behind the joke is there—heavy and unspoken.

Jaxon's eyes scan the group. Masks of tension. Lines of exhaustion. The bitter taste of failure clings to the air like smoke. The weight settles on his shoulders—deep, immovable.

But in that moment, it shifts.

Away from Caleb. Away from the young receivers trembling in the spotlight and doubt. The burden lands squarely on him—the captain bearing the brunt. A shield forged from silent promises and iron will.

Coach Hale's jaw remains tight. The eyes of the world narrow on this ragged collection of men fighting to stitch together something stronger than loss—something more than broken plays and ragged hope.

The huddle's tension thickens, but it's no longer a wall of blame.

It's a crucible—a moment hanging fragile between downfall and resolve. One man's sacrifice calls others to rise.

"Let's tighten it up," Jaxon commands, his voice low and steady, like a hand gripping the throat of doubt. The players shift, faces drawn but nodding, muscles tensing for the next battle.

Victor's camera clicks once more, capturing the admission, the acceptance, the burden carried alone. But the spotlight dims again, swallowed by grit and sweat—a team far from glory.

The timeout ticks down. The sideline hums low, buffered by heavy breaths and the scraped shuffle of shifting feet.

Jaxon's gaze flickers to Caleb, catching the ghost of a grateful nod tucked between the shadows.

The bench creaks under bodies tensed for war as preparation resumes—silent, uneasy, yet unmistakably united under a sky dull with promise.

The timeout expires.

The whistle blows.

The game demands their return.

###

The ball thuds hard against the turf. Brick barrels into the scrimmage pile like a freight train unleashed. His massive frame crashes through ankles and shoves shoulders—brute force meeting slippery determination. "Come on, make me," he snarls, his voice low and ragged over the grunts and heavy breaths. A defender dares to step in front of him. Brick doesn't hesitate. Teeth bared, he shoves the man hard enough to rattle bones. The crowd growls, and sharp clangs of pads echo across the field.

Other defenders feed off his fury, tightening their formation and banging bodies in a synchronized assault. The opposing running back staggers, drained of daylight and options.

Jaxon steps forward from the sideline, cold resolve knitting his jaw. Chatter over radios, whistles, and distant cheers all blend into a dull roar. He closes the gap to the line with purposeful pace. His hands move with practiced precision—the rhythm of taping wrists, tightening cleats, fingers steady despite the electric buzz under his skin. He casts a quick glance at his teammates and calls the huddle tighter.

"Alright, keep it clean. Slant route for Caleb," Jaxon says, his voice low but clear. "We don't need flamboyance—just fast, sure catches. Let's build from here." His eyes sweep the group, catching the faintest flicker of recognition in Caleb's pale, tense face. Under that gaze, Caleb feels it: the weight of expectation pressing down, the sharp edge of his own doubt. This is his chance; he can't afford to fumble it again.

Caleb's hands tremble visibly. His fingers jiggle as he tightens his gloves, nails biting into the fabric. His chest rises shallow and fast, his cheeks blank but drawn tight—like the whole game sits precariously on a wire he's terrified to walk. The snap comes. His legs spring forward with sudden, nervous propulsion—the fragile hope of a second chance carried in those shaky steps.

His route is clean, brief, and sharp. It slices through the defense's shadow like a blade. Air replaces the muffled silence that hangs over him. Jaxon tracks the arc of the ball, his arms curling upward, eyes fixed on the spiraling leather.

Caleb's fingers stretch, pale. The last crucial inches brush the ball's edge. The leather slips, then catches—finally. His first real grasp in a field full of misfires. Breath catches in his throat. He tucks the ball close, his legs pushing hard against the grass and dirt, breaking free into open ground.

On the sideline, genuine, surprised cheers unfold—raw and honest, echoing in chests that have been beaten down for too long by mistakes. Brick strides over, his colossal frame casting a shadow that seems softer beneath the lights. The corners of his mouth twitch upward, forming a rough, reluctant smile. Earned.

"That's how it's done!" Jaxon hollers, his voice slicing through the buzz. His grin breaks through armor—brief and genuine—directed at Caleb, who barely allows himself to nod. No smile yet, but the hardening in his eyes speaks volumes. Something is shifting. Something is taking root.

Caleb exhales slowly and shakily. The release carries weight off his shoulders, if only for a moment. The tension surrounding him seems to dissipate, replaced by something steadier, more concrete. Around them, players exchange glances—quick acknowledgments flickering between nods and clenched fists. The energy is different now. Lighter. Dangerous in a good way.

Brick slaps Caleb's shoulder with a grunt of approval before pivoting to ready himself for the next defensive stand. His role on this team goes deeper than tackles and sacks—he's the enforcer, yes, but he's also the heartbeat. His fiery physicality sets the tone, and when he backs a player, the rest follow. The team knows it, and Caleb feels it in that single gesture.

"You let that go; you're just giving them hope," Brick mutters to a nearby teammate, his eyes burning with controlled rage. His voice carries the kind of hatred reserved for opponents, sparking something in the defense's veins—a reminder that mercy isn't part of the game plan.

DeShawn catches the exchange and grins with the ease of relief. His nerves ease enough for him to throw in a teasing jab. "Man, I swear, Brick's got a vendetta. It's like he's the devil in cleats."

"Better the devil than the damn demon on their offense," Jaxon snaps back, smirking despite the ache in his gut.

Caleb moves closer to the line, adjusting his gloves once more as the huddle forms anew. Confidence isn't a lightning bolt; sometimes it creeps in slow and steady, forging solid ground out of shaky steps. The team feeds off that shift, their voices rising in clearer cadence, feet pounding with more purpose.

Jaxon draws a breath and lets it out in a small puff of cold air. His eyes scan every pair of nervous or determined gazes before diving back into the fray. For a fleeting moment, the game feels less like a burden and more like a chance—tangible, fragile, but real.

Brick exhales deeply, his chest heaving, muscles taut but ready. He locks eyes with Jaxon, and a silent acknowledgment passes between them—no words needed. The fire is ignited, and the fight reawakens. Around them, teammates trade quick, genuine exchanges: a nod here, a muttered "Let's go," a fist bump there.

The sideline hums low, a simmering promise beneath sweat and grit. In that crackling tension, brief triumph flickers, and hope sings its quiet, stubborn song.

The defense tightens like a steel trap. Players growl out coverage calls, their voices sharp against the humid tension thickening the air. Jaxon's cadence ripples through the line, echoed crisp and clear—a rhythm now more practiced than panic-stricken. Tackling snaps shift from loose swings to solid hits, chests thudding into torsos, helmets colliding with a determined crack—the kind that speaks of grit earned and lessons learned. The crowd, sparse and restless, leans in, sensing the shift, if only barely.

Jaxon's eyes scan the field—cold and precise. He spots DeShawn hovering near the line, ready. The moment opens like a pinhole, tight and fragile. With a quick nod and a breath, Jaxon releases a crisp pass—short, controlled, slicing through the damp air.

DeShawn's fingers snap around the spiraled leather, his muscles taut as he tucks the ball tight against his ribs. The thud of the incoming tackle hits hard, breath knocking loose, but he bends and battles upright—each step a gritty refusal to fall. His legs churn against the ache, pushing desperate yards forward. The sick scrape of cleats against turf fills the silence.

From the side, Eli mutters, low and sharp, "Got your six." His eyes flicker with quiet resolve and something akin to challenge. He shifts the line with a quick hand signal that steadies the chaos, offering Jaxon a flicker of assurance amid the storm's eye.

The clock's pulse pounds louder, seconds bleeding out like blood from a wound. Jaxon knows this drive demands everything—there is no room for error. He corrals the offense with a practiced edge, his voice low but fierce, pushing them forward with every breath.

And then—disaster.

A misread. The line falters, a crack in the armor exposed. Jaxon's hesitation costs them precious time—a split-second misstep that cascades into chaos. The pocket folds like a house of cards. He feels the heat rush past, the crushing weight of bodies converging. Momentum stalls. A violent clash sends a shock through his shoulders and ribs. Then he crashes—turf biting deep, air knocked clean from his lungs.

The whistle blows, shrill and final.

The scoreboard's glowing numbers mock him: the visitors hold the lead, the defeat carved deeper with each ticking second. A scattering of boos trickles through the stands, uneven and bitter, like a gust tearing through fragile hope. The hushed murmur of the crowd swells into a restless wave, punctuated by Victor Cross in the bleachers. The journalist's pen scratches furiously across the notepad, dark eyes locking onto Jaxon with the cold intensity of a hawk circling its prey.

From the edge of the field, Emma's gaze pins Jaxon like a silent verdict. Her eyes—soft yet sharp—hold disappointment, heavy but not without a glimmer of hope. Beneath that locked gaze lies something unspoken: her fragile belief in him is wavering but not yet broken. The weight between them is palpable, a quiet challenge neither is quite willing to break the silence.

"Did you see the line? They collapsed before the snap," Eli grits, his voice low but charged as he jogs up, adjusting his helmet with a frustrated swipe.

Jaxon groans, brushing turf off his palms. "Yeah, I missed the blitz. I thought I had time."

"You didn't."

Caleb shuffles closer, shaking his head, his face tight. "That mess? It can't be our signature."

Jaxon's jaw tightens. "It won't happen twice."

"They're breathing down our necks because our coverage is sloppy," Eli snaps, scanning the field. "If we let up, they will capitalize."

The weight settles deeper, sinking like ice-cold water into Jaxon's chest. The sting of failure isn't just personal—it's shared, magnified in the eyes of every teammate who fought raw and hard beside him.

"You called that last drive," Caleb says quietly, stepping closer. "You risked it. Maybe too much."

Jaxon meets his gaze, his voice steady but edged with fatigue. "I had to. Sitting back and playing it safe won't fix this."

DeShawn shuffles in beside them, rubbing a sore forearm. "Sometimes you need guts. Other times, it's just football poker. It doesn't always pay off, though."

Jaxon glances toward the bleachers, where Victor Cross taps relentlessly, then back to his team—bloodied, bruised, but still present. The sting of the game's end is sharp, the night wrapping around them like a shroud.

"Next time," Jaxon murmurs, breaking the heavy silence, "we'll get it right. We'll find that line. We'll hold."

A low groan from the crowd swells again, a rising storm of discontent and hope tangled into one.

Emma lingers at the perimeter, the faint scent of peppermint and antiseptic clinging to her like a shield. Their eyes lock longer this time—her steady warmth piercing through the brittle shell Jaxon wears like armor.

The players begin to shuffle off, shoulders slumped but unbroken. Jaxon pauses in the center of the fraying battlefield, the cold wind tugging at his sweat-soaked shirt. Around him, the crowd's uneasy murmur rises, then falls—a restless tide, mocking yet coaxing. Every moment here is a fight. The visitors celebrate quietly. Their victory flakes fall like cold snow, dissolving quickly into the night.

Emma's eyes don't falter. Not yet.

"We'll do better," Jaxon says to no one but the darkened field, his voice rough, carrying between the fading cheers and murmurs like a fragile promise.

The locker room door groans open. The first few players shuffle inside like shadows drifting through fog. Fluorescent bulbs flicker overhead, casting jittery pools of light over cracked concrete walls and battered green lockers.

The air hangs thick with the sour tang of sweat and liniment. Damp jerseys cling to tired skin. Showers sputter in the corner, their uneven bursts of scalding water adding to the hum of exhaustion that fills the space.

Silence presses hard here. Each heavy step and each sigh is muffled under the weight of unspoken disappointment.

Coach Hale's bulk blocks the doorway, his jaw clenched tight. He scans the room and lets out a slow breath. Then, gravelly and clipped, he says, "Tomorrow, we do it again."

No one answers. The sentence threads through the room, settling like frost on skin. It is both a promise and a challenge, cold with the expectation of early mornings and harder miles.

A tightening grips Jaxon's chest—determination trying to take root amid the exhaustion.

Players drift between lockers, their shoulders slumped as if carrying invisible weights, eyes fixed on the cracked concrete beneath scuffed cleats. Each carries the suffocating residue of defeat, the kind that seeps into muscles and lingers in the quiet spaces between words.

From the far corner, Caleb steps forward in that careful, almost hesitant way. His palms are damp, and his fingers twitch at the tape wrapped tightly around his hands. His eyes avoid the others, focused inward as he crosses the room. Without a sound, he extends the game ball toward Jaxon. It's untouched, pristine, except for the faint scuff of frustration engraved in its leather.

No words. No looks. Just a simple offering passed from uncertain hands to steady ones.

Jaxon's fingers curl tightly around the ball, his knuckles whitening. The cold, hard leather presses deep—heavier than any stone, laden with silent questions and missed chances. He shifts it thoughtfully, a quiet anchor in the storm of raw energy humming beneath the surface.

The air thickens.

From the bench, Brick rises. The scrape of his cleats is sharp against the cracked linoleum. His broad shoulders square, and his chest rises with tension. His voice rumbles low, almost a growl, breaking the stillness. "We fight as one. Or hell, we don't fight at all."

His words roll through the room like thunder after a long drought—heavy and unavoidable. Heads snap up, and eyes flicker away from the floor to meet his gaze—some sharp with fury, others raw with doubt. The silence cleaves between them, thick and sticky, but the statement hangs in the air, stubborn and true.

Jaxon exhales—a slow breath, a knot easing in his chest even as a fresh one tightens. His voice, when it comes, is rough and tentative, stripped of bravado but steady beneath the weight. "We own this loss. It's not the end—unless we let it be."

Hands pile in, one by one, flat against the worn wood of a scarred bench now turned altar. Calloused palms, trembling fingers—the strength of doubt and hope mingling in that fragile space.

Caleb's hand shakes, then stills. Steady.

Brick's grip is iron, grounding. DeShawn's is lighter but sure. Even Eli's reluctant fingers press in, the edge of old resentments softened beneath their shared burden.

A murmur rises quietly, ragged and raw—a low sound like fire crackling to life after months of rain. It is unity, fragile but fierce.

"Tomorrow," someone breathes out, voice rough but resolute.

"We make it count."

"Together."

The hands linger a heartbeat longer. Then they break apart like the first rays of dawn slicing through the night. Jaxon stands at the center, clutching the game ball—not a trophy, but a symbol. The room exhales as if released from a collective spell, the tightness easing from shoulders.

In that pause, a flicker of something new stirs—a quiet spark of resolve, born from shared loss but reaching for something beyond it.

Sunshine Has Limits

The locker room sweltered. Bodies, slick with exertion, pressed close together. The air was thick, filled with sweat, liniment, and damp jerseys mingling in every breath.

Emma slipped between clusters of hunched shoulders and silent faces. Her fingers traced the rough edges of scraped skin and the tight coils of muscle beneath wrapped tape. Some arms hung listlessly, while others trembled just beneath the surface—steady but breaking. The low murmur of voices—half-hearted grumbles and forced breaths—rose beneath the throb of fluorescent lights overhead.

The facility bore the weight of its age. Chipped paint peeled from the concrete walls. Lockers stood dented and worn, their surfaces scratched by years of seasons passing. Even the air felt gritty, as if the building itself carried the residue of every loss that had occurred within it.

She caught a flicker of a grimace from DeShawn as he rubbed a shoulder stiff from impact. Caleb sat nearby, absorbed in the dance of adrenaline and disappointment that played across his downcast eyes.

But Emma's gaze moved through the room, searching, until it settled on Jaxon.

Alone, on the far bench pressed back against the cracked block walls, his tall frame curled inward. His shoulders were tight, the sharp angles of his collarbones cutting a hard line beneath damp fabric. Hands clenched into slow fists rested over his knees, pale and tense. His head hung forward, eyes fixed on some mark on the scuffed concrete floor—avoiding hers. No energy to glance up. No will to meet the room.

Coach Marcus stood before the whiteboard. Ghostly traces of last season's play diagrams scratched beneath the surface—failures mapped out in faded ink, reminders of what hadn't worked then and what was failing now. His voice cut through the room: dry and terse.

"Execution was sloppy."

"Missed assignments and penalties killed us."

"We can do better."

A pause thick with expectation followed. The players didn't respond; only shuffles were heard. Some drifted toward the showers, steam already misting behind cracked glass. Others clustered quietly, blame unspoken, the space between them filled with the weight of harsh reality.

Emma lingered a few steps away from Jaxon, across the stretch of worn wooden benches and dented lockers. She watched the rigid line of his back. His entire frame seemed coiled with hardened defeat. The muscles in his jaw twitched briefly, almost imperceptibly, as if holding back the flood beneath. The fluorescent bulbs above flickered, casting a pale, sickly glow—but nothing softened the edge of his posture. He was a fortress.

A hush settled, broken only by the distant drip of water from a leaky faucet and the faint scrape of a cleat against concrete. The voices of the team had faded into scattered whispers and restrained sighs.

Emma's breath caught on the metallic scent of the lockers, mingling with the faint, sharp tang of eucalyptus from the small spray bottle she carried in her pocket. It wasn't enough to cut through the heaviness of defeat, but it grounded her and kept her steady as she moved forward, her eyes never leaving the figure who carried the weight of this room's fractures on his shoulders.

Jaxon pushes himself upright. The scrape of cleats against concrete cracks through the heavy stillness. His shoulders rise—then slump, like a loose coil unraveling.

He moves toward the cluster of guys near the lockers, his voice dropping low, laced with a brittle edge. "We'll get 'em next time. Or, you know, we'll trip over our own feet again. Same difference."

His smile doesn't reach his eyes—the kind that pulls a sting behind it, like a cracked jawbone aching beneath a forced grin. The words hang flat, empty as the air thick with sweat and worn leather.

Brick sidesteps through the shifting pack, his footsteps heavy but measured. He stops at Jaxon's side, closing the distance. His hand settles on Jaxon's upper arm—tentative, steady, weighty. "Tough break out there, man. We gave it our all, but the hits caught up with us."

Jaxon's eyes snap up, cold as winter steel, narrowing into a hard line. A smirk pulls at one corner of his mouth, sharp and brittle. "Yeah? Try not getting flattened on the first snap next time. Bet you'd look good dodging a hit for once."

The barb slides out easily, a scalpel slicing open old grievances. Brick's jaw tightens. His lips press thin against hurt and frustration, but he doesn't pull away. The heat in his eyes flickers—anger simmering beneath controlled breath.

A smaller figure stepped forward. Caleb's hands twitched at his sides, his voice dipped in careful softness. "Hey, Jax, about that last play... maybe if we had shifted the routes—"

Jaxon cut him off with a sharp shake of his head. "Focus on your own drops, Caleb. Don't go fishing for excuses right now."

His voice was cold and final—like a wall slammed shut. Caleb blinked, recoiling and sinking back into shadowed silence, where doubt curled like smoke. Around him, the other guys shifted, suddenly very interested in their cleats, their tape, anything but the fracture splitting wider.

From her spot on the bench, Emma's eyes moved between them, an unblinking witness to the undercurrents more telling than words.

Jaxon's irritation curled around his shoulders like smoke—sharp edges masking something bruised and raw beneath. She saw the way his voice held an almost bitter sarcasm, dipping into blame for bad luck and for the team's unpreparedness, as if shoveling dirt over any chance at collective healing.

"Yeah, like we're some kind of ready-made machine," he muttered, his voice low but biting. "Luck ran out, and so did the talent."

The locker room hummed faintly—soft shuffles, the scrape of tape being pulled, the dull thud of cleats being kicked off. The stale air carried a faint tang of liniment and sweat, a gritty perfume of defeat wrapped tight in silence.

Emma's jaw clenched, tight and silent. She felt the spiral before the words fully landed—how Jaxon's voice became a blade, slicing through the space between them, pushing everyone further out of reach. If this continued, the fracture wouldn't remain contained. It would splinter everything.

She rose smoothly, muscles coiled beneath her professional calm, and crossed the room with measured steps. The worn wooden benches creaked softly underfoot—a staccato accompaniment to the heavy quiet filling the space. The scent of eucalyptus from her kit mingled with the musk of damp jerseys, carving a fragile space of care amid the tension.

Every stride toward Jaxon felt like closing a distance not just measured in feet but in years of unspoken reckonings.

The tension in the air thickened, suffocating yet electric—like a storm gathering behind the cracked windows of this tired locker room.

She stopped a breath away, watching the rigid set of his shoulders. His hands were balled into fists over his knees, as if trying to crush the weight settling deep in his chest.

He didn't look up.

Emma's eyes softened, but her stance remained firm. The moment hovered, charged and waiting, as she prepared to break through the wall he had built anew, brick by bitter brick.

Emma lowered herself onto the wooden bench beside Jaxon. The worn grain bit into her palms—rough, steady, grounding. She left a deliberate gap between them. The cool air of the locker room swirled faintly, thick with sweat and liniment, with something else underneath: the ghost of old defeats.

The fluorescent lights hummed their jagged song overhead, casting jittery shadows across the peeling paint. Somewhere in the distance, a locker door slammed.

She had rehearsed this moment a dozen times and crossed the line before. This time felt different—heavier—because Jaxon had always been the one who pulled away first.

"Jaxon." Her voice dropped low, measured. "I can't watch this play out without saying something."

His jaw tightened, but she pressed on anyway.

"What you're saying in here—" She nodded toward the cluster of players drifting away. "It's more than frustration. It's wounding them."

His eyes flickered dark and guarded, but she held steady.

"When you snapped at Brick about getting flattened, that wasn't a bad joke. It cut." Emma's voice didn't waver. "And Caleb—telling him to focus on his own drops? Those kids are already drowning."

A muscle twitched in his neck.

"This team's on fragile ground," she continued, her tone shifting, pulling the space between them from tentative to solid. "Your words land like wrecking balls. They hear every one."

Emma's breath steadied. Her eyes, when they met his again, held no warmth now.

"It's the pattern. Just like before. You build walls so high that anything good—hope, accountability—bounces right off. You shift blame the moment things get real."

The slight narrowing of her eyes made something flicker behind his defenses.

"I'm here, Jaxon. But I'm done smoothing over what you won't face."

He scoffed. The sound was brittle, hollow as a shell. "Oh, therapy now? That's rich." His gaze darted away, refusing the pull of her eyes, then snapped back with a sarcastic edge. "Coming from the queen of pep talks and ice packs."

He leaned back, muscles coiling. "Maybe if I had a nickel for every time someone took my advice, I'd open my own clinic."

The shadow of a smirk flickered, then retreated behind that familiar steel.

"You think quick words can patch decades of screwing up? I'm some charity case you can fix if you just nag enough?"

Emma's lips pressed into a firm line. She didn't bite. The sarcasm stung—it was meant to push her away. But she held the silence, her steady breath cutting through his shifting tension.

When she spoke, her voice was low enough to slice through the quiet without rising.

"You're wrong. It's not about fixing you; it's about you owning what you let slip." Her gaze never wavered. "Your words don't float in the air; they land. And I'm not watching another game collapse because the captain won't face himself."

Jaxon's muscles tensed, and his fists barely stayed open. The tension stretched taut between them—a wire pulled tight, ready to snap. But Emma's posture didn't waver. The faint, acidic scent of old sweat and chalk hovered around them like a backdrop of unyielding truth.

"What, you want me to start sobbing?" His voice cracked sharply. "Own all six-loss nights? I'm not the team's damn therapist."

Emma's gaze sharpened, and her tone remained even, brushed with quiet resolve.

"No. I want you to stop pretending the losses aren't yours." She paused to let that land. "You're allowed to hurt, but you're not allowed to pretend that no one else does and that you don't matter to them."

His next words came fast, a shield of sarcasm. "Right. Because I'm the shining beacon this circus needs. Guess what? This season isn't about hope; it's about surviving wreckage."

Her eyes flickered with something older, deeper—a truth carved from their shared past.

"You've done this before, Jax. You hide behind anger because it feels safer than facing what comes after, but it never protects you." Emma's voice tightened, her patience folding inward but not breaking. "It just leaves everyone stranded."

She leaned forward slightly, enough to close the careful distance between them.

"I'm not your punching bag anymore. Not like I was before."

The weight of those words hung between them. They echoed off the scuffed lockers and the cracked tile. Dust caught in the light.

"If you want this team to rise," Emma continued, "you have to start by dropping the walls."

At last, his breath escaped in a brittle rasp. His shoulders trembled—just enough to crack the steel in his stance. His eyes flickered away, and his jaw clenched. But there was no retreat in Emma's steady presence. She waited, a quiet island amid the storm of frustration and defeat swirling around him.

The fluorescent lights hummed. Somewhere, a faucet dripped.

She held her ground, letting the space grow charged with the unspoken challenge: face it or keep falling apart.

The locker room hummed with brittle tension. Fluorescent lights flickered overhead, casting a sickly glow across the scuffed linoleum.

Emma stayed rooted on the bench, cold liniment mixing with the musk of damp jerseys and concrete gone sour with sweat. She watched Jaxon—the loss pressing down through his shoulders like lead, his jaw clenched so tightly that the muscles trembled beneath his skin.

"You lost the game," Emma said carefully, her voice low but unyielding. She didn't lean in or soften her words. This wasn't a space for sugarcoating. "You're allowed to hurt. Hell, you should hurt. But pretending none of this is on you, like you're just some bystander everyone has dragged down? That's poison."

Jaxon's head snapped up. His eyes flashed—something fierce, something raw beneath the surface. His fingers twitched against his knees, betraying the war happening inside him. The tight line of his mouth gave it away.

"Like I've never thought about that before?" His voice cracked against the hollow concrete, louder than the ghost of a whisper it had been moments ago. "You stand there, Emma, patching up scrapes and leaving the rest to 'the team,' like it's your damn job to care. Well, it is. You get paid for it. I'm the one who's already broken. I'm supposed to hold all this crap together. How about you cut me some slack?"

He rose, the motion sharp and sudden. His silhouette was framed by scuffed cleats, with lockers lining up like silent witnesses behind him. His pulse hammered visibly in his neck—the physical toll of holding himself together fracturing at the edges.

The room emptied of sound, save for his words bouncing off concrete and steel.

"You don't get it," he hissed. "Not really. You expect too much from someone who's been through hell and back. I guess that's your luxury. Me? I'm just trying to survive."

Emma's chest tightened, a sharp hitch in her breath beneath her steady words. Her fingers curled involuntarily against the edge of the bench, her nails biting into the worn wood. She pressed her lips tightly together, her eyes narrowing with a quiet fire that had been simmering well beneath the surface.

"Don't mistake my expectations for unfairness." She sat up straighter, her shoulders squared against his anger. "I'm not your damn punching bag, Jaxon. I won't be the fix-it for the mess you've made."

Her words carved through the thick air between them—deliberate, precise, and weighted carefully. The charge in her voice wasn't reckless; it was a boundary etched deep, a line drawn sharp and refusing to blur.

"The past? I carried it for you then. I'm not doing it anymore. Not because I don't care." She paused, letting the silence hang. "Because I do. Too much. But caring doesn't mean letting you stomp through my good faith like a storm. It means you own it. All of it."

Jaxon reeled slightly, his shoulders trembling as if the ground had shifted beneath him. His eyes darted away, something unguarded flickering across his face before the tough shell snapped back into place.

The silence that filled the locker room was not empty. It vibrated—heavy, thick as the breath they had both been holding for too long.

Emma watched him, her own breathing steady now, but her heart thundered with the gravity of what had just been laid bare. She understood the stakes. She understood what holding her ground meant—what it cost them both. But she also understood that she couldn't set herself on fire to keep him warm. Not anymore.

Without a word, she rose, her feet planted firmly on the cracked tiles. Her movements were measured, deliberate. Her silhouette cut a stark line through the dim light; the crisp fold of her jacket was the last thing Jaxon saw before she turned, the rustle of fabric punctuating the charged stillness.

She didn't look back—not once.

Emma's voice cut through the stale air like a lifeline—steady, unyielding.

"I'm not going to be the crutch you lean on, Jaxon. Not this time." Her eyes locked on his, searching for a flicker of acknowledgment beneath that iron mask. "I can stand beside you. I'll support you when you're ready to face what's real. But I can't carry your pain. You have a choice: you either drown in this alone, or you grab hold of something better."

Even as the words left her mouth, Emma felt the familiar ache twist in her chest. She had said versions of this before. He had nodded, promised change, then slipped back into the same patterns. This time had to be different. This time, she had to mean it.

Jaxon's jaw clenched so hard that his molars bit into his cheek. A dry scratch echoed in his throat as he swallowed, his eyes darting to the chipped paint beneath his palms. His hands unclenched, knuckles whitening as relief leaked out—if only for a heartbeat—before he pulled the armor back around himself like a familiar coat.

The locker room held its breath. Fluorescent tubes hummed their thin, anxious song. Somewhere in the distance, a shower dripped with metronomic precision.

Emma's footsteps broke the silence.

Heavy. Deliberate. She pushed off the bench and moved away, the soft thuds of her shoes ticking down the aisle like a countdown. Metal lockers caught her hand as she passed—cold, impersonal barriers, each one a small goodbye.

She paused where the concrete floor gave way to the hallway. Her chest rose sharply, her lungs drawing in a ragged breath. The air tasted faintly metallic, mixing with lingering sweat and liniment—the smell of effort, of struggle, of games lost and battles waged.

The ache behind her ribs wouldn't relent. It was a tug of war between turning back, reaching out, fixing what felt broken beyond repair, and the brutal necessity of walking away.

"I'm not here to bail you out or smooth over the cracks," she said, her voice low but firm, not turning around. "But I'm not giving up on you, either."

Jaxon's lips twitched—something like a grimace, something like acknowledgment. He didn't curse her or lash out with sharp words designed to wound and push her away. Instead, his eyes flickered with something raw and unguarded, a flicker of the man who still wanted to believe.

Emma's silhouette shrank down the hallway, swallowed by the dim light spilling from the locker room's open door. On the linoleum floor, scattered bits of grass from the field clung stubbornly to the soles of their shoes—remnants of a game lost, but a battle far from over.

The door creaked softly as it closed behind her.

The sudden quiet pressed against Jaxon's back like a weight.

She didn't look back. She wouldn't.

But the stillness she left behind vibrated with every unsaid word hanging in the sharp-edged air.

The door clicked shut behind her, and footsteps faded into the locker room's dull silence.

Jaxon didn't move. His eyes were locked on the water bottle beside him—half-full and untouched. His fingers closed around it, and the plastic crinkled under his grip, ridges pressing sharp divots into his palms. A tremor worked through his hands, creeping up his arms. His shoulders tightened and began to shake.

Grief. Raw and physical. It tasted bitter and cold, a knot twisting low in his stomach, squeezing like ice wrapped in steel.

The locker room smelled of sweat and liniment, sharp and sterile beneath the fluorescent hum above. His shadow stretched across the cracked concrete floor, fractured and long.

He couldn't look up. He couldn't face the hollow emptiness—the echo between cold lockers and peeling paint. Instead, his gaze caught the dented metal door beside him, its surface smeared with faded graffiti. The reflection staring back was a silent accusation.

His lips parted, and his voice came out rough and brittle.

"That's all I'm doing—hurting everyone." The words felt strange in his mouth, almost foreign, as if speaking them aloud stripped away the armor he'd worn for so long. He heard Emma's voice layered beneath his own—how she could still unsettle him, mixing resentment with something he wouldn't name, something that ached.

Restless anger bubbled beneath the surface. It swelled and demanded release.

He surged to his feet. His sneakers skidded against the scuffed floor. A sudden, sharp movement sent his duffel bag flying across the room. It hit the bench hard and burst open. Practice gloves spilled out with a muted slap. Papers scattered like leaves caught in an indifferent wind. A play sheet fluttered at the edge of the bench.

He bent down, his fingers brushing the scattered sheets.

Then he stopped.

An envelope lay among the debris, its edges frayed. The paper was yellowed like old leaves pressed between pages. Emma's handwriting curved across the front in looping script—delicate and deliberate. A fragile beacon pulled at something in his chest.

His breath hitched. His hand shook as he reached for it.

The faint aroma of peppermint oil lingered in the air—a ghost from her departure, woven into the sterile atmosphere. It was a reminder that she had stood here, that she had been real in this moment, in this place.

He turned the envelope over in his palm. Again and again, as if the motion might unlock a secret written between the folds. The texture of his weathered fingers contrasted sharply with the delicate paper. The weight of it was nothing; it was everything.

Should he open it?

Should he look inside?

A hollow rumble echoed through the room, the distant scrape of a cleat sliding across concrete, and the twitch of a flickering light in the corner. Life, stubborn and relentless, beat on beyond his fractured space.

He sank back onto the bench.

The cool metal bit into his shoulder blades.

He had been here before—alone in this room after failures, after losses that had spiraled deeper each time. This moment echoed those others, the weight of past collapses settling into his bones, a familiar despair that had only grown heavier.

The envelope rested in his palm.

Part promise. Part threat.

His shoulders sagged. The fierce grip on the bottle loosened. His fingers hovered on the threshold of choice, silence swelling around him like dusk seeping through grimy windows.

The questions hung thick and unyielding.

Will he face whatever truth waits inside?

Or will he let it remain a ghost between them—unread and untouched?

Becoming the Man They Need

The field lay empty, vast beneath the hum of the stadium lights. Shadows stretched long and trembling across the patchy grass—tired green bleeding into stubborn dirt scars.

Jaxon Reyes stood near the fifty-yard line, hands shoved deep into his worn leather jacket. A chill crept beneath his skin, relentless.

His duffel bag sat heavy at his feet, cradling the unopened letter—a silent weight pressing against his resolve. Emma's words from earlier clawed at the edges of his mind, sharp and unyielding.

"You can't keep hiding behind excuses, Jaxon. Not from me. Not anymore."

The sting settled like frostbite inside him: raw, relentless.

He shifted, his eyes scanning the cracked chain-link fence and the bleachers rattling in the restless wind. The Hawks' banner swayed weakly overhead—faded gold and navy, whispering stories he'd rather forget. Stories of a team in free fall, of seasons crumbling under the weight of dropped passes and shattered confidence. His own season had crumbled in the same way.

The faint smell of liniment and damp grass drifted with each exhale. Tension rippled beneath the stillness, thick enough to choke.

His steps started slowly along the sideline. The worn grass crunched beneath his boots. Eyes lowered, he tracked the faded fifty-yard line, its peeling stripes like ghosts of old seasons etched beneath scrape and scuff. Self-doubt dragged at his limbs with every hesitant step, and his shoulders sagged under its weight. The cold dug deeper into his bones.

Ahead, near a cluster of practice cones and a battered water cooler, a solitary figure moved: Caleb. The quiet kid lingered after drills, chasing something more than routine.

Jaxon slowed, his toes grinding into the dirt, his eyes fixed on Caleb's tense shoulders.

Caleb's fingers faltered. Ball after ball dropped—three clumsy fumbles in a row. His breath came sharp and quick. Clouds of mist swirled like ghosts of frustration in the biting air. His fingers trembled as they grazed the ball.

A tightening seized Jaxon's chest. Memories he kept locked away surfaced—his own stone hands, the pulverizing weight of failure, the sharp crack of a dropped pass that turned a season sour. He recognized that tremor, that particular brand of despair.

In the stillness, Jaxon exhaled hard, the sound low and measured against the quiet field.

He stepped onto the grass, the soft thud of his boots punctuating the silence as he closed the gap to Caleb. Each step was a promise—unspoken, yet sure.

The night wrapped around them, cool and watchful, as if holding its breath.

"Caleb."

His voice broke the silence—low and careful.

Caleb flinched, tension coiling in his guarded eyes. "Yeah?"

Jaxon's gaze held steady, softer than expected. His voice was rough, edged with something unsaid. "Let's try again. Together."

Caleb hesitated. His eyes darted away for a heartbeat before meeting Jaxon's gaze. "Okay..."

A flicker crossed the kid's face—a mix of hope and stubborn fear tangled together.

Jaxon nodded once, offering silent confirmation. It's not about perfection.

"Looks rough out here," Caleb muttered, his voice tight but edged with a tentative smile.

Jaxon shrugged. A ghost of a grin touched his mouth for the first time that night. "Been there. More times than I want to admit."

The letter still pulsed beneath his ribs—a weight, a burning. But he set it aside. For now, the field was enough. Here, under these flickering lights and worn stripes, second chances lived in every dropped catch and every earned bruise.

And for the first time in a long while, Jaxon thought maybe—for Caleb, for himself—redemption could begin tonight.

Jaxon stepped toward Caleb with deliberate calm, the cold night air crisp against his face, muting the distant rustle of empty bleachers behind them. At Redemption Valley, late-night practices carried a particular weight—the kind of silence that settled after hard sessions, when the field felt less like sacred ground and more like a place where mistakes lingered in the shadows.

His voice dropped an octave, carrying just enough to reach Caleb without breaking the quiet that blanketed the field.

"Caleb."

The name hangs there, simple but firm. Caleb's jaw tightens. His eyes snap up in surprise—a quick swallow follows, and his muscles brace for the brunt of Jaxon's usual sharpness. But it doesn't come. Instead, Jaxon stands still, letting the silence settle between them like something alive.

The faint whistle of a distant train threads through the air as Jaxon squares his broad shoulders and props himself two yards away from Caleb. He lifts his hands deliberately, fingers spread, pale under the harsh glow of the overhead lights. His eyes lock on an invisible target as he molds the motion he wants Caleb to learn.

"Catch soft," Jaxon murmurs, the sound barely stirring the night. "Hands like a cradle, not a claw."

He draws in a steady breath and snatches a crisp throw, fingers bending easily around the leather. Again. And again—each catch fluid, effortless, a quiet mastery echoed in the scrape of cleats against the dirt. Caleb watches, the tension in his jaw slowly slackening.

Then Jaxon crosses the final distance. His hands press against Caleb's forearms, firm but patient, thumbs adjusting with care. He shifts Caleb's grip and nudges his feet a fraction to the right. "Thumbs pointing in. Soft hands. Step to it—don't wait for the ball to find you."

The warmth of Jaxon's touch contrasts sharply with the night's chill, grounding Caleb in the moment. It steadies something within him—something fractured.

Jaxon steps back, his eyes steady but expectant.

Caleb exhales. His muscles release—just a fraction—but enough. That small loosening feels like surrender, like permission. He reaches out to catch the first pass, his fingertips grazing the ball before it slips through. On the next try, his hands close tighter, the leather settling into his palms as he collapses it inward.

"Better," Jaxon says, his voice low and precise. "Keep your hands relaxed. Don't squeeze too early."

Another catch, this one clean. Quick enough to make Caleb's shoulders, which had been stiff and hunched moments before, dip slightly, his grip loosening as ease creeps in. Step by step, his body lightens, attuning itself to the rhythm of the throws.

Jaxon's lips twitch. A rare flicker of humor softens his worn features. "Back in high school... hell, my hands were like rocks. I couldn't hold a hot potato, let alone a football."

Caleb cracks a soft, reluctant chuckle—the kind that surprises him, as if he's not sure he's allowed to laugh. The tight knot in his chest loosens, just enough.

"Guess that's why I'm the coach now," Jaxon adds with a dry edge. "I'm trying to teach my old mistakes."

The words hang between them like a fragile truce.

Caleb positions himself carefully, waiting for the next throw. The ball arcs through the frosty air, spinning with purpose. His hands meet it squarely, squeezing this time with quiet confidence.

The catch is firm. Unwavering. When he secures it cleanly, something flickers in Jaxon's chest—not quite warmth, but close. Recognition, maybe. He nods once, barely perceptible—a private acknowledgment without flair or fanfare.

"You got it," Jaxon says simply, stepping back and folding his arms. The air between them shifts, creating a crack in the usual barriers. Caleb's eyes trace the fading trail of the football, lingering longer than before, as if tasting the promise of progress.

The sideline hums softly with the distant ripple of nighttime insects. Cold breath plumes in the dark. The lone water cooler nearby shivers slightly, condensation droplets catching the faint glow. It feels different now—a sliver of hope nestled amidst the harshness of old mistakes.

"Alright," Jaxon says after a beat, his tone lighter. "Let's see if I can keep up with you."

DeShawn meanders onto the sideline, fingers brushing the sweat-darkened grass as if he's searching for something lost. He stops short of the water cooler, leans one shoulder against it with an easy grin, and lets his eyes flicker over Caleb's fumbling hands. "Man, those mitts of yours look like buttered popcorn tonight," he quips, his voice carrying just enough teasing edge to cut through the chill.

Caleb jerks his head toward DeShawn. His jaw tightens for a split second—ready for the usual ribbing. Jaxon stands nearby, a duffel slung over one shoulder, and chuckles softly. He flicks a glance at DeShawn, his thumb hooked inside his jacket pocket. "Alright, Mr. Showtime," Jaxon says, his voice calm but edged with challenge. "Show me if those hands can actually catch."

DeShawn's grin widens as he steps forward. Jaxon bends his knees, squares his body, and lobs a soft spiral just off the ground. DeShawn snatches it mid-air, exaggerating the catch with a dramatic, slow-motion cradle—one arm extended skyward as if he's sealing a touchdown in the Super Bowl's final seconds. His head tilts back, mouth open in a triumphant shout that cracks the quiet darkness of the empty field.

Caleb's lips twitch into a grin at the edge of his mouth. His shoulders drop slightly, and his breath smooths out in the cold night air.

"Not bad," Jaxon admits, tossing another pass. "But don't get too cocky. Even the pros trip over their own cleats sometimes." He hooks his hands behind his head, his eyes amused. "Remember that play where I threw a perfect lob… right into the opponent's hands? Yeah, that one. 'Jaxon Reyes: king of the interception.'"

DeShawn snorts and shakes his head. "Man, if I had pulled that jab... the crowd? They would have thrown tomatoes."

Jaxon shrugs, a ghost of a smile crossing his lips. "Tomatoes would have been polite." He lets that land. "I was the butt of every talk show in the state for a week. I thought I would never live it down."

But he had. That interception had burrowed deep, though—a small scar on his confidence that he still felt sometimes when the pressure mounted. Nights like this, when the drills felt heavy, that old mistake whispered in the back of his mind. Using humor to bury it had become second nature.

Caleb chuckles. The sound settles over the three of them like the first hint of warmth after a long freeze. The joke undoes some of the stiffness in his posture. DeShawn gives Jaxon a pointed look, and the banter shifts quickly—from mockery to something steadier.

Across the field, the faint scrape of cleats on concrete breaks the warm bubble forming between them. Brick, helmet off, watches from a distance—a shadowed figure outlined in pale floodlight. For a fleeting moment, a slow smile tugs at the corner of his mouth. Barely noticeable. But it is there. Then he turns back to gather his gear.

DeShawn flicks a grin toward Jaxon, tipping an imaginary hat. "Alright, coach. You've got some moves tonight." He jogs back to the cones, hands outstretched, ready for another round. His face is lighter, and his eyes are brighter.

Jaxon nods to himself, watching DeShawn slip back into the drill with sharper focus. His shoulders ease a little. The weight of the night's earlier tension loosens—pulled apart by shared jokes and small wins. The night air hums faintly with the rhythm of renewed effort, subtle as a breath, yet promising.

Brick stands off to the side, helmet cradled under one arm. His knuckles dig into the battered rim. The tension runs deep—each pressed finger a silent reminder of last season's weight on his shoulders, the battles etched into the helmet's worn scars mirroring the ones inside him.

His gaze is locked on the dull, patchy turf, brown and brittle beneath the cold floodlights. Cracked earth that might swallow him whole if he stares long enough. The steady rhythm of cleats thudding against the grass fills the night air, along with the muted clang of tackling dummies. But Brick remains still, detached.

Jaxon's eyes flicker to him from across the sideline, where he's corralling Caleb and DeShawn through another round of drills. He doesn't interrupt the momentum, letting Brick stew in his silence a little longer.

Jaxon bends to pick up a football. The worn leather feels rough against his palms as he spins it with a casual flick. Without looking up, he lobs the ball toward Brick's feet with a gentle arc. It lands with a quiet thump just inches from the defensive lineman's boots.

"When you're ready," Jaxon calls out—flat, neutral, neither a challenge nor a plea. Just an offer, hanging in the cold air like a solitary promise. Then he steps back, turning his attention to Caleb's fumbling hands and DeShawn's light-footed dance around the cones, careful not to crowd Brick's space.

The minutes stretch thin. Unseen clouds drift past the halo of circling stadium lights overhead. Brick's jaw tightens, and his hands clench around the helmet. Finally, after a pause that feels stretched taut between breaths, he sets it down with a heavy thud.

The rigid line of his shoulders slackens—just a fraction—as if a breath he didn't realize he was holding finally escapes. He squares his broad shoulders and strides onto the field.

Jaxon gestures—a quick, precise flick of his hand. "Get on the edge. Just one run."

Brick's voice is clipped, rough around the edges like gravel under a boot. "Don't get soft with me," he mutters, his eyes narrowing as he plants himself into position. His tone carries steel, but there's no spark of retreat. He's here, at least for now.

The drill kicks off with a burst of energy. Brick explodes forward—low, controlled, muscle and grit snapping into motion like clockwork. Jaxon watches silently. He doesn't interrupt; he just lets Brick find his rhythm and find himself in the work.

When the play tapers off, Jaxon nods once—not indulgently, but like someone registering a fact long known yet worth repeating in quiet confirmation.

"Last game—third quarter. You got outside and stopped their breakout run. That tackle?" He pauses. "That wasn't just any stop. That was the moment you proved you could still be this team's backbone when it counted. You saved the drive."

His voice is low, steady, and devoid of any need for grand applause—just an anchor thrown to a man who needs something real to hold on to.

Brick's rigid frame softens—a notch, two notches. The weight around his neck loosens.

Across the field, Caleb's shoulders stop twitching, and DeShawn's grin flickers wider. Even the night seems to hold its breath, as if the wound inside Brick's armor might just be starting to stitch itself closed.

Without looking away, Brick shifts his stance. His breath deepens—steady now. The smallest exhale of relief escapes him. When the final whistle echoes from the sidelines, he doesn't gather his helmet and retreat; instead, he stays, hands relaxed by his sides, chin lifted just enough to signal he's still in the game—ready to meet whatever's next.

Emma stands just beyond the cracked chalk line that separates the turf from the gravel, her fingers curling around the edge of a worn clipboard. The faint scent of peppermint—the subtle signature of the medical building behind her—rides the chill of the evening air. That sanctuary behind her holds the weight of every player's injury and every setback. Out here on the edge of the field, though, something tentative is taking root.

From this quiet vantage point, she watches Jaxon moving among the scattered players, his hands tucked deep into the pockets of his jacket, his voice low but clear as it cuts through the hum of the worn-out stadium lights.

Her eyes flick to the players. She traces the tentative arcs of their focus, the way their shoulders tense and then ease, breaths coming harsh and quick under the cold sky. She resists the impulse to step forward and intervene. Her job isn't to fix; it's to let them find their own footing and to trust them the way she needs them to trust themselves.

She taps a pen lightly on the clipboard, jotting down shorthand notes: "Player focus fluctuates—Jaxon's tone is growing softer but still firm." Her breath forms a small mist in the cold.

There. Caleb's hands snap out, fingers stretching, catching a well-thrown pass against the frigid wind. A brief smile cracks Emma's lips, softening the hard lines of the day's weight. Encouragement lingers in the crease of her eyes, though she says nothing aloud.

Across the field, beneath the sagging banner overhead, Jaxon meets her gaze. His jaw tightens, and his eyes flicker with unsaid words. Emma's breath catches slightly; the charged silence hums between them like the buzz of the overhead lights. Her expression remains steady, a quiet approval radiating beneath the surface, while his nod barely betrays the gratitude that tightens his jaw.

She tucks the pen behind her ear with a gentle click and writes one last line on the page: "Progress uneven but promising."

Folding the notes neatly, Emma allows herself a moment to breathe it in—the shift from fractured to something slowly coming together. The group on the field stirs, tentative warmth spreading. Fragments of connection merge, echoing Jaxon's measured cadence. Emma presses the clipboard against her side, her fingers lingering a beat longer as her eyes follow his lean frame weaving through the players.

The soft scrape of cleats on grass, scattered bursts of confident chatter, and the faint metallic rattle from a locker in the distance all stitch into the hum of fragile unity.

She stands for one more moment, tethered to this quiet witness. The night air brushes her cheeks, with peppermint mingling with musk and the sharp bite of impending frost.

Emma's gaze settles on Jaxon's silhouette—still strong, still guarded. For once, maybe this grumpy light has a chance to steady the dark.

Her breath exhales slowly and steadily, the clipboard now folded tightly under her arm. A quiet sentinel to hope unfolding on the edge of the field.

Caleb's fingers brushed the cold, slick leather awkwardly at first. The ball slipped against his palm. He yanked it in with a desperate squeeze, his teeth gritting against the sting of failure in the frosty air. His shoulders rose like coiled springs beneath his worn jersey, breaths sharp and fleeting. But the second catch stuck clean, nestled in the cradle of his hands. A crack appeared behind his guarded eyes. Not confidence—not yet—but something harder to ignore: a fissure in the dam.

Nearby, DeShawn darted low to the ground, his cleats carving into the frosted earth like claws. The cone-marked route directed him toward a precise spot. He snatched Jaxon's pass out of the air with smooth certainty. A ghost of a grin tugged at the corner of his mouth as the tight coil in his shoulders loosened beneath the black mesh.

A few yards away, Brick watched, fists clenched around his half-helmet.

When the moment came, he stepped onto the worn turf—a shape carved from muscle and stormy focus.

Jaxon's voice cut through the hum of the field—not sharp, but steady. "Square your stance. Lower your center. Drive with your legs."

Brick repeated the maneuver: a blocking drill, feet solid, arms locked. No outburst. No tension slackened the moment's gravity. Just a slow, deliberate nod as if marking a rare truce with himself.

Jaxon moved among them, matching each player's pulse like a careful predator. He crouched near Caleb, his voice dropping to a near whisper that floated in the cold air like breath on glass. "Keep your thumbs lined, like bookends—soft hands, not stone. Step into the catch. Don't wait for the ball to come."

Caleb's eyes flickered up, absorbing the detail as his hands closed around the next throw. Smoother now. More certain.

At DeShawn, Jaxon's tone lifted—lighter, almost teasing. "Good read on that break. Keep your head in the zone, eyes sharp, but don't tense up before the snap."

DeShawn bobbed his head, that half-smile widening as he thought, *Maybe you're not all business after all.*

At Brick's side, Jaxon kept it brief and clipped. "Less choke, more chokehold. Stay rigid through contact—like a wall, not a wobble."

Brick's jaw tightened. His next test held firm—a small victory in the ongoing war within.

A subtle shift rippled through the group. Other players picked up on the tone—the quiet competence replacing yesterday's stiff distance. Two teammates lined up side by side, sharing a look and syncing their footwork before a run-block drill. The nods between them carried weight without words, a growing hunger for connection.

From the corner of his eye, Jaxon watched the ripple spread—a quiet formation of allegiance, coaxed from shared effort rather than shouted commands. He recognized this fragile trust as the first real sign of progress—for him and for all of them—but he kept his wariness close, knowing how quickly momentum could shatter.

He resisted the urge to overpraise, knowing the sting of hollow accolades all too well. But when he gave credit, his words anchored firmly to skill, grounded and earned.

"Good feet on that snap."

A crack of approval flickered like a flame to the wary players, sparking something deeper than empty praise.

Hands unclenched. Backs straightened. The collective breath of the team seemed to shift. The air—once dense with tension and doubt—loosened, carrying a softer weight. Something finer took root beneath the chill: trust, tentative and raw, threading through the drumming of cleats and the faint rustle of the night breeze.

The final rep fell into place.

Caleb caught it with quiet confidence. The leather settled into his palms as if it belonged there, and for the first time in weeks, the old voice telling him he would fail went silent. That small victory chipped away at something deeper, something he had carried for too long.

DeShawn drove down the field, hitting every mark.

Brick held the line without flinching.

The circle tightened not with force, but with the quiet assertion of presence. Together. Not fractured.

In these small, earned moments, the fragile pulse of unity began to throb steadily under the waxing moonlight.

###

The clatter of cleats against cracked concrete fades as Jaxon raises a calloused hand, his voice dipping low, rough as gravel. The half-lit benches cast long shadows, fractured pools of pale yellow glow pooling like quiet islands beneath the wild night sky.

"Brick, that block on the third down? Cleaner footwork. You've got the muscle—now finesse it." His tone is clipped but steady, carrying more weight than praise.

Brick nods once, his jaw tight, eyes locked forward, no words but understanding simmering in that brief gesture.

Jaxon shifts his gaze, flicking over to Caleb, whose arms still tremble slightly from the afternoon's work. "Caleb, those catches by the sideline today—you stayed loose. Keep that hand position, and you'll own those routes."

Caleb's eyes flicker up, meeting Jaxon's for the barest moment before darting away like a startled bird. Hearing his name, the unease seems to settle like dust in a quiet room.

DeShawn leans on one knee beside him, wiping spit from his chin, the flicker of a grin tugging at his lips despite his exhaustion. "And you, Price, your cuts were sharper tonight. More snap. You didn't pull back once."

DeShawn bounces on the balls of his feet, the spark within him barely contained beneath layers of fatigued humor.

Jaxon's eyes narrow at the last few—a scattered collection of faces weathered by doubt, bruises, and long nights of questioning whether this team would ever hold together. His voice softens slightly, dipping almost to a whisper just for them.

"Eli, your reads were cleaner during drills. You're noticing the edges, and that timing? That's progress."

Eli shrugs, a small, reluctant half-smile curling at the corner of his mouth. The bitterness in his stare has faded with the drained light.

The huddle tightens with the subtle shift—worn shoulders straightening, a breath held longer, steadied.

Jaxon finally pulls back, his voice quiet but firm. "You stuck it out. Hard reps, low payoffs—tonight, none of you backed down. That's something. Thanks for that."

The words settle between them, more felt than heard. A murmur rises—nods and low affirmations sparking in the silence.

For a moment, Jaxon's guard fractures. He thinks of the fumbled plays, the playoff losses that still burn like fresh wounds, and the nights he'd questioned whether these boys had the spine for it. Trusting them had always felt like standing at the edge of something that could collapse. But here, in this thin strip of time before the tunnel swallows them whole, something tilts. Not certainty—he knows better than to mistake one good night for redemption—but a thin thread of belief he hasn't allowed himself to feel in months. The weight of it settles across his shoulders, unfamiliar and fragile, and he lets it.

Brick's eyes find Caleb's; for a flicker, the usual walls crumble. The two exchange a glance layered with unspoken promises—their shared weight lifted just a fraction.

"Guess that was harder than I thought," Caleb admits under his breath, exhaling a shaky laugh.

DeShawn elbows him lightly, his eyes twinkling with mischief. "Welcome to the world of 'harder than you thought.' There are no popcorn hands here, right?"

Jaxon lets a corner of his mouth twitch upward, a rare crack in the armor of his grumble. The tension loosens, fragile threads weaving warmth.

The players break their tight circle, but not apart—steps falling into rhythm, quietly linked. The group threads together, moving as one toward the locker room instead of splintering into solitary shadows.

Concrete echoes beneath their feet, a steady drumbeat that measures the night's shift—tentative yet determined.

Jaxon lingers a moment longer at the field's edge, watching their backs slip into the dull glow of the tunnel's gloom. The quiet confidence in his chest feels strange, like breathing through a deep, long-held silence.

A faint breeze stirs, carrying the scent of damp grass and faint liniment from the sidelines—reminders of battles fought both on the turf and inside.

He closes his eyes briefly, the night wrapping around him like a southern ghost, whispering possibilities beneath its vast, star-clotted mantle.

The field itself bore the scars—divots where seasons of fumbles had clawed at the earth, the yard markers faded from rain and neglect, and the worn patches where hope had been trampled more times than he could count. Every loss, every collapse, and every moment they had failed had sunk into this turf like blood into soil. Even now, those ghosts lingered in the dark corners, patient and watching.

The field, battered and bruised like its players, hummed with the first fragile pulse of unity. The scoreboard remained frozen, the ghosts of seasons past hovering like restless spirits, but tonight carried a different rhythm.

Jaxon exhaled, his shoulders easing for the first time in hours.

The team was moving—not just down the tunnel, but forward.

###

The bleachers sat empty now. Shadows stretched long under the dim glow of the stadium lights, and the bulbs hummed—a low, steady drone that mixed with the faint rustle of dry grass and the distant clink of a locker door shutting. The team's footsteps had faded into the locker room, their voices dropping off like whispers swallowed by the night. But Emma stayed behind, near the worn track that circled the field's edge.

She unwrapped the clip on her well-thumbed clipboard. Scribbled notes and hastily jotted observations from the evening spilled into view. The scent of peppermint from her diffuser clung faintly to the air—a subtle barrier against the cold and the tension lingering in the fading light.

Ink scratched softly across the paper as she wrote once more. Her hand remained steady despite the pull of exhaustion under her ribs and the crisp breeze that nipped at her cheeks, making her fingers ache.

Jaxon's presence—steady, commanding, but not heavy. The team experiments with trust, brief sparks of risk-taking together.

Her gaze drifted toward the equipment shed. Jaxon leaned back against the weathered metal door, his shoulders squared but tense. His breath puffed white in the chill. The duffel bag at his feet held more than just gear—unopened letters, words yet to be confronted. She could see the weight of it in the way he held himself and the careful distance he kept from the world. But beneath that tension, something else flickered—something like the faint outline of a man beginning to consider that change might be possible.

His head tilted slightly, catching the small movement of Emma's eyes meeting his across the darkened field. His nod was quick—barely there—but infused with a weight that felt like quiet gratitude.

Emma's lips tugged into a hesitant curve. Her eyes flickered away before meeting his gaze again, barely daring to trust the feeling stirring inside her. A silent pact passed between them, fragile and raw beneath the night air.

A staff assistant passed nearby, breaking the moment's hush. "Are you locking up soon, Emma?"

"Almost done here." Her voice remained calm, low but warm. "I'm just tying up a few notes."

The assistant nodded respectfully and moved on without pressing further. Emma closed the clipboard with a practiced snap. The sound cut cleanly through the evening's quiet. She slid it under her arm, steadying herself against the cool wind that threaded through the skeletal branches of nearby trees.

Jaxon shifted, stepping away from the shed. His boots crunched softly on the scattered gravel. The weight on his shoulders seemed a fraction lighter—a subtle lift in his head, like a man who had glimpsed a path he hadn't dared to consider before.

He walked toward the parking lot. The empty field stretched behind him, a canvas of worn grass and fading lines.

Emma watched from the edge of the lights, where the glow pooled softly against the dark. Her gaze held something deeper than approval. It was a quiet, reluctant pride tucked beneath layers of caution. Professional commitment tangled with personal hope—a combination she had fought hard to keep separate. But standing here in the cooling night, watching him walk taller than before, she felt the boundaries blur just slightly. No words spoke that hope aloud; it remained hers alone, a secret tether between them.

"You okay out here all alone?" Her voice barely broke the stillness.

Jaxon's eyes flickered in the shadows. "I needed the quiet."

"You got it." Emma stepped forward, the scent of peppermint briefly stronger between them. "I guess the night's good for thinking."

"Yeah." His voice was low, rough-edged but free of his usual bitterness. "Maybe it's good for starting over, too."

Emma's lips softened into the smallest curve—hope wrapped in silence. She didn't say more. Some things needed to grow quietly before they could be spoken.

Jaxon hesitated, then nodded. The night pulled him onward, away from the field and toward the uncertain future waiting just beyond the parking lot lights.

Emma stayed behind. The heartbeat of the field settled into calm. With the clipboard tucked beneath her arm, her eyes were fixed on the man walking taller than before—even if only by the smallest margin.

Almost

Emma's boots splashed through puddles, the water catching the harsh fluorescent glare. Her long coat clung to her skin—damp and heavy. Each step down the narrow hallway echoed softly against the scuffed tile.

Outside, the storm raged on. Raindrops snapped against the peeling windows like fingers drumming a frantic rhythm, demanding entry. She paused before the supply cabinet, her fingers numbly fumbling with the lock. Its rusty click echoed in the quiet space—too loud, somehow. She flinched.

The last fluorescent bulb buzzed overhead, throwing a sterile glow across the kitchenette as she flipped the switch. Shadows pooled in the corners, thick and patient. A quiet sigh escaped her lips.

The corridor held its breath. Outside, rain hammered the pavement in wild percussion. Emma moved toward the wellness suite door, and her clipboard finally slipped free from under her arm. Her fingertips brushed the worn wood grain—rough, familiar, and cold. Thunder rumbled low beneath the wooden beams, rattling the fragile panes. The vibration crawled under her skin.

She leaned in, listening. The storm's pulse thrummed against the windows. Beneath it, something more elusive—the unsettled echo of the building settling after hours, as if the place itself held its breath.

She flipped the clipboard open, her eyes scanning the handwritten schedule in the fading light. Late entries. Names underlined. Notes scribbled in cramped handwriting spoke of urgency and need. *Someone is still waiting. Someone who shouldn't be here this late.* Her stomach twisted tighter. The reality tugged at her unease—a knot that wouldn't loosen. She folded the clipboard shut and tucked it firmly beneath her arm, resolving not to retreat just yet.

Standing with her back pressed against the door, Emma watched as the corridor's edges darkened. The overhead lights flickered, stuttered, and surrendered to dusk's encroaching silence. The air smelled faintly of peppermint and antiseptic—a sterile sharpness clashing with the damp, earthy scent creeping in through cracks in the frame. She breathed it in; it made her chest feel tighter.

Her gaze dropped to the cold metal handle beneath her palm. The surface felt smooth, cool enough to sharpen the ache curling inside her chest. *Don't get involved. It's after hours. Keep it professional.* But the words felt hollow even as she thought them. Her ribs tightened as if squeezed by invisible hands, and her breath caught on a sharp knot of unease.

Fingers gripped the clipboard hidden beneath her arm as she hesitated—just for a breath, a heartbeat—before her hand rested there, suspended. The choice to enter weighed heavier than the storm itself.

"I should go," she murmured to herself, her voice low against the hum of thunder. But the words dissolved almost as soon as they left her mouth.

She had been here before—years ago. A patient left to sit too long in the dark, deteriorating quietly while the staff remained professional, remained distant, remained *safe*. That patient had needed more than professionalism. That patient hadn't come back. Emma had never forgotten.

Wet footprints trailed back toward the exit behind her—the echo of her own hurried steps. The building exhaled, empty yet alive with memories, a silent testimony to battles fought in these halls, with physical and invisible injuries tended to in shadows.

The fluorescent light flickered again, a brief stutter before silence wrapped around the hallway like a shroud.

Emma pressed her palm harder against the metal, grounded and anchored. Outside, the storm thrashed with renewed fury, rain hitting the windows in wild percussion, thunder rolling deep beneath the beams.

A delicate shiver ran down her spine—not from the cold, but from the weight of the choice cramped against the quiet pulse of the approaching night. She didn't move, rooted in the liminal space between entrance and retreat, between professionalism and something far more personal.

The corridor sighed beneath the storm's assault, dimming and swallowing the edges of the room where she waited—clipboard tucked firmly, coat still dripping—but the storm wasn't the only thing chasing her shadows tonight.

Her hand found the handle and turned it.

Emma's damp footsteps echoed down the narrow corridor. The fading storm whispered wet echoes through the windows behind her.

She clutched the clipboard against her chest, her fingertips tightening around its edge until the paper crinkled beneath her grip.

The overhead fluorescent lights flickered weakly, casting a wavering glow that was half-lost in shadow. She counted the reasons to turn away—she shouldn't cross the line after hours, not with him, not now. But her fingers tightened on the clipboard. Her breath was shallow. A brief tremor ran through her soaked coat sleeve.

Outside the small rehab room's door, she rehearsed a professional greeting under her breath. The words were stiff and clipped, like armor designed to hold back the storm building inside her.

This wasn't just any player tonight. Not Jaxon. Not after every-thing.

Her shoulder pressed against the cool metal frame. The chill seeped through the soaked fabric of her coat, grounding her amid the faint hum of the dim hallway. A faint melody slipped into the corri-dor—soft, distant music blending with the scrape of a rehab table being shifted. The sounds felt private, intimate, almost like a secret whispered across the rain-soaked night.

Late-night sessions weren't his usual pattern. Jaxon pushed bound-aries, tested limits, and moved through the world like someone certain of his place in it. But tonight, the quiet in his movements suggested something different: vulnerability, maybe. A desperation worn thin at the edges.

Her breath caught. She listened for another moment, letting those muted noises settle around her like a fragile promise.

With a slow inhale, she nudged the door open the rest of the way. The warmth inside reached for her instantly, thick with a hospi-tal-grade peppermint smell mingling with the musk of aged leather and fresh sweat. The faint scent of antiseptic cut through it all—sharp and unexpectedly comforting.

The wet hem of her coat dripped onto the dark mat just inside the threshold. Something firm tightened in her bones. She wouldn't turn away now—not after all the warnings she'd drilled into herself.

"You really know how to pick your hours, don't you?" she murmured, her voice low but edged with something between admonishment and concern.

The music faded slightly as she crossed the floor—each footfall soft and deliberate—closing the distance to where Jaxon waited in the half-darkness, where shadows clung to the therapy table as if they belonged there.

Jaxon perched on the therapy table, the cool vinyl pressing into his thighs beneath the loose weight of the bandage wrapped haphazardly around his shoulder. A slick of sweat beaded at his temple, tracing quick rivulets down his neck as he adjusted his posture. His fingers curled and unc curled against his thigh—a habit born of restlessness, of the quiet panic that comes with admitting you're broken enough to need fixing.

From the corner of the room, his phone hums softly. Low music drifts into the stale air, mixing with the steady drip of rain against the window. The rhythm outside mirrors his pulse, but it does nothing to untie the knot coiled tightly in his chest.

The door creaks open. Jaxon lifts his gaze.

His eyes narrow. The usual guarded steel shifts into something sharper—mirth flickering across his face like a match strike. Unwelcome. Surprising.

He crooks one corner of his mouth into a half-smile, rough with tension, effort, and days worn thin.

"Are you stalking me now, Caldwell?"

His voice rasps—a low growl. His jaw clenches tightly, words dragging like gravel across concrete, the weight of unsaid things settling uncomfortably between them. Decades of baggage compressed into five words.

Emma steps fully inside. Her damp coat drips faint puddles onto the mat beside the door. She brings the scent of antiseptic mixed with peppermint, warmth cutting through the clinical chill. The clipboard in her hand clicks softly as she sets it down on a rolling stool. The wheels squeak against the scuffed floor.

Her eyes do not waver from his.

She moves toward the table—deliberate. Unreadable. She kneels beside him, hands poised with practiced care, ready to start the assessment.

"Look, I'm just here to keep you from falling apart on duct tape and grit alone, Reyes."

Her words come out dry, but something threads beneath the surface: faint concern. A crack in the facade of professional distance. She says it the way someone does when they've already seen you at your worst and decided to show up anyway.

The air thickens, charged by unsaid histories, by the storm rumbling low in the distance, and by the weight of shared time neither of them knows how to name.

Their eyes lock, and hands pause mid-movement.

For a single heartbeat, something unspoken passes between them: recognition, familiarity, an old ache neither expects to confront tonight.

Silence presses in, taut as wire.

The distant thunder rolls—a warning, a heartbeat syncing two guarded souls. Outside, the rain falls harder.

Jaxon's gaze lingers, sharp as broken glass. Emma's is steady and warm, like sunlight touching cracked pavement—hesitant but unyielding.

The moment settles heavily between them. The storm outside echoes the tempest inside the quiet room.

###

Emma's fingers untangle the frayed edges of the loose bandage wrapped around Jaxon's shoulder, peeling it away slowly. The fabric clings, damp and worn from sweat. Her hands move with practiced precision—purposeful yet softer than the rigidity her training so often demands. Years of keeping distance had taught her to touch without feeling. With him, that wall cracked.

She presses lightly along the taut muscles beneath, tracing the shape of his deltoid and gently coaxing movement as she tests his range.

A flicker of discomfort crosses Jaxon's face when she lifts his arm a little higher. His eyes narrow to slits. He swallows past the sharp edge of pain and remains still, his jaw clenching like a trap being set. Emma notes the wince, then eases her hands, her touch becoming almost tentative as she circles the injury.

The sharp fluorescent buzz overhead hums steadily, mingling with the faint odor of peppermint oil and disinfectant. Beneath it all, the storm's distant growl presses against the building's skin like something alive.

Jaxon breaks the silence first. "Looks like I'm going to owe you more than I can ever pay back, huh?" His voice is rough from exertion, but there's a faint lift of humor threading through. They both know what he means—this isn't their first rescue. It is just the first time either of them has admitted it hurts.

Emma arches a brow, her lips twitching despite herself. "You haven't even started paying," she deadpans, smirking. "Think I should start charging overtime?"

He snorts softly, the sound damp but genuine. "Better send me the damn bill, then."

A sudden crack of thunder rumbles through the walls. The lights above flicker wildly, casting eerie shadows that dance across the worn linoleum floor. Emma's head tilts toward the dimming buzz. "Great. Classic horror movie timing."

Jaxon chuckles, a brief, rough sound that holds a sliver of ease between them. The storm hammers against the windows like anxious fists. Rain drums a relentless rhythm on the roof, mirroring the thud in Emma's chest as she holds her breath.

Somewhere deeper in the building, the scent of wet earth and ozone sneaks faintly into the air.

Emma's hand drifts, lingering a beat longer than necessary on Jaxon's forearm as she adjusts her position. His skin is warm beneath her palm, a faint heat against the chill creeping in from the storm.

Jaxon inhales sharply at the touch. His breath catches. The room narrows to that single heartbeat, charged and fragile. Her fingers tremble slightly. His eyes flicker down, then snap back to hers—charged with something neither of them says aloud. The storm's distant thunder seems to fold into the quiet hum between them.

Emma pulls back slightly, letting her hands rest lightly on Jaxon's forearm. Her voice drops to a cautious murmur. There's something more there—something she usually keeps buried beneath layers of professionalism. "Why won't you let anyone in? Not just on the field, but here, too. Outside of hours when no one's supposed to see you?"

Her eyes lock onto his, searching—not just for an answer, but for a crack in the wall he has built so meticulously.

Jaxon shrugs, the movement casual yet tight, as if the wound beneath his skin pulses with every breath. "I owe you, Cal. I'm not great at taking handouts." His smirk is brittle, a thin veneer stretched over something raw. "Besides, the last time I leaned on someone, it didn't end well."

His voice drops into a quieter timbre, the words dragging from a place he would rather keep locked away. "Scars don't show up just on my shoulder. They're... deeper than that."

The hospital room seems to tighten around them—those emotional wounds tied to the very public unraveling of his career, the failures he has shouldered alone before everything came crashing down. Emma would understand that without him spelling it out.

Emma's breath hitched. Her eyes glazed momentarily, clouded with a distant, unspoken memory. She threaded her fingers together, steadying the fragile moment between them. Leaning in, she fiddled with the edge of the now-loosened bandage, careful not to hurt him, but deliberate in breaking the silence.

"Trust doesn't mean you're weak," she said quietly. "It's how you start getting whole again." Her voice softened but was edged with steel, a rare combination that only he had heard before. "You've been running solo for too long, Jax."

There was a time—months ago—when he had tried to handle everything alone, when isolation felt safer than vulnerability. Emma had watched him nearly break under the weight of it.

His mouth tightened, and for a heartbeat, the weight of her words stalled the usual cage of cynicism. The rigid lines around his eyes softened, tension bleeding from shoulders that still cradled a weariness beyond muscle.

His chest tightened. Fingers twitching, he reached out—then paused, caught in the pull of old fears. His hand stopped inches from hers, trembling like hesitant birds caught between wire and sky.

He swallowed hard.

Instead of bridging the gap, his fingers clenched into a fist, curling tightly against his thigh. The air pulsed with the silence of what wasn't said, what almost happened.

"Maybe," he whispered, his voice rough and raw, "I'm scared. Scared to let people see what happens when I fall. Not just the body. The rest of me."

Emma didn't move. She didn't speak. She just let the moment stretch—profane and sacred all at once—as distant thunder rolled, a low, relentless growl that echoed the storm still raging outside the walls around them.

Lightning shattered the low rumble outside. A sudden crack snapped the facility into darkness. The overhead fluorescents sputtered and died, the rehab room dissolving into shadow. Rain pounded against the glass—a relentless percussion that filled the silence.

Emma's breath caught, and a sharp hitch tightened her chest. Instinct pulled her closer, her hand finding Jaxon's upper arm. The warmth of his skin grounded her, chasing back the cold that had begun to seep into the room. For a moment, it was only the two of them, suspended in the thick stillness between the cooling storm and something fragile.

Jaxon stiffened beneath her touch but didn't pull away. His eyes flickered, catching the faintest glimmer of the emergency exit sign beyond the door. Then, as if drawn by a gravity older than their fractured history, he leaned in. His fingers lifted, brushing a stray lock of damp hair from her temple with deliberate gentleness. Warmth bloomed across her skin, and her spine shivered in response.

The space between them shrank. Breath mingled, and pulses quickened. His voice dropped, barely more than a rasp: "You really planning on sticking around, Caldwell? I thought you'd have better sense."

Her lips parted, but nothing came.

The usual defenses—the decades of hurt and blame—dissolved for one suspended heartbeat. She felt the heat of his breath against her cheek, thick and real. Jaxon's walls trembled, a hairline crack exposing something raw beneath the hardened surface. The possibility hung in the humid air, electric and unguarded.

For a moment, the past seemed as if it might finally untangle, as if this fracture could heal. Emma tilted her chin ever so slightly, leaning in, willing the weight of years and silence to collapse into something softer.

Then his body tensed. His eyes flickered—a brief, raw break in the usual steely mask—before he blinked rapidly, forcing himself back behind the shadows he had built. Ghosts flared to life, memories sharp and unforgiving. His gaze hardened, the humor and openness snuffed out like a candle.

Jaxon turned his head, his jaw clenching in a slow, haunted beat. Regret etched itself across his features.

"You shouldn't..." he muttered, his voice low and gravelly, thick with warning and something that sounded like pain.

He stepped back—deliberate, composed—putting careful inches between them as if space itself could keep the past at bay. The warmth drained from the room like a tide retreating.

Emma's fingers fell away from his arm, lingering ghostlike for a breath before releasing. Her throat tightened, and a bitter ache coiled low in her chest. Her shoulders squared, her spine straightening as the familiar armor clicked into place—the quiet barrier she had worn for years, both fortress and prison.

She steeled herself, straightening the damp collar of her coat, the fabric stiff and cool against her skin.

One small step. Then another. Away from Jaxon, toward the dim outline of the door. The silence stretched between them, thick and unresolved. The storm's growl ebbed but never faded completely. The room felt impossibly empty now, the weight of that almost-touch settled deep in the spaces they couldn't yet bridge.

Emma inhales sharply. The last shadows of hesitation slip from her eyes.

She grabs the edge of her soaked coat and pulls her clipboard close. Papers rustle beneath her fingers—a sound like whispered doubts she refuses to hear. "Get some actual rest, Reyes," she says. Her voice slices through the quiet, brittle, like glass struggling not to shatter. Her heels scrape against the tiled floor as she takes measured steps backward, each inch away from him a careful retreat.

Jaxon sits motionless. The dim glow from his phone pulses weakly in his lap—a rhythm that mirrors nothing inside him. His eyes do not lift to meet hers, but his jaw tightens, and his shoulders curl inward. In that language of bone and sinew, an apology bleeds through—a silent plea she's not sure she knows how to answer. His fingers twitch against his thigh, almost reaching, then stilling.

Emma's hand hovers over the door handle.

The cool metal presses against her palm, grounding her like the last solid thing in a sea of storm-churned nerves. Beyond the threshold, the corridor yawns dark and cold. The hospital-grade peppermint diffuser mingles with distant thunder— that restless percussion that won't let her think. Her pulse throbs heavily at her throat, echoing the storm's rhythm. The near-kiss shadows her thoughts: the warmth of his breath, the fragile promise of something unspoken, almost within reach.

Outside, the hallway light flickers. Shadows dance across the cracked linoleum like ghosts refusing to settle.

Emma tightens her grip on the handle, willing herself to turn away. But the magnetic pull of that room—of him—won't release her. The memory sizzles beneath her skin, something she can neither dismiss nor fully claim.

"Why won't you take better care of yourself?" she finally murmurs, barely audible.

Jaxon's rough voice breaks the silence. He doesn't look at her. "Because sometimes... taking care means tearing the whole damn thing down. I'm not sure I'm ready for that."

Emma swallows. Her voice loses its edge but not its firmness. "You don't have to do every damn thing alone. Not anymore."

The storm's fury presses against the windows like a restless spirit. Jaxon's fingers twitch again, hovering just beside her coat's hem. A breath caught, then stilled.

"This isn't just about your shoulder," Emma continues, her chest tightening. "It's not about the team. It's about you—breaking your own rules."

He lets out a ragged breath. His eyes flicker toward her as if weighing the cost of every word left unsaid. "Maybe I'm scared... that if I let go this time, there's nothing left."

Emma's gaze holds steady. Unshed questions swirl between them like the thunder outside—heavy, charged, and dangerous.

Lightning splinters the sky, and the facility plunges into darkness.

The overhead hum dies. It is gone.

Emma's pulse jumps. She steps closer, her fingers pressing lightly to his arm, grounding them both in the dim void. The scent of peppermint and sweat wraps around them—an invisible tether pulling them together.

Their faces inch closer, and their breath mingles in the cool air. Jaxon brushes a stray lock of damp hair from her face. His rough fingertips tremble just enough to betray the walls cracking open inside him. The moment stretches—electric and fragile—as if the past and present could fold into one breath, one touch.

"Emma..." His voice falls low, threaded with echoes of old pain and something softer—almost hope.

She leans in, willing herself to believe in the flicker of repair.

Then he jerks away. His stare hardens like shuttered windows against the storm's lash. "You shouldn't..." His words come out clipped, brittle as shattered glass. He steps back, widening the space between them like a chasm carved by regret.

Emma's hand falls. The warmth drains from her skin. Her shoulders stiffen against the ache that blooms in her chest—sharp, spreading, undeniable.

With a slow inhale, she straightens her coat and presses her palms flat against the doorframe, a fleeting anchor before she turns.

"Get some actual rest, Reyes," she repeats, her voice clipped. What she's really saying hangs unsaid, thick between the words, heavy as storm clouds.

Jaxon says nothing. His eyes follow her every move, dark with regret, twisted with a quiet plea that winds through her gut like something alive, something dying.

She can almost hear the weight of the scars he carries—not just the one on his shoulder, but the ones buried deep beneath raw, taut skin, the ones he refuses to let anyone touch.

Emma reaches for the door handle, her fingers curling around the cold metal.

The distant quarter-light hum of the hallway seems miles away, a fragile sanctuary of solitude, of unspoken things. The echo of longing and loss swells inside her—a tight knot that won't unwind, won't release, and won't let her breathe easy.

She pulls the door closed behind her.

The lock clicks softly, a final punctuation in the silence.

Thunder rumbles low outside, rolling like a distant chant. The hallway swallows her steps as she walks away. The weight of everything unspoken lingers between the closing space and shrinking light—a presence as real as touch, as binding as any promise.

Both of them are left standing on opposite sides of a threshold neither dares to cross. Not yet.

They are haunted by the electricity of what might have been, by the impossible hope that lingers beneath the ache.

The Article

Dawn stretches thin fingers across the sky as Jaxon Reyes laces his cleats on the cracked asphalt parking lot. The scent of wet earth rises from the soaked turf behind him. Last night's rain lingers heavily in the dampness, the grass flattened and glistening with droplets that soak through the soles of his cleats with every step.

His shoulders are hunched, muscles coiled tight as silence stretches between him and Emma long after the door clicks shut. He dares not meet her gaze; she stares past him, distant and unreadable. A breath they almost shared. Too far. Then retreat.

The air tastes cool, sharp against his tongue, mingling with the faint metallic tang of sweat as he steps onto the field. Each footprint sinks slightly into the sodden ground, muddy residue sticking to the edges of his cleats. Around him, the empty stands rattle softly in the light breeze, aluminum benches humming an old, tired song.

Jaxon feels every bruise from the past twenty-four hours settle deeper into his bones. The weight isn't from the cold; it comes from the words left unsaid—words tangled with a promise they both dared to touch but never claimed. Words that terrify him. Words he can't take back, can't bury, can't pretend don't exist between them anymore.

His throat tightens. He clamps down on the urge to replay the moment again—the war fought between heart and authority, between wanting her and fearing what wanting her means.

He pushes through the locker room door. The musty odor of old sweat and leather wraps around him like a second skin. The locker room smells thick and heavy. The usual chatter is gone; only the faint scrape of cleats and a slow, steady breath punctuate the early morning hush.

A few players lift their heads, their eyes narrowing into cautious slits as they recognize him. Tension coils in their posture like a drawn bowstring. Some nod stiffly in acknowledgment, while others avoid direct eye contact altogether.

Jaxon's gaze sweeps the room briefly, taking in faces taut with anticipation. The unspoken questions hanging in the stale air taste like yesterday's rumors—invisible, hovering, persistent. His jaw tightens; he doesn't have the energy to explain or, worse, to admit what still roils beneath the surface.

He steps toward his locker. His fingers find the familiar grit of tape, sticky against his calloused skin. He methodically begins wrapping his hands. The snap of tape against flesh sounds louder than it should in the silence, marking a rhythm to bury emotion.

His jacket, soaked from the damp morning air, falls heavily onto the bench with a tired thud. He peels it off slowly, as if shedding a second skin weighed down by everything unspoken. The fabric slides from his shoulders, pooling at his feet. Cold air brushes against the sweat-slicked skin of his arms, a reminder that physical pain is easier to manage than the mental storm brewing inside.

He moves toward the corridor. Cleats squeak softly against the linoleum. His footsteps are steady—mechanical.

The sterile hall stretches ahead, with walls lined with faded pennants and peeling posters that whisper of better seasons. The school's losing streak is written in those worn banners, in the dents along the walls, and in the way the light seems to apologize for shining at all. A low fluorescent buzz hums overhead, flickering once. Once. Like a heartbeat disturbed.

The sounds from the locker room fade behind him. Only his breath remains—shallow and controlled. Only the soft scrape of tape tearing free. Beneath the surface, a pulse throbs, a reminder of the brush with Emma's warmth and the weight it carries.

He tightens his jaw and forces down the swell of feelings that threaten to spill over—those fragments of hope and regret locked in the space between what almost was and what can't yet be.

"Hey... can I ask you something?"

Her voice breaks through the barricade in his head: low, familiar, tentative.

He doesn't turn; his fingers remain quick with tape. "What?"

She steps closer, her voice barely rising above the fluorescent hum. "Last night... did it mean anything to you?"

He exhales a bitter laugh, his eyes narrowing. "You think I'd know?"

"That's not an answer."

"No." He cuts the tape clean with his teeth. "It's not. But it's the only one I've got."

Emma's reply is quiet but steady. "Maybe that's the problem."

Jaxon pauses, his breath catching as the echo of her words lingers longer than he wants. His body leans forward, the moment stretching thin before he breaks it with a harsh exhale.

"I'm not the guy you think I am," he mutters, his voice low enough that only he hears.

The corridor seems to constrict; the air thickens like static, pressing on his skin. He pulls free and strides toward the practice field. The damp grass shakes off droplets onto his ankles. Each step presses the muddy scent into his senses—raw, earthy, real—grounding him against the rising tide inside.

Distant birdcalls fracture the morning stillness. Light filters through the thinning clouds, golden and hopeful. Yet the ache from the almost-kiss remains, a ghost tethered to his fractured heart, slipping through his grasp with each step toward the relentless grind waiting on the other side of that battered goalpost.

He tells himself it's just another morning—another chance to focus, to fight.

But in the quiet spaces between the cracks, the truth gnaws: some battles don't start or end on the field.

The corridor's stale air bit at Jaxon's throat, thick with lingering sweat and a faint tang of liniment. Cold seeped into his soaked cleats, chilling his feet as he stepped forward. His mind still dragged him back to last night—Emma's face inches from his, that almost-kiss that wasn't, and the way she'd pulled away. It sharpened everything, made the fluorescent hum overhead feel more intense, and made the cracked linoleum tiles gleam like accusations.

Sterile pools of light reflected dully off the floor, casting the narrow hallway in washed-out grays and sickly whites.

A figure leaned against the peeling paint of the wall—a shadow carved in sharp contrast to the glare. Victor Cross, phone in hand, wore that same crooked smile: predatory, like a cat eyeing a trapped mouse.

Jaxon's breath hitched, and his jaw clenched so hard that his teeth pressed into his cheek.

Victor's green eyes sparkled with cold amusement. He stepped forward, shrinking the gap between them with deliberate slowness. His fingers drummed once against his phone—tap, tap—a sound that landed like a threat.

"Morning, Reyes." Victor's voice slid out smooth as oil over gravel. "I've got some fresh material you might be interested in."

Jaxon didn't respond; he just shifted to sidestep.

Victor's smile sharpened, a blade sliding free. "You've been keeping busy, I'm sure." He paused, letting the silence stretch. "But you might want to read tonight's headlines before practice tomorrow."

He tapped his phone again—deliberate, slow.

"New truths." His voice dropped, sharp. "Ready to surface."

The words landed heavily, like a shove that knocked the breath from Jaxon's chest.

"Cut the crap, Cross." Jaxon's voice came out clipped and hard. "I don't have time for your games."

He forced himself to pivot toward the open doors leading to the practice field, but Victor stepped in front of him.

"Hope you've told your new team everything." His voice dropped lower, laced with menace. "They're going to find out tonight."

His hand twitched, fingers curling into a half-fist before Jaxon forced them still.

The sting lingered—bitter ash on his tongue. He swallowed hard, his jaw flexed, wound tight like a spring.

Without answering, he forced himself forward, striding past Victor toward the open doors beyond. His mind raced, and his heart thudded with the pulse of old fears and new anxieties.

Behind him, Victor remained rooted to the corridor wall, watching and savoring the scene as it unraveled.

The turf beneath Jaxon's cleats glistened with dew, and the scent of damp earth and cut grass rose with each impatient step. His shoulders stiffened, tight with the aftershocks of last night's near-break—the moment when Emma's eyes had held something he couldn't quite name, when he had almost lost her. The bitter taste of it still lingered, coating his tongue.

The sky hung low and heavy, and lingering clouds stretched long shadows over the worn yard lines and scuffed goalposts. He blinked away the heaviness surging in his chest and snapped himself back. Focus. Damn it.

"Alright, Hawks. Circle up!" His voice snapped through the morning haze—tight, clipped, like a threadbare seam pulling apart.

The players shuffled in reluctantly, their eyes casting quick glances toward the fluorescent glow bleeding from the facility's corridor doors. Jaxon's gaze kept darting back there—restless, searching. His fingers tugged absently at the tape wrapped around his hands, as if trying to brace himself against something unseen.

He called the warm-up drills with an abruptness that jarred against the usual rhythm—sharp orders without their usual weight.

"Dynamic stretches. Move. Fast feet. Now!" He gestured sharply, masking the tremors beneath his surface calm. His voice sounded fractured, like a cracked horn.

From the edge of the circle, Brick's towering frame shifted. The defensive lineman's dark eyes sliced through the fog of distraction. He stepped closer, risking the quiet.

"You good, Jax? Your head in the game?" Brick's voice rumbled, rough and edged with genuine concern, but impatient underneath.

Jaxon's jaw clenched so hard that his teeth ached. "Always." The word came out sharp, like a snapped wire.

Caleb, quieter but no less sharp, hoisted his helmet, his voice barely above the soft wind stirring the ragged cornrows beyond the chain-link fence. "I saw Victor Cross near the sidelines. Thought you might want to know."

A ripple ran through the players—unease spreading beneath their calls and shouts. Faces tightened, brows knotted, and sideways glances met across the cracked asphalt.

The day's tension thickened, invisibly stitching itself into the fraying air.

Jaxon didn't answer. His eyes flickered involuntarily toward the darkened corridor where the threat had lurked. He couldn't shake the feeling that Cross was watching, waiting—that this thing between them would eventually explode in front of everyone. The thought twisted his gut.

Near the fence line, Emma stood like a quiet sentinel. The soft cotton of her jacket brushed faintly in the breeze. Her eyes held something deeper than concern—an echo of the night's charged moments and the burdens he carried, visible in the tight set of his jaw and the flicker of doubt shadowing his gaze. She folded her arms, masking any impulse to cross the barren stretch and offer sanctuary.

Today wasn't the moment. For now, she watched from the periphery, her heart pinched with unspoken words.

Coach Marcus Hale's shout clawed through the restless hum.

"Stop! What the hell is this? Sloppy hands, slow feet—it's as if you don't give a damn!" His voice cracked like iron over the field, booming and sharp like a hornet's sting. The players flinched, their shoulders dropping.

Jaxon sensed the fault lines beneath the outburst, the blame curling in quiet circles. His name was whispered in half-suppressed sighs and harsh breaths. Each botched handoff and every misstep fractured the fragile thread holding the team together. His distracted calls didn't help.

"Get it together!" Hale's eyes blazed as they swept across the field. "Discipline! This is weak. If you want to win, you need to start acting like it!"

The team stiffened. Caleb's fingers twitched hesitantly around his helmet. Brick tightened his fists, his jaw clenched, simmering rage edged with disappointment.

"You okay, man?" Brick's tone was gruff but laced with worry. "We can't have you zoning out on us."

"Don't let this become your problem, Jax," Caleb added quietly, his voice tight with uncertainty.

Jaxon's mouth betrayed a brief flicker—regret? Anger?—but he bit it back and hollowed his cheeks. He nodded sharply. The weight in his chest wouldn't let him lift higher. Not yet.

Practice grinds on.

Cleats clattered on the turf. Pads cracked sharply. Calls echoed beneath the bruised sky.

But something was off. The rhythm was lopsided. Each step felt heavier than the last, caught in a pulse nobody dared to name.

Conversations dropped mid-sentence. Sideline chatter faded to murmurs loaded with suspicion and whispered blame. Eyes flicked to Jaxon and then away.

As play after play faltered, the tension coiled tighter. The sun inched lower, casting a bruised glow across tired faces. Each whistle blow sounded like a countdown to the end.

When Coach Hale finally blew the whistle for dismissal, it sounded more like a takedown than a release. Feet dragged. Voices faltered. The usual locker room rush was stifled, strangled by the weight clutching their chests.

The players clustered in hesitant knots—some heading for showers, others lingering, reluctant to break the fragile silence. Caleb's shoulders slumped as he exchanged a look with Brick. The unspoken question lingered in the dusk: How much longer could they hold on like this?

Jaxon's figure moved through the scattered crowd, hands shoved deep in his pockets, jaw set like stone, determined to swallow the storm raging beneath his skin. The chorus of frustration trailed behind him like a storm cloud, heavy and unyielding.

Practice dissolved into a slow, reluctant retreat.

The locker room breathes low and rumbling as players peel away from the practice field. Rustling sneakers echo against cracked concrete. Voices ripple in hushed tones—cautious currents shifting beneath the surface. Groups cluster near weathered lockers, some heads bowed, others casting sideways glances. Whispers thread around late workouts, new drills, and the weight of an uneasy morning still lodged under their skin.

A pair drifts toward the cafeteria. Their footsteps fade into the corridor's diminishing light while others linger, muffled murmurs bouncing off graffiti-streaked walls.

Jaxon slides onto the splintered bench. The rough wood bites into his palms. Behind him, the door thuds shut, sealing him in. The locker room's cavernous silence drapes over his shoulders like a weight he cannot shrug off.

He leans forward, tugging at damp strands tangled at his temples. His throat feels raw, like swallowing grit. The weight of words stuck inside squeezes tighter with every breath. A phone rests in his grip—silent, dormant—its black screen reflecting his restless gaze.

Last night. Emma, warmth and sharp edges all at once. How the air buzzed electric between them. And Victor's words, slithering like poison, rattle in his mind. *Should he call her? Break the silence? Own the tangled mess they're both holding?* The question twists in his chest, with no answers rising.

A faint hiss from the distant showers punctuated the low drone of players packing up. Locker doors creaked open and slammed closed in rhythm with swallowed breaths. Somewhere behind him, laughter strained to pierce the heaviness but fell short—fractured and fragile.

Jaxon's thumb hovered over the phone's screen. He breathed shallowly, slowly, trying to tame the thudding in his ribs. *Call her. No—don't.* The pulse of indecision struck sharp as a spike.

"Why don't you just call her?"

The voice was rough and uneasy. Caleb settled onto the bench beside him, his eyes searching the trench of lines carved by doubt in Jaxon's face.

"Because every time I think about it, it feels like I'm walking blind into a storm I started," Jaxon admitted, his voice low. Something skittered near vulnerability but didn't yet land.

Caleb shifted, hesitation clinging to his youth. "Sometimes storms clear the air," he said. "But you can't fix anything by just pretending the thunder isn't there."

"And sometimes they tear everything to ruins," Jaxon countered, his fingers tightening around the phone like a lifeline—or a noose.

Caleb's shoulders tensed. The words hung heavy between them.

"Look," Caleb said, his voice steadier now, "no one's going to tell you how to make it right. But if you don't try, the silence becomes the real punishment."

The locker room hummed louder. Water dripped. Faint shouts echoed from distant hallways. The scrape and scratch of cleats against tile filled the air.

Jaxon forced a nod, but hesitation still tethered him.

"I don't want to make it harder for her," he said, his voice barely above a gravelly scrape. "The last thing I need is to drag her back into this mess."

Caleb's gaze softened. A muted kind of understanding resided in those eyes—the kind born from silent battles of self-doubt. "She's not a prize to win or lose. Emma's smart. She knows the stakes. You've got to believe she can handle the truth, even the ugly parts."

Jaxon's fingers finally twitched. They inched toward the screen.

Then, as if caught in slow motion, the phone slipped from his grip. It clattered softly on the cold floor. The sound snapped the room's fragile quiet like a wire stretched too tight.

Jaxon didn't flinch. The moment passed unclaimed.

He leaned back. The bench groaned beneath him. His eyes fixed on empty lockers lined up like silent sentinels. His breath clouded in the cooling air—shallow and uneven.

Around him, the locker room pulsed with life. Players shed their armor and tension in equal measure. But he remained still, suspended between action and retreat.

The faint sting of liniment and damp towels hung in the air, mingling with the distant clang of water faucets and the soft tap of footsteps fading into the hallways. A locker slammed shut somewhere, and the sharp crack sliced through the low murmur.

Like a warning.

Jaxon's pulse hammered in his ears, drowned out only by the slow scrape of leather cleats as someone passed by, dismissing him like a shadow clinging to cold concrete.

His eyes drifted back to the dark screen in his hand. The phone was an inert weight now. Between the clutter of what was said and what was left unsaid, he stayed rooted, caught in the quiet storm that neither time nor courage could easily calm.

He didn't call. Not yet. Not now.

Outside the locker room, the facility held its breath, waiting for the first thunderclap.

The locker room hummed with the distant drip of a leaky faucet, fluorescent lights flickering like dying stars overhead. Jaxon sat alone on a splintered wooden bench, the fading scent of liniment and sweat clinging to the stale air. His phone vibrated—a sharp, insistent buzz against the silence. Another. And another.

The screen blinked relentlessly in his palm, each ping a small drumbeat of inevitable trouble.

His thumb trembles, fumbling for the unlock. The cold glass presses against his rough skin, slick with nervous sweat. He swipes, his heart hammering a rhythm he can't escape.

The headline blares like a siren in the quiet room: *"Jaxon Reyes: The Full Story Behind the Fall — New Leaks Shake Redemption Valley."* It stabs at him, jagged shards of past mistakes and fresh rumors.

Leaked texts. Anonymous sources. Whispers of betrayal and back-stabbing. Everything he had buried under two years of sweat and careful silence is dragged back into the light. The article's words scrape his skin like dirt beneath fingernails. He scrolls down, his fingers twitching as the screen fills with accusations, each more scathing than the last. His carefully constructed redemption—fragile as it was—crumbles with every swipe.

His eyes darken, and his muscles tense. A flicker of panic surges, quickly drowned by a burn of anger that claws at his ribs.

Embedded videos demand his attention. The first flickers to life: grainy footage of his worst career moment. The snapped throw. The falling crowd. The crackle of failure frozen in time.

That throw. Six years ago. One moment when everything fractured—his confidence, his reputation, the trust of an entire town. The crowd's roar, once alive in his blood, now echoes as cruel mockery. Next, a montage of whispers—locker-room confrontations caught in shadow, teammates' voices heavy with doubt.

Hashtags cascade like a digital avalanche: #FallenStar, #ReyesReckoning, #RedemptionLost. The numbers swell beside them, ticking upward as if the world is watching. Waiting.

Jaxon's breath hitches. His fingers tighten around the phone until his knuckles blanch. His chest contracts, a sharp pinch where hope had tried to settle. He scrolls faster, as if speed could dodge the storm of words bearing down on him.

"#ThrowbackLoser shouldn't even be near the field..."

"Wasn't he drunk during that game? Hope they never forget."

"Redemption Valley? More like a graveyard of lies."

The comments gnash at his ego, tearing through years of painstaking rebuilding. Each insult wraps around his throat, squeezing until the air feels thinner with every breath.

His jaw clenches, teeth grinding until the pain shoots up like wildfire. The old shame rises again—more vivid, sharper, stalking him through the sterile locker room walls. The public humiliation he had tried to bury under sweat and grit comes clawing back.

He blinks rapidly.

The harsh light fractures into shards in his vision. His hands slip from the phone, trembling. The cold wood presses into his palms as he lowers his head between his elbows. The article's glow washes over his bowed shoulders.

Notifications keep pouring in, an unrelenting drumbeat that pulses in his ears even when the phone rests face down. Somewhere behind him, lockers rattle softly in a cold draft, as if the building itself is unsettled. The locker room feels suddenly smaller. Suffocating.

Far beyond these walls, somewhere in the town's streets, a distant cheer reminds him of what is at stake and what is slipping away.

Somewhere beneath the rubble of fury and panic, a single thought claws at the edges: Is this the final blow, or just another scar to carry forward?

He remains like that, face hidden, lost in the tidal wave of shame and noise—trapped in the silence that screams louder than any crowd.

The rec room hums with low murmurs and the buzz of phones lighting up in tight fists. Brick's broad shoulders are tensed, and his jaw is clenched as notifications scroll past—each one another spark in the gathering storm. A sharp curse breaks the uneasy quiet. He slams his phone against the worn table, the thunk echoing like a gunshot.

Caleb sits a few feet away, blinking rapidly. His eyes have gone glassy and distant. His fingers tremble as he scrolls through the flood of posts and articles, each one a small cut. Around them, teammates glance toward Jaxon's locker with shadowed eyes—wary and unsure where allegiance folds into doubt.

A ping cuts through the tension: a message from a sponsor representative—formal and as cold as winter. The text flickers across screens, concerns thinly veiled, with threats to pull funding hanging like a blade suspended overhead. From nearby offices, muffled voices rise in sharp cracks. Coach Hale's face darkens, and the lines in his forehead deepen as his phone rattles with calls from the athletic department and anxious alumni donors. Each ring is another weight, another ripple of tension spreading through the cracked hallways.

Nina Alvarez stepped quietly from a corner where she had been watching, her eyes sharp beneath the flicker of fluorescent lights. She moved toward Coach Hale, her voice low, urgency threading through each word as she outlined donor fears and sponsor pullbacks. The Redemption Valley program had always run lean—dependent on sponsorships to survive, especially after the scandals that had nearly buried them years ago. One major pullback could unravel everything. Their whispered exchange cracked openings in the air, drawing anxious ears.

Outside the staff room, the team's group chat erupted—a digital battlefield. Words flew fast and jagged. *Did you see this? Is Jaxon serious? We all knew the risks, but damn. Someone's got to tell him.* Caleb's muttered retort about loyalty was lost in the furious typing and the emojis turned sour.

The cafeteria filled with the heavy scent of reheated coffee and stale pizza. Players found separate islands to occupy. Clusters fractured. Whispered conversations. Sharp glances. Fingers drummed restless beats on tables.

Jaxon sank into a corner, alone. His eyes locked on the glow of his phone, where venom threaded down the endless scroll. DeShawn tried a joke—light, tentative. Laughter died before it could form. An oppressive hush replaced it. His smile faltered. The weight in his chest pressed down like the humid summer dusk outside the grimy windows.

Emma entered silently. The soft crunch of her footsteps barely stirred the tense air. She scanned the room, her breath catching as her gaze found Jaxon. His profile was rigid, his jaw set hard, but his eyes were shadowed and raw. She didn't cross the room; she didn't break the distance between them. Part of her wanted to, but part of her couldn't—not after everything left unsaid, not when approaching him now might only complicate what was already falling apart. Instead, she settled on watching. The careful balance of concern and respect played across her face as she let the space hold its quiet promise.

Voices trailed off, and conversations splintered into fragments. The cafeteria buzzed with quiet gossip and caution. The room breathed tension. Fractured loyalties stretched thin in the fading light.

Jaxon remained still. His hands clenched the cold plastic of the table. Anger curled tight in his gut, and humiliation clawed at the edges of his composure. Beneath his ribcage, panic swelled—a gathering storm unleashed but held back by sheer will. Around him, the facility pulsed with echoes of whispered betrayals, the cold click of keyboards, and the relentless thrum of a world tipping on the edge of unraveling.

Nina's shadow fell across the dimly lit cafeteria as Jaxon drowned in the glow of his phone screen. She approached with steady, purposeful steps, the quiet click of her shoes sliding over worn linoleum pulling his attention away from the relentless tide of notifications. "Coach Hale wants to see you. Now," she said, her voice calm but urgent.

Jaxon blinks and swallows hard. He pushes himself up from the cold plastic chair, his muscles stiff and aching from the day's stress. Without a word, he falls in step behind Nina.

The hallway envelops them in its fluorescent hum—buzzing and flickering. The lights above cast harsh, clinical shadows along the peeling paint and tarnished trophy cases, as if the school itself is holding its breath, waiting for what comes next.

As they part ways at the end of the corridor, Nina's footsteps fade. Jaxon is alone now, accompanied only by the echo of his own breath and the metallic scrape of his cleats against the scuffed floor.

His hand lingers on the door to Hale's office—cold and unyielding. The silence behind it feels heavier than the hallway—denser and suffocating.

He pushes open the door, and the hinges groan softly.

Coach Hale is already seated behind the heavy oak desk, a mountain of papers and a thick file sprawled in front of him. The man's gaze is sharp, his eyes like chips of steel under furrowed brows. Without a word, Hale closes the door with a deliberate click, locking the outside world away.

"Sit down," Hale commands, his voice low and steady.

Jaxon lowers himself onto the hard chair opposite. The leather creaks beneath him. The room smells of stale coffee and must—a scent that lingers after long, exhausting nights, after hours of strategy sessions and damage control. It clings to the walls like a warning.

Hale taps the file and flips it open.

"This," he begins, his voice tight, "is the fallout."

He leans forward slightly, fingers spreading across the papers as if containing something volatile.

"Sponsors are on edge. The administration is breathing down our necks. Morale is tanking. The team's frayed—some of the boys don't know where they stand anymore."

The words land like punches. Jaxon's ribs tighten. His fingers twitch on his lap as the silence stretches between them, heavy and suffocating.

"This isn't just about wins and losses anymore," Hale continues, his voice carrying the weight of institutional pressure—budgets, public perception, a program teetering on the edge. "Everything that happens on that field ripples outward. It has to."

Hale leans back. His fingers steeple, and his eyes narrow as he studies Jaxon with the intensity of someone who has already begun calculating costs.

"I'm not here to make excuses," Hale says. "I'm here to figure out if you're more trouble than you're worth." His stare sharpens. "If you belong here—or if this program is better off without you."

His jaw tightens. Not just challenging—searching. He is looking for an answer he hopes won't break him.

A bitter laugh escapes Jaxon's lips—short and hollow.

"You want me to quit? Is that where this is going?"

"No." Hale's voice hardens. "I'm saying you need to decide if you're ready to carry this, to be the leader they need, or if you're just dragging everyone down."

The file snaps shut. The sound cuts through the quiet room like a blade.

Hale stands, muscles taut beneath the worn polo, and paces once before standing rigidly behind the desk. "Don't say a word. Just sit on it. We'll finish this tomorrow."

He meets Jaxon's eyes. His voice drops lower but carries an unshakable weight.

"Think about what you want, Reyes."

With that, Hale turns and exits. The door clicks shut behind him.

The room plunges into silence.

Jaxon exhales—heavy and slow. He sinks back into the creaking chair, his body suddenly depleted. The window behind him reflects a shadowed version of himself: jaw clenched, eyes darkened with uncertainty. The night beyond is thick, the muted streetlamp glow casting fractured patterns on the glass.

His fingers uncurl on his lap, trembling slightly.

The last vestiges of confidence flicker and die, swallowed by the void of what comes next.

He sits motionless. The question beats beneath his ribs like a second heart: Is this really the end of his last shot?

The Cost of Staying

Emma steps into the locker room. The morning air settles heavily—thick as dust motes caught in flickering fluorescent light. The usual hum of locker slams and chatter has vanished. Players huddle in corners like wary animals, their faces ghost-pale under the harsh glow, eyes glued to glowing rectangles in their hands.

A few cast wary glances toward Jaxon's locker. Empty. Bare. The door hangs slightly ajar like a wound that won't scab.

She moves quietly between them, her footsteps muffled against the scuffed concrete. The sharp scent of sweat and liniment mingles with the faint medicinal tang of eucalyptus from her kit. She catches the fractured state of the team in the silence itself—the usual camaraderie replaced by suspicion and fear so palpable it coats her throat.

At Caleb's locker, she notices his trembling fingers scrolling mechanically through headline after headline. The bold print seems to stab through the room like broken glass. His breath comes shallow, and his skin looks almost translucent beneath the pale light.

"Caleb." She murmurs his name, her voice soft but firm, kneeling to meet his downcast eyes. "I know this hit hard. But whatever's out there—it's not who you are. It's not your fault to carry."

She presses a cool hand over his clammy fingers, steadying him. "Breathe. We'll get through this."

His lips twitch, but no words come. His hands still shake—a physical echo of the storm inside.

Her gaze drifts across the room. Brick stands like a statue on the far side, his jaw clenched so tightly that it threatens to crack. His fists curl at his sides as if grasping a blade too close. His eyes burn with frustrated fire, fixed on the door as if daring it to open or slam. His posture is taut, like a coiled spring barely restraining the chaos within.

Emma's fingers tighten around her roll of tape. Brick's clenched fists and taut jaw are textbook signs of fight-or-flight—anger barely restrained. A storm on the verge of breaking.

Near the water cooler, DeShawn forces a smile. His voice cracks—a mix of a nervous chuckle and something hollow underneath. "At least it isn't about laundry this time," he says, his eyes darting for any reaction.

A player's sharp intake of breath cuts through the room.

The punchline shatters like thin ice beneath a weight too heavy. His voice falters, cracking painfully mid-sentence. Silence crashes back—thick, awkward—filling the space like a tangible fog.

Emma swallows the lump forming in her throat. Her heartbeat ticks sharply now.

In the far corner, almost swallowed by shadows, Eli mutters low—just audible to himself, "Jaxon's gonna ruin us all." His shoulders curl inward, folding protectively as if trying to shrink from the words he has just birthed. Resentment etches the tight lines of his posture—quiet defiance brewing beneath a paper-thin calm.

The door creaks open behind her. Coach Marcus Hale's stern silhouette blocks the light. His face is a hard line, with eyes like cold steel beneath drawn brows. His voice cuts through the room like a whip crack. "Team. Meeting. Now."

The players shift reluctantly, their bodies stiff, and their eyes still sharp with unease. Voices murmur—whispers about sponsors already pulling their support, contracts dangling like fragile threads about to sever. A brief argument ignites, sharp and raw. The sting of betrayal lingers in every hushed protest. Losing sponsors threatens the survival of the Redemption Valley Football Program itself. What would that mean for their futures? For scholarship offers? For everything they had worked toward?

Emma weaves through the tight cluster of athletes again, spreading quiet reassurances with a soft touch and steady words. She finds a jittery player by the benches, his skin pale and sweat-slick. Her fingers trace a strip of kinesio tape along his shoulder, feeling the tremor beneath the muscle and the crackle of adrenaline in the air.

"You're stronger than this moment." Her voice is barely a whisper, but she feels resolve stiffen somewhere deep within him.

Yet beneath her calm, anxiety gnaws at Emma's ribs—a cold weight she can't shake. The room feels compressed by uncertainty and fractured trust.

Her eyes flicker toward the entrance again, toward the empty space where Jaxon should be.

The absence is deafening, hollow, and sharp.

Without him, the meeting fractures before it even starts, dispersing into murmurs and restless shuffles. The room is soaked with questions that hang too heavily to answer.

The chill slices through the thin fabric of Jaxon's jacket, gnawing at the exposed skin of his neck. He crouches at the scruffy edge of the practice field. The grass dips, patchy and stubborn beneath his boots, with dew clinging like fragile glass beads that threaten to break underfoot with every restless shift.

He pulls his knees tight to his chest. His knuckles crack in a slow, deliberate rhythm—the only sound except for the whispering wind skimming across tangled fenceposts and the distant howl of scavenging crows nesting atop the rusted scoreboard.

His jaw bolts shut, muscles taut like steel cables. He resists the deep sigh that wants to shake loose the tightness coiling in his chest. The sky overhead is a bruised canvas of gray, edged faintly with the pale blue of a reluctant dawn. The fluorescent hum and metallic clangs of the locker room fade far behind, replaced by the steady thrum of his own racing pulse.

A sudden buzz against his thigh yanked him from the cold quiet. Jaxon fished his phone from his pocket. The screen was ablaze with messages. His agent's name blinked urgently. A missed call was flagged in red. Then the phone buzzed again—his father.

He swiped to unlock the phone, and blinking notifications flooded in like a wound that wouldn't close. Headlines splattered across his lock screen: *"Scandal Rocks Redemption Valley"*—*"Reyes' Past Haunts Team Again"*—*"Exposé Digs Deep into Darkest Days."* A cascade of heated comments and buzzes from reporters. Victor Cross's latest article was cruel and relentless.

Images from the exposé replayed behind his eyes, slicing deeper than any wound: the headline screaming across local screens, the smirks of faceless critics, the players who had once laughed now bent with worry. The suffocating silence in the locker room where his name hung like a noose on an empty locker door.

It was all his fault. The toxic seed he had planted had sprouted into a cancer choking the team's breath.

He wanted to turn back time, to swear the mistakes had never happened. Instead, he was the sinkhole beneath their feet, dragging down every last hope. His hands trembled, fists snapping shut and then loosening, nails carving crescent moons into raw skin. A low growl tightened in his throat—frustration clawing its way through.

He pictured Coach Hale's stern face, the way it hardened when he heard the news. Frustration burned into every crease. The players' silent accusations and their haunted eyes. The sponsors threatening to pull away before the season even had a chance to breathe.

The team was fracturing, all because he couldn't keep the ghosts at bay.

He couldn't let himself be the wrecking ball these guys didn't need.

Slowly, a cold resolve settled beneath the storm in his chest. He straightened as the wind gusted around him—frostbitten fingers tugging at his jacket. His shoulders hunched, small against the morning's bite, but his spine stiffened with stubborn intention.

Words crystallized in his mind: *Coach, I'm stepping down. This isn't working. I'll save you the fallout.* They sharpened like shattered glass, ready to slice through false loyalty.

His boots pressed into the soggy grass—heavy and slow. Each footfall dragged him away from everything hollow and broken inside the walls of Redemption Valley. His mind recycled the weighty sentence he would deliver, the cold finality in the faces he imagined around the conference table. The locker room empty, the whispers stopped. Only the sound of his own retreat echoed like thunder.

He had done this before, felt this exact weight pressing on his shoulders—years ago, after the first scandal, when he had thought about walking away from football entirely. That morning, he had sat in his car for two hours, convinced he was a burden to anyone who believed in him. His ex-girlfriend had been right to leave, and his father had been right to question his judgment. Everyone would be better off if he just disappeared.

But he hadn't left that morning either.

The path to the parking lot stretched out, uneven and soaked beneath a sky struggling to hold back the first hints of sunlight. His breath formed ragged clouds as he edged forward. The dampness seeped into his shoes, slick with mud.

The metal guardrail came into view, cold and unyielding under his hand as he paused, pressing his palm flat against the chill.

His heart throttled—every beat a question clawing at his throat. Is this the end? The final door slammed shut on a future he barely clung to? If he walked away now, folded like a broken play, could he live with the silence that would follow? The shadow of what might have been pressed long and low behind his eyes.

The road called, empty and unforgiving. His hand tensed, fingers sliding over the frost.

He took a step forward. Then another.

The car waited, keys heavy in the pocket of a jacket that felt suddenly too thick—too heavy to wear.

He stopped.

His chest expanded with a breath that came ragged and uncertain. Maybe stepping down wasn't the answer. Maybe that was just another way of running—letting fear win without even throwing a punch. Coach had always said Jaxon fought hardest when his back was against the wall; that the team didn't need him to disappear. They needed him to stand and take the hit.

Maybe they needed him to stay.

"Maybe," he said aloud, his voice rough against the wind. "I'm not done."

He turned back toward the practice field, toward the locker room, toward the wreckage waiting to be rebuilt. His boots pressed into the grass with purpose now, no longer dragging but moving forward—deliberate, uncertain, but forward.

Jaxon stands at the far end of the practice field, his broad shoulders hunched beneath a threadbare hoodie. The cold morning breeze tugs at his worn jeans, and the sky above stretches pale gray—the color of old tin. The town hums in the distance, faint and muted through the damp air, mingling with the sharp tang of crushed grass beneath Emma's boots as she crosses the field. Her steps are measured. Steady. The faint roll of peppermint from the oil at her wrist trails behind her—a quiet thread amid the tension.

She stops a few yards from him. The silence stretches between them, taut and fragile.

Emma's chest tightens. She's rehearsed this a hundred times, but standing here now, watching him curve away from the world, she feels the weight of what she has to say. If she doesn't reach him now, he'll disappear. Not physically. Worse—he'll ghost the team, the season, and himself.

"Jaxon." Her voice comes out lower than expected, but firm enough to ripple through the chill. "You can't just quit—for all of us—without saying a word. Without talking it through first."

He doesn't turn. The weight of the world bends the slope of his neck. His teeth clench as he breathes.

"You don't get it," he finally says. His voice is rough, sharp with the sting of self-accusation. "I'm doing this for them. I'm toxic. Look at the stories. The exposé. How can I stick around and not drag this team down with me?"

Emma steps closer, matching the hard line in his shoulders with a steadiness that won't crack. "The team needs you now more than ever."

"No." He snaps the word like a whip, finally turning to face her. His eyes blaze—anger and exhaustion churning together, the familiar storm that keeps everyone at arm's length. "They need a clean slate. Not a walking disaster. I'm the reason everything's falling apart."

The words hang heavy between them, soaked in bitterness.

Emma has seen this before: good people drowning in their own shame. "I refuse to let you sabotage this together because you're scared." Her voice lifts, steady as the gentle pressure of her hands on a strained muscle. "You walk away out of fear, and that hurts more than any headline. More than any public shaming. This team is raw. Bruised. But it's not done. And neither are you."

His jaw tightens. His eyes darken as memories flash behind the pain—the fall from the spotlight, the searing shame of those nights against cold stadium seats, the echo of voices declaring him finished.

"You think you're the first to let down a team?" Emma's voice cuts through the frozen ground between them. "The first to drown in mistakes? I'm so damn tired, Jaxon."

Tired of watching good people run.

"I'm tired of watching good people run from what's hard. From what matters."

"Why does it always have to be me?" Jaxon's voice rises, cracking like a snapped wire. "The letdown. The scandal. The mess? I'm done being everyone's problem."

Emma meets his glare without flinching. She feels every fracture in him, the desperate need to disappear into the shadows.

"You're not done." She steps closer. "You can't be. They need a leader who owns it—the scars, the guilt, the whole damn thing. You."

He shifts back, his shoulders rolling under the weight of her words. His eyes flicker with doubt and something else—something almost like hope.

Their voices carry now, slicing through the quiet field, a beacon drawing curiosity from the players still inside and from the staff moving about near the locker room.

The first footsteps echo. Hesitant figures pause in doorways, watching and waiting.

Emma plants her hands firmly on her hips, a solid promise—a stance with no retreat.

"I will not let you quit because you're afraid. Not this time."

Jaxon steps back into the space she has claimed. The conflict roars in his chest like a caged animal—the weight of scandal and failure pressing down on him, the desperate urge to run colliding with something else she has ignited. Something that won't let him disappear.

Behind him, the first players emerge from the locker room, drawn by the rising voices and the promise of something unresolved.

###

The first heavy footfall breaks the tension like a wave crashing on cracked pavement. Brick emerges from the locker room. His broad shoulders square themselves, arms folded tightly across his barrel chest. His eyes—dark and narrowed—slice through the argument simmering at the field's edge. He plants himself between Jaxon and Emma and the sprawling stretch of turf beyond, a silent sentinel guarding a fragile front line.

His jaw clenches, the muscles twitching, ready to snap. The crease at his brow deepens—every inch of him screams watchfulness, like a predator marking territory yet holding back just enough.

Behind him, the locker room door creaks open again. DeShawn strolls out, a half-smile tugging at his lips but faltering just beneath his eyes. His grin tightens as the weight of the moment settles heavier. A bitter twist sneaks in—his coping mechanism kicking in, humor masking the anxiety coiling beneath his ribs.

"At least it's not about laundry this time," he calls, his voice rough but laced with dry humor. A few players nearby try to stifle their chuckles—strained sounds like dust scraping under boots. The effort cracks the surface just enough. DeShawn's fingers drum absently against the water cooler, producing faint clinks of plastic bottles. The echo of their collective breaths mingles with the distant call of crows perched beyond the goalposts.

Eli's arrival is less triumphant. He slips onto the grass last, shoulders hunched and arms folded with defensive sharpness. His eyes flick from Emma to Jaxon and back again, a skeptic's gaze soaked with quiet resentment. His posture spells it out: don't ask me to put faith in this. The way his feet root into the damp earth tells everyone he's ready to make himself scarce if the storm swells.

Caleb trails behind, his phone clutched like a talisman, the screen glowing faintly in the gray light. He pads forward hesitantly, a ghost moving through fog. His hands jitter, thumbs scrolling through headlines that have already tattooed fear and doubt beneath his skin. His eyes flicker between Jaxon's set jaw and Emma's steel-set gaze, trying to anchor himself somewhere safe in that silent standoff. There's a tremor in his breath as he licks his dry lips. The weight of unspoken questions presses down like the cold morning mist curling off the earth.

Through the locker room entrance, a final figure steps out—Coach Marcus Hale. His silhouette is a study in stoicism: broad, squared shoulders dusted in shadow, hands clasped behind his back. He watches the unfolding scene without a word. His presence commands attention despite the quiet. Players continue to emerge in a slow parade from the sanctuary of concrete and sweat, their faces taut with tension. Anxiety and defiance wrestle in their eyes. They drift into place, forming a loose semicircle around Jaxon and Emma. Coach Hale's gaze sweeps across them—cold, calculated—a silent nod, barely perceptible yet carrying the weight of unspoken command.

The circle tightens with murmurs—low, urgent, edged with unease. Eyes dart sideways in quick exchanges. Frustration curls in whispered syllables. A flicked helmet visor catches the light. Shadowed brows knit tightly. Someone mutters something too soft to catch. Heads nod, slow and reluctant. Brick's gaze flickers, hardened yet noticing everything—the way shoulders tense, the nervous smirks, the unspoken fears hovering just beyond reach. DeShawn slaps a teammate on the back with an awkward grin, trying to forge a connection through the tension.

Jaxon's stance shifts under the weight of dozens of eyes. His gaze sweeps the semicircle, catching the flicker of distrust from Eli, the uncertain hope quickening Caleb's breath, and the simmering loyalty hidden beneath Brick's guarded watchfulness. The muffled scrape of cleats on worn turf fills the heavy silence, followed by the swirl of tight glances, barely contained sighs, and hovered words left unsaid.

The semicircle draws in, crowding the space, the distance shrinking until all that remains is a shared heartbeat of precarious unity. Jaxon's shoulders rise slightly, as if bracing against an invisible wind. His breath releases in a measured huff. For a long moment, no one moves or speaks. Every pair of eyes hangs on him—a fragile weight settling into the air like static before a storm breaks.

"Look, man, this team's been a damn circus from the jump," De-Shawn finally breaks the hush, his voice rough but steady. "But none of this pie-in-the-sky crap, yeah? We need something solid right now."

Brick's roar cuts through next, low and rough: "Jaxon pushes us—throws us into the fire and expects us to crawl out better. Makes me hate him sometimes... but hell, he makes me fight."

Caleb's voice trembles from the fringe of the circle as he steps closer, his phone lowered now. "He believed in me when I was ready to fold. I owe him that."

Eli remains silent, his arms tight, eyes flicking across faces, weighing the room like a scalpel. He leans forward, tension pounding in his chest. Whatever he's about to say could tip the scales either way.

Emma's gaze doesn't waver from Jaxon, steady and unyielding, as if planting a stake in the ground. The men around her shift, their breathing caught between fear and defiance. The semicircle completes its journey inward, shrinking the gap until the team feels less like scattered fragments and more like a unit clinging to the edges of hope.

Silence tightens into something full. Alive. Waiting. All eyes settle on Jaxon. He lifts his chin, muscles taut, and meets their gazes head-on. No words yet—just the raw charge of collective breath held tight. The promise and peril of what is to come hang heavy in the air.

Jaxon's voice cracks, raw. The brittle morning air swallows his words whole. "If you want me gone, I'll go."

The semicircle of players holds its breath. Emma's eyes lock onto his—steady, unmovable—and something in him steadies too, if only fractionally. Around them, sidelong glances flicker like nervous fish. Cold gnaws at exposed skin. Each exhale materializes, faint and ghost-ly.

Jaxon's shoulders cave inward. Exhaustion has burrowed deep, settling into muscle and bone. His gaze sweeps the group, desperate, searching for the thing that might keep him tethered here.

The silence stretches—thick, suffocating.

Then Brick moves. His boot scuffs the turf. His jaw clenches so hard that the muscle twitches beneath his skin. He loosens his fists by degrees, fingers trembling as they uncurl. When he speaks, his voice drops low but burns.

"Jaxon... man, you piss me off like nobody else." He swallows; shame doesn't touch him. "But that fire? That grudge? It's making me better, pushing me to fight harder every single damn day." His sharp eyes sweep the group. "You want to walk? I vote you stay."

A murmur runs through the line—tentative at first, then growing.

DeShawn's easy smirk breaks through like the sun through clouds. He raises his hand, and a shadow crosses his eyes before he grins. "Yeah, pain in the ass? That's what you are." He laughs, rough and honest. "But nobody else is crazy enough to run this circus. It's a mess, sure. Our mess, though. I'm keeping you."

Caleb's fingers crush his phone, his knuckles blanching white. He swallows hard—a visible bob of his throat—before his voice emerges, fragile as cracked glass.

"Jaxon makes mistakes." His gaze drops to the fractured ground beneath them, then lifts again, something resolute hardening his expression. "But he believed in me when everyone else looked through me as if I weren't there. Like I was invisible." He straightens his shoulders. "I vote for him."

Eli steps forward, hesitation written across every angle of his face. His eyes dart from player to player—cautious, weighing, uncertain. His gaze flicks away from Jaxon's before he speaks, fingers tapping a nervous rhythm against his hip.

"I'm not there yet." His voice comes out quiet and reluctant. "I still don't trust you fully." A pause. His throat tightens. "But... I'm with the team. For now."

One by one, others fracture the silence with short declarations—clipped and honest. Boys who've tasted too many defeats and too many hollow promises. Some bury vulnerability beneath guarded words, while others lace their grudges with something that might be hope.

Each voice lands like a stone dropped into still water.

Jaxon exhales—long and low. The breath escapes as if he has been holding it since the moment he spoke. The weight around him begins to shift, that invisible pressure loosening with every spoken word.

Coach Marcus Hale steps forward then. His presence does not announce itself; it simply *is*, solid and unyielding. His eyes move across each face, reading the hardness that circumstance has carved into them and the softness that shared struggle has worn there. The nod he gives carries the weight of something complicated between him and Jaxon—years of friction, testing, and a loyalty that had to be earned and re-earned. No theatrics. No speeches. Just the steady gravity of a man who knows his players, who understands what this moment costs, and who stands with them anyway.

The semicircle tightens, drawing closer around Jaxon like worn armor—scarred, imperfect, but standing.

He exhales again. This time, air actually reaches his lungs. The support surrounding him tastes of salt, sweat, and something fragile—something that could shatter if they are not careful, but stands nonetheless. A tension held. A fragile hope shadowed by the hard work still waiting.

The brittle morning air settles around them, no longer empty.

The silence that follows the last reluctant voice hangs thick in the cold morning air. Emma steps closer to Jaxon. Her boots crunch softly on frost-tinged grass. She leans in, her breath a pale mist mingling with the sharp tang of earth and sweat. Her eyes narrow—not quite anger, but steel beneath warmth—before her voice slides out, low and steady.

"Staying here isn't going to be easy, Jax. This... this isn't just about the wins or losses. You're going to have to fight for every crumb of trust left in this place. Every single one."

He blinks. Her words hit him like cold water on bare skin. The weight settles deep in his chest—a familiar ache, one he remembers from years back when his father walked out, when silence felt like abandonment. But this time, there's no argument, no deflection. He nods, slow and deliberate, fingers twitching at his sides as if wrestling with something ancient inside. The grim set of his jaw blunts the usual flicker of bitterness. He pushes his shoulders back, standing taller despite the chill biting through his hoodie.

Turning toward the ragged line of players gathered in the pale dawn, his voice emerges hoarse, steadier—steady enough to crack through the raw morning.

"I'm not going to let you all down again. I'll be here—head in the game, no excuses. Practice, meetings, whatever Emma and Coach demand—I'll be there. All in."

The pause after his words feels endless. Then a few of them step forward like the first stones settling in a stubborn foundation. Brick's massive hand thuds firmly on Jaxon's shoulder, the weight grounding them both. DeShawn, arms folded with a half-grin that doesn't quite reach his eyes, sets his helmet down with a clang beside Jaxon's boots. Bit by bit, others close ranks, hands resting on shoulders, rough pads brushing, forming an uneven but solid circle. A tight huddle takes shape, breath mingling in clouds in the crisp air.

Coach Marcus Hale stands just beyond the ring, his silhouette stark against the pale dawn, muscles tense, eyes shadowed under a heavy brow. Staff members murmur quietly nearby, but none step forward—this moment is theirs. A few paces away, Nina shifts beside Emma, her posture protective yet visibly relieved, arms folded across her chest as if bracing herself against the storm but ready to weather it.

Within the huddle, voices dip below the rush of the wind. A low murmur swells, a blend of grit and quiet resolve. DeShawn breaks the tension, his voice clipped, dry, but somehow light.

"Well, at least it isn't about dirty laundry this time."

A brief spark of humor ripples through, pulling a few strained smiles from rugged faces. Brick grunts appreciatively, deep as thunder, his voice steady and slow.

"Yeah. It pisses me off how much this guy pushes us. But it's the only reason I'm not still stuck on the bench."

A few nods follow, small shields against the weight of everything—not just the morning's headlines but the history they carry in their bones.

"Jax isn't perfect," Caleb's voice quivers slightly, edged with nerves but firm beneath. "But he believes in us... even when we don't believe in ourselves. That counts for something."

Eli lingers nearby, his arms crossed and shoulders tight. His eyes flicker between hope and skepticism. Finally, his voice slips out, quieter but clear.

"I don't trust him all the way yet. But... yeah, we're better with him than without."

The cluster tightens, an unspoken pact forming like iron cooling in the forge. The fear that clung to their backs minutes before is shifting, morphing into something sharper—determination.

Emma watches from the outer edge of the circle, the sun breaking stubbornly through a quilt of clouds, casting pale gold on worn faces. The scent of crushed grass and liniment rises faintly, mingling with the salty warmth of sweat and breath. Her palms are slightly damp. The tension that gripped her moments ago still ripples through her limbs, a reminder of how fragile this unity truly is—how easily it could splinter if Jaxon stumbles again. She holds steady anyway, muscles braced, ready for whatever comes next.

Jaxon's wary eyes sweep the group, then flick upward, locking briefly with hers over the jumble of shoulders and helmets. The usual hardness softens into something raw and quietly hopeful. No promises are broken—just the fragile pulse of a new beginning.

The huddle draws tighter, bodies leaning in, voices low murmurs of resolve blending with the rhythm of steady breaths.

Hope lives here—in the cracks, in the grit, in the unpolished edges pressed close now against the cold morning. The bruised, battered team beats as one beneath their imperfect leader, ready to fight the hard road ahead.

Brotherhood

The thin edge of dawn hasn't grazed the sky when Jaxon's eyes snap open. 3:17 a.m. glows in dull red on the digital clock. He sits up, and the mattress creaks beneath him.

His breath comes shallow, and a cage tightens around his ribs. The weight from last night—the votes, the silent refusals, those raw looks in the locker room—drags heavily on his chest, a stone he can't shift. Sleep doesn't offer refuge; it just slips away.

His fingers curl tightly against his knees, rough with dry skin from hours of gripping. The dorm smells of stale sweat and cheap carpet, soaked into the threadbare floor beneath the fluorescent hum. A muffled thud from a late-night TV show bleeds through the walls—no one left to listen. Just him.

Jaxon's jaw clenches, and his fingers twitch, itching for control. But all he holds is tension, coiled tight and ready to snap.

He swings his legs over the bed's edge and plants his bare feet on the cold floor. The thin blanket pools forgotten on the mattress. Around him, the silence feels hollow—like this building breathes uneasily, waiting for daylight or disaster, uncertain which will come first.

Laced shoes brush against cracked linoleum with a muted whisper as he crosses the room. The hallway is a tunnel of shadows and cold echoes. Doors stand closed like mausoleum gates, their chipped paint hiding stories and secrets. Faint breaths of cold air slink from under them, but no light spills, and no voices stir. It's the desertion of midnight—a brood of waiting ghosts.

At the end of the hall, his steps slow. He halts in front of a narrow window, thin fingers pressing against the cool glass. Bleary eyes peer down at the field below, where pale gray movements dance near the locker room entrance. Figures shift and murmur, small and shapeless in the dark, but unmistakably present—teams already stirring in the bone-chill of early morning. His teammates: quiet conspirators of hope and fear.

The chain-link fence shivers faintly in the wind. Weeds scrape like dry bones against the concrete. The scoreboard looms—some bulbs dark, others flickering—frozen at 14–3. Mocking. That number haunts him; it represents everything they lost and everything they're fighting to reclaim.

The pennants flap limply, pale in the low light. The field wears its scars openly: patches of bare dirt and beaten paint fading into yesterday. Yet beneath that weathered surface hums a strange electricity, as if the ground itself remembers what once was—and what could still be.

Jaxon's lips press into a thin line. His nostrils flare at the scent of damp earth and distant liniment, memories mixed with the sharp tang of fresh sweat still etched in the air. His shoulders tighten under the weight of his hoodie, but the chill seeps in anyway.

A low breath escapes him. His hand drifts to the worn fabric of a jacket hanging near the door. The fabric is heavy and familiar—like armor shaped by late nights and hard truths. He pulls it on, letting the sleeves swallow his hands. His shoulders square beneath the bulk, and the hood slips up with a soft sigh.

The dorm stands silent behind him—a beast paused in its breath, suspended between what has been and what must come.

Jaxon steps out the door.

The faint scrape of his shoes on the linoleum trails behind him like a secret as he moves toward the field, his body taut and sure. The night still clings to the walls and the empty halls. But underfoot, the first shimmering hints of dawn begin to stain the edges of the cloud-heavy sky.

The locker-room vote, unresolved and raw, gathers into something quieter now—a promise, perhaps, or a challenge.

He pulls his jacket tighter—a stubborn barrier against the cold and the past alike. Ahead, the field waits: imperfect, scarred, alive.

And Jaxon steps into that waiting dark.

Grass clings to Jaxon's cleats, cold and soaking. He steps onto the practice field under a sky still sealed in shadow. The mist clings low, ghost-thin, curling around his ankles. His boots sink into the soft earth with each step. Dark, uneven footprints stretch behind him—echoes of every hesitant stride.

Part of him wants to turn back. Not today. Not now.

Ahead, a narrow bench rests at the edge of the field. Brick sits there, arms folded tightly, stripped of warmth except for the grit in his stare. The older man's jaw tightens as Jaxon approaches. A flicker of something unspoken passes between them. Jaxon's fingers curl into a loose fist, then relax. The tension lingers like a held breath.

A sharp nod answers Brick's silent challenge. His gaze locks onto Jaxon's like barbed wire—steady, unforgiving. Words don't come. Maybe they don't need to.

Around them, faint shapes ripple against the dark. Caleb emerges first, clutching a dented thermos like a lifeline. His fingers rub together for warmth, and his breath fogs in small rhythmic bursts. His eyes trace the horizon, wrapped in hope and uncertainty.

DeShawn follows, shuffling forward with a half-hearted grumble. His shoulders roll as if shaking off something heavier than a chill. His footsteps crunch against frost-kissed blades, louder in this quiet world.

Eli lingers at the fringe—lean and watchful. His arms are crossed in thought rather than defiance; the loner's posture is subtle but unmistakable.

The field stretches wide and waiting, the rustle of leaves stirred by the breeze, and the low hum of distant traffic mixing with the earthy scent of damp soil. Fresh paint wraps around the gathering like a secret.

In that quiet moment, heavy boots crunch softly against the frozen ground. Marcus Hale emerges from the shadows like a fixture carved into dim light—the coach's sharp gaze slicing through dawn's murk. His nod is rare, approval heavy but whispered without ceremony. He kneels and sets down a crate weighted with spray paints and buckets splattered with urgency and color. The hiss of paint cans waits like a held breath at Jaxon's feet before Marcus drifts back into darkness.

This field meant something once. Three years ago, they had owned it. State semifinals, adrenaline burning through their veins, believing they were unstoppable. That was before everything fell apart. Before Jaxon left and the team fractured. Now they gather in pre-dawn shadow, trying to piece something back together.

Jaxon stoops and lifts a can of spray paint. The cool metal hums softly against his calloused skin—a fragile anchor.

Around him, the team settles into thick silence. Shifting weight, nervous glances, jackets rustling against wet grass. The air tastes bitter, sharp with expectation and old scars barely buried under fresh hope.

"You actually showed," Caleb's voice cuts through the hush, breath hitching in the cold. "I thought you'd pull a Houdini on us."

Jaxon grunts, his eyes fixed on the spinning can. "I'm here. Don't expect a pep talk."

Brick's chuckle rumbles low and dry, but his words remain locked tight.

DeShawn steps closer, wiping his paint-smudged hands on his pants. "We cruise out here because it's a damn party."

Jaxon lifts his gaze to meet DeShawn's. The edge is blunt but not unkind. "This better mean you've got a plan. Chaos doesn't win games."

Eli's voice drifts from the sidelines, calm and guarded. "Plans mean nothing if we can't hold it together. Your coming back was the first piece."

A pause stretches. The mist curls tighter as if it is listening.

"That crate has more than paint, huh?" Brick nods toward the supplies.

"Symbolism," Jaxon mutters, tightening his grip on the can. "A fresh start with a mess waiting to happen."

Caleb swallows, rubbing his hands again. "We need something to believe in. Something real."

The cold settles deeper. The field stretches vast and unknowable beneath heavy skies. Jaxon's fingers tighten around the spray can, the metallic hiss barely breaking through the pre-dawn stillness. Every drip of paint that will come is a chance—a stubborn, messy confession that they're here together, not quite broken.

He looks back at the team. Each face is pale in the dim light, unreadable but raw. The weight of their presence presses heavier than any scoreboard. The moment beckons with a quiet roar—a call to stake the ground beneath their feet and lay claim not just to a game, but to something more fragile: trust.

Jaxon's jaw clenches. Something fierce and uncertain stirs within his chest. He deliberately turns the can, the cool metal whispering under his calloused palm. The team holds its breath, poised on the edge of what comes next.

The cold air bites through Jaxon's jacket, sharp against his skin as Brick's heavy hands drag the warped plywood from its hiding spot behind the bleachers. The wood groans, and splinters catch at the frayed edges. Brick props it upright on two sawhorses. The faded grain and chipped paint catch the soft pre-dawn light like a challenge waiting to be answered.

The sudden clatter shatters the hushed gathering. Heads lift, and eyes snap toward the makeshift altar beneath the empty stands.

Brick wipes his paint-slick palms on his jeans, his jaw clenched tight. His grin appears shaky, like a mask barely holding. "Well, boys," he says, his voice tighter than usual. "Here's our permanent mess."

DeShawn's face contorts into mock horror as he leans back, shaking his head. "Permanent mess? Man, maybe I should bolt—this finger-painting gig is too damn serious for me."

DeShawn's low chuckle breaks free, rippling through the group. Shoulders visibly loosen, and a few stray smiles flicker uncertainly, tentative as dawn itself.

Jaxon steps forward, the heel of his boot crunching softly on scattered gravel. He stares at the blank canvas—massive and awkward, daring him to ruin it. His hand sinks deep into the bucket of electric blue paint, the cold oozing up his wrist, slick and tacky against his skin. He's owned worse messes than this. This one, though, matters.

He drags the paint slowly onto the center of the wood, pressing down with a grunt. The print blooms—raw, uneven edges swallowing the sun-faded scratches beneath.

"Gotta own our mess. All of it," he mumbles, his lips barely moving. "Leave a mark that can't be wiped clean."

Caleb's fingers tremble as he steps up next, dipping into a jar of bright red that stains his skin like fire. His print blooms beside Jaxon's—roughly shaped, the paint slurring where sweat glistens on his palm. Eli follows, quieter and deliberate, rolling his hand in a sober gray that coolly contrasts with the other hues. His imprint is smaller, pressed with cautious precision, edges jagged and unfinished.

Brick's jaw tightens. He swipes a fist thickly coated in forest-green paint and slaps it onto the plywood like a gauntlet thrown down. The green spreads in a messy, rebellious smear, consuming half the board.

"That's ours," Brick rasps, his eyes daring anyone to argue against the chaos beneath their fingertips.

Then it breaks loose.

DeShawn flicks a glob of paint toward Caleb, streaking it across his shoulder. Caleb yelps, wiping at the sudden wetness. Laughter explodes around them, sharp and wild. Jaxon dodges a playful swipe that leaves a streak of blue across his cheek, the cold paint prickling his skin. He doesn't retaliate—not yet. The dusty grass beneath their cleats bears traces too—smeared colors rubbed raw from fingertips that dart between faces and sleeves.

"Hey!" DeShawn shouts, his voice bright with mischief. "Do you think Captain Reyes here can keep up with us, or will he just boss us around with paint?"

Jaxon snorts, gruff but amused. "Lucky it isn't permanent. Otherwise, you'd be on the hook for scrubbing."

Laughter ripples, echoing over the field's jagged edges as the team dives into the mess, their hands soaked and smeared like artists gone wild. The heavy scent of oil-based paint mixes with the damp earth—sharp, acrid, and intoxicatingly real.

Masks of color bloom on faces, with streaks of red across foreheads and smudged gray fingerprints on sleeves rolled up past elbows. Green splashes dot hair like rebellious streaks of moss. Even the sky seems to brighten, the early clouds pulling back as if to watch this messy ceremony unfold.

Amid the chaos, something shifts. The rough edges of the group begin to blur. Distance folds into something less guarded, less fractured.

The plywood becomes a riotous mosaic—overlapping prints layered like imperfect promises, smeared edges bleeding into each other, colors clashing and mingling in defiant patterns. The air hums with unspoken words laced with shared laughter and fresh hope.

DeShawn slaps his painted palms together, sending droplets of blue and green arcing with a hiss through the morning air. He grins widely, his eyes gleaming.

"This," he calls, his voice loud enough to catch every ear, "is more than paint. It's us—our screw-ups and stubborn fights. And yeah, our chances. Right here."

Brick's nod is slow and steady. His gaze locks with Jaxon's, a spark crackling in the cold air—part challenge, part truce. The hardness in their eyes softens for a heartbeat, and the old walls between them creak open.

No words are needed as the group surrounds the board, this patchwork symbol catching every hand—paint slick, rough, and eager.

Their breaths cloud in the cold air, forming small ghosts that vanish beneath stirred-up laughter. The scent of wet paint lingers, a sharp tang—a quiet defiance against the gray, the doubting whispers in town, and the scars no one talks about.

Jaxon stands still for a moment, scanning the faces ringed around the board. Each streak and smear is a fingerprint on his own fractured hope. The tattered plywood holds their marks, their voices, and their claim to this fractured field. It is messy and imperfect—but it is theirs.

The air hums with something electric and fragile. The team—knit together by splashes of paint—grins back through the residues of their fight, hands sticky with color and unspoken promises.

Brick stands solid beside the plywood board, his palms still dripping with vivid green paint. The color starkly interrupts the dawn-gray sky. His gaze locks on Jaxon—steady and unflinching.

The cool air carries the scent of wet grass and acrid paint fumes, mixing with the distant hum of the waking town.

"I ran into some folks down Main Street yesterday," Brick's voice rumbles low, steady as the ground beneath them. "They were talking trash about you, saying you're washed up, done. That maybe you don't belong here anymore."

He swallows and keeps going.

In Brick's experience, captains crumbled under pressure. He had seen it before—big talk, hollow spines. But Jaxon had never bent that way.

"But I told them—Jaxon's here because he doesn't quit. And the way I see it? We aren't either."

A silence stretches between them, thick and expectant. Around the board, the others shift quietly. Dew clings to blades of grass, peppering their shoes with cold drops. The handprints layered across the wood—crude and overlapping—tell a story of effort and messy beginnings. Brick's words sharpen the outline beneath the haze.

"For real," Brick says, his voice folding softer but no less certain, "I've never trusted captains before. Too many come in talking big but fold when the pressure hits. But you?" He pauses. "You don't quit. Not until it's damn near embarrassing. That's the kind of real I respect. That's the kind of real we needed."

Heads tilt—some lowered, some lifting to meet Jaxon's face. The word "real" hangs heavy in the air.

Jaxon snorts—a rough sound caught somewhere between surprise and something nearly vulnerable.

It wasn't much, but it cracked the armor.

His jaw twitches. For a moment, the hard line between humor and pain blurs.

"Yeah, well. 'Bout time someone said it right." The grumble is low and rough, offhand but honest beneath the edge. He steps forward, scanning the faces and holding each gaze deliberately, as if trying to siphon courage from the group.

Nods thread through the circle—a quiet respect settling in. Caleb's head dips once in slow recognition, a brief but sincere gesture. Eli shifts his weight, pausing the instinct to drift away and grounding himself beside the team. DeShawn's usual loose grin tightens into something quieter and more respectful. The light teasing pauses between breaths.

They're choosing this: to lean on each other's strength, to stitch together ragged confidence with shared sweat and paint.

The cold settles into every muscle, but somewhere inside Jaxon, something uncoils.

He had spent years building walls high enough to keep everyone out. Trust had always been a liability, a weakness that got you hurt.

Yet here, with paint drying on his hands and these men watching him with something that looked like belief—it terrified him. And maybe that was the point. Maybe belonging meant being terrified together.

Jaxon presses his fingers—still slick with blue and red paint—against the plywood again. Smaller this time, near Brick's bold green smear. The texture of the wet paint cools his skin. The second handprint rests just beside the first.

A silent, unspoken pact.

Brick cracks a tight smile, wiping his hands on his pants. His eyes flick around the group. The dawn leans into the promise of something rough-hewn but real.

"You know I've got your back," Brick says, his voice low but carrying a fierceness beneath.

Jaxon lifts his gaze, catching Brick's meaning in that look. Fewer words. More weight. "Damn right."

DeShawn pipes in, wiping paint off his forearm with the edge of his shirt. "Guess maybe trusting you isn't the worst idea yet, huh?"

Caleb laughs quietly, his eyes bright despite the cold. "It's about damn time someone said that."

Eli's voice cuts in, more reserved but present. "We all have scars. It ain't about pretending they aren't there."

Jaxon's jaw relaxes slightly, his eyes lingering a moment longer on each teammate before flicking away. The hard set of his lips softens, just a fraction. He looks over the growing mess—crimson, blue, gray, green—a chaotic testament to stubborn loyalty and bruised hope.

"It's messy," he admits, his voice rough but steady. "Like us. But it means something."

Brick nods, stepping back as the weight of the moment sinks in. The others add more prints—each stroke and press drawing tighter lines between fractured pieces.

A flicker moves through Jaxon's chest. It is not quite peace, but perhaps the slow stir of belonging.

"Never thought I'd see the day you let yourself be part of the team like this," Caleb murmurs, half a smile breaking through his usual reserve.

Jaxon's eyes catch the fading space between words. He finds more in Caleb's gaze than encouragement—a quiet challenge and a shared struggle.

"Yeah," Jaxon says, his voice catching the dawn's uncertain light. "Me neither."

The board wobbles on makeshift sawhorses, coated with smeared colors and sweaty smudges. Barking laughter mingles with the morning chill. The first warmth of the day casts long shadows as the men hover close, paint-clad hands bristling with raw hope.

In that space, thick with silent promises and scraped knees, the team begins to bind—not just to a game, but to each other.

Jaxon presses one last finger to the board, a small imprint beside Brick's green mark, sealing a fragile moment of trust under the waking sky.

DeShawn's forearm gleams with streaks of bright paint—green bleeding into blue. He ducks in front of the plywood board. The buzz of restless energy dies instantly.

His usual grin fades. The joking mask slips away, replaced by a tight line that cuts across his face like a scar. He straightens, and his throat clears with a roughness that snags everyone's attention.

"I need everyone's ears for a second."

His voice cut through the cold dawn, stripped of warmth. The team turned, caught off guard. DeShawn's eyes pushed through the mist, but something flickered there—raw and nearly cracked.

He had spent the whole season hiding behind jokes and laughter. Those shields had once felt safe; now they just felt suffocating.

"This shit," he said, jerking a thumb toward his paint-splattered arm, "isn't just fun. The jokes? They're walls—shields I slap on to hide from the things I'm actually scared of."

His hands trembled, fingers twisting and untwisting, as if they wanted to grasp something solid.

"I'm terrified."

He swallowed hard.

"Terrified of failing. Of letting down my mom. All the damn sacrifices she made." His throat tightened, and a sharp catch broke his voice on the next word. "For me to mess this up. For her to think it was all for nothing."

The crack hung in the air—raw and unguarded.

Caleb stepped forward, his warm hand pressing firmly against DeShawn's shoulder. Steady. No announcing flourish—just quiet grounding. A soft clap on the back, a brotherly anchor.

"We all have fears," Caleb murmured, his voice low and steady. Around them, small ripples of agreement sifted through the circle.

Eli's usual silence fractured. His voice came out hushed but clear.

"Yeah." He paused, his gaze sliding away, betraying the unexpected weight of his confession. "Even me."

A hush fell.

Thick as fog over the grass, silence was heavy enough to drown a thousand doubts.

Jaxon stepped forward. The usual tight line of his mouth softened, and something like empathy shaped his face. He had spent the whole season running, trying not to let his fears break him. But standing there, watching DeShawn's vulnerability crack open the air between them, he couldn't hide anymore.

"I've been running from my fears all damn season," he said, his voice rough—closer to a whisper but fiercer than the dawn wind. He met DeShawn's eyes, then the faces around the board: paint-smeared and shadowed by exhaustion and honesty.

"I'm just as scared as you."

The confession felt like a hand breaking through ice—fragile but real.

The team shifted, and the air loosened. The weight of their shared vulnerability knitted quiet threads of understanding between them.

Paint-spattered hands hovered, hesitant, before reaching toward the board again.

A low murmur swelled from the group—a collective breath held and released. Then came a sound like a wave breaking: soft cheers rising from their chests, raw, unpolished, and fierce.

Laughter mingled with cheers as the lingering cold was shaken off. Paint splashed—scarlet, cobalt, green. Fresh handprints blurred and bled into one another, creating a chaos that somehow felt perfect.

DeShawn exhaled, releasing a breath he didn't know he was holding. His lips twitched upward, faint but genuine.

Around him, the team's hands moved across the board, leaving a mosaic alive with flaws and faith. The dawn deepened, and the paint, like their stories, refused to be wiped clean.

Eli stepped forward, a towel draped over his forearm as if it were the last thing he was comfortable holding onto. His eyes flickered with cautious curiosity beneath tired lids as he offered the cloth to Jaxon, who was still gripping a smear of blue paint across his palm. The nod Eli gave was small—almost hesitant—but there was a glimmer of something begrudgingly respectful in it.

"Maybe we make this a thing," Eli said, his voice low but steady. "Like—every captain's got to leave their handprint. Not just paint. A real promise."

Jaxon scowled, halfway to brushing the paint off, but something in Eli's tone pulled at the edges of his resolve. A tradition wasn't exactly what he had imagined under the flickering dawn sky, but damn if it didn't sound necessary.

From the corner of his eye, Caleb leans forward, stepping cautiously into the space between player and promise. His voice carries quiet certainty, soft with the dawn but sharp with hope.

"Yeah," Caleb says, rubbing his chilly hands together, streaks of red paint still glistening on his fingers. "Each captain has to leave their mark right in the center of the board, surrounded by all of us. That way, it's not just a name on a jersey—it's a stake in the ground."

Murmurs tumble across the group—quiet but rising, a tide of agreement washing over the frost-tinged grass. Jaxon glances down at the plywood: a mosaic of smeared colors, overlapping handprints like fractured fingerprints fused in defiance against lost seasons and ruined reputations.

Before he can shrink into silence, rough hands—paint-slick and sure—settle firmly on his shoulders. Brick's grip is steady, a tether pulling Jaxon toward the makeshift altar.

Other hands join: Caleb's warm, DeShawn's smudged with green paint. Even Eli's tentative fingers brush Jaxon's back.

The insistence is gentle but relentless. There's no escape.

Jaxon swallows the familiar impulse—the urge to pull away, to retreat into cynicism—and steps forward until his chest nearly brushes the board.

A bucket of blue paint sits at his feet. He dips his other hand, the cold liquid seeping between his fingers. The chill bites at his skin, and for a moment, he stands suspended, feeling the weight of every doubt and every promise pressing down through his palm.

He raises his hand and presses it squarely against the center. The texture is gritty beneath his skin, heavy with the morning's dampness and dust.

In that moment, the world narrows to the weight of his palm imprint.

Then comes the chant—a hesitant murmur at first, barely more than Jaxon's name caught in the rustling air. Brick threads in, his voice gruff but steady, pulling the rest into rhythm.

"Jaxon... Jaxon..."

The call builds and grows louder, a chorus rising like a storm rolling in over damp fields.

His name bounces from mouth to mouth, echoing off the battered bleachers and settling into the crisp mist. A weight settles deep in Jaxon's chest, making it hard to draw a full breath. His eyes press closed against the chill, the chant crashing over him like relentless waves.

Usually, it would grind him down. But now? There's a thin thread of something else—quiet, almost fragile—that twists free.

He stands still beneath the rising chant, his shoulders trembling slightly, his breath shallow but his embrace widening. His hand, the one stamped on the board, tingles with cold, paint, and something heavier—acceptance.

The chant swells, reaching a jagged crescendo before dissolving into ragged laughter and heavy slaps on mud-caked shoulders.

The team leans into each other, a rough mosaic of painted palms and weathered grins. Brick catches Jaxon's eye across the gathered bodies and gives a slow nod—no words needed. Caleb exhales, long and deliberate, his shoulder brushing against Jaxon's. They breathe together, a shared moment that conveys more than any promise could.

Jaxon exhales, long and slow, the tension igniting in his chest like embers settling after a fire. Around him, bodies radiate warmth against the chill, voices and breath misting into the crisp morning air.

He stands framed—literally branded—by color and comradeship, their handprints a messy testament to the damage endured and the battles still to fight.

For a heartbeat, he lets the exhaustion roll over him, feeling the strange ease of standing among them not as a burden but as their chosen leader.

"Looks like you're stuck with us," Caleb jokes, nudging Jaxon's elbow with a grin that's pure sunshine after the storm.

"Don't get comfortable," Jaxon shoots back, his voice rough but lighter, his eyes scanning faces gleaming with paint and promise.

Eli smirks from the edge of the circle, folding his arms with a slow nod. "We'll keep you honest. No slipping back."

"That's the plan," Jaxon replies, his gaze harder now, braced for the road ahead.

The morning mist curls low, dew spilling over the grass like liquid silver beneath the bleachers. The board, chaotic and vivid, catches the pale light—every handprint a story, every smudge a vow. Around it, the team breathes, a slow ritual sealed in paint, trust, and dawn.

Jaxon straightens, shoulders steady, imprint pressed firm like a pact.

No more running.

Only forward.

Golden light spills over the horizon. The field's ragged edges ignite in a quiet blaze. Morning mist clings to the painted plywood board near the locker room entrance, catching the sun's first breath and wrapping it in a shimmering halo that feels almost sacred.

The wild mosaic of handprints—blue, red, green, gray—gleams in the soft light, each smudge carrying the faint smell of latex paint and nervous sweat. Raw. Chaotic. Electric. Every mark is a silent pledge pressed into wood by trembling fingers the night before.

Players lean into the warmth, their breath mingling with wet grass and drying paint. Caleb tucks the battered thermos deep into his jacket pocket, fingers tight around the worn cap. "Gotta call Grandma," he mutters, already turning toward the field's edge. "I hope she's up." His voice carries nervous optimism—the edge of a kid sneaking out after a midnight pact.

Brick lingers, his palms stained a lurid green. He flicks the lids off paint cans with practiced patience, moving with the steady deliberation of someone who knows his place. "I'll handle cleanup. No fuss." A hint of a grin breaks through the tension wrapped in his thick frame. His promise is a quiet anchor; he is the storm's steady eye.

DeShawn shuffles close to Eli, balancing the easy grin that usually masks his worries. "Man, check out these tiny handprints," he teases, elbowing Eli's side where the gray smudge sits—an awkward, imperfect stamp. "You sure you're not afraid to get dirty?" Eli just shrugs, folding his arms beneath the rising sun. "You're talking big now. Just don't get caught under pressure," he says, his voice low but edged with a grin that doesn't quite reach his eyes. They drift toward the locker room, light banter weaving through the morning chill.

At the far edge of the field, Emma steps forward. The golden haze parts around her deliberate posture—composed, measured. But something softer flickers beneath the professional mask: a wariness mixed with restrained hope. She pauses, her arms crossed loosely, as if weighing the warmth against the memories the light stirs. Her eyes scan the group—a healed distance between her and the chaos, but not quite a wall. Not yet.

Jaxon's cleats crack the softened earth. Mud sticks cold and stubborn in the seams. His palms remain tacky with drywall-blue paint, fingerprints smeared in streaks of refusal and hope. Every step toward Emma thrums with the sharp pulse of a heart too heavy to hide, anticipation winding tight in his ribs.

Her gaze meets his—not a reprimand, but a question honed by battles neither wants to relive today.

"I'm not here to argue," she says, her voice low, almost lost in the morning breeze. "I want to hear it. Really hear it. After practice."

Surprise flickers across Jaxon's face. The usual gruff guard loosens like cracked leather. His throat tightens. Words hover unspoken as he nods once—a gesture steeped in cautious relief.

"I'll be there," he replies. His voice is rough but steady, a promise and a challenge wrapped in a single breath.

She turns away then, her heels crunching softly over scattered gravel. She disappears slowly into the burnished light that gleams like a second chance.

Jaxon lingers, watching the long line of handprints shimmer—a riot of colors bleeding together, wild and imperfect, much like them all. The sun warms his back. For the first time that morning, his chest feels a little less like a cage.

He closes his eyes. His fingers trace the ghost of green paint—Brick's mark—and press his own beside it, sealing the fragile bond: brotherhood, hope.

For a long moment, Jaxon stands there, shoulders squared and heart exposed to the dawn. The field exhales around him, alive with possibility—a promise yet to be redeemed.d.

Second Chances Hurt

The chill of night settles over Redemption Valley's worn turf. The air cuts sharp enough to catch in the lungs, painting pale ghosts where breath curls upward beneath the harsh stadium lights. Emma stands near the fifty-yard line, fingers locked around her clipboard, the paper edges stiff under pressure. Behind her, the field stretches into shadow—cracked earth punching through worn grass.

Practice has dissolved into memory. The grunts, the slap of cleats, the whistle's sharp bark—all swallowed by stillness now. Emma scribbles her final note. The pen scratches quietly against the paper, a small anchor of order in the raw cold. Her coat pulls snug. Eucalyptus lingers from the training room, mingling with fresh-cut grass and sweat that still clings to the air—sharp, metallic, alive.

Footsteps cut through the silence. Steady. Deliberate.

Jaxon emerges from the shadowed tunnel. Tension weighs on every movement. His broad shoulders stiffen as his boots crunch on brittle grass and scattered leaves. A line of scars traces his jaw, tired hardness carved into bone. His leather jacket creaks softly as he stops a few yards short of her.

Emma straightens, pushing a curl of hair from her face. She squares her shoulders like a soldier readying for battle—no hesitation, no retreat. The clipboard becomes a shield, her knuckles pale where her fingers curl tight.

She had been bracing for this moment all day. Her hope and dread twisted together, threatening to reopen wounds she had spent years stitching closed.

Emma's pen stopped. The scrape of ink faded. She inhaled deeply, a breath heavy with resolve. Ready. No matter what came next.

Her lips parted, just for a flicker—then snapped shut, holding back words that might soften the edge.

Jaxon's jaw twitched. His eyes flicked down, then back up, catching the stubborn fire in hers. He nodded once—a taut gesture, tight with force—before shifting a hesitant step forward, muscles coiled beneath the cold light casting long shadows across the cracked field.

The step forward felt like exposing something fragile inside him. Years of armor stripped away in a single motion. His breath came shallow, his chest tight with the vulnerability he had spent so long hiding. One foot in front of the other. That's all it took to undo everything.

She watched him closely, gathering all the years of fractured memories and loaded silences into that one moment. The space between them crackled, charged with the weight of truths ready to spill.

"I'm here. No more running." His voice was rough and low—barely more than a thread in the stillness.

Emma exhales slowly. She meets his eyes fully. Nothing in her posture shifts. She is resolute, demanding honesty—not distractions or deflections.

Jaxon shifts his weight, his eyes narrowing as though weighing hard truths against fragile hope. Her presence pulls at some raw edge inside him, the quiet ache of regret settling beneath his skin and scars.

"No easy answers," he finally admits, his voice tight around the words, "but I'm done hiding."

The thin winter air brushes against their faces. Empty bleachers rustle behind them. Liniment and old leather hang in ghostly wisps.

Emma taps her clipboard once, a subtle signal—a line drawn between denial and confrontation. "Then start talking."

A pause stretches between them.

Jaxon nods, slower this time. The stadium lights blaze overhead, cold and unforgiving, spotlighting two figures anchored in the empty field—a pair caught between past errors and the fragile chance for something more.

His next step cracks the silence: deliberate, cautious. His boots crunch on the brittle turf, sending a sharp chill through the soles—like the weight of all he has carried settling, at last, between them.

Jaxon's footsteps crunch over the worn grass. He stops just shy of the bleachers. The empty stands loom behind him—silent witnesses in the night.

His chest tightened as he approached her. He had rehearsed this a hundred times, each version crumbling the moment he pictured her face. His hands flexed at his sides, then curled into fists that he forced open again.

The floodlights cast his shadow long and sharp across the field. When he spoke, his voice came out low and clipped, stripped of warmth. "Practice is looking better. The guys are moving faster and making reads quicker. Brick is pushing harder, and Caleb is starting to catch on. It feels like something might stick this time."

Emma's eyes flicked up from her clipboard, sharp and assessing. She caught the tightening around his mouth—the desperation lurking just beneath his words. Without missing a beat, she cut him off, her palms flattening hard against the clipboard. The slap of paper punctuated her next words like a gavel.

"Enough with the rehearsed lines, Jaxon." Her voice was calm and steel-threaded. "I'm not here for feel-good updates about the team. I want to know why you disappeared when it mattered. Not now. Back then. During my mom's sickness."

The question landed like a fist. Jaxon's jaw tightened, skin pulling taut. The stadium lights didn't just glare—they seemed to suck the heat from his skin, leaving the night sharper and biting. He cocked his head slightly, eyes narrowing as they locked with hers. Fierce. Unwavering.

Slowly, a nod parted from the tight set of his jaw. No excuses. No deflections.

Emma lowered her clipboard with a measured breath, shifting the weight from her hands to her sides. Her shoulders squared, carving a line of resolve against the chill crackling in the air. The hurt was there too, etched into the set of her jaw—this was the reckoning she had been waiting for, the moment he would finally have to answer for vanishing when she needed him most.

She let the silence stretch, unyielding. The unspoken demand hung between them, heavy as the cold air itself: *Speak now. No more hiding.*

His breath misted faintly in the night.

"Alright," Jaxon started, his voice rough, each word slow and deliberate. "I'll say it plain."

The grass beneath Jaxon's boots was uneven, scuffed from hours of practice. Crushed earth and sweat hung thick in the cold air.

He shifted his weight. The stadium lights hummed in the distance, casting sharp shadows that stretched long and thin across the worn field. His voice was low, rough as rusted wire—brittle one moment, barely holding together the next.

"I heard them. Every night." He breathed it out slowly, as though speaking faster might choke him. "Your calls. The ones you made when you thought no one was listening." He swallowed hard, his eyes flickering to the field. "I just stopped answering. I saw the messages light up my screen and hid from them. I turned my back because I didn't know how to face it."

His eyes lock onto the cracked, fading fifty-yard line, where ghosts of broken promises are etched deep in the peeling paint.

"Hospital visits? I didn't show," he says, his voice fracturing. "Not once. The funeral—I was there in everything but body." His fingers curl tightly, nails gouging into his palm. A tremor shudders through his hand, a small, involuntary betrayal of the guilt weighing him down.

"I wasn't there when you needed me."

The cold air swirls faintly around them, carrying the distant tick of traffic and the phantom of a whistle from somewhere unseen. Emma stands silent, her clipboard forgotten at her side, her eyes locked on him—sharp and impossible to look away from.

Jaxon's jaw clenches. When he speaks again, his voice is raw, stripped bare.

"I was frozen inside. Not worried—frozen. Terrified to walk into that storm because I didn't have my own shelter." He pauses, struggling for the words. "I thought if I just kept away, closed my eyes and ears, maybe it wouldn't sink in so deep. But it did. It buried me alive."

His shoulders tense, the tremor of vulnerability flickering in the harsh gleam of the lights.

"And shame," he exhales, the word like poison. "Shame was a brick wall I couldn't climb. You were carrying a world I couldn't touch, and I felt useless. Like a fraud. Like I owed you something I didn't have left to give."

His hands clench again, fists tight against the cold.

"I made up reasons to stay away. I told myself things to soften the blow: 'I was protecting myself.' 'I needed to get my head straight.' 'I didn't know how to help.'" His voice turns hollow. "But all those justifications? They were just failures—excuses wearing different masks."

His shoulders slump, tired and heavy, as if the past itself is dragging him down through the frost and mud. "You deserved better than silence. You deserved me showing up, laying down the fight instead of stepping aside."

He looks up then. His eyes are glassy but steady, meeting Emma's with an honesty that is raw and unmasked.

"Every day, I watched from a distance. I heard bits of stories. I caught the hospital smell in your voice. Those quiet sobs behind closed doors that you tried so hard to hide." His lips part as if to say more, but the words choke back.

A fragile silence settles between them, heavy as stone.

His chest rises and falls with a pained, ragged breath—the sound sharp against the night's chill. The confession hangs in the cold white blaze of the stadium lights, waiting to be caught or to fall. Jaxon's gaze drops again to the battered grass underfoot, his shadow bleeding long and thin, stretched by the harsh glow above.

The weight of all those empty nights lingers between them, a ghost neither can yet chase away.

Emma stands still, her jaw clenched tight, her breath shallow and brittle in the cold air. Her fingers curve rigidly around the clipboard's edge, her nails digging in just enough to crease the paper beneath. Each revelation from Jaxon's mouth weighs heavier in the night, folding into the empty hush lingering between them. Stadium lights slant across her face, catching the hard lines of tension etched around her mouth and eyes. No softness. Only quiet steel.

When Jaxon falls silent, the stillness fractures, like ice cracking beneath sudden weight.

Emma's shoulders shudder first, a subtle tremor masking the storm inside. Her voice, when it breaks free, is sharp lightning against the vast dark sky of the empty field.

"You left me." Her voice comes out tight, almost brittle—a whisper at first. "At my weakest, Jaxon. You were gone when I needed you most."

Her hands tighten, clutching the clipboard like a lifeline. One corner bends crazily beneath her fingers. "I spent nights curled up on those hard hospital chairs, my phone clenched so tightly I thought it might shatter, waiting for a message that never came, for a call you couldn't bring yourself to make."

Her gaze lashed to his, cold and accusing under the bright lights, daring him to meet the full weight of her hurt.

"And then the lies—telling my family you were busy, unreachable." Her jaw worked. "You don't know how humiliating that was: to have to cover for the one person who should have been there."

Jaxon's eyes flickered, tight and unyielding. Emma didn't soften. Anger threaded through her words now, raw and ragged, but trembling too—the fragile edge of vulnerability that had taken years to surface.

"I waited for you to show up, to come back." Her voice dropped lower, cutting through the night air like broken glass. "But I got nothing. No apologies. No explanations. Just silence."

The clipboard slipped from her fingers and thudded against the thick grass beside her.

"It didn't just hurt; it broke something inside me." Her breath caught. "It was another kind of betrayal because I believed in us, even when you stopped believing in yourself."

Her body convulsed in a silent shake, shoulders rocking as if trying to carry the weight of years all at once. She turned her face away, fingers trembling as they lifted to wipe at her cheeks. Hot, salt-heavy tears refused to fall, smudging the scattered notes instead. Her lips pressed thin, quivering, desperate to hold the flood behind the dam for just a moment longer.

The field held its breath. Artificial light washed over them, catching dust motes dancing like ghosts in the chilly night. Somewhere in the distance, a night guard's whistle cut through the quiet. The stadium fixtures hummed like a heartbeat—steady and relentless.

"Did you even care?" The question sliced through the cool air, less a demand now and more a crack in the armor.

Jaxon didn't answer immediately. His jaw worked, muscles twitching beneath taut skin as he fought the urge to retreat under the weight of her gaze. The silence felt too loud. Finally, he exhaled—low and ragged. A surrender laced with raw honesty.

"I cared." His voice came out rough, wrapped in something close to shame. "Maybe not the way I should have, but I cared."

He paused. His hands fumbled at the edge of his jacket, pulling at the fabric as if it might steady the tremble in his voice.

"I didn't deserve your grace, Emma. Not after what I did." He swallowed hard. "I watched from the sidelines—too scared and too selfish to step into your pain. I thought sparing you would protect you, but all I did was make it worse."

The memory crashed over him then—a specific night, weeks into her hospital stay. He had sat in his car in the parking lot, engine running, warming his hands on the steering wheel. He could see the lit windows of her floor. He had sat there for an hour, never going in.

Emma's lips parted, a strangled sound catching in her throat as the hot tide behind her eyes threatened to spill again. Her fingers fluttered uncertainly, trembling as she clutched the damp pages, ink bleeding with each new tear.

"You left me to fight alone." Her voice emerged thick with grief and fury intertwined, barely a whisper but fierce. "And that's the hurt I carry—the part you never touched. Not because you weren't there."

She looked at him then, truly looked at him. Her eyes were red-rimmed and defiant.

"Because you chose not to be."

Another shudder rattled through her frame. She hitched a shaky breath, peering out from behind a veil of lashes heavy with silent tears. The clipboard lay forgotten by her side, notes stamped with the imprint of heartbreak and anger.

Between them, the ground felt sacred and shattered all at once, lit harshly and cruelly by those unforgiving stadium lights. Each waited, breath fogging in the dark air, the ache between them as vast and silent as the empty stands that ringed the field.

Jaxon's eyes never left her, taut with regret and the fragile thread of hope tangled deep beneath the surface. On this hollow night, beneath the flickering blaze of broken dreams and quiet truths, the past and present collided—raw, unguarded, and demanding reckoning.

"Did you even care at all?" Emma's voice cut sharply through the cold night, like a blade finding its mark. Her clipboard crumpled slightly in her trembling hands, the paper rustling loudly in the heavy silence between them. "Or was it just easier to watch from some safe distance while I crumbled?"

Jaxon clenched his jaw, the hard line trembling for a beat. Then he exhaled—low, rough, weighted with years.

"I cared," he said, his voice raw. "God, I did. But you're right. I didn't deserve your grace. I never did."

The sky hung heavily above them, clouds swirling low and catching the glare of flickering stadium lights. Long shadows stretched across the worn grass where they stood, frozen in the ache of unspoken truths. Jaxon's fingers fumbled with the hem of his jacket, the leather stiff and cold beneath his rough touch, seeking something solid to hold onto. His eyes darted up to meet hers—desperate for something she wouldn't yet give.

Permission to cross the chasm between them.

"I watched," he confessed, his voice barely above a whisper but thunderous in the hollow emptiness of the field. "I watched you fight through it all. The calls you made in the middle of the night. The hospital halls were empty except for your shadow."

Emma had memorized those hallways: the particular squeak of the third door in the left wing, the smell of antiseptic that never quite masked something darker underneath. She had learned to walk those corridors in her sleep, her mother's name a prayer worn thin from repetition. The fluorescent lights had bleached the color from her skin, and somewhere between midnight and dawn on day forty-three, she had stopped expecting him to find her there.

"I read your texts," Jaxon continued, each word seeming to cost him. "Your pleas. And I—"

"You fled." Emma's voice snapped like ice cracking beneath weight. Her eyes blazed with the fire of every sleepless night and every lie she had told to cover for his absence. The clipboard rattled against her trembling palms as she clenched it tighter, the edges digging cold into her skin until the paper began to blur beneath her grip.

"But I was drowning," Jaxon said. His voice broke. "I was scared shitless. Ashamed of my weakness, my uselessness."

He swallowed hard, the words tasting bitter as old wounds peeled raw.

"I thought that if I got close, I'd drag you down too."

Jaxon had spent those months convincing himself he was being noble, that his absence was a kindness. But the truth was uglier—he had been terrified of watching her slip away and discovering he couldn't save her. He was terrified that his helplessness would become her burden. So he had chosen a different kind of drowning: the slow suffocation of shame, the weight of knowing she had needed him and he had chosen the easier path of running.

Emma's breath caught. Her shoulders jerked in uneven breaths, tears slipping past clenched lashes even as she fought to keep her voice steady. They streaked across the notes she clutched, smudging letters into watery ghosts.

"You left me alone in the dark, Jax," she whispered fiercely, her voice cracking like thin ice underfoot. "Alone with a pain that was supposed to be ours to bear together."

Her fingers trembled, threatening to drop the pages at her feet.

Jaxon stepped closer, but the distance remained—a canyon carved by years and countless silences.

"I thought I was protecting you," he rasped. "Instead, I just broke us both."

Her eyes flickered with agony and something fragile—hope, maybe. Or the desperate gasp of someone drowning but still reaching for a lifeline.

"How do we move past this?" she asked, her voice barely a breath on the cold wind. "When the damage feels so damn permanent?"

Jaxon shook his head slowly, his lips pressed tight, as if holding back might keep him from shattering entirely.

"I don't have the answers," he admitted, the simple truth laid bare like bone. "But I'll keep trying, for however long it takes."

A long silence stretched between them, thick with the scent of chilled earth and fading sweat. The distant whistle of a departing coach drifted across the empty field. Above them, the stadium lights hummed their steady, harsh song, casting their glow over cracked paint and weathered bleachers.

The night held its breath.

Two fractured spirits hovered on the edge of something both terrifying and necessary: a chance to heal or finally fall apart.

Emma breaks first. She turns her back sharply away from Jaxon. Her shoulders tremble with ragged breaths that come in uneven waves. The clipboard slips from her hands. Her fingers had clenched its edges until her nails grazed the paper's thin surface, trembling as if holding onto something ready to snap. Now it falls. Papers rustle against the dry grass as she stumbles, taking a few unsteady steps toward the sideline—as if physical distance might dull the ache knotted deep inside her chest. The sharp scent of sweat and earth clings to the air, mixing with the distant clatter of cleats and muffled whistles from the far end of practice, reminders of a world moving on without them.

Jaxon steps forward, tense. His fingers stretch out reflexively toward her, light catching on his knuckles. But uncertainty freezes him. The motion halts just inches short of contact. The heat of the stadium lights throws his shadow jagged and long across the field. Does he still have the right to reach for her? His hand falls slowly to his side. That unspoken question hangs heavy between them. The silence that follows is thick, punctuated only by the faint hum of the scoreboard and the occasional murmur from the distant field.

After what feels like an eternity, Emma turns. Her face glistens with tears—her eyes swollen and raw. Salt streaks run unnoticed down her cheeks. The brittle veneer of composure shatters. Vulnerability stands stark, exposed beneath the harsh white glare of the lights. Her voice cracks—brittle yet steady. It threads through the heavy quiet, fragile but fierce, cutting through the dark.

"Why did you never trust me? Why was I always left... cleaning up the mess you made? Why wouldn't you let me in on your pain?"

Jaxon's breath hitches—ragged and unsteady. His gaze dips, caught in the grip of his own guilt. When his voice finally emerges, it is hoarse, raw with years of buried regret. "I thought... sparing you was mercy. I didn't get it—I didn't see that what you needed was for me to be there. Hell, I was scared. Scared I'd break too." The confession trembles on his tongue, the weight of selfishness heavy in every syllable.

They linger in that space between them—bare and quiet. The world shrinks to the place where their shadows meet on the grass. Neither dares to speak again just yet. The brokenness they share settles like frost on everything beneath the relentless stadium glow—delicate and raw, but not altogether without hope.

Jaxon's voice cracks under the stadium lights. It is raw. The words tremble like a whispered prayer beating against the cold night air. "I'm sorry," he breathes through it. "I don't expect forgiveness—not now, maybe not ever. Saying sorry isn't enough. I know that. But you had to hear the truth before anything else."

He meets her gaze. His eyes are haunted yet desperate, the weight of confession hanging between them like mist curling off the worn grass.

Emma's shoulders straighten. She presses her palm over her face, wiping away tears that blur hot and fierce. When she looks up, her voice cuts clean. "I wanted you to fight. Fight for us."

Her eyes search his—sharp and unforgiving.

"The betrayal wasn't just in how you left." She swallows hard, her throat tight with years of swallowed words. "It was in how you judged me, as if I couldn't bear the truth, as if I wasn't strong enough to stand beside you when everything was falling apart."

He inhales sharply. The muscles along his jaw tighten, clench, and release.

"I've changed." His voice lowers, measured now. "Staying here—that's not something I'm entitled to; it's something I have to show every day." He clenches his fists and then unclenches them. The gesture shouts his uncertainty. "I need to earn your trust, not demand it."

Emma's hand rises again, trembling. She drags it across her cheek, clearing away heat and sorrow. Her nod is slow and deliberate, anchored in both caution and tentative hope.

"Old wounds don't vanish just because you've said sorry," her voice is soft but edged with steel. "They need time—a hell of a lot of time—and steady, consistent proof that you're different now. Confessions won't cut it."

A long breath escapes Jaxon, silent. The tension gripping his shoulders loosens just enough to reveal fragile relief. Emma mirrors that—her chest rising and falling. Two weary souls exhale shared burdens into the vastness of the silent field.

Between them, the night swallows the echoes of raw confession. Anger fades, and pain recedes. A tenuous calm settles—strange yet necessary.

"I don't expect you to forgive me tonight," Jaxon says after a pause. His voice is cracked but honest. "But I needed you to know where I've been and why I disappeared."

Emma swallows. When she speaks, her voice catches but holds steady. "I needed you to fight for us—not just here on the field, but when it mattered most." She looks away briefly, her fingers trembling at the edge of her clipboard. "When I was breaking, alone in those sterile hospital hallways, clutching my phone and hoping you'd show up."

The silence stretches.

"You weren't there." Her eyes return to his, raw and unforgiving. "You judged me, Jaxon, as if I were too weak to handle reality by your side."

His gaze drops. His fingers twist awkwardly at his belt loop, betraying his calm words. "I was terrified, ashamed, and selfish as hell." The words spill out in a rush, barely contained. "That fear kept me from being there. I thought I was sparing you more pain by stepping away. Instead, I left you hanging."

He breathes and struggles.

"I couldn't face the truth. But that wasn't fair to you. Not then. Not ever."

Emma's voice trembles, but she holds her ground. "The betrayal wasn't your absence." She wipes a tear that slips free, her ink smudging beneath damp fingers. "It was the silent judgment that said I couldn't bear the truth with you. So you ran."

Her voice cracks slightly.

"That cut deeper than any night alone could."

Jaxon steps closer under the gleam of the floodlights. He stops short, unsure. His hand hovers in the space between them before he pulls it back.

Emma breaks the silence. "Why didn't you trust me with your pain?"

The question hangs, fragile and exposed.

"Because I thought I was protecting you." His voice shakes, stripped bare. "I believed I was shielding you from a storm I was too scared to weather myself. I didn't realize that what you needed most wasn't protection."

He looks directly at her.

"It was my presence. My willingness to stand in the mess with you, not to disappear from it."

Her throat tightens. The honesty unravels the old armor she wasn't ready to abandon. She wipes her face again, and the gesture sows a quiet connection, bridging the chasm carved by silence.

A cool breeze stirs across the field, carrying the scent of damp grass and crushed earth. The stadium lights cast harsh shadows across their faces.

Jaxon breathes out. His voice is barely above a whisper but filled with raw resolve. "I'm sorry it took me so long to see that. I don't expect that I can fix this tonight, maybe not ever. But I'll spend every day trying."

He pauses.

"I'll show you through every decision, every word, every moment that I'm here, that I'm different."

Emma studies him. The cool night air wraps around them like a shield. Her nod is slow, deliberate, anchored in both caution and tentative hope.

"Words sounded hollow before," her voice is barely steady. "Empty promises replayed like a broken record. This will take more than apologies. It'll take time, consistency, and a willingness to face the ugly parts with me."

She looks down at her smudged clipboard, then back up at him.

"The real work starts tomorrow. And the day after. And the day after that."

For a moment, the world narrows. Two figures are framed beneath the vast sky, the stadium lights serving as their harsh, unlikely witness. Time seems to slow.

In the pause between breaths, they find a fragile accord. It is not easy, not whole, but it is real.

Neither rushes to break the quiet as the night folds around them. Instead, they share the steady cadence of acceptance—each exhale loosening the weight of what has been and what must come. A shared vulnerability, delicate yet fierce, settles softly like dew on the struggling grass beneath their feet.

The night air hums low and cool against their skin. Chalk dust and grass mix beneath the harsh stadium lights. Emma stands rigid near midfield, her breath forming fragile clouds that drift and vanish in the stillness.

The clipboard weighs heavily in her hands. Pages tremble as she folds her arms tightly across her chest—a wall she has built brick by brick from years of silence and waiting. Her chin rises, sharp and steady. Her hazel eyes fix on Jaxon, who stands yards away, shoulders squared but not quite guarded.

"I forgive you." Her voice breaks slightly, rough from holding back years of hurt. "But I don't trust you. Not yet."

The words hang between them, thick and real. Emma's arms remain folded tightly, muscles taut beneath the fabric. Her jaw tightens. Her eyes flicker briefly to the sidelines before locking back onto Jaxon. In that silence, something slower beats underneath—a faint, fragile hope she doesn't fully dare to claim yet.

Jaxon's gaze drops to his worn cleats digging into the uneven turf. His fists ball tightly, knuckles white. Relief crashes through him like a cold wave, tangled with a sharp stab of pain. A slow exhale trembles from his cracked lips. His voice emerges low and deliberate. "I'll earn it." He swallows hard. "However long it takes."

The words fall like a solemn vow, quiet but unwavering.

The field stretches between them—scorched and scarred by yesterday's mistakes—but in this moment, the distance narrows, bridged by something raw and honest. Neither speaks again. Empty bleachers hum softly. Cicadas chirp in the distance. The pause stretches and breathes.

Jaxon watches as Emma folds the clipboard neatly and then turns away.

Her footsteps press softly and deliberately into the patchy grass. Each step is hesitant yet certain. The night has cooled further, biting gently at the thin jacket slung over Jaxon's shoulders, but he doesn't move. Watching is all he can do.

Emma nears the edge of the field, where faded lines give way to cracked concrete and shadows that stretch toward the tunnel. The distant rustle of dry leaves skitters across the pavement. Before slipping into that murk, she pauses, her silhouette outlined by cold floodlights. Her expression is fragile—eyes searching, vulnerable, holding the question of what comes next without speaking it.

Then, with a tilt of her chin, she releases the weight of the past one small step at a time. She moves toward the lockers and the sparse glow of the hallway beyond.

Jaxon stays rooted beneath the glare of the stadium, fingers curling into fists at his sides, knuckles raw. The tension coiling in his chest unwinds just enough to fill that empty place with something new: resolve. He wonders if this fragile bridge could hold or if time would shatter it. The thought terrifies and anchors him equally. Distant thunder mutters softly over the valley, a dark accompaniment to what feels like the first breath of fresh air after a storm long overdue.

"I forgive you, but I don't trust you. Not yet."

Her voice still echoes—an unsteady promise carved into the night.

He doesn't answer aloud, but in the quiet swell of possibility, Jaxon knows this isn't the end. Not by a long shot.

The Rival Game

The bench creaked under Jaxon's weight. His fingers, nimble but cautious, peeled the edge of the athletic tape, wrapping it tighter around his ankle until the pressure felt just right—a fragile cradle against the lingering ache. His ankle pulsed with that familiar dull throb, the ghost of an old wound that had never fully let go. He had learned to live with it, the way one learns to live with doubt. Some days it whispered; other days it screamed.

He flicked his gaze up, catching snapshots of teammates scattered like ghosts through the cramped locker room—each lost in their own quiet ritual before the storm.

Brick limped through the door. The leather of his cleats cracked against the linoleum. His knee wavered for a fraction of a second before he slammed it hard against a dented locker, bracing himself with a grimace. The stubborn set of his jaw was carved by something deeper than pain: defiance. He pulled his pads over broad shoulders, each strap tightened with the knowledge that surrender wasn't an option tonight. Shadows clung to him, but he pushed forward anyway.

DeShawn sank onto the cold bench near the showers, cracking a joke that bounced off the concrete walls. His words tumbled out fast—a burst of warmth cutting through the tension—but damp palms clung to his knees, trembling beneath the bravado. The nervous energy clawing at him had nowhere to hide.

Caleb stood a few lockers down, earbuds securing him in his own world. His lips moved in silence, rehearsing routes and plays with precise rhythm, his eyes locked on the fluorescent-lit wall ahead. The geometry of the game was imprinted in his mind. Everything else fell away.

The door creaked. Coach Hale's voice cut through like a sharp blade—commanding attention without raising its volume.

Eli stretched near the threshold, each muscle unraveling beneath his damp jersey. His eyes never left the window, where thick clouds folded heavy and low into the night, swollen with rain. A growl of thunder rolled through the sky. The storm was coming. He tightened his jaw, understanding the weight of those darkening heavens.

Coach Marcus Hale strode to the center of the room. The rumble of the incoming storm underscored his words. His voice was stripped of flourish—raw and unyielding.

"We've fought through worse than a little rain and mud. This team—this family—we've built something no one believed in."

He had weathered worse himself: seasons that crumbled, teams that fractured. But he had learned that storms didn't break you if you knew how to stand. That was what he was here to teach them.

Silence pressed thick against those words, and Jaxon felt it like a physical weight settling squarely on his shoulders. No more hiding. No more running.

DeShawn broke the quiet, nudging Brick with a grin. "I guess rain is the only thing that hasn't beaten us yet, huh?"

Brick snorted—a muffled sound—and nodded, his eyes alight with fierce resolve.

Caleb stepped away from his locker, his earbuds slipping free. He rose to his feet, his face sharpening with renewed focus.

Jaxon tightened the last loop of tape as the team began to gather. The stale air smelled of sweat and old leather, sharp and alive, mingling with liniment from Emma's treatment kit nearby. He breathed it in; this smell meant something.

They lined up in a ragged formation, helmets pressed tight, visors lowered against the first drops spattering the floor. The roar swelled beyond the cracked locker room walls—a low tide of voices, hope, and desperation.

Jaxon met Eli's glance, a brief exchange under the flickering light. No words were needed—just the silent pact of men about to step into the storm together.

The locker room door swung open, and cold air rushed in—a sharp slap of wet, soaked grass and rain pelting down in curtains. The team jogged through, feet pounding the corridor, spilling out onto the slick field. Rain was immediate and relentless, turning the turf into patches of black mud and forcing players to grip their helmets harder.

Half-filled stands rumbled with cheers—hesitant but fierce—as bodies surged through the downpour. Jaxon's footsteps pressed steadily into the wet earth, each one echoing the rhythm of his heart: fast, steady, like an ancient drumbeat beneath a swelling storm.

Cold rain stung his face, seeping past the visor and mixing with the grit on his skin. His ankle hummed with dull anticipation—a reminder of battles past and the fight still to come.

The roar of the crowd swelled, a tidal wave of noise crashing across the wet stadium. The moment froze into sharp focus as Jaxon crossed the sideline, shoulders squared, jaw clenched, and eyes burning through the sheets of rain.

This is it.

###

The referee's whistle cracked through the steady drizzle—sharp and cold. It cut across the rumble of rain against the turf.

The rival team exploded off the line, a wave of aggression crashing into Redemption Valley's defense. Brick planted his feet on the wet turf. His knees buckled as a powerful shoulder slammed into him. A grunt slipped from his throat—low and guttural. The ache in his knee flared razor-sharp, but he stayed upright, teeth clenched, pushing back against the surge. Rain splashed off his broad shoulders, mixing with sweat. Mud slicked his cleats, and the world narrowed to the roar of bodies colliding.

Jaxon's voice cuts through the chaos as the offense forms a tight circle. Their breaths steam and spiral into the cold air, even as rain soaks through their jerseys and skin. He slaps the ball sharply against his palm, his eyes flicking over the lineup.

"Trips right, DeShawn, quick out. Caleb, stay sharp—eyes on me."

Caleb's glance darts too quickly. It flickers between Jaxon and the snapping ball. The center's hands are slick, and the snap spirals unevenly toward Jaxon. DeShawn takes off like a shot, his cleats slipping. He plants awkwardly on the slick grass and pushes forward, but the gain is stunted—one yard.

The crowd's murmur is swallowed by the rain, but the weight of the rough start presses on the team's shoulders like a hand pushing them deeper into the mud.

Along the line, rival players exchange words sharp enough to cut through the patter of rain. Eli's jaw tightens, and a flicker of heat ignites behind his eyes. When a rival leans in with another taunt,

Eli shoves hard, his chest rising. The motion is quick but burning with anger. A sharp whistle cuts through the downpour—a sideline warning. Eli swallows, turning away with his fists clenched. He steps back into position, his jaw tight.

On the next snap, Jaxon steps back into a rain-lashed pocket. Slick leather slips from his grasp. The ball squirms free—slanted and wild—hurtling past Caleb's outstretched hands. The rival corner's arms shoot up, his fingers scraping desperately as the ball skews wide, splattering onto the soggy turf.

"Damn it!" Jaxon growls, his knuckles white around the wet ball as he spins back toward the huddle.

The team pulls together near their forty-yard line, soaked to the bone. Mud spatters their knees and elbows. There is no warmth in the sloshing heaviness of their cleats, only cold adrenaline sparking beneath drenched skin.

A harsh wind pushes rain sideways, plastering jerseys against ribs and slicking hair flat.

Brick wipes mud from his eyes, his breath hitching. His voice is rough but steady. "We've got to shake that off. The play's not over."

Jaxon squares his shoulders against the cold, grinding a fist into his palm. The scoreboard glows distant and relentless—zeroes blinking back at them. Each missed opportunity carves deeper lines of pressure across his face. His ankle throbs faintly, a constant reminder of every past mistake piling up, every moment he has failed them before.

"Alright, listen—one thing at a time," Jaxon says, his voice low enough to carry the weight of command. "We control what's in front of us. One play. That's it."

DeShawn pulls at his jersey, slipping a grin through chattering teeth. "Yeah, yeah. One damn play. It's not like we haven't been saying this for weeks."

Caleb lowers his gaze. He swallows hard before meeting Jaxon's eyes. The dropped passes haunt him—each one a fresh failure layering atop the last. He nods. "We've got this."

Eli, shoulders rigid, digs his cleats into the muddy ground. His glance flickers toward the rain-darkened sky as if searching for a crack in the storm.

The mud soaks deeper into their clothes. Cold seeps beneath their skin. Every body shifts with restless energy.

"You see that?" A voice snaps near Caleb. "Your guy's got no grip tonight."

Caleb doesn't respond. He swallows the rising heat of embarrassment and doubt. The slick ball slips again and again in these conditions. The margin for error shrinks to a razor's edge.

"Keep your head, man!" DeShawn throws an arm around Caleb's shoulder, his voice rough but steady in the stinging rain. "We're rough out here. It's still ours to win."

Jaxon pulls his chin down, watching the scoreboard's cold glow. Every missed pass feels like a crack spreading through the fragile shell of the team's confidence. The wet chill wraps tight, pressing on their minds as much as their muscles.

Rain beads on the wire-rimmed glasses of the sideline staff. The half-full stands blur into streaks of color and sound—hoots, shouts, and the stomping of boots on metal bleachers.

Leather smacks against pads. Cleats skid on sodden grass. Lungs burn in crisp, rain-drenched air.

"We tighten up next round," Jaxon murmurs. "No more freebies."

A tense silence gathers before the snap.

"You think we'll make it out of this one?" Caleb whispers low, his eyes scanning the dripping bleachers.

"We have to," Jaxon replies, his voice barely audible over the downpour.

Slap. The ball presses into Jaxon's hand. The weight. The slickness. Both remind him of every gamble, every crack in his armor.

The quarter bell sounds, mingling with the throaty rumble of thunder. Players slip and skid, soaked and jittery. Lungs burn. Spirits remain stubborn.

Jaxon's jaw tightens as his gaze locks on the blinking scoreboard. Each error echoes. The weight of a hundred mistakes pushes down. But beneath it all, the faint pulse of resolve stirs—quiet, steady, and refusing to break.

"Let's go," he says, stepping toward the sideline. Rain spits freeze and fire across his face. The promise of the game still flickers wild and fierce beneath the storm.

Brick's heavy boots scrape against the slick turf as he limps toward the sideline, his breath ragged. The rain hammers down like a drumbeat on soaked canvas. His broad shoulder bumps the locker fence as he leans in, dark eyes flashing with grit beneath the dripping hood of his jersey. He raises a hand—sharp, final.

He's done.

Pain gnawed at his knee like fire beneath ice. But backing down wasn't an option—not when the team was fracturing like thin glass. Coach Hale's voice cut through the storm, gravelly and steady.

"You think you can give us one more series, Brick?"

Brick ground his teeth, his jaw clenched tight enough to crack bone. The rain traced rivulets down his face, mingling with sweat and mud. Fear flickered beneath his ribs—not of the pain, but of failing them—but he buried it deep. He spat a shard of defiance with a slow nod.

"Not sitting. Not. Tonight."

Back in the huddle, Jaxon caught Brick's grim nod and met his locked gaze. No words passed between them—just the weight of silent understanding, a baton handed off in the chaos.

Jaxon slid to the quarterback spot. His eyes traced the muddy field, the way dew and dirt clung to cleats, droplets trembling on jagged grass. He felt it then—the suffocating weight of holding this together. One mistake, and everything crumbled. DeShawn lined up beside him, nerves masked beneath a forced grin and the glint of stubborn hope.

"Shotgun formation," Jaxon muttered.

Then he pivoted, veering from the scripted play. Impulse. Desperation. The snap shuddered from his hands, slick and barely controlled. DeShawn took the ball—

A rival linebacker slammed into his ribs like a battering ram.

The breath left him in a gut-wrenching thud. The ball slipped free, a slick spheroid twisting in slow-motion chaos.

Time stretched. The fumble skittered over wet blades and drowning dust, raw and cruel. Hearts pounded audibly. The rain's roar swallowed everything.

Then DeShawn dove, arms outstretched. His soaked jersey clung to mud-caked skin as his fingers clamped desperately onto the rolling ball, pinning it to his chest like a lover's last embrace.

The sideline erupted—a strangled cheer swallowed instantly by the rain's roar—but raw relief bled through their soaked voices.

Boots stamped in driven rage, hurling mud mechanically as the players circled tighter. Their breath misted in sharp bursts of cold. The downpour thickened, stealing color from the world. The field turned into churned chocolate mud, each step a wrestle with an unyielding foe.

Rain's cold fingers clawed at faces. Hands and helmets gleamed, slick with wetness. Muscle and bone strained against the relentless gray wash.

Caleb stood alone, shoulders slumped beneath his drenched jersey, earbuds still anchored deep in his ears. His lips moved silently—whispers of routes and plays running through a private cinema in his mind.

A high, clean pass arced toward him. It should be routine. Easy.

The rival cornerback's eyes glittered with petty malice, baiting.

Caleb's hands fluttered, uncertain. The ball slipped like a ghost through his fingers and thudded hard against the soaked turf.

His breath caught, and his shoulders stiffened. Fingers twitched at his sides as the world crowded in—faces, voices, the rain's relentless percussion. Desperation flared, nerves snapping raw. He was sinking fast.

Jaxon's boot splashed toward him on the sideline. His rough hand pressed gently on Caleb's soaked shoulder. His voice dropped low, almost a whisper over the rain's roar—meant only for Caleb's ears. Jaxon needed this too; he needed the team to hold together just a little longer.

"You got this."

Caleb swallowed the lump in his throat, forcing the corners of his mouth into a stubborn, brittle smile. The wetness in his eyes didn't quite reach that smile, but it was there—fragile, unyielding.

Nearby, Eli crouched in shadow near the sideline, frustration twisting his lean frame like a coiled spring. His hands flashed urgent signals. The trick snap formed in his mind like a whispered promise.

Then he burst upfield in an explosion of motion—his shoulder smashing into a rival defender with crushing precision. The pathway opened. Jaxon, freed from the grasp of the rushing storm, scrambled forward, limping but alive with cold fire.

Every step is a battle. Every yard is won hard and ragged.

The drive stalled. Mud clung to him like a second skin.

Coach Hale's sharp bark cut through the fading roar of the crowd.

"Composure! Keep it together!"

The team broke from the huddle, stepping back into the relentless assault of rain and fatigue. Brick limped back toward the line, his gait uneven but unbowed—a sentinel bearing more than just his own pain. Each man wore his personal stakes like armor, rain dripping and plastering jerseys to bruised skin, faces set against the pounding storm.

The rain drove down harder. Each drop was a hammer striking the forge—the team welded tighter, tougher, damaged but undiminished beneath the storm's furious weight.

The rain blurred the edges of the stadium lights, droplets pelting the soaked faces of fans crowding the bleachers. Their shouts sliced through the wind, sharp against the low rumble of thunder and the soft splash of cleats on wet turf. Redemption Valley's defense scrambled. The rival offense ground forward like a slow-moving freight train, pounding the soaked ground with relentless momentum—a reminder of every resource they had that the Hawks didn't, every perfectly maintained field and state-of-the-art facility working in their favor. The running back burst through a shaky hole, muscles straining and boots slicing through the mud, crossing into the end zone as the scoreboard tilted further against the Hawks. A muddy splatter of cheers and groans filled the air while the cold rain washed over everything like a relentless tide.

Brick's leg buckled just before the pile-up. Pain flared sharply beneath his skin, familiar and biting. Double-teamed, he bore down, teeth clenched until his jaw ached. Blood throbbed warmth in his knee—but he wouldn't relent. Slamming into the opponent's ribs, he wrapped himself like iron bands around the runner, muscles tensing with raw determination. A guttural howl tore from his throat, sharp and ragged, as he dragged the man down, agonizingly short of the goal line. Mud splashed against his soaked jersey, rain stinging his eyes, but the fire in his stance didn't waver—a fortress of resilience against the storm.

Jaxon limped toward the sideline. Each step was a battle against the throb in his taped ankle. Emma waited beneath the skeletal shelter of the worn bench, rain tracing rivulets down her face, damp strands of hair plastered to her temples. Her hands moved deftly, pulling fresh tape from the slick roll, fingers warming the sticky strip before pressing it tightly around his swollen joint. The sharp smell of liniment blended with the earthy scent of wet grass and leather. Their eyes locked across the downpour. Emma's fingers pressed the tape tighter; Jaxon's breath hitched, a tremor running through his frame. Neither spoke, but the weight between them hung heavy—unspoken, steady, a fragile truce forged in rain and pain. They were both fighting to keep him on this field, and they both knew how thin that line had become.

He straightened, nodded once, and turned back into the tempest. The razor's edge between pushing through and breaking was something he lived with now—one twisted ankle away from being benched, one bad throw away from losing the team's faith. He wiped rain from his face, water pushing past his collared jersey and pooling in the crease of his brow. Cold air filled his lungs in ragged gulps. He called the play—not the safe, predictable throw, but a daring arc downfield; the kind that could change the game or shatter his confidence on the muddy grass. Dropping back, he navigated the pocket. Water stung his eyes as rain lashed like needles against his skin. The crowd's roar was muffled by the storm, but adrenaline surged sharp and bright against the chill.

Third down. The world narrowed to the seam of the rain-smeared field and the target rushing into view. Jaxon released the ball with a stiff wrist, threading a tight needle through drops of water and grasping defenders. The leather spiraled with precision, cutting through cold air and pooling water to land squarely in Caleb's outstretched hands. Caleb's body twisted midair, drenched fingers clawing at the impossible catch. He crashed hard into the soaked mud with a victorious grunt. The crowd exploded—a wash of cheers that pierced the downpour—and somewhere deep in the team's collective spirit, a spark flared bright.

DeShawn took the handoff on the next snap. His boots slipped on the slippery grass as he shimmied left, evading a grasp that threatened to topple him. For a heart-stopping second, the wet ball slipped loose, sliding like a slick shell across the field. DeShawn lunged, his arms wrapping tightly around it. The leather pinned against his chest as he clutched it fiercely, his teeth gritting against the sting of rain and mud thrown in his face. He shoved forward, muscles coiling with effort, climbing into the red zone as the rain intensified, soaking through every layer and blending sweat with the storm.

A shadow of pressure pushed against the line, and Eli's sharp eyes caught the shift. Calling a quick audible, he snapped his helmet on and gestured, his voice cutting across the tumult. The play shifted like a living thing. Jaxon pivoted on his heel, slipping a tackle by inches, his body bending with calculated grace in the chaos. His arm arced, releasing a sharp, short pass to DeShawn just before the whistle blew. DeShawn caught it, turned, and charged ahead, a flash of defiance burning in his soaked, mud-splattered face.

"Not here to fold now," Eli shouted, his voice steady beneath the storm. "We finish this."

Brick gritted his teeth, dragging the pain from his trembling leg back into the fight. "Every yard counts. Every damn yard. No exceptions."

Jaxon wiped a line of rain from his eyes, his gaze locked forward. "Let's finish what we started. No backing down."

The third quarter wound down with Redemption Valley perched deep in enemy territory. Boots were heavy with mud. Jerseys clung tightly and were streaked with earthy grime. Hearts pounded. Breaths billowed in ragged clouds. Bruises bloomed beneath soaked fabric. The storm showed no mercy, but something new hummed beneath the mud and rain: grit. Fight. The unspoken promise that they weren't beaten yet. The catch that sparked hope. The grit that kept Brick standing. They carried each other forward, battered but alive.

###

Rain slammed down in sheets. Each drop hit like cold needles against skin and slick fabric. The fourth quarter began under a curtain of gray, the stadium lights refracting off rivulets running down helmets and sticky mud clinging to jerseys. Visibility faltered as rivers of water carved deep trails through the churned earth. Breath fumes rose and disappeared swiftly into the damp air—tangled with the sharp scent of wet grass and sweat.

Brick's boots ground through the muck. He pulled his teammates close, his voice ragged but fierce against the storm's roar. "This ends with us. All of us."

His chest heaved. Each breath was a rough rasp. Pain spiked beneath his skin—his knee swollen, protesting every movement—but the fire in his gaze refused to dim. Years of fighting through family hardship and past injuries that should have broken him all fueled this stand. This is survival. This is pride.

He barrels forward moments later, his massive arms wrapping around a charging running back. The crunch of bodies in the mud echoes like thunder. His teeth are gritted tight as he drags the opponent down just shy of the goal line. His grin—cracked and stubborn—flashes through the rain-drenched haze, a defiant promise forged in agony.

The whistle blares.

The offense assembles, dripping and raw. Jaxon shifts his weight. Cold water snakes beneath his tape, biting sharply. His ankle flares, a sharp, familiar fire racing through the joint. He grits his teeth and shifts his weight forward anyway. A low hit cracks through the rush. Searing agony shoots up his leg like wildfire. He staggers, clutching his side for balance.

Coach Hale's sharp eyes catch the falter. He flicks a nod toward Eli. Substitute ready.

Jaxon shakes off the signal with a swipe, grimacing but resolute. Limping back into the huddle, his voice cuts through the storm's symphony. "They need us."

Eli's gaze flickers sideways. His jaw tightens. "You sure? You look like hell out there."

"I'm fine." Jaxon's glare cuts through the rain. "They need us."

Eli's eyes darken, shoulders tense beneath soaked fabric. But he nods once, slow and steady. "We ride this out together."

The team knows the weight each step carries. Jaxon's leg bears battle scars far older than this game—years of wear, emotional ghosts beneath the physical pain. Past mistakes. Past betrayals. Each injury is a reminder. The lineup forms, a broken but unbowed unit, muscles coiled for the drive ahead.

The ball snaps.

DeShawn charges through the trembling muck. His legs plow through the thick sludge. His lungs burn with effort—and pain. He forces his way forward, yard by yard. His chain inches closer. His breath is steady but ragged. The crowd's muted roar seeps through the rain, a distant pulse against the night's madness.

Jaxon retreats into the pocket. Rain stings his face. His muscles scream with each movement. The pass rush closes in like a wave, crashing down heavy and relentless. He pivots and spots Caleb darting through the storm, his gloves slick with rain and mud. Time fractures.

Caleb launches upward—a desperate, soaring figure cleaving through the storm—and miraculously clutches the ball just as a defender crashes down. Mud and water explode around them. The crowd surges, and a wild flood of sound breaks the tension momentarily.

Chaos erupts. A blitz barrels in on third down. Eli's sharp eyes lock onto the incoming danger. Without hesitation, he lunges forward, throwing his weight into the defender's path. The hit pulses through him—a sledgehammer through bone and muscle—but it buys Jaxon the split second he needs. Limping and with his teeth clenched, Jaxon slips from the collapsing wall of bodies, shoving forward despite the ache that threatens to buckle him.

The huddle breaks with storm-born urgency. Jaxon commands the play. Risky. Reckless. But it's the only shot.

Each planted step feels like a fracture. Every inch is made of iron will. He coils, releases, and the spiraling ball arcs through the rain, piercing the gloom with a promise. Caleb, soaked to the bone, meets it with bent knees and outstretched arms, dragging heavy feet across the sodden end zone line. Mud clings like battle scars. The touchdown blares into the storm's fury.

The kicker steps forward, a small figure against the vast wetness and whipping wind. Twilight lashes his face as rain mixes with grit. He plants, swings, and sends the ball rising, spinning true over the struggle beneath. The ball thuds through the uprights with a crisp, perfect note. The scoreboard clicks: a tie. Time lingers in the wet, charged air.

Jaxon's breath forks in the cold air. Every muscle trembles with exhaustion and pain. The world narrows to slick mud and pounding heartbeats. He folds to his knees, soaked and shivering. The storm batters but cannot break something old and fierce inside.

Hands grip his shoulders—calloused hands, steady pressure. The unspoken message: *we're here.* Teammates close in, forming a tight circle. He's pulled upright into their battered but unbroken embrace. The rain taps relentlessly on helmets, on turf, on bare skin.

The game isn't over. Not yet.

Eli's voice cuts through the downpour, rough but edged with concern. "Jax, you gotta sit this one out."

"I said no." Pain bites through Jaxon's words. "They need us. All of us. Are you ready for this?"

Eli's eyes flicker away, then back. His voice drops. "We ride this out together."

Jaxon nods. Pride and raw hope flicker beneath the grime and the storm's black embrace. This night isn't just about football anymore; it's about blood, grit, and bone-deep heart—something no mud or rain could wash away.

Lightning fractures the sky. A jagged crack illuminates the mud-smeared faces gathered beneath the stadium lights. Wet grass gleams under the pounding rain—slick and unyielding. Mud clings to jerseys, spills over cleats, and streaks skin like war paint. Each mark tells the story of a fight hard-fought. The referee's arm slices up-ward—overtime. The crowd erupts, a single rising roar that pulses through the soaked air and rattles inside Jaxon's ribs.

The players cluster tightly in the center of the field, breath carving small clouds in the cold night. The huddle's circle shrinks, cramped with bodies, sweat, and urgency. Jaxon slips into the center, his voice rough and cracked from hours of shouting commands. Pain radiates through his ankle, sharp and insistent, but he pushes it down—letting it sharpen his focus instead. Doubt flickers at the edges of his mind. He swallows it whole.

"No one's here alone," he rasped, catching each man's eye. "No one."

A low chorus rose from the circle—a thread of nods and gruff murmurs, pitch-worn by cold and mud. Breath billowed in puffs as voices held firm, steady against the storm's chill.

Brick flexed his knee, his face tight as steel. "We finish this together. No excuses." His voice cracked but held firm as iron.

DeShawn winced, clutching his ribs as if to quiet the ache. "Can't let this slip," he muttered, his voice rough but resolute.

Caleb's chest rose in sharp heaves, adrenaline and fear mingling bitterly on his tongue. "We've worked too damn hard to blow it here."

Eli stood rigid, then grinned—a quiet fire beneath years of skepticism. "Let's seal it."

The huddle broke as one. Helmets rose, serving as armor against the rain slicing into their skin. They shuffled forward, their bodies slick with muddy water, blades of grass sticking to clenched fists. The turf drank the storm, spongy now—every step splashing in pooling darkness. Rain hammered against helmets with a steady drum; mud sucked greedily at cleats as players shifted their weight. The sharp sting of cold wind mixed with musky sweat and liniment.

The stadium lights glared off wet plastic and shining helmets as the team lined up, shadows stretched and blurred by falling sheets of rain. The crowd—a sea of umbrellas and drenched cheers—rose as one, a wild, undeterred beast holding its breath. Wet earth and adrenaline hung thick in the air, mingling with distant echoes of lightning and the sharp zing of cold.

On the sideline, Emma stood alone, her fingers numbed by the cold, damp strands of hair plastered to her forehead. The steady drum of rain masked the distant thunder rolling through the valley. Her concern for the team twisted tightly in her chest, sharp and personal. Fear flickered for Jaxon—what he carried and what it might cost. She folded it down and locked it away. Her gaze burned through the mist to the huddle, her breath catching as their communal heartbeat rose. A flicker passed between her and Jaxon—words unspoken, electric and raw, charged by proximity and the storm's fury.

Jaxon's gaze flicked to the swirling clouds overhead and then squared on the field ahead. His ankle throbbed beneath the aching tape, dull but insistent, tying him to the moment with a fierce pulse. His fists tightened, knuckles whitening beneath his gloves. The noise surged around him—mud, sweat, thunder—but inside, something hardened steadily.

The referee lifted his arm higher, muscles taut in the cold. The silver whistle cracked sharply, breaking the storm's rhythm. The world narrowed to a pinpoint of shared breath and unspoken promises.

Everything hung on what came next.

The Last Yard

The rain still whispered its final taps against the stadium lights, slanting through the mist like cold fingers reaching for the field. Jaxon's cleats met the soaked turf with a tired squeak—slick, unforgiving. Each step sent a sharp pulse of ache up his left ankle, a stubborn, throbbing reminder of hits that had kept piling up through the night. Mud clung to his soles, slick ribbons pulling loose as he stomped toward midfield. The weight of everything tangled in his muscles, dragging at each stride. This ankle had held him back before; tonight, it couldn't.

Above him, the stands were packed—faces blurred, streaked with glinting rain and the stadium's glow. Shadows rippled through flashing cameras and flickering phones, eyes heavy with hope and doubt.

A tension so thick pressed into Jaxon's chest like iron bands. The crowd's hum swelled, raw and expectant, rising around the floodlights' cold ring. His ribs tightened, and his breath caught in the damp air. Overtime clawed at the edges of every breath, every muscle waiting for that impossible line between triumph and collapse.

Jaxon's gaze sliced through the chaos: worn jerseys soaked through, heads tilted forward, voices swallowed in the roar. Familiar faces, strangers, foes—all caught in the same suspended beat. Time contracted, and his mind sharpened. This one drive pulled at every fiber inside him; this moment cracked open all their fragile dreams.

He dropped into the huddle, the tight circle of bodies pressing close, breaths steaming in the humid night air. His heartbeat drowned out the rain and cheers. Thud. Thud. Thud. A war drum pounding with urgency, pushing past his control. The mud seeped cold through his socks, the grit beneath burning in contrast to the slick wetness on his skin.

Around him, the team locked eyes—roughened, battle-worn, every man carrying his own cracked hope and desperate will. Jaxon sensed the brittle thread holding them together, taut and trembling, stretched by every fumble, every loss, and every setback this season. This drive couldn't falter. It had to end with a touchdown. Anything less, and everything fracturing inside him—the team, his last chance, his own battered pride—would crumble.

He planted his cleats firmly into the softened grass, his boots sinking slightly in the mud as his ankles protested. The huddle tightened. Helmets bumped softly. The warmth of sweat and shared determination mixed in the heavy air. Jaxon drew it all in—the smell of damp earth, the sharp sting of liniment from last-minute treatment, and the faint metallic tang of something older, deeper underneath it all.

Exhaling slowly, his breath scattered in quick, white wisps, vanishing into the rain-streaked night. His voice broke the suspended silence with gravel and steel as he called the play—a sentence carved from countless drills, battles, regrets, and grudging hope. The words cut through the tension. Solid. Sharp. A beacon in the storm.

"This is it," he said, not just to the team but to himself, steadying the wild storm in his chest. "Make it count."

"Are you really sure about this one, Jax?" Eli's voice slipped through, cautious beneath the rain. "Caleb's route is tight—and that ball is slick."

"It's the only shot we've got. Trust it. Trust him." Jaxon's eyes narrowed against the stinging drops sliding down his face.

Brick's jaw tightened beneath his helmet. "It's going to rain fire. Nobody gets through this time."

The circle tightened. The team leaned in, lungs burning with cold and fire, ready to wrest victory from the slick, unforgiving turf. Jaxon's foot pressed deeper, digging into the mud like an anchor, grounding him in this sliver of chaos. The moment stretched taut—one play, one chance, a heartbeat away from redemption or ruin.

"Let's finish this," he said, his voice raw but unwavering.

The huddle broke. Feet splashed through puddles as they surged forward. The cold rain met him like a challenge. The air crackled with the sharp promise of something larger than all of them, forging strength from the storm.

He could feel it now: the weight, the urgency, the unspoken pact between every player circling him, riding this razor's edge. The crowd's tension wrapped tighter, ready to snap or roar.

Jaxon steadied the ball in his hands—slick and heavy—and planted his feet, ready to lead the final charge beyond the rain, beyond the past, beyond every shadow drawn tonight beneath these relentless lights.

Coach Marcus Hale's cleats scraped sharply against the soaked turf as he strode onto the sideline, the rain still hanging in the misty air like a whisper clinging to muscle and cloth. His eyes locked onto Jaxon near the fifty-yard line, past the edge where the mud blended into lighter grass, slick and bruised from the game. Without a word, he cut through the hum of the stadium—fans shouting, the steady drip from helmets, the odd groan or grunt—and pulled Jaxon aside.

The coach's voice dropped low, gravelly but steady beneath the overhead glow of floodlights smeared by rain. "It's a hairy play," Marcus said, fingers curling into a tight fist at his side. His breath clouded in the chilly air, sharp and thin. "Caleb can hit the window. But only if you trust his split-second timing on that slant through the middle. It's tight." He paused, his eyes hardening. "Our best shot."

Jaxon watched Marcus outline the play with quick hand motions—a slash across the middle, a darting break, a split-second decision that could shatter this stale deadlock or bury them deeper. The ball's weight pressed cold and slick against his fingers, the leather damp enough to slip but familiar all the same. His leg throbbed, a dull drumbeat beneath his knee, seconds after that brutal hit, but he clenched his jaw and matched the coach's intensity.

The timing had haunted Caleb all season—routes half a step too late, receivers expecting the ball elsewhere. But last week in practice, something shifted. Jaxon had felt it in the precision of the breaks, the way Caleb's body language screamed readiness. If anyone could thread this needle, it was him. That flicker of certainty steadied something in Jaxon's chest.

"For Caleb, huh?" Jaxon's voice is rough, barely breaking past the roar rising from the stands.

Marcus's eyes bore into Jaxon's for a long beat. The coach's jaw tightened; the faintest twitch at the corner of his mouth hinted at the stakes they both carried. His hand settled heavily on Jaxon's shoulder, a silent plea and a weight neither would speak aloud. Legacy. The future. The last burning chance to claw back something worth fighting for.

This program hadn't seen a winning season in three years. With Jaxon's scandal hanging over the town like storm clouds, tonight felt like the final crossroads—the moment that would define not just their season, but what they were made of underneath.

Jaxon swallowed, the taste of rain mixing with grit at the back of his throat. Doubt clawed at the edges, but he pushed it down deep, digging through muscle memory and years of broken dreams to find the flicker of stubborn fire still twisting inside him. Slowly, he nodded back.

"Alright," he says, his voice low but certain. "We run it. Tight window. I'll trust Caleb's break."

Marcus's hand leaves his shoulder. "Good." His eyes are steely. "We're counting on that. No second chances tonight."

Jaxon squares his shoulders, the cold mud squelching beneath his cleats, the lights flickering with the storm's dying pulse. He turns back toward the team, who are already shifting toward the fifty-yard line, gathered in that tight huddle like soldiers bracing for a final charge. The sounds of the crowd fade into the rain tapping softly but insistently on helmets, pads, and grass.

He steps back into the circle, the pressure settling around him like thick fog—every eye fixed, every breath measured. Inside, his heartbeat drums the rhythm of focus, a steady cadence that drowns out pain and fear. The ball finds its home in his hands once more, and something hardens inside him: resolve tempered like steel in the storm's cold fire.

"Caleb's route—slant middle. Quick break, sharp timing," Jaxon murmurs, his voice still hoarse but firm. "We've got one shot. You trust me, I trust you."

The team breathes in unison beneath the glow of those snowy-white floodlights, the rain blurring edges into shimmering halos. The field lies before them—raw, unforgiving, the very heart of redemption bleeding through every soaked blade of grass.

Jaxon's gaze flickers to Caleb; the wide receiver's eyes are sharp and focused, a calm pulsing beneath nervous fingers tightening gloves. It's a quiet affirmation in a storm of doubt.

Then Jaxon draws a breath, the cold air sharp against his lungs, and his voice slices through the turbulence: "Let's make it count."

The rain hasn't stopped—it hisses off helmets and streaks down faces trapped under slick visors. Jaxon can taste the damp sharpness in the air. The turf beneath his cleats is soft and slick as mud, threatening to swallow his boots whole with every planted step. His throat rasps with each breath—hoarse but steady—cutting through the chorus of rattling pads and ragged pants.

"Alright," he says, his voice low but firm. A pause. "We're running slant-through. Caleb—eyes sharp. You've got this."

The words hit Caleb like a beacon. Jaxon has noticed it before—how Caleb's self-doubt can creep in during moments like these, how he second-guesses his hands when pressure mounts. But now, under Jaxon's steady gaze, something locks behind those jittery fingers twitching inside wet gloves.

Caleb meets Jaxon's gaze. His shoulders stiffen before a slow nod. His fingers twitch in the damp leather, the jitters clawing at his calm. Swallowed confidence bubbles to the surface like a storm surge. The weight of the moment settles into his shoulders—tight but unyielding.

In this circle under the bruised sky, everything boils down to trust forged through endless sweat and pain.

Brick's jaw clenches beneath his helmet. His voice cuts through—just a growl under the roar of the crowd and the rain drumming against the field. "Nobody gets through." Even in the drizzle slicking everything and clinging to his eyelashes, his fire burns hot. His fists curl tightly at his sides, muscles coiled. He'll throw himself against whatever walls the defense sends. Double up. Guard that slant route like it's the last line of defense for more than just a game.

Eli leans in from the edge of the circle, his eyes sharp as a hawk catching a shimmer of movement just beyond the huddle. His fingers sketch subtle commands through the damp air—nods, taps, shifts in stance—directing blockers like a conductor managing chaos. The glint in his gaze holds calculation and warning, threading precision into the protective web they'll weave around Jaxon. His voice remains buried. This quiet language suffices.

DeShawn hobbles into position. Pain draws through his step, but iron lines his jaw. He swallows a grimace and buries it deep—the kind that colors his face a shade harder than he lets on. His eyes flash a sharp, silent promise: this pain won't write the story tonight. His fingers flex around the ball, dusted with dirt and rain. Steady enough to run the first play. Keep the gears turning. Keep the momentum alive.

Jaxon tightens his grip on the ball. The leather's cool slickness seeps into his palm, soaking up the tension like a sponge. Around him, breaths gather—ragged exhales and sharp intakes blending with the wet slap of cleats shuffling on gravel and grass. The huddle narrows. The world beyond the circle shrinks to a blur of mist and distant shouts.

An unspoken pulse thrums in those few seconds. Countless games fold into one moment. Every heartbreak. Every blistered hand. Every moment clawed back from the edge.

A steady burn in his gut calls up the fight buried deep beneath the cynicism.

He locks eyes with Caleb one last time. No cracks. No second-guessing.

"We take that yard. We take the damn game. Together."

The circle tightens. A breath is held before the storm breaks.

Jaxon steps back. The world snaps open again—a flood of noise, rain, and cold biting at exposed skin. Beneath it all, a steadiness anchors him. A resolve sharp as the cut of a knife in his chest.

Feet pound. Hands throw up signals. Jaxon Rees, bruised, battered, and determined, charges into the waiting darkness of the field.

Mud clings to Jaxon's cleats as he crouches low, the sodden turf slick beneath the weight of the cold rain. The ball, swollen with moisture and slick like wet leather, presses cool and unforgiving into his palms, the faint squeeze of soaked laces rough under his fingertips. Stadium lights flicker, casting shards of silver across the glistening field. Raindrops hammer the pitch—sharp as footsteps in a cavern. At his side, DeShawn shifts his weight, jaw clenched so hard that his jaw muscles twitch, each step swallowing the ache in his stiffening leg like a simmering vow he wouldn't break. Jaxon's breath hitches in the damp air.

He snaps the ball to DeShawn, who plants his cleats firmly, muscles coiling like springs. Brick surges forward—a wall of raw power driving two defenders back with punishing force. The line wrinkles and folds around Jaxon. Pockets flicker like mirages. Defenders snap close until Brick's shove holds firm. DeShawn charges, legs thundering through mud and muscle, carving forward three hard-won yards before the defense swarms too late.

Rain lashes at Jaxon's face. He resets under center, the stadium's roar a distant swell, punctuated by sharp whistles and the slap of cleats. He catches the tight end's route—a quick out breaking clean through the thunder. With a sharp, low throw, the ball arcs like a silver comet caught in soaked fingers. The catch draws a brief exhale from the crowd. The clock spins down, and the offense huddles tight again beneath the pulsing floodlights. The ticking clock isn't just time slipping away; it's the weight of every missed chance crashing down, reminding him that this drive is more than just the game.

Inside the pocket, Jaxon leans into the cold sting of raindrops, tuning out the squall of wet leather and padded breaths. DeShawn's hands close around the ball, plum-smudged and heavy with soaked grit, slipping just a moment before he pins it tight to his chest. The running back dives forward, crunching into the mud, an inch gained through clenched teeth and sheer will. Another push. Another breath. The drive is alive, heartbeat pounding beneath the rain.

They line up again. Midfield. Fourth down. The weight of the moment nestles deep in Jaxon's chest, twisting tight. Across the line, Caleb flexes his fingers in gloved hands, a tremor beneath steel resolve. Jaxon catches the slight nod Caleb gives—barely there, a whisper of trust amid the rising storm. The crowd's roar folds into rain and anticipation, threads knotting the night into a taut wire.

Brick's shoulders square beneath his helmet. Eli's eyes flicker, calculating protections and reading the dance of blitzers and stallers on the opposing line. DeShawn sets his shoulders, the limp faint beneath a mask of determination. Jaxon senses it all—the fragile structure of men and moments compressed into this single, looming play.

Fresh mud clings to shoulders and helmets, seeping cold into soaked skin, a reminder that this isn't just sport; it is grit and endurance battling the elements and each other. The offensive line tightens, a living wall ready to meet the chaos creeping forward like hungry shadows. Dripping rain scours faces. Cool hands grip leather slick with memory and hope. Every breath drawn, every taut muscle, and every restless shuffle holds the suspended silence before the storm breaks once more.

The snap cracks through the night like a pistol shot. Brick detonates off the line, a vanguard cannonball barreling into two defenders. His arms crash into their chests with the weight of iron, driving them backward and cracking open a jagged lane right through the center. Jaxon's eyes lock on the gap that widens, the brief promise of red turf swallowed by mud and rain. His breath mists in the cold air, heartbeat hammering against slick ribs.

Behind Brick, Eli's instincts flare—a blitz coming from the blind side, a shadow lunging through the storm. Without hesitation, Eli lowers his leverage and dives, his arms shooting out like a surprise dagger. His shoulder crashes into the attacker's knees—wet flesh and bone meeting with a sickening thud, muffled only by the rain pelting the turf. His breath hitches, every nerve straining to maintain balance, the sting of sacrifice sparking through his arm. But the sacrifice grants Jaxon a precious heartbeat more in the pocket. Eli's body sags under the impact, muscles screaming with the cost of his choice, knowing the pain would come later—knowing he doesn't care.

DeShawn's limp holds tight beneath the surface, like a secret knot in his gait. His jaw clenches, eyes narrowing as he steadies his grip, refusing to let the pain betray him. He darts as if to take the handoff, a phantom rush that pulls the linebackers forward like ships drawn to a mirage, their attention snapping to the fake. The defenders bite, east coast sweat mixing with cold rain, leaning into the ghost of a run. Meanwhile, Caleb crouches deeper, muscles coiled like springs waiting to launch on a slant route—his silent, desperate chance slipping through the night.

Jaxon feels the ghost of last season's injury. White-hot shards shoot beneath skin so raw it burns. Still, he plants his foot like a stake in this mud-soaked battlefield. The motion doesn't come easily—it is carved from muscle memory and stubborn will, driven by a heart desperate not to fail again. His arm whips forward in a tight arc, fingers releasing the wet ball with a spin that cleaves through the rain's hiss. His hand flicks at a slight angle, the slick leather thudding against his palm and fingertips, an uneven farewell.

The ball cuts across the darkened field. Caleb explodes off the line, a streak of raw tenacity threading through a shroud of mud and rain. His fingertips stretch wide, desperate, claws extended for salvation, even as a defender closes in fast, breath fogging in the cold. The world tilts in that moment—the collision of hope and doubt, inches and seconds, breath and battle.

Without warning, a brutal fist crashes into Jaxon's ribs. The air whooshes out of him—a staccato slam that folds him backward like a rag doll. The earth meets him hard. Slick turf, cold and unyielding, climbs his shirt, mud painting his cheek with grit and rain. His vision blurs, the flight of the football snatched from sight as his lungs rebel in sharp, aching gasps for breath. Silence cracks across the shattered noise—a singular, suspended instant stretching before the eruption.

From the wet earth below, the referee's whistle slices through the tension, a sharp line cutting through the night. For a heartbeat, the world stills, hanging fragile between triumph and collapse. Then the roar tumbles in—wild, raw, a fierce surge of sound crashing over the field like thunder breaking a storm's pause.

Caleb's hands clamp around the slick leather like a lifeline. The ball slips through his rain-soaked gloves, but he catches it, pinning it hard to his chest as gravity yanks him toward the grass. Mud clings greedily to his jersey, cold and heavy like a second skin, while the slick grass presses into his palms as he hits the ground. The world blurs into a wet smear of light and sound. Every heartbeat thunders in Jaxon's ears, deafening and steady.

One yard. Everything hinges on it.

Caleb carries the ball like a promise, dragging himself the last agonizing inch beyond the chalked line. The end zone bleeds out beneath him, a patchwork of muddied grass and fading white paint. He sprawls, breath ragged and soaked through, yet victorious. In the smoky floodlight, his face breaks into a fierce, stunned grin, his eyes wide with disbelief and something deeper—hope clawing free.

A sharp whistle slices through the roar. The line judge's flag arcs into the sky, a sudden flash of red against the smoky haze. "Touchdown," the official calls, his voice clear and final.

The scoreboard groans and shifts, the numbers recalibrating to show Redemption Valley ahead by a sliver—one yard, the margin between despair and glory. More than just points, this narrow lead symbolizes the fragile turnaround of an entire program, the thin thread holding a broken team together.

The stands erupt like a breaking dam. Hoots, shouts, and pounding feet tear through the rain's hiss, creating a chaotic symphony of raw pride and relief. The crowd's wild energy crashes over the field, propelling the team forward.

Caleb lands on heavy feet amidst the end zone's soggy battlefield, his body trembling with exhaustion and something fierce and bright.

Then the floodgates burst.

Brick crashes in first, his massive frame folding to the ground in a slow, shuddering cascade of release. His helmet falls askew as he raises a clenched fist—a primal roar muffled beneath his breath. Every muscle goes slack, the weight of the fight suddenly lifted.

Eli's hand punches the air, a quick, sharp motion against the gray sky. His dark eyes gleam with hard-won satisfaction, and the usual bitterness softens just a fraction.

DeShawn falls back, shoulders shaking as laughter turns into tears. His hands cover his face to hide the sudden crack in his armor, his body caught between disbelief and release. He shakes his head at the improbability of it all, at the cruel, beautiful mercy of the moment.

The muddy end zone transforms into a sanctuary of joy and shattered exhaustion.

Teammates swarm Caleb like a wave breaking on jagged rocks, hands grabbing, pulling, and lifting him high despite soaked gloves and slick jerseys. The mud stains their skin and clothes but cannot dull the fire pooling behind their eyes.

"Did you see that, man? Fuck—did you even see that?" Brick growls, his voice thick with disbelief and triumph.

Caleb catches Jaxon's gaze from across the field, still tangled in the slick turf, his body aching but alive. An entire season of struggle passes between them in that glance—of broken moments made whole in this wild, fleeting instant.

"You carried us here," Jaxon wheezes. His eyes never leave Caleb's, conveying what words cannot.

Caleb's grin widens, vulnerable and fierce. "We earned it. All of us."

The sky opens again, rain hammering down on the helmets, the grass, and the wild surge of celebration. The crowd's roar swells, a living tide that carries the team into something beyond victory—into redemption, into a moment where the impossible feels just within reach. The muddy field, the exhaustion, the aches and doubts—they all fall away, leaving only the raw, fierce heartbeat of triumph.

Jaxon pushes himself up from the ground, his body trembling with weariness but his heart hammered full. Around him, the noise rises and crashes, the smell of wet earth and sweat thick in the air. He knows this win is more than just points; it's the fragile thread of hope pulling his team—and himself—back from the edge.

And in that charged, chaotic end zone, Caleb's battered face shining with mud and rain, lifted high by his brothers in arms, the impossible finally feels real.

The world tilted beneath Emma's feet. Relief crashed down like the rain still drumming at her back.

Her knees gave way almost without warning, folding like brittle branches. The cold mud splattered up her calves—sticky and raw against her skin. She pressed a trembling hand over her heart as her chest tightened with a rapid ache, a sensation that lifetimes of clinical care had never prepared her for.

One solitary tear carved a warm trail through the rain and dirt smeared across her cheek, its heat stark against the chill settling into her bones.

From the corner of her eye, Nina appeared. Her stride was steady through the mud-slick sideline. She closed the small distance between them, her arms circling Emma in an unyielding, breathless hug.

There was laughter tangled with tears—sharp, ragged sounds that scarcely held back the swelling surge of pent-up hope. They grasped at each other like lifelines, shaking with a palpable need to believe that this moment was real.

When Emma pulled away, her therapist's instincts sharpened. The chorus of jubilation faded into a clinical checklist in her mind: injuries, status, safety. Her gaze flicked past the crowd, measuring and assessing.

Her focus swung to the muddied end zone.

Shapes jerked and moved—messy, urgent, alive. There, beneath the harsh floodlights that gleamed like watchful eyes, Jaxon lay sprawled. His silhouette folded outward as he laboriously pushed himself up. Each motion was a battle—deliberate and slow. His mud-streaked hand dug into the soaked turf for purchase.

Emma felt the twin pull of competing truths: the professional healer who saw pain written in every stuttered breath and the woman who believed in impossible second chances. She had spent years keeping those two parts of herself separate. In this moment, they collided.

Not far away, Caleb was swallowed by a human wave—a frenzy of mud-splattered jerseys, cups flying as teammates hoisted him into the air. The scent of damp grass mingled with musk and liniment, heavy and comforting in the night air.

Emma's breath puffed out in short, visible bursts. Cold mist curled before her lips. Her fingers twitched around the clipboard she had been clutching too fiercely. The tension held for a moment—then loosened. The clipboard slipped from her grasp, forgotten on the sodden ground.

A shudder of raw adrenaline coursed through her. She pressed both palms down on the rough grass, grounding herself against the chaos. Her eyes locked onto Jaxon—fierce slits of amber hidden beneath rain-streaked strands of hair. Every movement was a silent reckoning; every breath, a whispered vow.

The rhythm of her heart stuttered and caught as hope and fear battled inside her.

"Is he going to be okay?" Nina's voice was low but trembled beneath the roar of the crowd. Her eyes sought Emma's, full of fierce worry and reluctant optimism.

Emma swallowed hard, her voice a quiet rasp. "He's pushing through it. But there's pain beneath that grit. I can see it in his breathing."

Nina chuckled—a dry rasp barely holding back tears. "Every damn play, right? What's his secret, anyway? You?"

Emma shook her head, a wry smile teasing the edges of her lips. "If I had Jaxon's resilience, I'd already be selling skincare in some spa town."

The crowd's chant swelled, first a low rumble beneath her feet, then a full-throated roar pulsing across the field. The floodlights cut through the rain in spattered shards, illuminating the mud-caked warriors at the center of victory's storm.

Emma's jacket clung wetly to her skin. Cold droplets pricked like pinpricks along her neck as the rain painted the night sharp and metallic on her tongue. Somewhere deep inside, a fragile ember breathed to life, fueled by the raw energy shooting through the players around her.

She glanced across the end zone. Caleb's grin was wide, soaked through with exhaustion. His teammates' hands were steady and sure as they lifted him. Brick collapsed to one knee, his massive frame sagging with released tension, shoulders heaving heavy breaths that spoke volumes of battles won and lost. DeShawn let himself fall against the damp earth, laughter and sobs twining as relief flooded through him.

Emma's fingers twitched. They settled briefly into tight fists before loosening—a tremor of tension beneath the surface that she refused to show. She pushed off the wet ground and steadied herself, her back straight and her gaze fixed unwaveringly on Jaxon.

He staggered upright, each step heavy with the weight of pain and pride. The mud masked cuts and bruises, but Emma saw the worn lines mapped across his face—the quiet, stubborn flame still burning behind his eyes.

"Hey, Emma." The voice was rough, barely a whisper carried by the wind and the distant calls of celebration.

She turned sharply, her heart lurching, but it was Nina. Her grin was wide and breathless as she brushed raindrops from her brow.

"I'm not crying," Nina insisted, her voice cracking just a little.

Emma let out a short laugh, which was quickly swallowed by the night. "Right. Not crying."

The sideline pulsed with strange electricity—a lamprey glow powered by hope mixed with fatigue, tension, and years of failures hanging too close. Emma's throat tightened as the sea of faces blurred. Fans drenched in team colors sprayed cheers and raised their fists aloft.

Her eyes never left Jaxon. She mapped the slow reclamation of his strength, measuring the cost that no one else could see.

She crouched slightly, an ache threading through her limbs. In the rawness of this moment, the healer and the girl who once believed in impossible second chances collided quietly.

The crowd's noise faded beneath the pounding rain and the blood in her ears, distilled into a single steady pulse: his name, whispered—unspoken promises lingering like the scent of wet grass after a storm.

"I swear, if you go down again..." She breathed it out, her eyes flickering to the fractured scoreboard and then back to the center of the field.

Nina laid a hand on her shoulder, steady and grounding. "He's not alone—not this time. Neither are we."

Emma drew in a trembling breath. The wet night air was sharp and invigorating in her lungs. Her gaze sliced through the chaos like a beacon, cutting straight to Jaxon's worn figure rising—a man reclaimed from the ashes of doubt. Fragile. Fierce. Unfinished.

Her heartbeat thrummed loud and fierce in the storm's roar. Hopeful. Raw. Real.

Jaxon's chest heaved beneath soaked pads, rain and mud clinging stubbornly to his skin and jersey. His shaking hands pressed against the sticky turf as he pushed up. A sharp ache curled through his leg beneath the grime. The crowd's roar crashed—distant thunder in his ears—but his head lolled up just as the lights sliced through the mist and steam rising from the field.

Across the chaos, Emma stands rigid by the sideline. Her eyes are wide, locked—impossible to miss even through the storm of shouts and wet bodies surging around her. Every muscle in Jaxon's body screams exhaustion, bruised and spent from the relentless grind of the game and everything he has fought to rebuild beneath the surface. Yet her gaze finds his, a thread pulling through the noise that thickens the air between them. His lips part. Breath comes shallow. No words form—only the raw pulse of the moment.

Mud streaks his left cheek, glinting faintly under the amber floodlights. His body sags—a quiet testament to battles fought both on the field and beneath the skin. Emma's instincts tighten. Her fingertips brush her lips—a trembling barrier against the storm of relief and fear rising inside her. She swallows, but the words dry up before they reach him.

The crowd's roar muffles, pressing far away—like waves crashing beyond thick glass. Time stutters. Nothing exists but their shared breath and wet, gleaming eyes. There is neither blame nor regret here, just raw survival. A quiet understanding sealed in that suspended instant—fights waged on grass and beneath skin, battles no one else sees.

His gaze burns through the distance, questioning, promising, exposing the soft edges he has fought so hard to hide. Her steady hands tremble, betraying a hope she has kept locked down. The world narrows until there is only that electric connection pulsing between them, fierce and fragile all at once.

Then—like lightning splitting the sky—the moment shatters. Teammates avalanche toward Jaxon, yanking at sleeves and helmets, their voices hoarse with victory and disbelief. The tide of bodies swells, pulling him from the edge of that charged look, an invisible tether stretching taut and loose at once.

His eyes flicker back to hers just before the wave of celebration crashes over him. Her figure blurs beneath the rain-slicked floodlights, but the imprint of that gaze remains seared into his chest, a quiet anchor amid the frenzy.

"Glad you're still standing," Emma breathes, her voice low, so close it might float across the field like a secret.

"I was counting on it," he replies, his voice rough, almost swallowed by thunder and cheers.

"You don't get to do that alone anymore, you know."

"I'm learning."

Their eyes hold one last trace of that unsaid honesty, a fragile truce born from bloodied cleats and shattered doubts. The crowd's roar surges back, snapping the spell into jagged fragments.

Jaxon exhales, muscles tightening for the next wave, but inside, the ghost of that glance lingers—a promise that no matter how hard the storm, some connections don't break.

Caleb's teammates hoist him into the damp air, their hands gripping muddy jerseys and sweat-slicked arms. Higher and higher. The flickering stadium lights catch the moisture on their skin. His breath comes in ragged gasps, each exhale mixing with the drizzle that hasn't let up since the final whistle. The crowd's roar chokes the cold night air—a tidal wave of sound swelling and crashing around the cracked concrete stands. Overhead, the scoreboard glares bright: Redemption Valley Hawks. One yard ahead. The red digits feel like a promise and a verdict all at once. Around Caleb, voices tangle in a chaotic chorus of victory, hope reborn in ragged cheers and pounding fists.

From the mud-caked grass, Jaxon blinks up at the field. Every muscle screams in protest as he pushes himself onto trembling hands. The cold slickness of the wet turf seeps through his uniform, clinging like a second skin. His ankle throbs—a dull, relentless ache that tightens whenever he shifts his weight. But the pain is now background noise, somewhere beneath the pounding in his ribs where excitement and exhaustion combust. He straightens slowly; every movement is a negotiation between desire and limitation. A sharp wince crosses his face. Then, faint but growing, the sound swells—the chant rising from the stands, a steady beat carrying his name for the very first time tonight. Jaxon's chest swells, hollow and full all at once.

On the sideline, Emma stands still as stone. Rain weaves through her hair, dampening the edges of her jacket. Her fingers press to her mouth, nails digging into warm flesh. The sharp sting grounds her. A single hot tear trails down her cheek, mingling with grit and drizzle. She lets the wave of relief wash over her—raw and fragile. Her shoulders relax just a fraction. Her breath catches, then eases, as her gaze never strays from the figure struggling to rise: Jaxon, battered but unbroken. Her heart strikes a relentless rhythm against her ribs. She studies the heft of his shoulders, the stubborn set of his jaw, and the dark smudges of mud streaking a face roughened by minutes that stretch like hours.

Somewhere across the field, Nina's quick footsteps approach. Her breath mists in the cold air as she wraps Emma in a fierce, trembling hug. The tension between them folds like paper in a breeze. Laughter breaks free—half joy, half disbelief. Emma untangles herself, her fingers loosening from warm skin. The clipboard falls, forgotten, at her feet, with protocol abandoned in the face of pure, unfiltered humanity.

Jaxon's hands settle on his hips as the cold rain slicks his skin beneath the jersey. The sharp scent of damp earth and turf rises with every exhale. Distant echoes of the crowd's cheers ripple through the night. His teammates cluster around him, laughter and shouting threading through the humid air. Brick's heavy shoulders heave with relief, while Eli pumps his fists like pistons of renewed fire. DeShawn's weary grin breaks into a lopsided smile despite the limp he masks with every step. Their faces, etched with grime and triumph, carve a circle of belonging that presses against the fatigue pooling in Jaxon's limbs.

The rain runs in threads down his neck, slick fingers tracing the line of his jersey. The floodlights burn down, casting long, stretching shadows that dance over the grass like restless spirits. He senses the weight of the moment, with so much hanging on this fragile win. A pulse of something unspoken threads through him, the taste of victory sharp on his tongue—sour and sweet, mingled with the bitter edge of what still lies beyond reach: what this win doesn't erase, the past mistakes, the media scrutiny, and the longer fight ahead.

"There's a storm coming," Jaxon mutters under his breath. "And we're the ones holding the line."

"We've got this," Brick snaps beside him, his voice rough but steady. "One yard."

"Feels like a thousand." Jaxon's eyes narrow toward the distant stands, where the crowd's roar swirls like a living thing.

Emma's eyes flick to the huddle, then back to where Jaxon stands firm amid the shifting pack. Her voice is barely audible as she speaks to Nina, filled with brittle hope stitched with caution.

"He's not just standing. He's fighting. For more than us. For himself."

Nina replies, her tone measured but warm. "We all are. Every damn one of us."

Jaxon scans the faces pressed close. The grime and sweat meld into a rough mosaic of second chances and unspoken promises. Flickers of vulnerability lace his guarded countenance—shadows behind the hard edges. Yet he stands, the embodiment of a program clawing its way back from oblivion. The crowd's chant licks at his skin, a tidal pull pushing forward even as doubt tugs beneath.

His gaze shifts and catches Emma's across the field. Her fingertips brush her lips. Her eyes are wide and luminous in the rain's gleam. In that suspended heartbeat, the cacophony falls away. Only the rough, ragged pulse of shared survival remains. Neither speaks, but the promise hangs in the air—unsaid and undeniable.

They hold that silent communion until bodies surge between them. Teammates shout. Laughter rings like broken bells. The adrenaline spike crashes over them all. But the electric tether between Jaxon and Emma remains—a thin thread shimmering beneath the storm.

Jaxon breathes in the night: the sharp tang of wet earth, the sting of rain against cracked lips, and the distant, echoing stomp of feet on worn asphalt outside the stadium. His body aches in ways that go deeper than muscle and bone, caught somewhere between triumph and the gnawing uncertainty that the win has only just begun a longer, harder fight. Yet here, under the bright, searching lights—the muddied sanctuary of their battered field—he stands unyielding.

Victory wraps around them like a threadbare cloak: heavy, real, and impossible to ignore. But inside that heat beats a quieter question, tangled like the rain-darkened grass beneath their cleats.

What comes next?

Jaxon tightens his jaw as rain streaks down his face like slate tears. He lets his teammates pull him into the fold. The field holds its breath with him—a battered but steady heart ready to carry the fight forward into the unknown.

After the Whistle

The final whistle slices through the damp air—sharp, abrupt—a note that leaves a rippling silence just before the storm.

Jaxon Reyes lies sprawled on the slick turf, every breath a ragged scrape against the ache knifing into his ribs. Mud clings to his jersey in dark streaks, the dampness seeping through the fabric and cooling the fever burning beneath his skin. His fingers press into the grass—slick, uneven—grounding him even as the sting radiates from the last brutal tackle.

Somewhere beyond the iron chain-link fences, the crowd explodes. But here, on the field, time stretches thin. Each second fills with the heavy drum of Jaxon's heartbeat thrumming in his ears, like a restless drumline marching a hard victory anthem.

The sharp scent of damp earth and crushed grass floods his nostrils, mingling with the metallic tang of sweat and liniment drifting from the sidelines. Sweat mingles with grit on his skin. The floodlights flicker against the swollen sky, casting long shadows across the field like silent witnesses to their fight.

Across the fifty-yard line, Caleb cradles the football to his chest, his eyes wide, disbelief and triumph blazing across his face. His teammates—mud-caked, panting, wild-eyed—swarm him like wolves, hands slapping backs and shoulder pads in gleeful frenzy.

The sideline erupts. Shouts shatter the stunned silence. In seconds, the roar crashes over the field like a tidal wave. Voices collide and blend—the sharp whistles of coaches, laughter, and hoarse cries of sheer exhilaration.

"Reyes! Reyes! You did it!" Brick's voice cuts clearly through the tumult as he wrenches himself free and jogs toward Jaxon's prone form.

Jaxon pushes himself up. Every muscle screams in protest. His ribs jab like splintered glass with each movement, but stubbornness anchors him. The cold, sticky mud presses against his palms while blades of grass jab into his forearms. He forces a grin—slow and raw, tugging at the corners of his bruised face. The sharp stab in his ribs tightens the smile, a silent testament to the fight he just survived.

Brick looms over him, the giant defensive lineman's hand thrust out without hesitation. Their fingers mesh into a vice grip—hands rough and solid, forearms locked in mutual respect. Brick's gaze is fierce but carries something softer: an awareness of what this win means beyond yards and points.

"You still breathing, man?" Brick's voice rumbles low, soaked in relief and quiet pride.

"Like a freight train ran me over," Jaxon admits, his voice rough and laced with fatigue. "But yeah—I'm here."

Brick pulls him to his feet with a grunt. Their shoulders brush—both steadying and electric. Around them, the team surges forward, breaking free from the cluster around Caleb. A living wave of navy and gold charges toward the end zone like hunters scenting blood.

The crowd noise swells—miles of cheers mixed with stomped feet and frantic clapping. Thunder made human. A tempest of hope and disbelief seeps into Jaxon's bones and lifts his bruised spirit. He stands unsteadily at midfield, chest heaving, the cool night air brushing wet against his skin. His eyes scan the flood of faces, lit in flashes by camera phones and the glow of stadium lights.

Teammates pour past him, laughter spilling, voices cracked from shouting. Caleb, still clutching the game ball, dances near the goalposts—the epicenter of their victory. Arms raised. Lips moving in silent thanks to something bigger than four quarters of gridiron combat.

Jaxon's gaze latches onto Brick, who is now cracking a rare, broad smile. Teeth flash bright beneath smudges of dirt. Though they have clashed in practice and words, Brick's rare smile tonight is a quiet salute—a battle-hardened respect forged in shared struggle. Nearby, DeShawn mimics a dance move, lightening the charged air, while Eli stands back slightly, eyes sharp and calculating but unmistakably pleased.

The ground beneath Jaxon still feels uncertain. His legs tremble. Yet something steadies him—this moment, raw and improbable. He inhales deeply, savoring the sharp tang of grass, sweat, and victory. His thoughts flicker between the present chaos and the slow, grinding journey that brought him here: a climb from ashes, somewhere near the edge of despair and hope.

From the sidelines, voices rise again. Cheers layer with the distant bark of Coach Hale—the hard-nosed commander who expects nothing less than grit and guts. That mixture of noise is a soundtrack Jaxon hadn't thought he would hear again. After years of disappointing seasons, this sudden victory feels less like luck and more like a long-awaited turning tide.

"Did you ever think we'd get here?" Brick asks, his voice close and gruff.

"Not a damn chance," Jaxon replies, the smile sharper now, flickering with something almost like pride. "But here we are."

A sudden blast of cold wind rips across the field, carrying the taste of rain from the dark horizon. Jaxon lets it sweep over him, the sting biting into his cheek like a reminder. Mud and sweat mix into the scent of old leather and liniment—a familiar perfume of battles fought beneath lights and stands.

He watches Caleb, like a lighthouse guiding their ragged ship back to shore, as the team crashes into him—a pile of bodies and raw laughter that echoes into the night.

"Next time," Jaxon murmurs, more to himself than to anyone else, "we finish it sooner."

Brick laughs, low and rich. The sound folds into the night like a benediction.

Suddenly, Jaxon feels a hand on his back—firm but steady. It's Caleb's. The kid's smile is messy, flushed, and hopeful, radiant like the sunrise breaking through storm clouds.

"You did good, Reyes. We all did."

"Yeah," Jaxon breathes out, his voice rough but steady. "We did."

The heavy door to the locker room slams open. The team floods inside like a tidal wave. Mud-caked cleats strike the worn concrete. Dust puffs rise, mingling with damp patches where rainwater still clings. Jerseys cling to skin, soaked through and splattered with dark earth and grass stains. There's a whoosh of icy water and the sharp crack of Gatorade bottles opening. Players whoop and laugh, their backs slapping with the force of release and triumph.

Jaxon pushes through, his skin slick with sweat, ribs thudding with a dull ache—there but drowned beneath a rush of adrenaline and a grin he can't hide. His fingertips catch a rough slab of peeling paint on the bench as he moves. The gritty tang of sweat and leather mingles with the sharper fizz of spilled sports drinks, coating his tongue.

Brick's voice slices through the chaos—raw, deep, and commanding. "One, two, three—Hawks!" The rallying cry echoes off the cold concrete walls, igniting a fire beneath the team. Voices rise in thunder, a swelling chorus drawn from every ragged breath filled with hope and relief. Like moths to a flame, the players funnel toward the center of the storm: their shared sanctuary.

Jaxon's feet find the circle before he knows it. His arms suddenly lift, spinning into the heart of the huddle. Grimy hands grab his shoulders and ribcage in a chaotic embrace. Their warmth grounds him amidst the roar.

The clang of the outer door draws all eyes. Coach Marcus Hale looms in the frame—his solid form rigid, his face a carved mask of discipline. But as the cacophony swells, something cracks through the hardness: his tight lips twitch upward for the barest moment, a flash of softness beneath the iron. His booted step carries weight as he crosses the threshold.

Years of coaching had taught him to wear that stone face, to keep a distance between himself and the boys. Yet standing here, watching them celebrate—these kids who had fought through doubt and whispered uncertainties from the town—something in his chest shifted. They weren't just a team anymore; they were proof that second chances, real ones, could still exist.

His hand clamps onto Jaxon's shoulder, steady and firm—a grounding force. The room drops into a tense hush, expectant and raw.

"Second chances," Marcus's voice cuts through like sharpened steel, "don't come by accident. Nobody handed this to us—this fight, this blood, this victory—we earned it with every damn breath. You fought not just for the win out there; you fought for redemption, for yourselves, for this team, for this town." He breathes deeply, his chest expanding as his eyes scan the sea of mud-streaked faces. "You keep that fire burning. Don't let it die here."

The weight of his words settles, thick and real in the damp air.

Then, breaking the fragile tension, DeShawn leaps onto a battered bench. He shrugs off the grime, his wide, mischievous eyes flashing. A grin spreads across his face as he breaks into a laugh-igniting dance. His arms flail with practiced exaggeration, and his feet drum a wild rhythm on the wood.

Laughter crashes across the room—boisterous and free—cutting through the earlier sharpness like a blade through fog.

Brick roars, slapping his thigh. "Come on, man! Show us those moves again!"

"We did it! We did it!" Caleb's voice pitches higher, his eyes bright as he claps. His hand comes down hard on the locker beside him.

Hands clap. Echoes bounce between the walls. The tide of noise swells—a ragged symphony of cheers, stomps, whoops, and the slap of sweaty skin on backs and shoulders.

Jaxon's breath runs ragged. A raw mix of exhaustion and exhilaration rises in laughter from his chest. Mud-crusted fingers press into his shoulder as teammates launch themselves onto benches and the pinnacles of concrete lockers. The air is thick with the sharp tang of sweat and spilled Gatorade. His lips twitch upward, tight with fatigue but unguarded in the flood of joy.

"We iced that game, man." DeShawn hops down, breathless, his grin infectious as he slaps Jaxon's arm. "Nobody saw us coming."

Jaxon nods, his voice gravelly. "Not just iced it. We froze everyone solid."

Brick claps him hard on the back, rumbling, "That's what happens when we stop pretending and start fighting like we mean it."

DeShawn jumps back on the bench, dropping into exaggerated moves that have half the room doubled over.

"You really pulled it off out there, huh?" Caleb shouts over the din, wiping mud from his forehead. His smile stretches wide, unburdened.

"Hell yes." Jaxon breathes the words between gasps, his smile breaking free—unguarded and real for once.

Brick bawls, "Next thing you know, they'll be writing songs about the Hawks again!"

Coach Hale steps forward quietly, his eyes glinting with something fierce beneath the weariness. "Damn right," he murmurs.

The locker room hums and roars—a raucous blend of voices and pounding hearts. Water sprays, and cheers thunder. Somewhere beneath it all, the promise of a new dawn threads its way between the players. Jaxon stands, breathless and laughing, the noisy heat of the moment settling around him like a shield forged in mud and sweat.

Phones buzzed, vibrations rattled pockets, and alert chimes pinged against lockers and benches in quick succession. Caleb yanked his phone free, his thumbs flicking across the glowing screen as notifications cascaded in a relentless flood. The headlines had flipped; the sharp edges of past condemnations blurred into phrases like "comeback king," "redemption story," and "unlikely hero." Bold voices online whispered of something new—something worth watching.

Outside, rain-dampened asphalt gleamed under flickering streetlights. Camera crews huddled beneath battered awnings, their equipment glinting wetly. This town had hardened itself against the team; years of economic struggle and media brutality had calcified skepticism into the very soil. That skepticism was cracking now. The usual cold calculation in reporters' eyes softened, sharpening instead into something hungrier. Whispers rippled through the press pit as a victory narrative began to form.

Caleb scrolled through multiple feeds. Sponsor accounts he had never seen before retweeted highlights—hesitant but interested. Fans flooded timelines with messages soaked in hope and surprise. Hashtags climbed the trending lists: #RedemptionRun and #JaxonReyesReturns. A tide was turning—slow and undeniable. But even as Caleb's chest tightened with possibility, something darker coiled beneath it. This euphoria wouldn't last; it never did. The town would turn again if Jaxon stumbled. They always did.

The locker room door slammed open.

Nina Alvarez stumbled inside, her cheeks burning and her chest rising in quick gasps. Her eyes darted around the room, sharp as a blade. Without a word, she jabbed a finger toward her phone, her lips mouthing "sponsors." The screen buzzed relentlessly in her palm. She moved through the locker room like electricity—urgent and commanding.

Phones lit up in waves—half a dozen without warning. Teammates glanced down, their eyes quickening as unread texts and buzzes cascaded. The air hummed—electric and alive. The usual heaviness of doubt pulled back just a fraction. Buzzing alerts, low murmurs of conversation, and the faint, tentative glimmer of something like hope stirred between walls stained with grit and hard-fought battles.

Caleb's voice cut through—quiet and charged.

"Looks like the town's starting to believe."

A grin spread across his face. His phone blinked with another notification—a direct message from a local brand this time. Meet next week. The tentative voices online, the pause in the media's usual attack—they were listening now, really listening. His fingers hovered over the screen, excitement warring with caution as he typed: *Last night's heartbreak turned into this morning's promise. Redemption isn't given; it's earned. #RedemptionRun.* The post hit the feed and ignited instantly.

Across the locker room, DeShawn nudged Brick, who nodded slowly, watching the flood of messages scroll across his own screen.

"So, do we finally catch a break, or what? Do you think they'll cut us some slack now?" DeShawn grinned, his voice flowing easily, though hope trembled beneath.

Brick shook his head, a low laugh rumbling out. "Peace? Nah. Respect is one thing. We earned every damn bit of that."

Eli shrugged off his soaked cap. A rare smirk tugged at the corner of his mouth.

Even in this raw space filled with sweat and mud, the hard lines of suspicion and old battles began to blur, like dawn after a long, dark night.

Nina caught Caleb's eye and threw a quick nod. "We need to ride this wave. Get ahead of it before Victor Cross smells blood again. Jaxon is on the edge—he needs this win to stick, but it won't hold itself."

The muffled cadence of camera shutters drifted from outside, accompanied by the soft tapping of feet and the faint hiss of rain on concrete. The scent of damp grass crept beneath the door. This mix of raw emotion and nascent triumph pressed in—thick and palpable—anchoring the team in the moment before the next storm.

"Jaxon's no angel," Caleb muttered, his eyes still glued to the rolling updates. "But maybe... maybe this time, he's got a shot."

Restless energy wove through the locker room. Players crowded closer, phones raised, capturing the scene—their laughter, their mud-streaked faces, and the rising chorus of acceptance pouring invisibly from glowing screens. The sudden optimism dripped like electricity, prickling the skin and warming the grit caked on tired muscles.

Near the benches, a quiet conversation unfolded, just loud enough to reach listening ears:

"Did you see that headline? 'From Scandal to Savior'—they actually used that."

"Yeah, but there's a line beneath it: 'Not yet forgiven, but the fight's worth watching.'"

"Better than 'washed up,' right? I'll take it."

"Trust me, it's a start."

Voices rose and fell, creating a mosaic of hope and caution that settled unevenly. But for the first time, it felt real.

The phones vibrated again, a fresh chorus lifting beneath the stale fluorescent glow. The glare from the screens reflected off faces that were dirt-smudged and shining with sweat. It was a break in the clouds—fragile, trembling, but unmistakably there.

Nina stepped back near the door, scanning faces. A quiet smile flickered—professional, guarded, yet undeniably proud. This moment was raw, unfinished, and precarious. But it was theirs. The fight wasn't over. For now, the tide had turned.

Caleb pocketed his phone, his voice low but steady as he met Brick's eye. "We ride this. No turning back."

Brick nodded once. His expression was grim and fierce.

Outside, the media crews shuffled slightly, their senses alert. The predators had paused, replaced by curiosity. Somewhere within the chatter, a story about redemption began weaving itself through the night, through rain and shadow, and the fragile, electric hope that now hummed inside the locker room walls.

The cacophony of the locker room celebration distilled into a muffled heartbeat as Jaxon slipped away. Each step was soft on the scuffed tile of the training wing. The distant roar of laughter, shouts, and slapping backs faded into a strange kind of quiet—the kind born from thick walls and corridors that hold secrets.

He leaned against the cool concrete, his eyes closing briefly. He felt the slick weight of mud still caked to his cleats and the sharp sting in his ribs humming low beneath bruised muscle. That ache was old company now, a constant whisper of limits pushed and prices paid over years of carrying more than most.

The cold air didn't soothe it, but it steadied his breath and slowed the pulse hammering against ghosts that wouldn't let go.

Footsteps echoed from behind—a softer rhythm cutting through the corridor's stillness. Emma appeared around the corner, her presence folding into the space like warm light filtering through smoke. Her jeans were flecked with stubborn specks of sideline mud, and the watchful crease in her hazel eyes softened as she approached. Pride anchored her smile—quiet, measured, with no grand gestures—just the unspoken acknowledgment that this moment was hard-earned.

Their proximity contracts, a breath's length between them where the noise of the world can't reach.

Emma's gaze lingers a moment longer, searching his face for a sign she can trust. Jaxon's jaw tightens as he swallows, suddenly keenly aware of the warmth radiating from her before she speaks. Her voice breaks the hush, steady and lined with iron beneath the warmth.

"That was real today, Jaxon. You gave them something new—something you've kept hidden."

He lets the words settle, heavy but true. The rigidity in his shoulders softens, a slow uncoiling of the tension he's carried since he walked onto that field. His eyes trace the lines of her face—the faint crease at her temple where she's fought long battles, the set of her jaw that mirrors his own stubbornness. He hears more between her words.

"But don't let this win convince you that the work's over. Not when the real fight is still ahead. You can't let the rush of one game undo the changes you've made."

Jaxon nods. The gesture is small but full. There's relief hitching in his chest, a fragile opening beneath the armor still in place. The scars—visible on his ribs and invisible beneath the surface—whisper cautionary tales. He's learned to respect their warnings.

"I'm trying," he mutters, his voice barely above a whisper, yet honest.

Emma's fingers find his forearm. Her touch is grounding and sure—tender but commanding, a silent promise woven through the brief squeeze. Jaxon feels gratitude unfurl, a fierce, quiet flame burning away the last remnants of doubt.

For a heartbeat, the world narrows down to that touch.

The steady beat of their shared history threads between them.

Then, with careful deliberation, Emma releases him gently. She steps back with the grace of someone who knows exactly when to hold on and when to let go. Each step toward the doorway is a quiet declaration of trust and respect—giving him space to reclaim this victory as his own. There's a complexity woven through this gesture, an unspoken understanding between them born from years of tangled moments and choices made. She trusts him in a way that costs her something, and they both know it.

Jaxon watches her silhouette fade into the dim light. A tightness works through his chest, accompanied by undeniable clarity.

This moment, soaked in fleeting warmth and the soft hum of burgeoning hope, feels like a pivot—a line drawn between what has been lost and what might still be saved.

His hands curl into loose fists at his sides—not from anger, but from resolve—the kind forged in the crucible of mistakes and hard-won lessons.

This is his win; it is now his burden to hold steady under its weight.

"You don't get to forget," Emma's voice lingers as she pauses at the frame, "but you get to decide what comes next."

Jaxon breathes in the quiet and nods once more, slower this time, as if sealing a pact with himself.

"I'm ready."

Behind him, the echoes of celebration drift down the hallway—wild, joyful, alive. Ahead, the door stands open, waiting for him to step back through and claim the path he has chosen.

He straightens, pushing the ache in his ribs aside like a stubborn shadow. With one last glance into the fading light of what is left behind, Jaxon moves forward..

A cluster of overhead lights stabbed into Jaxon's eyes as the door clicked shut behind him. The press room felt smaller than he had expected. Faded foam panels hemmed in the walls. Charcoal-gray carpet stretched beneath his feet, stained dark from years of spilled coffee and nervous sweat. Microphones crowded the table like sharpened teeth, while wires tangled beneath them—creeping roots in the shadows.

Victor Cross stood near the back, leaning forward with that familiar calculating tilt. His green eyes gleamed under the harsh lighting, cold and sharp. His fingers were already poised over his notebook.

A dozen reporters crammed into the space. Cameras pointed like spears, and lenses glinted with suspicion.

"Jaxon Reyes! Over here!" someone called, their voice crackling through the charged air.

"Congrats on the win. What does this victory mean for you after everything?"

"Jaxon, can one good game really erase the shadow of your scandal?"

The questions volleyed back and forth, some edged with cautious praise and others loaded with suspicion.

Jaxon's jaw tightened. He tasted grit. His breath came slow and forced—each inhale steadying the storm beneath his surface. Dozens of eyes burned into him, sharp as hot spotlights, tracing every twitch and tightening muscle.

He pulled his shoulders back, squared his stance, and stepped forward.

His hand brushed the cold microphone stand. The buzz of the room settled into expectant silence, thick enough to taste like iron and sweat.

"I won't pretend I'm not aware of the past." His voice dropped, steady but rough with fatigue. Each word landed deliberately, measured. "Redemption isn't a one-game fix. It's a road I'm walking—fully, honestly, no excuses."

His eyes swept the room, a flicker of doubt appearing in some faces and something like hope in others.

"To those I let down—teammates, fans, my family—I'm not here to erase the mistakes. I'm here to own them and to build from them."

Victor's hand shot up, and his voice sliced through the stillness with surgical precision.

"Isn't it naive to think a single comeback game can overwrite years of scandal? Doesn't the damage run deeper than today's scoreboard?"

Jaxon met Victor's gaze evenly, the sharpness in his own eyes tempered with quiet resolve.

"Naive? Maybe. Or honest." He paused. "The past? It's always there. Scars don't fade overnight. But I'm done running from it. This win isn't a clean slate—it's a promise to face what's behind me without flinching, to prove that growth is possible even when the scars are visible."

The silence stretched taut, like a prowling predator's breath. Then, tentatively, applause began to peck out. Soft claps bloomed into a steady rhythm—hesitant but genuine. Some reporters exchanged surprised glances, while others lowered their pens, caught off guard by the unexpected candor.

The room hummed with a subtle shift, a fragile unspooling of tension.

Jaxon stepped back from the microphone. His breath held steady now, but a ghost of vulnerability still patrolled the edges of his composure. Flashbulbs popped, and camera shutters snapped to life, encapsulating this rare moment of truth like a fragile orb.

Victor watched, his lips pressed thin and his brow furrowed beneath the weight of reconsideration—or perhaps calculation. The intensity of his gaze suggested something deeper: a professional drive tangled with a personal stake in Jaxon's story, a tension that had been building long before this moment.

Jaxon's jaw loosened just enough as he turned away. The heavy spotlight chased him to the door.

The press room exhaled, quieter still. A void between judgment and hope lingered in the air.

The door creaked open, and Jaxon stepped back into the locker room. The sharp clang of lockers, the faint smell of sweat and liniment, and the lingering sting of eucalyptus from Emma's supplies—all of it hung in the air like a held breath. But the raucous frenzy from minutes ago had folded into something quieter, something more tightly knit. Boots slapped the stained concrete floor in a steady rhythm. Players breathed hard but with a new focus. The room still hummed, like a gathering storm calmed before the next wave.

A sudden hush sweeps through the circle as Jaxon crosses the room. Every eye, once wild with victory, is now sharp and serious, tracking his approach.

The weight of their gaze settles on him—half expectation, half reverence. He feels it like a hand pressing against his sternum, and something inside him shifts. For months, he has been clawing his way back from the wreckage of his own mistakes, and now, watching their faces follow him, he understands: they have already forgiven what he has not yet forgiven himself.

Mud splatters his jersey, mixing with the sweat that clings to his skin, streaking dark beneath the harsh fluorescent lights. The injury in his ribs throbs dully, but it is nothing compared to the hunger blooming in his chest—a need older and deeper than pain.

Brick's mouth quirks upward, the corner twisted into a grin that barely tames the storm in his eyes as he leans toward DeShawn. With an elbow jab, a silent challenge flickers between them—fierce and brotherly.

"Let's do it," Caleb mutters, already shifting to set the rhythm. His fingers snap in a quiet cue, low and steady.

Eli, ever the watcher, smirks—a slow tilt of his lips that carries both mischief and respect. His fingers find the rim of his cap, pulling it free like a crown trembling in anticipation.

Without a word and without hesitation, the circle bursts.

Rough hands curl beneath Jaxon's ribs, gripping his arms and shirt. His boots leave the gritty floor, lifted by the force of their belief. He's hoisted high, his weight suspended on shoulders as solid as bedrock.

Laughter spills out, raw and unbridled, pulsing through the walls. The room shakes with cheers—wild and free. They echo around battered lockers etched with years of frustration and hope.

"Cap-tain! Cap-tain!" Caleb's voice slices through the air, sharp and ringing, the call picked up and multiplied by every throat.

"We did it! We did it!" roars the chorus, carrying Jaxon in a swirling tide around the benches, close enough to scratch the cracked green paint and bruised wood.

Even Eli—usually reserved—flings Jaxon's cap toward him, a teasing salute caught midair. The cap lands crooked but precious atop Jaxon's damp, disheveled hair.

"Alright, knock it off," Jaxon grunts, his voice gravelly, laughter tangled with a cough—the kind of rough warmth only a man half-drowned in sweat and disbelief could muster. His hands claw gently at the air, trying to reclaim some control.

But the hands on his back, the tight grip around his calves, and the laughter that isn't mocking but fierce with loyalty—all of it presses against him like a wave breaking over a shore. Relentless. Warm.

He stops fighting and surrenders to the weight of the moment, of belonging.

Coach Hale's boots click against the floor, steady and deliberate, drawing attention away from the chaos. He appears in the doorway like a sentinel, arms crossed, the hard lines of his face softened by something rare—a slight nod, a hint of a smile tugging briefly at his lips.

The team stills, sensing the shift. In that pause, something unspoken passes between them—Hale's quiet recognition that Jaxon has become more than the player he was before the injury, more than the mistakes. He has become what they needed: someone worth following.

"You've earned it," Coach says, his voice low but carrying like thunderclaps in the sudden silence.

The room, energized yet attentive, seems to hold its breath for a heartbeat before exploding back into noise—cheers, claps, and shouts.

Jaxon sits tall on their shoulders, breath catching in his throat, heart hammering with a yearning older than the injury in his ribs. A hunger for this, for them, for the chance to be more than the sum of his mistakes.

Mud runs down his cheek, mingling with sweat and something harder to name—the raw ache of hope.

Laughter curls around him, voices lifting in unison, a ragged symphony of redemption.

"Cap-tain! Cap-tain! Cap-tain!"

He closes his eyes for just a flicker, his arms dropping limply to his sides, letting the moment bury him whole. The world narrows to the rhythm of their voices, the sureness of their hands, and the steady beat of a team claiming something bigger than themselves.

And for a fragile second, just one, he feels it.

Belonging.

The tumult in the locker room begins to ebb. It does not fade into silence but stretches thin like a slow-motion film. Sweat and spilled Gatorade catch the harsh fluorescent light, shimmering on skin and slick concrete. Camera flashes pulse at the doorway—bursts that fracture through the damp air, scattering reflections against scuffed gray lockers and cracked tiles. The hum of victory swells like a rising tide, voices converging into a ragged, raw chorus that rattles the locker room walls.

Up above it all, Jaxon rides the power. With his arms slung heavily across the shoulders of his teammates, he feels their weight—iron and steady, anchoring him. The clamor fades into a soft roar in his ears as he closes his eyes. The ache in his ribs dims. Shadows seep from the corners of his mind. And for once, the tension between hope and fear slackens.

A tear slipped free. Cold. Salty. Its trail cut through the dust and mud on his cheek, leaving a path that felt like both shame and release. Raw and honest—a small surrender to the unexpected lightness blooming in his chest.

From somewhere above, nestled among faces blurred with joy and relief, Emma craned her neck. Her hazel eyes caught the dim overhead shadows. They locked with his. No words. Only a small nod, slow and steady, like a lighthouse flickering through the storm. That quiet signal carried weight—all their tangled history folded into a single gesture: caution, pride, and something like forgiveness. She had kept her distance for months, watching him stumble, wondering if this moment would ever come. Now it had, and the sight of him here, finally believing, made her breath catch. She stepped back gently, letting the crowd press in, drawing a veil of space around him.

The noise swelled again—a living thing. The chant rippled on—ragged and beautiful. "Captain! Captain! Captain!" Voices cracked with emotion, raw and unpolished yet unwavering. Every chant carried the weight of battles fought—the grueling practices, the blown plays, and the comebacks that had nearly broken them all. But they had endured. And now, in this moment, their captain was finally standing tall.

Jaxon spread his arms tentatively, like a boy testing the sky for wings. His palms lifted upward—vulnerable and willing to catch whatever gravity this moment offered: the tentative promise that forgiveness was no longer a question mark. The air smelled of sweat, triumph, and faint liniment, reminders of every bruised muscle and stubborn yard earned. The locker room felt like both a sanctuary and a battleground, every breath thick with the scent of grit and redemption.

A slow smile tugged at the corners of his mouth—careful and uneasy. The weight of years pressed against him, memories jangling like loose chains. But here, right now, he let them rest. Not forgotten, not erased, but held at bay by something more powerful: the raw, messy, unguarded pulse of belonging.

Then his voice broke through the chant—low but steady, carrying the fragile sound of a man daring to believe. "We did it. We really did."

Brick's laugh boomed beneath him, a deep rumble that shifted into a shout. "That's right, man! You earned every damn bit of this!"

Caleb's grin spread wide, echoing in the half-lit room. "We ride or die, Jax. This is just the start."

"Cap-tain, Cap-tain!" Eli threw his cap up in salute, defying the gloom with an irreverent spark.

Jaxon shifted slightly, feeling the rise and fall of chests and the beating of hearts. The solid weight of his teammates anchored him. His arms stretched wider—not out of pride, but out of surrender. To them. To this moment suspended between the past and the future.

Near the stands, Emma watched him dissolve into something new—a man no longer defined by scandal or self-doubt, but by the slow, steady beat of trust rebuilt. The chant spiraled upward, carving a slow arc into the night air, drowning out every harsh whisper that had ever said he was finished.

She lowered her gaze, quiet now, knowing this victory was his alone to hold.

The crowd's voices folded into the locker room's dim glow as the night stretched on—endless, pregnant with promise.

"Do you think this changes anything?" Emma's voice dipped low. "Or does it just give you a moment before the next storm hits?"

Jaxon's grin was wry and tired. "The storm is always coming. But maybe this time, I'm done running. I'm ready to stand in it."

She studied him, her eyes sharp yet soft. "Are you sure you're not fooling yourself?"

He shrugged slowly, heavily. "Maybe. But hell, I'm done hiding. It's time to fight."

Her smile was small and cautious. "Good. Because whether you like it or not, you're not doing this alone."

His lips quirked, a shadow of the old charm. "I wouldn't want it any other way."

Jaxon inhaled deeply, pressing his face upward where the locker room light softened just enough to catch dust motes swirling in lazy spirals. The chant pressed inside him—a living pulse moving through every fiber. His fingers twitched as if reaching for something unseen, a tether woven from voices, from sweat and mud, and countless last-yard fights. The ache in his ribs was a distant whisper now, out-matched by the fierce beat of this fragile redemption.

With his eyes closed and arms open wide like wings in tentative flight, he let the moment hold him—a man broken and rebuilt, imperfect but willing, forgiven, if only for now.

Beneath the bright buzz of overhead lights and the endless echo of teammate voices, the locker room chant rose again, spilling into the night and weaving a thread of hope through all the scars and shadows.

What Comes After

He fluorescent light above flickers and hums, a low, persistent drone filling the quiet of the nearly empty training facility.

Emma sits rigidly in her well-worn chair, the coffee cup—half-empty, disposable, and with a cracked lid—balanced precariously next to a stack of personnel folders resting on her knees. The sterile scent of antiseptic mingles with the fading warmth of the cup, carrying a subtle bitterness that matches the knot tightening in her chest.

Her security badge pulses on the monitor beside her, a quiet heartbeat in the silence.

She traces her eyes over the glowing screen once more: the email from the prestigious sports clinic, an offer blinking with possibility. The generous sign-on bonus, the travel allowance promising escapes into new cities, and better rehab resources shimmering like a distant shore. Each promise feels like a thread inviting her away from here, away from the cracked linoleum floor and the faded walls of Redemption Valley's worn medical bay.

She scrolls, hesitates, and then clicks.

The email shrinks but doesn't disappear. The possibility hangs just out of reach, caught in the corner of her screen like an unfinished thought.

Her phone buzzes sharply against the cluttered desk. She taps the screen and reads Nina's message: "Decision's overdue, Emma. The board's watching. You know how this works."

The words land like a stone dropped onto her shoulders. Muscles she didn't know were holding tension tighten in response.

She shifts her gaze to the photograph taped crookedly to the edge of her monitor. The color has faded with time—embers of a memory worn soft around the edges. The team picture. Jaxon Reyes stands there, jaw tight, his smirk barely reaching his guarded eyes. Beside him, her arm snakes around DeShawn's broad shoulders, his grin easy and wide.

A flash surfaces unbidden: DeShawn laughing during a late-night recovery session, his voice carrying that infectious warmth that made even the worst injuries feel survivable. Then Jaxon, jaw clenched as she adjusted his shoulder wrap, his resistance softening just slightly when she met his eyes. The snapshot carries the warmth of nights now past—echoing laughter, shared victories, and the complicated threads tying her heart to this fractured family.

Coach Hale's voice surfaces from earlier in the day, slicing through the haze of memories. "Emma," he had said, his tone rough like gravel but sincere, "don't let personal feelings cloud your judgment about them. Especially not Jaxon." The gratitude in his eyes had softened his words, but the warning lingered—a subtle undercurrent gnawing at her resolve.

She chews the inside of her cheek. The small bite grounds her as she weighs the pull of loyalty against the promise of escape.

Her fingers hover above the keyboard. Tremors betray the tempest beneath her calm exterior.

The clinic's offer glimmers with stability—a future unmarred by scandal or broken hopes.

But Redemption Valley wraps around her, with tangled roots deep beneath her skin. Broken yet stubbornly alive.

The late-night silence presses close. The hum of the fluorescent light feels like a metronome counting down a choice that no amount of reflection can lighten.

A soft sigh escapes her lips. She shakes her head, a fleeting smile ghosting across her face before vanishing as the fullness of what awaits settles around her like night shadows pooling at the edges of the room.

"Maybe they want an easy fix," she murmurs quietly, not quite daring to hope. "But this mess? It's not their game to clean up."

Nina's text buzzes again—urgent and unyielding.

Emma closes her eyes for a moment. She feels the sterile chill of the training table across the room and the faint smell of peppermint oil lingering in the air. The quiet here holds the echoes of the past: the crack of the pigskin, the scrape of cleats on the field, the low murmur of players healing and hurting—all mingling like a distant storm of life she's come to shield with care.

Her voice breaks the hush, steady but laced with an edge. "Do they think I'm just some nurse for broken toys? Someone who will pack up and leave when things get rough?"

The room remains still, except for the persistent hum and the blinking light marking her presence in this place.

She straightens, her gaze snapping back to the folder on her lap—a list of names, faces, and stories. A patchwork of pain and promise under her fingertips.

"If I leave," she confesses softly, "who is left to pick up the pieces when the spotlight fades?"

Her phone vibrates. Her fingers twitch toward it, but she resists. Her breath catches somewhere between fear and resolve.

She leans forward, her hands splayed over the keyboard.

The clinic's promises dazzle, but the weight of familiarity binds tighter than any contract.

"You're making this harder on yourself than it needs to be," she whispers to the empty room.

The words hang there, raw and unanswered.

Easy never fixed anything. You know better than that.

She exhales, deeper this time—a breath pulled up from her core.

Her fingers find the keyboard and press one key.

Just one.

The minimized offer waits quietly in the corner of the screen, neither accepted nor rejected—a fragile thread to a future not yet claimed.

The shadows creep closer, swallowing the edges of the quiet room. Emma sits caught between two worlds: the glittering chance of elsewhere and the sticky, undeniable roots of Redemption Valley pulsing beneath her skin.

A sharp rap on the door breaks the fluorescent hum. Nina steps inside, her worn clipboard clutched like armor. Her eyes flicker—concern etched in the tightening of her brows—as she closes the door with deliberate care.

"We can't risk another scandal, Emma." Nina's voice holds steady, but urgency threads through it, tightening the air between them. She taps the clipboard—a metronome. "They want someone unbiased. The board's definition mostly means staying clear of Jaxon—too many eyes watch their every move."

Emma leans back against the unforgiving chair. The sharp tang of antiseptic pricks her nose, mingling uneasily with the faint, soothing trace of peppermint—her small rebellion against this sterile, suffocating room. Her gaze doesn't waver from Nina, cold clarity sharpening her words. "So I should what—pretend he doesn't exist?"

Nina's jaw stiffens. Her eyes flick away, then refocus. "Or at least don't be obvious." The warning remains etched in every syllable, though her tone softens. "The program can't survive another exposé. Sponsors are already skittish. The staff is nervous. And the players—they watch everything. Every choice you make echoes far beyond this room."

Emma's throat tightens. She presses her lips together, her fingers curling into a quiet fist in her lap as the restless papers of the clipboard stir—a whispered reminder of the political storm gathering beyond these walls. She feels the squeeze tighten, not just from the board's demands, but from the silent ache of choosing between what is right for her and what the program requires.

"So, what do you suggest I do?" Emma presses, her voice low but edged with exhaustion and frustration.

Nina's eyes remain unyielding. "I'm not the one to tell you that." She sets the clipboard down, and the faint scrape echoes—final. "But know this: if the board sees risk, they won't wait for you to make a move. They act, Emma. And whatever you decide, it won't just affect you; it ripples through everyone connected."

There is a long pause as Nina gathers herself. The silence hums, broken only by the fading echoes of celebration elsewhere in the building.

She picks up the clipboard, pausing at the door. "You carry this more than most."

"Remember: mistakes cost more than just you."

The door clicks closed—muted, final.

Emma remains seated, the weight in the room heavier now, shadows pooling beneath her tired eyes. Footsteps recede down the hallway. All that is left is the fluorescent hum and the faint scent of peppermint swirling in the tunnel of quiet.

Emma's fingers hover over the phone's keypad before pressing a number with an impulsive breath. The receiver feels cool against her cheek as the soft murmur of distant celebrations seeps through the sterile walls of the training facility. Somewhere down the hall, faint laughter and the clink of soda cans ripple like ghosts of the night's fleeting joy. Here, in Emma's quiet office corner, the world shrinks to the crackle of the line and the steady rhythm of her heartbeat.

"Hello?"

Her mother's voice flows in warm and steady—a river that never dries up. It carries a gentle strength, something carved from years of weathering storms and loving unconditionally.

"I wasn't expecting to hear from you so late," her mother says, a smile woven into each word.

Emma's breath falters for a moment before releasing slowly, her shoulders sagging just enough—as if the weight she has been holding shifts, barely, but enough to matter. "Yeah, I... needed to hear a familiar voice."

There's a pause. Faint. Full of unspoken understanding.

"You know, Emma, ever since that heartbreak a while back, you've grown into someone I'm really proud of." The words land softly, and Emma feels the sting of them—how they contradict the doubt that has been coiling tight in her chest. "You're stronger than you realize, even if you can't see it yourself right now."

Emma's eyes trace the jagged outline of a dried paint chip on the far wall, the same subtle imperfection she has noticed every night here.

Her voice is low and hesitant. "Do you ever think running away is the right choice? Walking away from everything when it feels like too much?"

Her mother's reply is tender yet edged with pragmatism: "Sometimes running feels like the easiest way out. But that run isn't just from the pain—it's from the chance to find something real. Something worth sticking around for. I remember a time when I thought packing it all in was the only way. But bravery doesn't always roar in the spotlight. Sometimes it's the quiet, steady choice to stay and face what's hard. Don't just be brave—be wise, too."

Emma presses her free hand against the cool desk. The faint scent of peppermint oil swirls around her, mingling with the musk of sweat and old leather lingering from the day's work. Her mother's words settle—a slow warmth blooming beneath her skin.

"Thank you, Mom. I needed that."

The click of the receiver echoes in the small room as Emma sets the phone down. She folds her hands atop the cluttered desk, the edge of a scarred notebook grazing her skin. Outside the window, the world is swallowed in deep shadows. Only a faint glimmer from distant stadium floodlights throws shards of silver across the dark glass. Her gaze catches her own reflection—tired eyes, curtains of hair loosely pulled back, a face both familiar and strange.

Her breath fogs the pane.

For a moment, the hard lines of doubt soften. Something fragile—a thread of quiet hope—slips through.

She squeezes the phone, her knuckles whitening. A small, private smile ghosts her lips—barely there. It flickers. Then the shadows at her heart stretch longer, pulling it under once more.

Emma's office door clicks softly behind her. The fluorescent bulbs overhead cast everything in gray. From the locker room, the team's laughter echoes in faint bursts—distant thunder rolling away. Her footsteps trace the familiar path along worn linoleum, muted beneath heavy, thoughtful soles. Shadows twitch beneath flickering lights. Metal plaques and glass catch the occasional buzz.

She turns a corner and slows.

Her fingertips brush the cool glass separating her from the past—a long trophy case housing battered helmets, skewed medals, and brittle ribbons. Behind them, the faded "Home of the Hawks" banner drapes like a relic from forgotten wars, its edges frayed and curling. Emma's hand lingers as she traces invisible words etched into the dusty sheen.

The first day at Redemption Valley crashes back—vivid and sharp. New sneakers squeak against the floor. Her heart thrums wildly in her chest like a drum struck too hard. Faces are bright-eyed with hope and skepticism alike. The weight of that moment settles against her ribs, cold and heavy as the steel of a helmet resting too long on her skin.

Her gaze drifts to a worn, crooked plaque: "Dedicated to those who never gave up."

A sharp hitch tightens in her gut. She swallows, forcing herself forward. Her footsteps fall lightly, nearly soundless, as if afraid to disturb the memories waiting in the shadows.

The training room door stands ajar, its walls steeped in the scent of antiseptic mixed with liniment oil. She pauses at a narrow shelf lined with manila folders stacked like fragile bones. The files bear faded marks of battles fought in silence—rehab plans scribbled in hurried script, X-rays taped like ghostly maps of injuries, and charts lined in careful ink cataloging struggle and resilience. Each one represents a person she carries: silent stories she won't abandon.

She smooths her palm over the papers. Beneath her fingers, she imagines the pulse of bruised muscles and aching joints. Each injury is a testament to the players she works for, each one a fragile thread of their strength.

As she steps back, faces surface. Brick's steady nods—never loud but always sure. Behind his stormy brow flickers a quiet fire, sparked by her gentle encouragement. DeShawn's easy grin cracks open hardened moments like shattered glass catching the sun. Caleb's hesitations, softened over time into tentative thank-yous, reveal his guarded steps edging toward trust.

And then there was Jaxon.

Fierce. Bristling. A man she had circled cautiously at first, wary of the walls he had built. Those walls had shifted. The lines between them blurred with unspoken questions and uneasy truths. She wants to say yes. She wants to believe she can hold this fractured place—and the people in it—together. But doubt flickers beneath her ribs like a stubborn bruise.

Pale hallway light catches her breath. Night seeps deeper into the building now. Her breath clouds the air, soft and momentary. The world feels suspended—neither retreat nor advance. Just a fragile hesitation where everything balances.

Her fingers curl. Unclench.

The choice ahead glimmers. It is not just about her career, but about the shape of herself with these broken, fiercely human people who have found cracks of light in the shadows. Her steps slow until stillness finds her.

"I don't know if I'm ready," she murmurs. Her voice disappears into the hollow space.

The corridor hums. Memories crowd in, alongside challenges and the relentless beat of second chances.

And in the cool light along the endless hallway, Emma realizes that choosing isn't just about leaving or staying. It's about who she allows herself to be. For the first time in a long while, that terrifies her. And maybe—just maybe—that's exactly how she knows she's ready.

The chilly night wraps around Emma like the stiff fabric of her coat as she steps onto the cracked concrete steps behind the training facility. The stadium floodlights spill harsh white pools across the empty asphalt, casting long, lean shadows that stretch into the dark. She pulls the collar of her coat higher. The wind bites.

Out here late, the cold always reminds her of how fragile everything is—this life she has fought to build, the careful architecture of promises and presence she has constructed in Redemption Valley's worn-down soil. One breath wrong, one hasty decision, and it could all shatter like ice beneath weight.

Her fingers close around the phone, her thumbs poised above a draft—the resignation email, still unsent, bright against the dark screen. She imagines the clinic waiting on the other side of that message: sterile hallways, equipment gleaming under fluorescent panels, a city she has never walked at dusk, no familiar faces, no weight.

Her eyes flicker over the message again. She taps, and the clinic's offer blinks back at her: a sign-on bonus generous enough to soothe a bruised pride, travel allowances to whisk her far away from the weathered buildings of Redemption Valley, and promises of cutting-edge rehab equipment and resources no halfway town could dream of. The words look perfect. The clinic's neat lines promise security, but beneath them gnaws the fear: leave, and she loses this—loses them.

Emma scrolls carefully, the screen reflecting brief bursts of light onto her creased forehead. Stability. Boundaries. Better options. But there is also the sense that walking away might mean abandoning something worth fighting for. She chews the inside of her cheek, thinking of the stakes—the team's fragile heartbeat, Jaxon's taut silhouette shadowed in her memory, and the weight of promises made and broken.

Her thumb hesitates, then slides to her contacts: Jaxon Reyes. She taps, bringing up the string of texts, the call logs, and the moments etched sharply between them. That one night, when he had finally dropped his walls enough for regret to snatch his voice—an apology raw and breathless. The memory stirs anew—a trace of his cologne, a cracked edge to his voice—that both soothes and unsettles. She feels the ache coil in her chest again, that bittersweet tether to the steady presence he had been trying hard to become. The night she thought he might shatter, and somehow didn't.

Her fingers waver over the screen, a tremor betraying the weight of the choice, before they retreat—reluctant and uncertain. The screen waits, blank and expectant. She begins to type:

"No. I'm not leaving. But I'm not hiding who I am, either."

She sends it. Her breath catches as if exhaling into the pressure that has been mounting all night. A flutter of relief mingles with fresh, jittery anxiety—like standing on a precipice and knowing the fall is both terrifying and necessary.

Her shoulders slump, finally letting go of the tight coil of tension that has clenched through hours of silent wrestling. The cold taps sharper now. But under the stadium lights, Emma feels something loosen—an invisible weight easing, replaced by a fragile spark that might just endure.

She slips the phone into her coat pocket, her fingers brushing over the fabric as she rises from the step. The night hums softly around her, distant echoes of the team's fading celebration mixing with the steady buzz of the floodlights. Alone beneath the vast, indifferent sky, she grants herself a quiet moment—a small, secret ember of hope warming her from the inside out.

Moonlight spills across cracked asphalt, the outlines of long-abandoned parking stripes barely visible. Emma steps quietly into the stadium lot, the cold air biting through her coat as she scans the assortment of vehicles until her eyes settle on the familiar silhouette of Jaxon's battered truck. His broad frame is slouched against the hood, shoulders rounded as if he's trying to disappear into himself, a sports bottle cradled in one rough hand. The bottle—scuffed, dented, half-empty—moves to his lips with a slow, deliberate rhythm, as if the water inside is the only thing keeping him steady.

She hesitates, letting the weight of the night drape over her before moving closer, each footfall muted by a layer of gravel and shadow. When she reaches him, the air smells faintly of leather and gasoline, a stubborn scent that clings to the truck like memories cling to skin. The distant hum of the stadium's scoreboard blinks in orange digits, inert but watchful, casting a ghostly glow over the horizon.

Emma settles beside him on the hood, the cold metal pressing through the thin fabric of her jacket. Her voice is steady and low—but her fingers twitch slightly against the metal, betraying the tremor she can't quite mask.

"I almost left," she says, her eyes fixed on the distant 14-3 score, a reminder neither of them can ignore.

Jaxon's jaw clenches tight. His gaze remains fixed on those bleary numbers. The scoreboard's weight presses down on him—that number, that final tally, a monument to everything he has failed at. How is he supposed to stand here in front of her, knowing what he has cost them both? The cold metal beneath his palms feels like punishment. Like penance.

Then he answers without looking away.

"I... wouldn't have stopped you."

His voice cracks, rough like gravel with raw edges, catching her off guard.

"But—" His breath hitched, the fortress around him cracking just enough to reveal something buried deep. "I'd have been broken if you'd walked away."

The confession pulsed in the cool air between them, fragile and tentative, as if saying it aloud might shatter whatever delicate truce they were trying to forge.

Emma leaned back, letting her weight settle. She searched for words that wouldn't crumble under the tension coiling between them.

"No promises," she began, her voice soft but deliberate. "We both know better than that. Whatever this is—whatever we're trying—it's got to start from now, not from some perfect past that doesn't exist."

Jaxon finally turned, his eyes dark and steady, hunting hers for truth beneath the surface.

"What if I let you down again?" His question hung heavy like a challenge, like a plea.

Emma met that fear head-on, with no theatrics and no sugarcoating.

"Then we start again—or we stop. But neither of us runs."

The words settled into the night like a solemn vow, simple and raw. Neither retreat nor surrender, just this: a shared willingness to face whatever comes, without illusion or guarantee.

Their breaths mingled in the cold, plumes frozen for just a moment before fading to nothing. The silence between them stretched, unspoken but whole. It was in that quiet where the weight of their fractured history lightened, just slightly, making room for something new and fragile at the edges.

Crickets hummed faintly under the distant buzz of the stadium floodlights, casting halos in the mist. Jaxon shifted, the muscles in his neck tight but no longer tense. His hand rested near hers, the gap closing without words.

Emma let her gaze drift for a heartbeat to the worn grille of the truck, the chipped paint a testament to battles survived. Each scratch mirrored something in Jaxon—the dents from collisions he couldn't avoid, the rust creeping in where he had been exposed too long to the elements. The truck had endured. He had endured. And somehow, standing here beside him now, she understood that survival itself was a kind of victory.

Somewhere beneath it all, hope—thin but stubborn—tingled at her fingertips.

Between the steady beat of their breathing and the placid night around them, something unspoken stirred. Not a promise. Not a certainty. Just a beginning.

Emma slid her fingers into Jaxon's without a word. Gravity. That's what the gesture felt like—quiet, inevitable, pulling them together. His hand was warm. Strong. Her skin tingled where their fingers intertwined, a sensation that made her acutely aware of how long it had been since they had touched like this.

They stepped off the cracked concrete onto grass damp with dew. The blades whispered beneath their worn sneakers, cool and sticky. The night air wrapped around them—sharp, crisp—carrying the faint scent of crushed earth and sweat, ghosts of the day's battle lingering just beyond the floodlights.

They moved slowly, unhurried, letting silence stretch between words until Emma broke it, her voice low but steady.

"Morning drills are killer," she said. "Brick's already hyping Caleb up—'Superstar in the making,' he says, as if he has some magic touch. I don't know where Caleb finds that courage every day."

Jaxon chuckled, the sound rough but genuine in the muted space beneath the lights. "Caleb's got jokes too. DeShawn's got him laughing about some mop bucket prank. I missed that one."

Emma's smile flickered. "DeShawn pulled it on Eli. Poor guy was slipping everywhere, almost face-planted in front of Coach Hale." She paused, watching the light trace across Jaxon's dark eyes. "Did you stay up with the team afterward? I heard some of the guys kept celebrating past midnight."

Jaxon shrugged, his gaze steady on the goalposts glowing dimly in the distance. "I stayed late enough. I needed a moment to clear my head before the quiet." He glanced at her. "You?"

"I mostly worked—filed notes, called my mom." Her fingers squeezed his. "Last night felt different, though. Like we're standing at the beginning of something. Or maybe its end."

He exhaled, the sound heavy. His eyes darkened as if he were swallowing a weight he wouldn't name. "We've still got unfinished work here. Not just wins on the board, but the players—us." His voice dropped low, roughened like gravel. "You and me. We're tangled up in this too. I won't pretend it's easy."

"No," Emma's breath rose in the cold. "But neither of us has to pretend anymore. Not about what we want. Not about who we are."

They drifted toward midfield, their footsteps soft on the worn grass where the lines faded into patches of bare earth. The silence thickened again, comfortable now—like the space between heartbeats. Jaxon reached up and tucked a damp strand of her hair behind her ear. His fingers brushed her temple, gentle, almost reverent.

She leaned into the touch, closed her eyes, and let the moment linger. No promises. No words were needed.

Emma's foot nudged something firm and round. A weathered football rested near the sideline, forgotten like a relic. She stared at it.

Then she laughed—light, unguarded—breaking the quiet spell.

"What if we just walk forward?" Her voice lifted on the night breeze. "As far as it takes us?"

Jaxon tightened his grip on her hand with a simple squeeze. It said everything.

Together, they followed the faint outline of the practice field, their steps slow and sure, hands clasped against the shadowed stretch of grass and night sky. The stadium lights hummed softly overhead, and the world around them faded into the small space they carved for themselves.

Step by step, they walked forward, not knowing what lay ahead, choosing to face it side by side.

Home Isn't a Stadium

The tables groan softly as Jaxon shoves them together in the dull hum of the dorm common area. The two folding relics are chipped and beaten by years of use, their laminate surfaces scarred with the history of careless hands and late-night frustrations. He adjusts their alignment until the gap between them disappears, his fingers lingering on the worn edge like a player tracing the broken-in leather of a football. Above, the low ceiling looms close, paint peeling in thin strips, and Jaxon pulls a string of fairy lights from his duffel—an eccentric tangle of mismatched bulbs, some clear and some stained faintly blue or amber—and pins them across with thumbtacks. The lights droop and swing unevenly, casting playful shadows on the cracked walls.

He moves to one of the nearby chairs. Its bent leg wobbles beneath the faded red paint, with flakes of color lifting like autumn leaves. He straightens it twice and leans back to test it. It sways slightly, not quite steady but close enough. Around him, the other scratched chairs form a haphazard circle—a deliberate kind of chaos that feels less like neglect and more like a long-awaited invitation. He pulls one nearer, wipes grime from the seat with his hoodie sleeve, and drags it patiently into place.

The air smells of stale sweat and old liniment, with a stray hint of damp fabric. Jaxon inhales deeply, the sharp tang catching at the back of his throat. The room's stale warmth settles heavily on his skin, pressing in like the day's weariness. Outside, golden light retreats behind the bare limbs of skeletal trees visible through grimy windows. The dorm has the feel of a skeleton patiently awaiting flesh and spirit—the kind of place that has seen better days, years when the program still mattered to more than just him.

He moves toward the kitchenette counter, a thin strip of cracked laminate etched with the ghost of spilled coffee and uncounted crumbs. The takeout containers radiate warmth. He cracks the lid of one, steam rising and curling toward the fluorescent lights, bringing a sudden sharp tang of soy and sesame. With practiced ease, he scoops forkfuls of stewed vegetables onto crumpled paper plates, stacking them with quiet reverence. A smear of thick red sauce clings to the edge; he wipes it away with the hem of his shirt, leaving faint grease marks on the faded fabric. The plastic scrapes lightly against the laminate—almost rhythmic.

He arranges the plates on the battered table with the same quiet care, grouping them as if conjuring order out of disorder. Fried chicken sits in one corner, a bowl of coleslaw hastily slapped in plastic wrap, and a container of mashed potatoes cooling rapidly in the draft. He shakes out a crumpled napkin and tucks it beside the plates—a final gesture of preparedness. The room shifts from cold, impersonal utility toward something half-formed, half-warm, half-home.

Jaxon collapses onto the splintered edge of the ancient couch. Wood pokes unexpectedly beneath the thin layers of torn upholstery. The cushions sag under years of borrowed weight, their fabric rough against his skin. He pushes his phone from his worn jeans and flips it open, fingers tapping out a message he rewrites half a dozen times before sending it.

The screen buzzes instantly. Emma.

Her reply flickers like sunshine breaking through clouds: *"Bringing dessert. See you soon :)"*

He reads it twice. His lips twitch into the ghost of a smile. His shoulders sag ever so slightly, and he exhales slowly and unguarded, as if shedding weight he hadn't noticed before. The invisible tight coil inside his chest loosens—just a touch.

He pockets the phone and reaches for a half-empty bottle of water on the nearby side table. The cool plastic is slick against his palm. Raising it to his lips, he drinks deeply, the liquid bitter with the metallic tang of the dorm tap. It grounds him, pulling his thoughts away from the sharp edges of regret and the gnawing doubt that had shadowed him for weeks—the fear that tonight might not be enough to fix what he had let break.

His gaze lifts to the room again. The crooked string of fairy lights winks overhead. The scattered chairs wait for their occupants. The smell of old wood and takeout hangs thick in the twilight. The place is far from perfect, but something has shifted. For the first time in a long while, it looks like something worth building.

He stands. His feet scrape softly against the worn linoleum. A beat of silence follows. The fridge hums low. Footsteps echo down the hall. A neon sign flickers, matching his quickening heartbeat.

Jaxon shifts to the front door, fingers brushing the chipped paint as he pulls it open just enough to peer into the cooling dusk. Fading light slips behind the dorm walls, swallowing the horizon in bruises of purple and indigo. He collects the stray hum of distant cicadas and the soft clinking of keys from nearby rooms.

A pulse of anticipation rides the evening air—the promise of company, the fragile hope that tonight, maybe they would all find something worth fighting for.

"Guess this is it," he mutters under his breath, his voice low and rough, eyes scanning the shadows beyond.

He tucks his hands into his pockets and waits.

###

Brick's footsteps thud heavily across the worn linoleum. The soda case crinkles beneath his grip, its plastic sleeve squeaking—a nervous tell he cannot quite shake. He has come to belong here, though part of him still braces for rejection.

The dorm common area smelled of stale popcorn and sharp cleaning spray. Late evening quiet hummed under flickering lights. Jaxon arranged chairs by dented tables. The sagging couch in the corner looked lived-in now—real.

Brick's grin cracked his usual sternness. He charged forward, wrapping Jaxon in a bear hug—solid weight, genuine warmth. Jaxon ducked under the embrace like a cornered cat. Instead, he settled for a stiff clap on Brick's shoulder.

"You trying to crush me, Brick?"

"Only trying to remind you I'm still standing." Brick ruffled his hair—a rare gesture. Brothers in arms. "And thirsty."

The door crashed open. Caleb and DeShawn barreled in, dragging their voices like cargo.

"*Inception* is the only pick!" DeShawn's laughter echoed off the cracked concrete.

"Nah, man." Caleb tossed a scornful look. "Blade Runner or bust."

They dropped their backpacks, and dust kicked up. Grins twisted their faces into genuine smiles as they jabbed at each other.

Jaxon wiped his hands on his jeans. DeShawn swaggered closer, the air thick with bravado.

"Speaking of chef skills..." He nodded mockingly toward paper plates crowded with leftovers. "Jaxon, when you say you cook, do you mean you order?"

Caleb snorted, collapsing beside him on the couch. "Hey, *chef*, did you forget the toast earlier?"

"Five-star meal if you don't ask what's in the can." Jaxon's smirk widened, and the tight line around his eyes softened for the first time.

Eli slid in quietly, a shadow peeling from the dark hallway. He took a corner chair, unobtrusive, until Jaxon's eyes found his.

A slow nod passed between them—recognition, respect, an unspoken truce forged in shared battles, threading a new tone forward.

Eli's gaze steadied, warmer than suspicion. A quiet warmth threaded through the chill settling in Jaxon's chest. Not much was said; the moment stretched, a mutual acknowledgment of the hard road traveled and the uneasy hope ahead.

A heavy knock sounded at the doorway. Coach Marcus Hale stepped inside, his rigid posture and arms folded like a barrier. His gravelly voice cut through the banter without missing a beat.

"Proud of you all. Don't trash the place."

Half teasing, half serious, his gaze swept the room, lingering on Jaxon with something deeper than authority—respect, maybe. A mentor conflicted but invested, his rare, brief smile cracked the stern face.

Laughter sputtered free—rough and uneven at first—then spilled over like sudden summer rain, loosening tense shoulders and lighting tired eyes. Marcus turned on his heel, his boots thudding down the hall and leaving behind a pulse of steady strength.

FIFA's electronic bleeps buzzed from the television. Halftime chaos fueled the room's soundtrack. Paper plates clinked as potluck slices passed from hand to hand. Warm pasta mingled with the sharp sweetness of soda fizz.

Laughter erupted sporadically—unpolished but heartfelt—a tapestry of voices reclaiming space.

Jaxon leaned back against the worn couch. The rough fabric scratched through his shirt. Fatigue ebbed into something strange: comfort. The room that once felt stiff blurred into rhythms of movement and sound. Friends, not strangers.

It smelled like possibility, like late nights when mistakes fade into hope.

"Man," DeShawn elbowed Caleb as the screen flashed a critical goal. "If this game doesn't get intense, I might actually sleep."

"Please," Caleb shot back. "You're just scared I'm going to wipe the floor with you in the second half."

"Keep dreaming, rookie."

Brick clapped for both of them. "Alright, cut the crap—let's just kick back tonight, no beefs."

Jaxon watched the easy truce settle. His shoulders loosened, and the tight knots of the day began to unravel.

A low hum of belonging thrummed through the space—an unspoken promise. They were building something fragile and real.

The noise stretched and flowed, breathing life into tired walls. Caps, cleats, and past mistakes fell away. It was just them—the team, clinging to second chances and the stubborn hope that maybe, just maybe, this was where they came home.

The room hums with the clatter of plates and the low murmur of voices as everyone sinks toward the pushed-together tables. The common area smells like every compromise ever made—worn carpet, layered dust, and the ghosts of a hundred meals soaked into concrete walls that can't decide if they're gray or just tired. Paper plates bristle under an eclectic spread—spicy wings that sizzle with lingering heat, tangy coleslaw dotted with flecks of carrot and celery seed, and a mountain of mac and cheese oozing creamy gold. Hands reach and reclaim, the scent of barbecue mingling with the sharp tang of soda fizz. It's the kind of place where rough edges live comfortably alongside hope.

DeShawn leans forward, a wide grin cracking across his face as his fingers pinch the corner of a chicken wing. His voice slides into the space, cutting through the murmur like a lightning strike.

"So, y'all know why a football team makes terrible bakers?"

A dozen heads turn. A pause—the kind that says, *here it comes.*

"Because every time they get a good mix going, someone fumbles the dough."

A burst of laughter ripples forward, forcing loose smiles from even the most stone-faced. The tension lifts like morning fog burned away by the sun.

Brick clears his throat. The sound is rough, thick like gravel under leather boots. He shifts, takes hold of his plastic cup as if it were a fragile trophy, and his eyes sweep the room with slow, steady fire. Before he speaks, something flickers across his face—a tightness at the corners of his mouth, a vulnerability he doesn't usually allow to breathe. He's built walls so high for so long that opening them feels like stepping off a cliff.

"Alright, listen up." His voice is thick, coated in a weight that draws them still. "Thanks for sticking with a screw-up like me. Growing up, I didn't have much—I got thrown out more times than I can count. I've never sat at a real table with people who cared. This crew? This room?" He pauses. His jaw tightens. "Feels like the first family I've ever had."

The room falls silent. Brick's words hang heavy in the air, raw and fragile—like the faint buzz of those fairy lights above, barely holding the darkness at bay.

Jaxon meets Brick's gaze. He catches the dark storm swirling behind those eyes, a flicker of something unspoken passing between them—an invisible thread knitting two worn souls tight. His nod is slow and deliberate. Something heavy coils in his chest: gratitude, and the sharp sting of knowing how rare this kind of loyalty can be.

Caleb fidgets, tugging at a loose thread on his sleeve. His throat tightens. He stands, and the movement feels enormous—like climbing out of something deep. When he speaks, his voice is steady but low.

"Thanks, Jaxon." His gaze drifts away, then returns. The shimmer of vulnerability is clear in his eyes. "For giving me a chance. I—" He swallows as if it's the first time he's ever been heard. "I finally believe I belong here."

The common area quiets like a breath held. Every pair of eyes fixes on Caleb. The weight of his words draws out a hush that feels rare and real, heavy in the chill evening air.

Jaxon offers him a faint, approving smile—the kind that says, *I see you.* Caleb's shoulders loosen. He sinks back down.

DeShawn adds his own twist, standing with exaggerated swagger before dropping his voice like a well-timed punchline.

"Guess that means I'll be using my voice even more now—applying for a summer mentorship in sports broadcasting." He shoots a sideways glance at Jaxon. "Gotta say, team jokes and your advice about following my voice got me thinking it's time I shine off the field too. Who knew?"

Laughter bubbles up again, loose and easy this time, filling the old room with warmth and the faint clatter of soda cans opening.

Eli, usually a shadow in the background, cracks a rare smile. The edges of his mouth twitch as he catches the group's attention. He leans forward slightly, his voice low but clear.

"Remember that night... when I was ready to storm off after that Cross exposé—thanks to you, Jax? You didn't need to stop me, but you did." His fingers drum once against the table. Stop. "I'm not sure I ever told you that."

His words hang there; it's not a direct thank-you, but it lands just the same. The gratitude rings clear in the tight line of his jaw and the light in his dark eyes. Jaxon senses it and feels the slow thaw around Eli, a bridge stretching from silence to something closer—understanding.

"So," DeShawn grins, popping a chip into his mouth, "we're all a bunch of misfits glued together by grilled chicken and desperation, huh?"

"Speak for yourself," Brick replies, nudging DeShawn with a smirk. "I'm a solid gold enigma."

"That's the nicest thing anyone has said to you all season," Caleb chuckles, shaking his head.

Jaxon leans back. The bench creaks beneath him, splintered and worn. The noise swells—half-laughter, half-conversation—as stories start spilling out like an opening floodgate. Shadows dance on cracked walls. Gray concrete swallows warmth but never quite smothers it. A stubborn smell of leather, sweat, and cheap cologne mixes with fading traces of peppermint from Emma's diffuser—a ghostly presence that lingers in the corners.

This great mess of voices, food strewn across a worn table, and quiet confessions is different from the loneliness Jaxon has carried. It crackles with something unfamiliar and sharp, tangled between past regrets and a hope he has refused to speak aloud. Here, in the low light and half-eaten wings, is belonging—tangible, rough around the edges, and real.

He swallows hard against it. His eyes catch the flicker of smiles around the room and settle on Brick's steady gaze. The ache inside him loosens. Thread by thread, story by story, laugh by laugh—for the first time in a long time, the hard knot in his chest begins to unwind.

Emma's footsteps echo softly in the dorm's worn common area. The spring of her step is light despite the weight of the tray balancing homemade cookies—still warm, their sweet aroma weaving through the room's stale air. Conversations falter and then dissolve as every eye shifts toward her entrance; the scattered laughter and murmurs hush into a respectful quiet.

Brick, still clutching his case of sodas, grins widely, stepping forward like a proud older brother welcoming home a long-awaited family guest. Caleb's tentative smile brightens as he spots Emma, and even Eli's usual watchful reserve softens near the doorway. The room's scattered energy shifts, folding in on itself as if the glow from the fairy lights mingles with a deeper warmth—recognition, and maybe something more.

Emma lowers the tray onto the scratched wooden table with careful hands, the cookies arranged like peace offerings. She places them gently; it's an offering.

She clears her throat, her voice steady, carrying the kind of quiet confidence that pulls people in effortlessly.

"I'm officially in," she says, her eyes sweeping the room and catching faces lit with surprise and hope. "Permanent. Redemption Valley's new full-time sports therapist."

A beat of stunned silence stretches thin before the team bursts into cheers, laughter ringing off the cracked walls as if shaking loose some of the past's grit. Plastic plates clatter against the worn table, soda cans hiss open, releasing sharp citrus scents that mingle with the sweet warmth of freshly baked cookies. Voices surge in celebration, raw and unguarded.

Relief floods through Emma's chest, warm as the cookies she had baked at three in the morning, her hands trembling as she made the decision final. This was real now. This was hers.

DeShawn leans forward from the splintered couch, one brow arched and a teasing smirk tugging at his lips. "So, Em, permanent now? That's got to mean more ice baths, right? Or, hey, maybe fewer?"

Laughter rolls through the room, easy and genuine, like an old rhythm rediscovered. The tension that had clung to shoulders unwinds, a shared joke softening the edges of hard-fought battles.

Emma rolls her eyes, a knowing smile flickering. "It depends on how well you all behave," she says, a playful spark in her hazel eyes. "But don't get used to mercy."

Jaxon remains near the back, leaning against the dented edge of the table, watching Emma take in the room. Months ago, she had stood in this same space like an outsider, uncertain and tested by every glance. Now, the players circled her as if she were something essential, something they had been waiting for without knowing it. The distance between then and now tightened something in his chest.

His jaw tightens, a faint curl at the corner of his mouth betraying a rare smile. He lets his eyes linger on Emma a moment longer, reluctant to look away.

Their eyes meet across the room—his guarded, hers open—and in that glance flows years of tangled history, regret, and a fragile hope neither dares to speak aloud yet. A silent reprieve.

Caleb nudges forward, breaking the moment, his voice trembling just enough to sound raw. "Thank you, Emma... for staying. For believing in all of us, even when we couldn't."

The room stills again.

The weight of those words settles like quiet snow.

Brick claps a heavy hand on Emma's shoulder, his voice rough but sincere. "We don't say it enough, but you're one of us now—no take-backs."

Emma looks around at the faces circling her—some marked with fatigue, others brightened by this newfound sense of belonging—and she allows herself to breathe in the acceptance. She stands at the center, solid and steady, finally home.

DeShawn, catching her eye, adds with a grin, "And just so you know, permanent means you're stuck with our shenanigans forever."

A low laugh ripples through the group, wrapping around them like a thread weaving fractured lives together.

Jaxon steps forward then, his voice low but clear enough to cut through the chatter. "We're lucky to have you."

Emma meets his gaze, her smile softening into something heavier and gentler all at once. "No, Jax. We're lucky because you let me."

The room leans in closer, the circle tightening as congratulations echo in waves. Hands reach out, clapping backs and brushing shoulders, the steady pulse of a team no longer strangers but something fiercely earned.

Emma stands rooted amid the circle of worn jerseys and hopeful eyes, her presence sealing a new chapter—not just for herself but for every one of them. Under the flickering fluorescent light, their laughter blends with the lingering scent of vanilla and cinnamon from the cookies—a fragile promise baked into that small dorm room.

Redemption Valley doesn't feel quite so distant tonight.

Brick steps forward. His broad hands hold out a smooth, rounded stone that catches the light—its surface a canvas of vibrant colors, blues and reds swirling beneath a glossy seal. In the center, a small handprint smeared in white paint presses out like a ghost of future victories. "First handprint for next season, captain," he says, his voice rough but warm. "Caleb already signed it."

The rock is more than just paint and stone. It is tradition—the team's way of marking growth and cementing legacy before the season even begins. Jaxon understands that weight.

Jaxon's fingers brush the cool rock. Weighty. Real. He sets it down gently on the scratched coffee table, its chipped edges catching little flakes of grit from the wood. The splash of color feels like a soft challenge—a promise etched in paint and sweat.

The sudden buzz of a phone slices through the quiet. DeShawn's grin spreads wide as he pulls out his device. "Group selfie! Come on, get in here."

Brick shoves the circle tighter—bodies bumping, arms draping over shoulders, a tangle of jerseys and laughter. DeShawn puckers his lips, twisting his face into a ridiculous mock-snarl. Caleb throws his head back, laughter shaking the room. Even Eli, usually stone-faced, breaks into a rare, easy smile. His laugh tumbles out like a secret. The camera flash ignites a brief burst of light, immortalizing the mess and joy—the crooked smiles, the scrunched-up eyes. A perfect imperfection.

Jaxon sinks back into the couch. His phone buzzes with a new message. He swipes it open.

Proud. You built something real. — Coach Hale

Coach Hale's words settle over him like a warm cloak—soft and steady. A balm after months of cold doubt. He reads them again, slower. His lips twitch into a rare smile that softens the usual hardness carved into his jaw. It's not just praise; it's recognition—the kind that roots deep, claiming space in his chest where hope fights to grow.

One by one, the others drift toward the door. The energy shifts from boisterous to quiet as the night wraps around them. Eli lingers behind, shoulders squared but hesitant, hands stuffed deep in his pockets.

He has been fighting respect for Jaxon all season—respect tinged with lingering resentment and fear of what it meant to finally let that wall down. But something has shifted. Maybe it was watching Jaxon lead. Maybe it was simply time.

His voice is low but steady. "This might never be easy between us, Jaxon." He scrubs a hand over his face, his eyes flicking away before locking back. "But if you've got any offseason drills—nothing crazy—I wouldn't mind hearing them."

Jaxon's eyes flicker—a quick catch of surprise disrupting the usual steel. His guarded jaw loosens just a fraction, like a wall briefly cracked but not yet fallen. "Yeah. We'll dial you in. Smart. Steady. No hero moves."

Eli's fingers twitch. "That's all I'm asking for."

The room breathes easier as Jaxon moves toward the counter. His shoulders shift under the weight of fatigue and something gentler. Emma is already gathering empty plates, a mountain of paper tossed with casual precision. The faint scent of peppermint lingers like a signature. Jaxon grabs a few cups and stacks them neatly.

Together, they fold the remnants of the night. Paper plates bend, and cups click as they stack. Moving in quiet unison, they don't break the rhythm. Their hands brush—brief contact that carries everything left unsaid, the air thick with steady warmth.

"Thanks for sticking around," Emma says softly, her eyes catching his in the dim light.

"Had to make sure Brick didn't steal the rock for good." He offers a tired grin.

She laughs, her breath light and sincere. The sound slips easily into the settling night.

The last shuffled footsteps fade down the hall. Laughter dangles in the quiet like a breath caught between them. The common area, once noisy and alive, now hums with gentle peace, the air tinged with the faint musk of spilled soda and lingering spices from the meal. Jaxon and Emma stand together, the dull hum of fluorescent lights above the only witness as the doors swing shut with a soft, definitive click.

The heavy wooden door creaks open. Cool, damp air spills out, wrapped in the scent of wet grass and fresh earth. Jaxon steps through first, the quiet night pressing around him like a physical presence. Emma follows closely, her breath visible in the chill that hasn't yet surrendered to dawn. The campus lies hushed beneath a thick veil of dew, each blade of grass tipped with diamonds that catch the errant glow of a flickering streetlamp. They stride side by side, in no rush to pull apart after the night's confessions, the tension between them softened by the fragile peace of this moment.

Underfoot, gravel crunches. Sneakers slap the pavement. The sounds mingle with distant bird calls waking to the half-dark. The sky overhead is a deep, bruised purple, slow to surrender its hold. Ahead, the practice field waits. The goalposts stand stoic against the horizon, as if keeping vigil over something lost and not yet found.

Jaxon's jaw tightens. A low knot twists in his gut as the empty stands loom—a weathered concrete graveyard where faded cheers whisper in the cracked shadows. The echoes still cling, stubborn things. He can almost hear them if he listens hard enough.

No words break the silence until Emma's voice slips softly beside him.

"Feels different out here. Like maybe second chances really mean something."

Her hand hovered near his for a fraction of a moment, trembling just slightly. He felt it before she made contact—that hesitation. Then her palm brushed against his as they climbed the worn aluminum steps of the bleachers. Jaxon's breath caught. He let his rough fingers curl over hers in a deliberate reach, a silent truce between the pieces of themselves they had spent the night confessing.

A subtle spark bolted through the contact. Neither of them pulled away.

They settled into the hard seats, their shoulders barely touching, the wood creaking softly beneath them with each shift. Above, stars winked out one by one, swallowed by the gradual blush of pink seeping into the horizon. The sky stretched wide and forgiving, painted in strokes of amber and slate. The field below shimmered with a thin mist, the grass laid out like a secret canvas awaiting dawn's first touch.

Jaxon's gaze lingered on the fading shadows. A quiet reverence tied him to this battered patch of earth—far more than a playfield. Far more than the roar of crowds or the weight of a championship. This was where he had learned to stand back up.

He exhaled, his voice low but steady. "Home? It's not some big stadium. It's this. Right here."

His words rippled in the cold air. Not an evasion, but a truth worn hard by loss and hope.

Emma's lips curved upward, a small smile that didn't quite reach her eyes but felt like a promise made without sound. She squeezed his hand, their fingers slipping into a shared rhythm—a subtle refusal to let go, even if the past hummed quietly between them.

"You've built something here," she said. "Not just for the team, but maybe for yourself too."

Jaxon's gaze dropped to their entwined hands. The rough calluses of his palms contrasted with the smooth resilience of hers. He shifted closer, their shoulders brushing, the nearness knitting a fragile thread of warmth through the cool predawn. Around them, the world waited, suspended in that balance between night and day, hesitation and potential.

"I don't know what tomorrow brings," he murmured, his voice rough like gravel softened by something tender beneath. "But I'm willing to find out."

Emma's eyes caught his. A flicker of something unspoken passed between them—an acknowledgment of broken pieces, of scars still tender but held with care. She leaned just enough to press her head lightly against his shoulder. The space between them vanished. The tension that once crackled with electric sharpness now hummed like a slow-burning fire.

"Me too," she breathed.

The sun crested the horizon. A flood of liquid gold spilled over the field and bleachers alike, washing away shadows and doubt. The light warmed their skin, wrapped around their linked hands, and filled the empty seats with a quiet hope that felt as fragile and fierce as new leaves in spring. They sat unmoving, savoring the slow birth of day—two figures carved into the rising light. Together. Fragile. Unguarded.

Jaxon caught the fresh scent of earth and morning dew mingling with the faint trace of peppermint from Emma's coat, grounding him in the present. The soft rustle of a breeze whispered through the chain-link fence, carrying promises they both hesitated to name aloud.

"It's not the crowd," Jaxon said finally, his voice steady with conviction. "It's the fight. The standing back up. This. This is home."

Emma's smile deepened, and her fingers tightened in his.

"You're not alone now."

He turned his head so their profiles nearly touched, the space between them charged yet gentle.

"Guess I'm finally ready to see where this goes," he said quietly.

Her laugh rippled softly through the dawn silence. "Good. Because I'm not walking away."

They settled into the rhythm of the waking world, palms pressed together beneath the endless sky, letting hope fill the spaces that doubt once claimed. The field sprawled before them, empty but brimming with possibility. In that stillness, wrapped in the glow of a new sunrise, they found something neither had dared to name before: a beginning.

The Next Season

J axon blinks awake. Pale light seeps through the thin curtains of his cramped apartment. The creak of aging hardwood beneath his bare feet feels familiar, grounding after a restless night. He stretches long, the muscles in his shoulders and back stiff but willing under his fingertips.

The phone buzzes softly on the bedside table. He grabs it, his thumb flicking through the team chat—already buzzing with rookies bragging and veterans tossing dry, sarcastic quips.

"Anyone else bring their own helmet, or are we running 'bare skull' this year?" a rookie pipes up.

"Bare skull? Always. Adds to the cardio," a grizzled lineman fires back.

Jaxon smirks. Last night's dinner with Emma, that quiet dawn walk—the warmth of it settles beneath his ribs like an easy melody. He lets the feeling linger there, something rare in mornings that usually mean silence and solitude. Emma had a way of cracking open the small, locked places in his chest without forcing it. That kind of disruption, he was learning, wasn't always dangerous.

The city outside hums with quirky energy. But here in this small room, a settled calm weaves through him—fragile, but real.

He glances at the calendar app. No distractions today. The tryouts loom. Emma's steady presence looms too, a balm to the ragged edges in his chest.

Down the hall, sunlight pools through the narrow window of the medical facility, casting warm gold onto the scuffed linoleum floor. Emma moves through her morning ritual with practiced assurance—peeling tape from the roll with quick fingers and stacking ice packs like fragile icebergs in clear plastic bins. Her clipboard clutches neat lines of fresh evaluation forms as her eyes scan the rows one final time.

Peppermint oil hums softly from the diffuser, mingling with the faint tang of antiseptic. She sets down her polka-dot thermos, a small rebellion of cheer against the clinical stillness.

A sunbeam catches motes of dust. The quiet in this corner of the chaos has always felt like a promise. Today, something shifts. She can feel it.

Outside, the practice field stretches in golden readiness. Blades of freshly cut grass catch the light like emeralds on fire. The air bites lightly with late-summer crispness, nudging the skin with whispers of coming change.

Cones stand like tiny sentinels in neat rows, marking lines for drills and hopes made tangible in sweat and grit. This field has swallowed broken dreams and unfinished stories—Redemption Valley's heart, layered with loss and the fragile, shimmering weight of second chances. Today, it will demand everything again.

A breeze rustles the chain-link fences, carrying the faint, distant call of crows not yet ready to leave their morning posts.

Jaxon hoists his rugged duffel onto his shoulder, his fingers brushing over the worn leather as he steps out into the mellow wash of dawn. The slow creak of the door echoes behind him, and the lock clicks into place with finality.

Not far down the path, Emma's footsteps tap a steady rhythm as she secures the medical room's door. The weight of the scene ahead threads thin electricity between them.

Both moving toward the same battlefield of second chances and hard truths, their paths converge under the awakening sky.

"You're up early," Jaxon's voice cuts low as they cross paths.

Emma adjusts the strap of her bag, a slight smile tugging at her lips. "Wouldn't miss rookie chaos for all the coffee in my thermos. Besides, someone needs to keep the team from killing themselves before noon."

He chuckles dryly. "Hell, I thought I was the only one plotting my early demise. Don't suppose your coffee stash survived last night's scavenging?"

"Only thanks to my well-placed polka dots. They keep it safe from the 'new dad' with covert caffeine thievery."

Jaxon raises a brow. The corner of his mouth twitches into a half-smile that softens his usual scowl. "Guilty as charged. Are you awake enough to forgive me?"

"Maybe. It depends on how many times you steal it before you quit pretending that leadership comes from caffeine alone."

He grins, his eyes softening as the rising sun gilds the edges of his face. "Teach me your ways, then."

The silence that stretches between them carries more than words—an unspoken truce sewn tight with cautious hope.

Jaxon laces his worn sneakers tighter. Gravel crunches beneath his feet. Emma brushes a stray lock of hair behind her ear, her gaze fixed on the horizon where pale blue trembles into gold.

Together, they step forward—two halves of a whole reckoning with the ghosts of past mistakes and the fragile, shimmering promise of what might be born anew.

"Ready for another round of 'mess it up first, fix it later'?" Emma teases, nudging him lightly with her elbow.

"That doesn't sound like a plan, but it's the only one I've got."

They share a fleeting grin before moving toward the tangled hum of the waking football field, shoulders squared against the chill and history, hearts caught between fear and fierce, flickering hope.

The locker room door creaks open on its rusted hinge. Jaxon steps inside. His boots thud against the cold concrete, the sound swallowed by the hive of activity humming around him.

Nina Alvarez anchors the registration table by the entrance, her fingers darting over stacks of paperwork. The clipboard shakes slightly as she corrals a swirl of rookie players. The sharp scent of freshly printed forms mingles with the heavy blend of old sweat and liniment—clinging to these walls like a lived-in shroud.

Jaxon nods in her direction. His eyes flicker—recognition laced with an unspoken thanks—as she keeps her fingers flying over the paperwork without breaking stride.

"Morning, Nina." His voice comes low but steady.

She flicks her eyes up just long enough to return a brisk nod. "You know the drill, Reyes. Sign these in before they melt into the woodwork." Pragmatic efficiency. A shield against chaos.

Behind her, clusters of returning players throw barbed jabs across the room. The thud and scrape of cleats against tile echo off dented lockers. One linebacker's laugh rumbles—a deep, rolling thing—bouncing off the cinderblock walls like a defiant thunderclap.

Leather footballs thump against worn benches. Guys dump gear, slam locker doors, and flex knuckles. The air is thick, buzzing with anticipation—for glory, for greatness. Or maybe just the sweet ache of belonging.

New faces linger near the entrance, clutching playbooks like talismans. Fingers twitch around equipment bags. Eyes flicker around the room with that fragile edge—hope tangled with nerves and self-doubt. A freshman's shirt sticks damp against his back as he shifts his weight from one foot to the other, his jaw clenched tight against the fluttering tension in his chest.

Jaxon moves toward the far side, where Brick stretches out his long hamstrings beside Caleb. Brick's massive frame looms, scarred forearms gleaming faintly under the fluorescent buzz. His usual intensity softens slightly—he's no longer just raw power but something steadier: a mentor offering a foundation. The anger he once wore like a second skin has begun to lose its grip on him, replaced by something harder earned: restraint. Control. It shows in the way he holds Caleb's hesitation without judgment, in the steady grip with which he steadies the younger receiver's shoulder.

"You ready to lead the front?" Jaxon asks, his voice low but edged with encouragement.

Brick grunts, smearing chalk dust from his fingers onto his shorts. "Been waiting for this. Time to show them what self-control means around here."

Caleb glances up, nerves writhing beneath a thin grin. The easy awkwardness of a fledgling player trying to find his ground ripples through his hesitant shoulders.

Nearby, DeShawn weaves through a knot of rookies, one hand flailing with exaggerated glee while the other clutches a helmet. His grin is a beacon, teasing and warm all at once.

"Hey, y'all ever wonder why our team got bounced from the library?" he calls, his voice dropping into a mock-serious growl.

"No idea—why?" a kid quivers.

"'Cause we were makin' too many incomplete passes," DeShawn cackles, snagging a loose helmet from a rookie and spinning it like a prize.

The rookies laugh, a relieved break in their tight shoulders. Smiles crack open shy expressions.

Not far off, Eli lowers himself beside a young, shrinking freshman. His tone is quiet, a soft current beneath the locker room's roar.

"Take it one snap at a time," he says, his voice low and steady. "You've got this." He taps the kid's shoulder—brief, steady support.

The freshman's lips twitch, hesitant but grateful.

Jaxon watches the scene, the dynamic. This mess of raw energy, nerves, and rough-around-the-edges banter is the fragile skeleton of something more: a team.

Old ghosts of losses and scandals cling to the peeling paint and scuffed floors. But in this moment, something new breathes between these walls—something that feels like redemption, not just for the program, but for him and for all of them.

The feel in the room is electric and tentative, a charged pulse that hums beneath every grunt, laugh, and rustle of a playbook page.

Stepping toward the scuffed exit, Jaxon pauses at the threshold. His gaze sweeps the room; Brick's shadow leans heavily over Caleb's hesitant posture, while DeShawn's ringing laughter ripples through the cluster of newbies. Eli's quiet steadiness anchors the shy ones.

The edges of his mouth tug upward—briefly, a crack in the armor.

As he pushes open the door, the morning air slides in, cool and sharp, carrying the faint scent of cut grass and sun-baked dirt. Out on the practice turf, cones dot the field like a constellation of promise beneath an endless blue sky.

The buzz of the locker room fades behind him, replaced by distant shouts and the rhythmic thud-thud of footballs.

Jaxon shoulders his duffel and strides toward the chaos waiting on the field, his heart beating to a rhythm stitched with hope and hard-earned trust.

The team is alive again, and maybe—just maybe—so is he.

###

Emma stepped out of the medical facility, the clipboard snapping crisply against her palms. Gold sunlight spilled across the practice field, warming the exposed skin of her forearms. The air carried the faint scent of fresh-cut grass mixed with the lingering tang of antiseptic from the clinic—a contrast she had come to recognize as the pulse of this place.

Just past the goalposts, Jaxon stood tall amidst the stretching play-ers, his broad shoulders rolling fluidly despite the early chill. His voice, low and steady, carried the measured count of warm-up reps. Emma's breath caught, and her fingers tightened reflexively on the clipboard as the morning breeze teased loose strands of hair. Seeing him here—commanding and unguarded—flickered a familiar ache beneath her calm. For a moment, a shuttered window opened: mem-ory, possibility, and the weight of what had been left unsaid.

A cluster of returning players wove toward her, their faces etched with the gritty lines of seasons past. Brick led them, his massive frame leaning slightly as he carried that cautious but hopeful energy. "This year's gonna be different, right, Ms. Caldwell?" Caleb's voice, softer and almost vulnerable, threaded through the group.

Brick's low rumble followed. "We're ready this time."

Caleb shifted, his eyes searching her face. "Feels different already."

Emma crouched slightly, locking eyes with Caleb first. "It has to be. Hydrate early. Tape your shoulders well. No shortcuts this time. And—remember—it's not just about muscle; it's about heart." Her voice was calm but emphatic, sharp as a whistle, slicing through the thick, sweet air. "I'll be here for every step, but you've got to hold yourselves accountable." The nods she received felt like a quiet oath.

From the corner of her eye, Jaxon's figure cut a silhouette against the sky—commanding and steady. Something hummed beneath her calm exterior: a fragile, growing hope.

Coach Hale stood nearby, hands tucked into the pockets of his worn jacket, his eyes bright behind furrowed brows. He had fought battles alongside her for years—quiet ones, the kind that left no visible scars but shaped everything. His faith in her, even when she doubted herself, had become the foundation of what they were building here. When he caught her gaze, he lifted his chin in a muted nod. No words were exchanged, just a silent connection thick with the weight of shared burdens and miles yet to run. The faint crease around his eyes softened. A rare, fleeting smile played at the edge of his lips—as if the ghosts in this field were, just for this morning, watching quietly from the sidelines, willing change. Emma returned the smile, embedding that brief connection deep inside, a small balm for the heavy legacy they carried together.

She moved to the folding table just off the sideline, setting her clipboard down with purposeful care. The old plastic groaned slightly beneath the weight, its worn surface scarred from a hundred players' sweat-dampened palms. Her fingers trailed over the fresh evaluation forms stacked nearby and then over the cooler, where ice packs rested in cold promise. The clipboard's snap echoed softly amid the murmur of warming muscles and the faint, sharp scent of tape unraveling nearby. Her eyes surveyed the drill stations, already humming with soft footfalls and the faint rustling of cleats against synthetic turf. The field awaited its proving.

The scuff of footsteps drew Emma's attention to a nearby player adjusting his knee wrap with trembling hands. Without a word, she offered a quick, reassuring nod, moving forward with practiced eyes trained to spot the subtle signs beneath bravado and grit. The morning sun pressed a gentle warmth against the back of her neck and hands, anchoring her between clinical precision and the raw human stories woven into every snap and shout.

She breathed in the mingling scents—grass, sweat, and faint peppermint from her diffuser. The air hummed with quiet anticipation as she bent beside the first drill line.

Players ran their routes, muscles coiling and uncoiling, voices rising in competitive bursts. Emma's gaze narrowed on technique and movement, but also on the tremble of nerves beneath a wide receiver's practiced routes. Her lips pressed into a thin line, the weight of countless seasons folded into measured observation.

From the corner of her vision, Jaxon called out encouragement, his voice carrying the gruff warmth of a leader who had earned every inch of respect. A faint smile tugged at Emma's lips, her hands steady as she jotted down notes—a delicate balance of critical care and fierce hope. The hum of anticipation thickened, the heartbeat of Redemption Valley beating steadily beneath the clamor, as if the field itself held its breath, waiting for the next play to define them all.

Jaxon's voice cut through the restless chatter, steady and sure as he pulled the ragtag crowd into a tight huddle on the turf. Early sunlight bounced off helmets and painted eyes, casting narrow beams across the worn grass. "We keep the tradition alive," he said, scanning the faces—new rookies wide-eyed and veterans with the corners of their mouths tugged into reluctant grins. "Every handprint tells the story of who we are. So, let's make some marks."

A low murmur rippled through the group. The unspoken weight of that history settled between them, heavy and crisp as the morning air. Brick, towering with arms already stretched for warm-up, pivoted on one heel and motioned toward the locker room hallway. "The paint's ready for us," he called, his grin suggesting that something fun was about to break through their usual grind.

Inside, the hallway walls gleamed white, freshly patched and begging for color. Brick spread containers of thick, glossy paint across an aged counter: navy blues, golds, and whites—the hues of fierce loyalty. The acrylic smell hung heavy and chemical, mixing with the metallic tang of sweat already soaking the humid air. These colors meant something. They had watched generations press their palms against these walls, witnessing the paint dry into a permanent record of belonging.

Veterans and rookies clustered together, trading teasing jabs.

"Hey, Brick. Are you planning on keeping it neat this year, or just slapping paint on like usual?" Jaxon smirked as he approached the tray.

"Since when do you care about that?" Brick shot back, flicking paint onto Jaxon's palm with a lazy grin before smearing an intentional streak across the back of his hand. Goofy. Imperfect.

The first handprint pressed against the wall with a quiet pop—a navy silhouette against sterile white. Laughter bounced off the lockers as cautious rookies watched, then steeled themselves to join in. Some palms were wide and strong, leaving deep, confident impressions. Others were tentative and small—like Caleb's, whose fingers hesitated before pressing down, cheeks flushed under Emma's encouraging smile.

A veteran patted Caleb's back. "You're part of this now. Own it." The words were soft, solid as stone.

Emma lingered near the doorway, her camera steady in her hands, though her breath caught at times. Her fingers tightened briefly around the grip as she framed each splash, each smear—the mingled colors forming a tapestry of struggle and hope. Her eyes softened at the faces: Brick's controlled fire, Jaxon's shadowed intensity, and the rookies' hesitant sparks, each etched with unspoken stories. Through her lens, hands layered atop hands created a patchwork of narratives.

When the last handprint dried under the glow of a flickering hallway bulb, Emma tucked the camera away and turned to the growing circle of players. "This," she said quietly, "is what the team looks like: strength in every shade, every size."

Jaxon wiped paint from his palms onto his jeans. His eyes flicked up to see the wall transformed. The uneven handprints—a wild brush of rebellion and hope—stretched across the lockers like a living banner. Laughter and easy banter still pulsed in the air, replacing the weight of quiet nerves from before.

"Alright, Hawks," Jaxon called, his voice deeper now, steadying like the ground beneath them. "Let's take that energy back to the field. It's time to show what we're really made of."

The crowd fractured with renewed purpose. Boots scraped against the concrete. Voices climbed above the fading hum of paint cans. The locker room, once sterile and somber, now hummed with life. A gallery of palms spoke volumes—unity, trust, and fight.

Brick clapped Caleb on the shoulder, then caught Jaxon's eye with a grin that said, without words, *we're getting there*. Emma lingered a moment longer, her fingers tracing the worn spine of the scrapbook stuffed with these moments—each snapshot a promise, each handprint a whisper of the story still unfolding.

Outside, the practice field beckoned, awash in gold, waiting for the next chapter to be written.

"Do you think the rookies will keep the tradition alive?" Emma asked softly as they moved toward the door, her eyes flickering from the wall to Jaxon.

Jaxon shrugged. A fleeting softness broke through his usual stubborn mask. "They don't have much choice. It's in the blood of this place."

Emma smirked, nudging him playfully. "Well, don't go stealing all my credit for the pep talk."

He chuckled, shaking his paint-smeared hands free. "Nah, that's all you. Me? I just show up."

She stepped toward the threshold, then half-turned with a grin. "You better show up early tomorrow. We're building more than a team here."

"More than a team," Jaxon agreed, matching her stride out into the sunlight.

The locker room wall stood tall behind them, each handprint a silent cheer—an unspoken vow to carry the storm together, no matter how fierce the wind.

###

The sharp blast of Coach Hale's whistle cut through the morning air, taut and commanding. "Alright! Let's keep it tight! Focus on form—cover those yards like your life depends on it!" His voice rumbled over the bleachers, sending a ripple of energy through the scattered groups on the turf. Boots rhythmically pounded the sun-baked grass, and the scent of sweat and fresh-cut greenery swirled in the breeze.

Jaxon stands at the sideline, a duffel slung over one broad shoulder, his eyes narrowing thoughtfully as he tracks the plays unfolding before him. Emma, clipboard in hand, surveys the drills with quiet intensity, her gaze flicking from feet pounding on cones to grimaces of effort. They alternate their focus—sometimes on body mechanics, other times on the fire in a player's eyes. No detail escapes them.

Jaxon's jaw tightens as he watches a linebacker stumble through his footwork. Hope and cynicism war inside him—these last-chance recruits carry stories of washed-out dreams and second winds, and he has learned the hard way that desire alone doesn't translate to performance. Yet his guarded skepticism sharpens every observation, cutting through the noise of empty effort to find those with genuine fire beneath the sweat. He doesn't trust easily, not anymore, but when he does, it means something.

A newcomer wide receiver darts downfield, his strides sharp and purposeful, snapping into crisp cuts that slice the air cleanly. Yet each time he turns his head before the catch, his eyes search nervously for approval. His fingers twitch, almost hesitant, when the ball arcs his way. On the sideline, Jaxon's gaze tightens. He knows that runner's hesitation all too well—that need for external validation before committing.

Across the field, a transfer quarterback swaggers with effortless charm. His throws streak with calculated precision and casual arrogance as he tosses quick jabs of banter at Eli, who leans into the easy crackle like a wary sparring partner.

"You're not rusty, are you, Brooks? Gonna let the new guy steal your throne?"

Eli smirks, stepping up to return fire.

"Keep dreaming. The throne's mine—until you drop the snap."

Their exchange is brief but charged, a silent contest that unfolds in well-worn rhythms only teammates know. Nearby, Emma catches sight of a slight figure slipping through cones with an almost liquid grace. The girl is diminutive, perhaps barely past high school, but her speed curves around the course like wind threading through cracks in stone. Emma's gaze softens, an approving flicker crossing her face—a rare, quiet smile hinting at undisguised respect.

Emma's mind drifts as she watches the girl complete another drill flawlessly. Talent like that doesn't announce itself; it whispers, moving with the kind of economy that suggests years of discipline rather than raw athleticism alone. What strikes Emma most is the absence of ego—the girl doesn't celebrate her clean cuts or glance sideways for validation. That humility, paired with such skill, is rare—a combination that could reshape the program's future if nurtured with care rather than worn down by pressure. Emma finds herself hoping the girl's resilience matches her gift, and that whoever guides her next won't mistake hunger for need.

On the far edge, a shy kicker lingers, shoulders hunched as if he is carrying the weight of unseen eyes. He draws the ball back, his breath steady but his fingers trembling. The kick sails true—a booming 45 yards that cuts through a sudden hush like a promise. Heads lift. Even Coach Hale's steely eyes betray a flicker of surprise.

Near the sideline, the returning players have shifted roles, turning into reluctant guides. Caleb's voice is low and patient as he crouches beside a rookie, his fingers tracing imaginary routes over the turf.

"You've got to sell it harder, make the defender think you're every-where before you're anywhere."

The rookie nods, swallowing his nerves as he mimics the cut, his feet faltering a beat before finding their rhythm.

DeShawn circles a cluster of rookies, laughter and easy jokes slipping between whispered fears. "Hey, if you trip, make it look like you meant to. Confidence beats clumsiness every time."

His grin is contagious, shaking off tension like dust.

Brick's booming presence cuts through the chatter as he slaps heavy hands onto a young linebacker's shoulders. "Remember, it's us against the field. No egos. Team first—that's the only way we win."

The rookie stiffens, meeting Brick's fierce gaze and drawing a steady breath beneath the sudden weight. Brick's nod feels like an unspoken oath.

From the sideline, Jaxon steals a glance at Emma. Their eyes flicker—a shared understanding, a silent cataloging of promise and risk, all wrapped into this ragtag batch of hopefuls.

Coach Hale's clipped commands punctuate the drills, his clipboard capturing the flashing movements of players who shine through merit and spirit—not just raw speed or size. The weathered coaching staff gathers in tight clusters, scribbling notes and exchanging terse nods. Veteran players lean in with sober assessments—whispers of names and potential murmured against the backdrop of relentless effort.

Jaxon's mind traces the outlines of futures in the dust kicked up by pounding cleats—the ones who carry fear behind their eyes and those whose blaze threatens to ignite the whole field. Each moment is an opportunity; each misstep is a lesson etched in sweat and resolve.

The sun climbs higher, warming the space between promise and reality as drills continue without pause. The chatter, the laughter, and the muted groans of exertion all coalesce into the living heartbeat of a team shaping itself anew.

A fresh roster is emerging, painted in sweat and determination under the wide, open sky.

Jaxon's boots crunch against the dew-stiffened turf. He shifts his duffel from one shoulder to the other. The hum of voices swells around the field—sharp commands, nervous laughter, and the thud of cleats digging into the earth. This year feels different. Last season's collapse still hangs in the air, but today there is a bristling energy, a hunger in the way the rookies move through drills. Second chances don't come often at Redemption Valley.

He rounds the corner near the sideline and comes face-to-face with Emma, clipboard clutched in one hand and the other tucked into her windbreaker pocket. For a heartbeat, the noise dims, and the world narrows to this quiet collision.

"Hey," she says, her voice low. Her eyes catch the sunlight like fire, pulling a reluctant smile from deep inside him.

He tilts a dry smile at her, the faint crease lines at the corners of his eyes deepening. "Morning, Emma. The team's already buzzing."

She nods, glancing toward the drills unfolding like a slow-motion ballet of sweat and grit. "It feels different this year. Like they actually believe it can change."

Jaxon watches a rookie weave uncertainly through cones, chased by Brick's booming encouragement. "Yeah, the weight of the past is lifting. Or at least, we're starting to stand taller beneath it."

Emma steps closer. The scent of peppermint oil mingles with the crispness of freshly cut grass and the sharp tang of liniment from the medical kit behind her. "You're leading with something new, Jax. That new dad energy."

He laughs—short and rough, catching her off guard. A faint blush rises on his cheek before he speaks. "Guilty. But only because I've been stealing your secret coffee stash. I figured that's the real leadership edge around here."

She lifts the thermos, the cheerful polka-dot sticker glinting. Mock offense flickers across her face. "Is that what you call it? I just wanted something to keep me upright before you showed up."

Their shoulders brush as they lean in. The soft electric charge between them hums quietly—the kind that settles after years of silence, replacing doubt and regret with something steadier.

The whistle shrills, slicing through the bubble.

Emma glances toward the field where Caleb breaks down route footwork with a nervous rookie, while DeShawn's laughter bubbles easily. Even the gruffest veterans smile.

She sets down her clipboard on a folding table and moves toward the first drill station. For a moment, she holds the weight of this fragile season—the hope balanced against the very real possibility of another collapse. She braces herself to support these players, to protect herself from disappointment, and to believe anyway.

Jaxon shifts. The weight of the moment lightens.

"It's not just a game anymore," he says, meeting her eyes again. "Something's actually growing here."

Emma's smile is gentle, touching the corners of her eyes. "Yeah. It's hope. And hard work. A damn good mix."

Their arms brush once more—intentionally—a quiet tether amid the chaos. They stand side by side—two halves of a fragile whole—before stepping back to their corners of the sideline.

Jaxon hefts his duffel. He narrows his eyes at the scrimmage, then glances over at Emma. Her focus has already settled on the next set of drills scheduled for medical observation.

They share a glance—easy, full of quiet promise. No grand declarations, no flash of old flames rekindling, just the simple certainty of a partnership renewed—the hard-earned kind that doesn't need words to hold its weight.

Around them, the field pulses with life and possibility. The day's heat hums beneath the sun's growing fire. Fresh shouts break loose again.

Side by side, they turn back to the game—two custodians of this fragile rebirth, ready for whatever comes next.

The heat clung to the slick turf beneath booted feet, barely touched by the early autumn sun. Coach Hale paced the sideline, pen sharp against clipped paper, his jaw tightening with every snap of the ball. Every scribbled note felt like a lifeline—for him, for the team, for Redemption Valley's last shot. Sweat beaded down young faces as timed routes tested muscles forged in whispered gym myths and grit. The air hummed with panting breaths, the sharp slap of cleats on grass, and occasional barks of encouragement.

On the line, a cocky rookie—a wide receiver with swagger too big for Redemption Valley—cut through his routes as if he owned the field. Brick and DeShawn stood nearby, exchanging easy smirks, their voices low but teasing.

"Look at Sparky over here," Brick said. "It's like he's auditioning for a highlight reel."

DeShawn laughed, nudging his teammate. "That boy's hips have more snap than a fresh jar of peanut butter. I bet he's already bragging in the locker room about how fast he ran."

Brick shook his head with a grin. "Speed is one thing. Heart? That's a whole other game." Years of fighting to keep his temper in check had taught him that skill could win battles, but only grit could win wars. "We'll see if he's still smiling when the pressure hits."

The duo's ribbing set a rhythm—a mix of competition and camaraderie—mingling with the restless energy vibrating from rookies gripping playbooks like lifelines. Yet beneath the bravado, nervous tension pulsed strongly.

Emma's eyes caught a quieter figure. A receiver shifted uneasily near the cones, his frame slight against the hulking veterans. His hands twitched as he adjusted his gear strap. Her breath caught. Something in the way his shoulders hunched—the shallow breathing, the tight knot behind his gaze—sent a warning through her chest. She leaned forward, muscles taut, watching as the boy squared off.

Jaxon stepped forward, catching the rookie's eye. His voice slashed through the murmur of the crowd—calm but commanding. The football arced from his hand in a perfect spiral, tracing a graceful parabola over the turf.

The world narrowed.

The ball sailed toward outstretched hands trembling with tension. Then it slipped. The ball wobbled, skidding off trembling fingers. It thudded lightly onto dew-mottled grass.

Silence crashed over the field.

A heartbeat fractured the moment. Nerves tightened like drawn wire. Hope hung in the damp air, mingling with the metallic tang of adrenaline.

But instead of scorn, Jaxon's lips curved into a sly grin, his eyes twinkling with something almost conspiratorial.

"That's why we have practice! Again—let's see it."

The statement rode the breeze, a buoy pulling the rookie above the weight of failure. The boy's shoulders squared, and his jaw set with renewed resolve. He nodded—sharp, small movements that gathered quiet determination like thunderclouds on the horizon.

Emma exhaled, tension unspooling as the boy turned for another run. This time, he moved with steadier footing, tracking the ball like a hunter honing in on prey. His hands curled confidently around the leather—more certain, more fierce.

The crowd exhaled as drills resumed their steady cadence. The pulse of the field returned to life.

Jaxon's gaze lingered on the rookie, an approving lift of his brow almost a benediction. The man's face, lined with silent scars and unseen battles, reflected a rare softness beneath his hardened exterior. Without a word, he nodded—the kind of affirmation that sparks whispered promises between fighter and fight.

The dusk-stained sky faded behind clouds, but the field remained alive—an orchestra of sweat, grit, and second chances. The muddy earth rose with each footfall, mingling with the sharper breath of effort and determination. Every mistake became a lesson carved deeper into striving souls.

"Think you can handle the pressure after that one?" DeShawn grinned, clapping a hand on the rookie's shoulder. His voice carried a challenge wrapped in warmth.

The boy forced a smile, his lips trembling, and his eyes flickering with both fear and something brighter.

"Yeah," he breathed, his voice barely above the turf's damp whisper. "I can."

Brick threw an approving nod toward Jaxon, then glanced skyward, shoulders squared, embodying the relentless heart of this imperfect team.

The drills rippled forward as new plays unfolded. Shadows stretched across Redemption Valley's worn turf—a testament not just to the game, but to the fragile, stubborn hope that every drop and catch holds the promise of something greater.

Coach Marcus Hale's whistle sliced through the thick midday air. Sharp. Final.

The clang reverberated against the bleachers, cutting off the steady rhythm of heavy breaths and thudding cleats. Players paused mid-move—some still bent low in a lunge, others blinking against the sun. Sweat traced salt-etched paths down their necks. A veteran lineman's clenched jaw slackened, his brow smoothing as he let out a breath he didn't realize he had been holding. A few rookies exchanged wide-eyed glances; the tension finally peeled away like shed skin.

Behind the huddle, Emma slides her clipboard into her bag with a snap while Jaxon lingers, his eyes scanning the field one last time. His jaw tightens as he nods toward several names in the notes—Caleb and two others flagged as standouts with raw spark, the kind of hunger that reminds him why he took this job. DeShawn and Marcus are tagged differently: raw potential shadowed by injury concerns, the fragile edge between breakthrough and setback that makes every decision feel weighted. Emma steps closer, her voice low and practical.

"Caleb's foot looked solid after a deep sprint. There are no signs of that nagging strain. But DeShawn's shoulder is still tight. I'll arrange some manual work for tomorrow. We have to be ready come game week."

Jaxon's gaze flicks to the cluster where rookies have started gathering near the sidelines. The mix of apprehension and hope is nearly tangible—the scent of fresh-cut grass mingling with liniment and the faint tang of sweat hanging in the air.

"Yeah. We can't afford another injury, especially not now." His hands disappear into the pockets of his hoodie, his posture softening. "These guys... they want it. For real."

She studies him for a moment, arms folded, but her fingers twitch as if reluctant to let the moment slip away. Then she steps back, letting their careful silence hang between them.

Jaxon clears his throat and steps forward to the center of the turf. The buzz hushes as all eyes pivot toward him. The sun beats down warmly, glinting off the dew-dried grass, with shadows pooling beneath helmets and scrunched brows.

"Look around." His voice carries a gruff weight, hard-earned lessons etched into every syllable. "This isn't just another tryout. It's a chance—a real one—for second chances. For proving what resilience means in a place where so much feels like it has been lost."

He paces slowly, watching faces flicker with recognition, some nodding.

"We're not just rebuilding a team. We're rebuilding trust. Trust in ourselves. In each other."

Emma steps beside him, her voice clear and firm, a calm anchor cutting through the lingering tension. "We're here to support every single person on this field. Not just through drills, but through the hard days ahead. Building strength isn't just physical. It's about community. About accountability. About knowing you're never alone in this."

A ripple of agreement spreads, faint but powerful in its simplicity.

Off to the side near the bleachers, Victor Cross leans back against the chain-link fence, his camera clicking softly as it frames moments—players wiping sweat-dampened hair, hands clasped in encouragement, laughter breaking through the usual grit. His notepad lies closed, tucked away like a temporary peace treaty. Jaxon catches

Emma's eye as they both observe him, and for a moment, he wonders: is this a new chance for peace, or just a fragile ceasefire before the next storm? Emma's expression mirrors his uncertainty, but she says nothing. For now, that quiet observation is enough.

The locker room echoes with the familiar strains of camaraderie. Veterans gently shove rookies, ribbing them about the "rookie hazing" they are about to endure—smirks hiding both challenge and welcome. Gatorades pop open, the faint hiss mixing with bursts of laughter and the shuffle of cleats finding footing on cracked concrete. The air hums with heat, thick with the tang of sweat, while dust particles catch the late-afternoon light filtering through high windows.

Rookies buzz in tight clusters, nerves jangling, but excitement prickles the skin like electricity. Some practice launches with makeshift balls, while others exchange tentative high-fives. The veterans, weathered and gruff-eyed, wear open arms as invitations to this rough-hewn family, their teasing edged with protective warmth.

From the fading crowds, the timid rookie from earlier remains—a silhouette against the sprawling green. Alone but unhurried, he launches into smooth routes, each cut sharper than the last, a quiet determination carrying him past the usual fatigue. Jaxon stands nearby, his hoodie wrapped around him, hands plunged deep into his pockets. An approving smirk tugs at the corner of his mouth. Emma is beside him, arms crossed, eyes bright with encouragement—her smile soft but steady, a silent cheer.

A hush falls between them, the kind that speaks of futures not yet written but already hoped for.

Jaxon breaks the silence with a low chuckle.

"You know, I never thought I'd call this 'new dad energy,'" Emma teases quietly, nudging his side with her elbow.

He snorts, shaking his head. "Stealing your secret coffee stash is probably why I'm still standing."

"Good thing you're not stealing my patience." Her eyes gleam with something sharper than mere teasing.

Jaxon's smirk softens. He says nothing for a moment, then his voice drops to a murmur.

"Maybe this season, we both get a little of what we need."

Emma's grin deepens, her gaze lingering on his face before she nods. The field stretches ahead—the fading echo of cleats and foot-steps mixing with the rustle of late-summer wind through the grass. His shoulder nearly brushes hers, close enough that she can feel the warmth radiating from his hoodie, but neither moves.

They exchange one last look. No promises. No doubts.

Just steady, shared readiness. The season waits, and with it, every hard-fought yard beyond the last.

Epilogue

The final whistle echoed, sharp and clean.

Jaxon stood on the field longer than he needed to—not because he was afraid to leave, but because for the first time, he wasn't running from anything.

The team laughed behind him. The town felt different now. So did the future.

He hadn't erased the past.
He hadn't rewritten history.

But he had earned something better.

A place.
A purpose.
A life beyond the game.

And this time, when he walked away from the field, he did it whole.

Final Thoughts

The Last Yard is a story about more than football.

It's about standing back up when the world expects you to stay down.

About found family where you least expect it.

About love that doesn't fix you—but walks beside you while you heal.

Thank you for stepping onto this field with me.
I hope this story reminds you that no matter how far you've fallen, there is always one more yard left to fight for.

Request Review

Thank You for Reading!

Your support means the world. If you enjoyed this book, would you leave a quick review? Even one sentence helps other readers discover the story.

★★★ **_CLICK HERE TO LEAVE YOUR REVIEW_** ★★★